# SORA'S QUEST

## THE CAT'S EYE CHRONICLES

## BOOK 1

### T. L. SHREFFLER

www.catseyechronicles.com

## *The Cat's Eye Chronicles*

*Sora's Quest* (Book #1)
*Viper's Creed* (Book #2)
*Volcrian's Hunt* (Book #3)

# PROLOGUE

There was blood on his hands. Blood and flowers and the sickly smell of spilled perfume.

Volcrian grasped the body, crumpled in front of the apothecary, cold and limp in the doorway. Petals were strewn around the cobblestones, glints of yellow, blue and white. It had been a horrible mistake. He had warned his brother—but his brother had not listened.

He had hoped to meet him here on these steps, to convince him to leave the city, but he was too late. Etienne's enemies had arrived first. His brother had been too friendly, spreading word of their practice to the wrong people. There were dangers in using magic, risks that one should not take, especially in a world where magic was thought dead.

*"We're the only ones who can use it, Volcrian,"* his brother said, his eyes gleaming with a passionate light. *"Don't worry! Humans are weak. It will be like the olden days, before the War, when Wolfies were powerful."*

But magic was dying for a reason....

Two days ago, a member of the nobility had bought a potion from them. A tonic to make a woman fall in love. But young Etienne botched the tonic; he had forgotten a key ingredient, and it hadn't worked as planned.

He read of the woman's death in the papers: a well-respected noble Lady, suddenly taken with a mysterious illness. The paper insinuated she had been poisoned. With a gut-sinking dread, he immediately realized the truth.

And, knowing the nobility, he knew there would be repercussions. He raced back to the apothecary...but not fast enough.

Volcrian's nostrils flared as he touched his brother's face, and then he saw the sticky red pool of blood on the ground. His brother's blood crowned the tips of his fingers like expensive paint.

Something trembled within him, crawling from the tips of his fingers to the back of his throat. He could feel his brother's blood like a rush of heat, an itch, a knowledge carried as deep as his bones. On the outside he was silent, calm, still...but inside, magic surged through him, thick like black water. He was drowning in it.

*Who did this?*

Suddenly Volcrian didn't see the apothecary, or the cobblestone street; his eyes clouded over, turning from ice-blue to chilly silver. A vision came to him of his brother's final seconds. He saw the bushes across from their shop, the long stretch of paved road, a clutch of stars high overhead, twinkling in the solemn night, and then—a shadow. A knife. A face. The last image that had flashed before Etienne's eyes: his killer.

Volcrian memorized what he saw: a man dressed entirely in black, a veil hiding the lower half of his face. A knife: long, wicked, curved to a vicious point. The man fleeing down the road.

Then the vision slowly faded, leaving him dizzy, momentarily disoriented. He blinked, his eyes dry from staring, his nose filled with the fresh scent of his brother's blood. He glanced down at the body again and watched the slowly widening pool of blood on the ground. His brother had only been dead for minutes. It should take no longer to catch up with the killer.

Volcrian leapt to his feet. There was no time for funeral rites; he would take care of that after he took his revenge.

He took off running in the same direction the assassin had fled, racing down the cobblestone side streets. Volcrian's body hummed with energy, with the ancient power of his race. This magic was his birthright, his heritage—his blood—more natural than learned. His eyes were lined with silver, and he could see the assassin's trail like a bright light against the ground. It led straight and true, no alleys, no jumped fences. Perhaps the killer did not know he was being followed.

Mist rose with each breath he took. Volcrian passed scores of sleeping houses. The only light was from the moon overhead. *Faster. Faster.* There was a beast inside of him roaring to be released, tearing up the ground in fury. If the assassin got away, it would be the worst disgrace, a complete dishonor, a final insult to his Wolfy kind.

Suddenly the city gates rose before him, giants in the night. Two guards stood silently outside the gates. Yet the blood-magic resonating in his veins said that the killer had passed this way. His eyes flicked to the left, where a dark alley cut between the houses. He saw a large stack of crates leaning against the wall.

Volcrian ran into the alley and up the pile of crates, then leapt over the wall, landing smoothly on the ground. He stumbled slightly, unprepared for such a long drop. Then he paused in the darkness. No human would have been able to hear, but he had Wolfy ears: keen and pointed. He noted a disturbance in the forest, felt the path that the assassin had taken, and followed.

The woods were dark and tangled, heavy with the scent of

spring. Pine needles brushed his face. He pushed his way through the trees. No sooner had he entered the forest than a figure leapt out before him, as silent as a ghost. A glint in the darkness indicated a knife—probably the same poisoned blade that had killed his brother. Volcrian was no warrior, but he had the advantage of magic and rage. All of his senses were heightened.

With incredible swiftness, he knocked the knife away from the assassin's skilled grasp and pulled his own knife from beneath his cloak, then lashed out wildly. The Goddess was on his side, and his blade sunk deep into flesh, striking the man just above his hip. Bearing his fangs, Volcrian dragged the knife up the man's body all the way to his neck, gutting him from navel to jaw. He smiled grimly.

A true human would have collapsed within seconds, but not this assassin. Instead, impossibly, he grabbed Volcrian's hand and twisted it back. Volcrian heard his bones crunch, saw his fingers twist into unnatural shapes. Excruciating pain shot through him as his strength crumbled. He screamed and fell.

The man yanked the knife out of his own flesh and threw it into the darkness. Then he turned and fled, darting into the shadows, swift as a phantom. Volcrian hit the ground hard, stunned and breathless, his mangled hand cradled to his chest. He stared after the man who had killed his brother.

The assassin left a trail of blood behind, marking a clear path through the trees. Its scent was overpowering, clogging Volcrian's nostrils, imprinting his mind. He tried to climb to his feet and stagger forward, but he was in too much pain; he could barely focus his eyes. Wearily, he sank back onto the dirt. In that moment he hated his body, his weakness, his powerlessness to control his own limbs. Guilt clawed at him, mixed with the cold knowledge of failure.

It would be impossible to follow the assassin now. He had to find a Healer, someone to bind his hand. He wanted to slam it on the ground in frustration, or else cut off his arm with the missing knife.

He would have to return to Etienne's body, bury his brother while the killer still lived. And afterward...he would slit the noble's throat, at least partial justice. The guilty must be put to rest.

He was alone now, friendless, a stranger in the world. Etienne was his only family, his sole companion, one of the few remaining from the Wolfy race. How long had they struggled? How long had they fought to stay alive, to survive in human cities, to protect their lineage and magic?

*I failed him.* The thought crushed him like an avalanche, pressing him down into a pathetic, bestial position. He wished for his own death; perhaps it was only seconds away, lying in wait, eager to pounce. "Finish me," he grunted, eyes darting about the bushes, desperate. "You coward! Kill me and be done with it!"

But the woods did not answer.

Something dark writhed in his gut, something wrathful and ravenous. He bared his teeth. The mage raised his head and howled to the trees, to the moon, to the cold silence of the night. *I failed him.* Etienne was dead, never to grow old, never to find peace. *I failed him.* All of their plans—gone, blown away. *Nothing left....*The overwhelming thought kept spinning around him, flashing. The vision of Etienne's face, curved into a smile. His smooth, clear voice.

"Nothing left," Volcrian murmured. He felt himself slipping

from reality. Spinning, falling...."Nothing left...Etienne...."

No, nothing but revenge. His brother deserved as much. Blood demanded blood. The noble would die first...and then he would follow the assassin's trail, crystal-clear through the trees.

A rictus of pain split his face, the gaping mouth of a predator.

*Oh, no, Etienne. I will not fail you again.*

# CHAPTER 1

Sora looked in the mirror, staring at the swirls of face paint and the long, layered, elaborate dress. It was burnt pink, a shade too close to her skin tone, with sparkles and sequins. Several crystals were expertly sewn into the neckline.

"It's hideous," she finally said, tugging at the long, ruffled skirt.

"No!" cried her handmaid, Lily, bursting from her side. "No, not at all! It's...decorative. You're beautiful."

"I look like a smoked salmon."

"My Lady...."

"Honestly, Lily?" Sora turned to look at her maid, one sleek blond eyebrow raised. Her expression bordered on comical, exaggerated by her gold-flaked eyebrow paint, which arched dramatically across her forehead. She hadn't been able to touch her face all day. The artisans had come that morning to paint her skin in rich, deep tones, all in preparation for the Blooming. The makeup had taken hours to apply. "I don't want to go through with this," she said. "I've never had a birthday party before. Why start now?"

Lily opened her mouth, but no words came.

Sora turned to face her maid fully, her solid blue eyes lit with a sudden idea. "Let's cut out, Lily!"

"What?"

"Leave the ball! Forget the Blooming! Let's just go!" Her eyes returned to the mirror, to the thin gold clay that caked her face, the silvery powder overlaying her cheeks. "I've never gone to town before," she murmured. "It's my birthday, isn't it? Let's go exploring."

Lily, a frail young woman with bobbed black hair, seemed rigid at first, like a ruffled swan. Then her shoulders slowly melted. Her face softened. Her long, pale neck lost its tension. She took her mistress gently by the arm, turning her toward the antique vanity, perhaps the least decorative article in the room. It was broad, standing on four solid oak legs, the bases carved to appear like lion's feet.

Sora's bedroom was large enough to house several families. The rich, heavy rug that covered the floor was a deep rouge color, far more vibrant and beautiful than her salmon-pink dress. It was thicker than grass and softer than wool. Her massive bed took up an entire corner of the room, enclosed by red drapes, decorated in smooth silks, thick furs and a dozen pillows, all of the softest goose down. The furniture, ornately carved of dark cherrywood, had been passed down for generations. Frivolous silks clung to every surface. Intricately detailed tapestries covered the walls, portraying outdoor tea parties, great hunts, dashing hounds and a giant, rearing stallion.

"It's not just a birthday party, you know," her handmaid said, assisting Sora into her chair. Lily was five years older than Sora and knew her mistress's moods as surely as the weather. She undid Sora's hair, a cascade of deep golden waves, and combed it out with a boar-bristle brush. "Your father has been preparing for this all year. He's invited half the royal court and almost the entire Second Tier."

"Second Tier, that's fine. I am one, after all," Sora murmured, rolling her eyes. "Country nobility I don't mind. It's the city nobles that I can't stand. Snooty gossips, the lot of them. I hope they don't show."

"Oh, hush. Your father invited a few. Marrying into city nobility would be quite a dream come true..."

Sora turned in her chair, staring up at her maid—who also happened to be her closest friend. "Truly?" she exclaimed. "Have you forgotten every other conversation we've ever had?"

Lily shrugged in exasperation. "I still don't understand it! Any normal person would jump at the chance to marry city nobility. You would never have to lift a finger again, not even to eat your own breakfast! Huh, what I would do with that kind of coin...." Her eyes glazed over, as they always did when Lily thought about money.

Sora sighed and turned back to the mirror. She understood as much. As country nobility, or the "Second Tier," she lived with comfortable wealth. Just not *considerable* wealth. Noble blood didn't guarantee fistfuls of money, after all. Her family's nobility had been won through military service. The Fallcrests had spawned several generations of Captains and Generals. But now the times of war and battle were long past. Peace had flourished in the Kingdom of Err for five hundred years. It had been a long, long time since a Fallcrest had done anything of note.

Her father would be ecstatic if she landed a city noble. Rumor had it that Sora was beautiful enough to slip into the highest ranks, the First Tier, second only to the King himself.

But she wasn't like other country nobility, who daydreamed of the Royal City of Crowns, of riverboats, masquerades and, of course, the yearly Carnival. An entire four weeks of mystifying feats, fine wines and legendary debauchery. No, Sora's experience of city nobility was much the opposite, and it had left a bad taste in her mouth.

The memories brought on a momentary pang of embarrassment, and she bit her lip, her brow furrowed in thought.

"This birthday has nothing to do with me," she finally grumbled.

"Well, of course not!" Lily replied, rolling her eyes.

"Then you'll admit that this is all about my father! And...and marriage."

"You're seventeen, 'tis tradition!" Lily nodded, and glanced up, catching her mistress's eyes in the mirror. Then she recited in a singsong voice, "On a noble Lady's seventeenth birthday, she must show the kingdom what she is worth! All families with eligible bachelors are invited. They dance with the Lady and make their suits."

"Make their suits...." Sora muttered, cutting off Lily's tirade. "It's like they're buying me. That's what the kitchen staff say."

"Yes, well, that's the kitchen staff for you. Be thankful you're not one of them. Have you ever thought they might be jealous?" Lily gave a firm nod and began braiding Sora's hair in a series of small, neat rows. Her fingers moved deftly through the blond locks. "But you're country nobility, and this is how it has always been. You have an estate to worry about. And marriage is not such a bad thing." Her maid tapped Sora's shoulder knowingly. "Your Lord father wants to ensure the future of his House."

"Ugh! *Enough!*" Sora threw up her hands and jumped out of the chair, yanking her hair from Lily's grasp. It was so long and thick, she hardly felt the pull. "*His* House," she mocked. "His lineage, his marriage, his grandbabies, his future—all *him!* When was the last time my father even spoke to me, Lily?"

There was an awkward pause. Her maid glanced away.

"Am I ever going to get the chance to leave this place?" Sora continued. It was an old song, one she had sung before. "Hells, I am seventeen years old and I've never ridden off my father's lands!"

Her maid looked flustered. She fiddled with the ivory comb, running her hands along its length. "Your father doesn't want you befriending the wrong kind of people...."

"I don't care what he wants! A few common friends are better than complete solitude."

"Solitude? Excuse me? Aren't you forgetting someone?" Lily replied with a wry smile. She smacked Sora playfully on the arm with the flat of the comb.

Sora's mouth opened slightly. She flushed in embarrassment. "I...I'm sorry, Lily."

"It's all right. You just need to calm down," Lily said, and waved her hand in the air dismissively. "You'll dance with handsome suitors. The Ladies will all be jealous. Everyone will have a great time. You're just nervous."

"I hate being the center of attention...." Sora muttered.

"I know," Lily assured her. She went to place a hand on her mistress's shoulder, then paused, her palm hovering over the body paint. "Here, I'll do you a favor. I'm going to nip down to the kitchen for a calming tonic. That will take the edge off." Lily finally found a place for her sympathetic hand, resting it gently on Sora's upper arm, then running it down the smooth silk dress. "I'll be back in a minute, all right? Don't go anywhere."

Sora gave her a pained look in the mirror, and Lily smiled in return. Then, with a click of her black boots, she turned and walked quickly to the door, her deep blue skirts swaying with each stride. A second later, she was gone.

Sora let out a long, slow breath. Her eyes turned to the distant window, watching the sun set in a blood-red glory, a sacrifice to the coming night. Far down in the courtyard, a dozen stable boys ran back and forth along the front drive, trying to keep up with the constant arrival of carriages and guests.

She twisted her hands around her boar-bristle brush. Lily had a point. She *was* nervous—about her dress, her body paint, the Blooming she would have to perform. And, of course, the hundreds of eyes that would be staring at her. All for what? A hand in marriage? *When do I get to live my life?*

Up to this moment she had put off thinking about the birthday, the suitors, the whole damn thing. She had focused instead on all of her usual activities: flute lessons, schooling, riding her horse through the vast acres of her father's estate, fishing in the peaceful streams, painting, weaving crowns of wildflowers, romping in the meadow, on and on and on until finally, the day had arrived. It seemed too soon. She felt bushwhacked, betrayed somehow.

*I can't do this anymore. I don't belong here,* she thought, gazing out the window across the open meadow behind her father's house. The city nobles laughed at her—the country nobles avoided her. And now her father wanted to get rid of her.

*I hate him,* she thought, reflecting on her father's two-year stay in the City of Crowns. He sent cold, disinterested letters, addressed to Lily, about her studies. She had felt this several times, but now she could finally confirm it: *I really just hate him.* It didn't matter who attended the party or how much body paint she wore. The

First Tier would never want her. Not with a damaged pedigree.

On a sudden inspiration, Sora rushed across her room to her nightstand, where an ornate musicbox sat, a remnant from her childhood nursery. She glanced at the door, poised, listening for the maids. They couldn't know about her secret.

Turning the musicbox upside down, Sora thumped the heel of her palm against its base. An object rattled inside the box. She slipped her lithe fingers through a crack at the bottom and dragged the necklace out from its hiding place, holding it up to the light.

A single stone hung from a long silver chain, shaped like a perfectly round marble, sparkling in the sunlight like an expensive gem. She had never been able to identify the stone, though she had looked through countless books. Green-tinted, a yellow swirl shifted and swam inside it, as though alive.

It was her mother's necklace, or so Lily had confirmed. Her mother, common-born and now disappeared. And Lord Fallcrest's greatest mistake....

She didn't know if the rumors were true. If her mother truly was peasant-born or if that was just vicious gossip from the First Tier. Looking at the pretty green stone, she felt certain that it was rare, not something that a mere peasant would own. The musicbox, the only relic left by her mother, was forgotten in the nursery for years. Sora found the necklace about five years ago.

Lily had admitted to seeing it before. "She never wore it," her maid had told her. "Only held it. And sometimes, she would speak to it. But I was very young. I thought the stone was magic, but...well, that's just silly."

*My mother left this to me. I know she did,* Sora thought, staring at the bright green bauble. She had  never worn it, worried that she would lose it somehow. But tonight seemed appropriate.

She fastened the clasp around her neck, careful not to smear the body paint.

Chills flowed over her as the necklace settled in place. A shudder ran down her spine. She jerked, resisting the urge to rub her arms, feeling as though a thousand needles were piercing her skin. She glanced around. Had there been a draft?

Sora frowned, jarred from her memories. Her hands traveled to the stone, which was warm to the touch, warmer than a stone should be.

*By the six gods...if only I was free to do as I wish.* Her eyes found the small bells and tassels that hung from the bed frame, tokens of the Goddess. She had waited long enough. She wanted to find her mother. Perhaps it sounded like a fanciful dream—the woman could have been a harlot, a wandering gypsy who had caught her father's eye—but she would never know unless she found her. And sitting around in this manor house, waiting to be married, wouldn't help find her.

*But how?* Sora's hand trailed along the side of her bookshelf, running over the old leather and gold-leaf titles. The bookshelf was an easy reach from her bedside, jam-packed with every single book she could get her hands on. Some were in languages she couldn't read, yet she kept them anyway, for love of leather and ink. The top shelf was dedicated to the mythology of the War of the Races, stories of heroism and adventure.

She wished she could be strong like the warriors of old, braving the wilderness, plunging into the unknown. She imagined hundreds of years ago, when legendary fighters had walked the lands, wielding deadly broadswords and enchanted arrows. Back in the time of the races, before city and country nobility, before mundacity, before magic had drained from the world....

Sora's hand paused on a title. *The Wanderer.* Hadn't her favorite warrior—Kaelyn the Wanderer—left her family behind? The first warrior of the Goddess, she who was chosen to save humanity. She had been a true adventurer, someone worth looking up to. Strong enough to follow her own path....

Sora's hands stilled in shock. *Gods, how could I be so stupid?* The answer had been right in front of her the entire time!

Run away.

*It's so obvious! If I just run away and disappear, I won't have to get married, my father would never find me, and I'd be free to find my mother....*

Brilliant

It was also a very desperate plan, but Sora was as desperate as one could be. *If not now, when?* she thought, her breath quickening with possibilities. She had considered the idea before, when she had been very young. But at that age, running away meant camping in the woods for a night. Not forever.

And yet, it felt right.

She only had three hours before the Blooming and about a thousand details to cover. It was already growing dark; the lanterns were lit across the front drive. She began ticking off a mental list of supplies she would need. *If I can gather them quickly enough, I can stash the bag somewhere in the hallway. I could slip out of the ballroom after the festivities...during my father's speech, mayhap. That's the ticket!* Then no one would suspect.

She felt that icy sensation again, as though a cold draft of air had struck her feet. But she pushed that concern aside. There was no time left for hesitation. Lily would return any minute!

Rushing to the other side of the room and yanking open her wardrobe, she pulled out an old, worn leather bag, one she had often used while riding or hiking in the forest. A small hunting knife rested at the bottom of the bag, along with her travel flute, a wooden pipe she had whittled by hand.

She reached far back into the recesses of the wardrobe and pulled out a pair of muddied riding pants and a stained shirt, which she also threw into the sack, followed by her riding boots, a light cloak and compass. Then she stood for a moment and racked her brain, trying to imagine what else she would need. A waterskin, certainly. She had one of those stashed under her bed. Money, of course. She had that under the bed too, a heavy purse of gold coins, bits and pieces she had tucked away over the years. Her lifesavings were the perfect funds for an adventure. *To find my mother,* she thought with a thrill of excitement.

She dashed quickly to the bed, clumsy and awkward in her tall shoes, dragged out the flask and coin purse from beneath her mattress and tossed them in her satchel. Then she stood up with a triumphant grin. It was all so perfect—why had she not thought of it sooner? She would wait until everyone was dizzy from dancing and dead drunk, then slip out and never return.

"Milady! Your paint is smeared!" a horrified voice exclaimed behind her.

Sora whirled around, nearly falling over her nightstand. She tossed the satchel under the bed before Lily could see it. "I didn't hear you come in!"

"I should have come back sooner," Lily said, her voice strained. She stood in the doorway with a pinched mouth. "Did you touch your face? Your hair is sticking to your forehead! Here, I think I can fix it. Sit down and drink this—but don't let it brush your lips!" Her maid handed over a frothing green glass. Sora took it gingerly, staring at the dark, syrupy liquid. A short reed straw stuck out past the rim.

Sora sat down obediently as Lily broke out the jars of paint. She wanted to groan in frustration. She had been forced to stand stiffly for most of the afternoon as the body artists had painted her chest, arms, neck and face—any patch of skin that wasn't covered by the dress. Supposedly, she was to symbolize the fertility of the Wind Goddess. The custom was so long-standing that no one questioned it. The artists had left some paint behind, just in case something like this happened.

Lily went about her duty, untangling Sora's hair and gently extracting it from the paint. She then got out a tiny paintbrush and started dabbing at the red splotches and thin purple lines. As Sora stared at her face in the mirror, she felt another lurch of horror and anxiety, imagining the ceremony to come. She was already messing up. *This evening is going to be horrible.*

But her eyes focused on the green stone necklace, which glinted and twinkled secretively, and she felt a smile come to her lips. Tomorrow...who knew where she might be? She had her bag packed, ready to go at a moment's notice. A seed of hope bloomed in her heart. Tonight was it. The end of nobility, of stuffy parties and snobbery...and the beginning of her true life.

A sense of relief flooded her. Now that she was finally committed to leaving, to heading out on her own, it was as if a fresh wind had blown open a stuck window. She couldn't wait.

Lily began braiding Sora's long, rich hair, looping the strands expertly atop her head, pinning them in place with fresh flowers.

Sora stuck the straw in her mouth and slurped the liquid. She grimaced. It tasted like rotten plums.

One hour down. Two more to go.

# CHAPTER 2

Sora wished—really, truly wished—that she had not drunk that tonic.

Three chimes of a bell initiated the birthday ceremony. The guests had all gathered in the ballroom. The lanterns were dimmed, the musicians assembled. The stage was large and circular, crowded on all sides by rich nobility. The most eligible bachelors got the first row; as she performed, they would be admiring her grace and muscular calves from every angle.

Lily rushed Sora onstage once the lights were low. The room was purposefully darkened so the audience could see nothing until the performance began. The bells chimed once. There stood her father, front and center, his lined, plump face drawn into a discouraging frown. *Of course he's right in front. Wouldn't want to miss a wrong step,* Sora thought, resisting the urge to touch her hair nervously. Any small mistake would be immediately noticeable. And thanks to the tonic, she was wobbling. Off-balance. The drink had been more than just pungent...it had been tipsy-strong as well. And the six-inch heels on her shoes weren't helping, either.

The bells chimed again. Lily clasped Sora's hands one last time, gave her a slight squeeze for strength, then deposited her in the center of the ring. She scurried off-stage, disappearing into the deep shadows toward the musicians' pit.

Sora readied herself, heart pounding, poised in the starting position, left foot in front, waiting for the music.

A hollow drum began to beat a slow, meditative rhythm. It echoed around the ballroom, thudding deeply against the walls. Then a low flute joined in, weaving its way up through the drumbeats like a sleepy serpent.

The chimes struck a third time.

Sora stepped forward and back in measured intervals, swinging her hips slowly, rolling her body, twisting her arms into the air in snake-like patterns. It was a dance of the Goddess, of the Wind, of fertility and light, of midnight fields and deep forests. She followed the intricate melody.

Her dress was specially designed for the ceremony. It was supposed to be peeled apart, layer by layer, as the dance progressed. The dance itself was called "The Blooming," like a flower opening for the first time.

As the rhythm increased, she snagged one of the cloth layers with her fingers, slowly pulling upward, unraveling the length from her body. She bunched the strip of sheer silk in her hands and tossed it to one of the onlookers, a particularly well-dressed man standing in the front row. She hadn't truly aimed, so she was surprised to see him catch it. He was tall and broad-chested, and stared at her with a strange light in his eyes, magnetic.

She turned away, her heart in her throat. The wind instruments escalated and Sora's movements followed the tempo. She spun, smooth in the giant shoes, and glided to the opposite side of the stage. She allowed the music to direct her steps, move forward, backward, side to side, then turn, arms out, in, up....The bells chimed again, and she whirled, pulling off another layer, the dress clasping her body like a tight glove. She tossed the silk to the crowd, not caring if someone caught it.

Now the wind was becoming a cyclone, picking up ferocity and passion. She rolled her head, moved her arms to the left, to the front. *Shoulders back, look up....*Her eyes landed on the skylight, the gorgeous expanse of clear glass that encased the ballroom, her father's crowning jewel. A net of stars sparkled back at her, winking, twirling.

She had practiced the ceremony since her first blood appeared at thirteen. Now, despite her shaky balance, the moves came like second nature. She barely had to think about them.

The third silk wrap came off a minute later. She spun around one final time and tossed the last layer of skirt into the darkened crowd. Her dress was still mostly intact, just smoother and thinner than it had been, hugging her figure.

It seemed like a lot of to-do for such a short performance. The dance was less than three minutes long. Then the musicians entered into their final refrain, and Sora made one last turn, whirling elegantly to the cascading flutes. A few people had already begun to applaud.

Just as the final chime was struck, her six-inch boot caught on the hem of her dress. Sora wobbled once, twice. Carried by the momentum of her fall, she felt everything spiral out of control.

The crowd gasped as she tumbled across the stage, her ankle twisting underneath her, her boots clonking loudly against the wood. She collapsed awkwardly into a sitting position, the dress gripping her legs, the body paint smearing all the way down her left arm.

As she looked up in horror, her gaze landed immediately on her father; his face was absolutely livid.

She opened her mouth.

Then, blessedly, the lanterns were doused, signaling the end of the performance. The stage was plunged into instant darkness and she was hidden by shadows.

The ballroom was silent. Someone snorted nearby.

A few scattered claps came from the back rows, Sora suspected from the manor staff, although she was too shaken to care. The applause built again, though not nearly as enthusiastic as before. She could detect a few outbursts of laughter and muffled giggles. Her arms trembled. *I can't believe I just did that.* She fell! Fell at her own Blooming! *No!* It was the one thing her dancing instructor had repeated at every single lesson, every single day, for the past five years. *Do. Not. Fall.*

Not only was the fall clumsy and undesirable...it was just plain bad luck.

Sora managed to drag herself to her feet and stumble offstage, as fast as she could before the lanterns were re-lit. She slipped through the crowd of musicians before anyone could catch her eye. Now would be the perfect time to disappear. No one would expect her to show her face again after that performance....

Just before she made the hallway, she was blocked by someone.

She looked up, shocked. The room was still very dark, though a few lanterns were starting to glow on from the walls. Who was this?

"A beautiful—if flawed—performance," a voice said. A deep, masculine voice.

Her heart tripped. "Uh, thank you," she said, averting her eyes, and curtsied automatically. "If you'll excuse me, I...."

"Actually, I was hoping to ask for your first dance, once the stage is cleared."

Sora looked up, shocked. The lights were still dim as the servants cleared the dance area and set up the buffet. She could hardly see the man's countenance, although from the glint in his dark eyes, she thought she might have recognized him from the front row. "Who....?"

Sora was diverted from the conversation by the sound of a wine glass being struck to get people's attention. The ballroom was illuminated once again with low, romantic lighting. The crowd moved toward the sound. Her father stood at a long table. After he struck the wine glass again, the chatter dimmed and everyone turned toward him.

She watched her father's gray head from a distance. *Ugh, a toast.* No, worse, it was an apology. For her, of course. For being undesirable, clumsy and peasant-born.

He opened his speech with some sort of joke and motioned in her direction. She was too far away to hear it, but a ripple of laughter moved through the room. Her gut lurched and she blushed. For a moment—a terrible, stifling moment—she wanted to give the whole room a piece of her mind.

But, of course, she couldn't. The stranger at her elbow made a comment, but she was incapable of listening. A strange numbness washed over her. There was a dull buzzing in her ears from the droning of her father's voice. Sora's eyes drifted upward, focusing on the stars through the skylight.

This was it. Now she would have to run away. Nobility be damned! There was no way she could show her face again before the Second Tier. *Bad luck,* she thought. *Worst luck of all.* Forget marrying into city nobility. She would be surprised if she got a suit from the horsemaster's son....

Then she blinked. Was it her imagination, or had she seen something move beyond the distant glass of the skylight? A shooting star, a cloud, or some sign from the Goddess....?

One second later, the world shattered.

Her father's grumbling voice was suddenly cut off by an ear-splitting *crashhhh!* The skylight exploded into a million pieces. Glass shards, some as sharp and heavy as swords, rained down on the ballroom.

Sora's mouth opened. She could scarcely breathe.

There was instant chaos. The guests screamed and dove in every direction, squeezing under tables and dodging the deadly glass rain; servants dashed around, trying to escape. Men collided into each other, women tripped over their hems, screaming at the top of their lungs.

Ironically, the calming potion decided to kick in again, and Sora found herself distant and fuzzy as she looked up at the broken skylight. She felt dreamlike. Part of her wanted to laugh at the outrageous sight. *As though things could get any worse!*

And there stood her father at the head of it all, unmoved, a Lord to the very end. He waved his arms around and roared out orders to the servants. *Doesn't the man ever give up?* she thought. *Gods, this is terrible. Just tell everyone to go home and come back next week. This ceremony is over....*

Suddenly his words were cut off.

Sora blinked in surprise. She couldn't quite see what had happened; the room was too crowded. Then people started screaming. Suddenly her father was on his knees, scrabbling at the ground, dark red blood staining his shirt.

The room grew dim. Sora heard a dull rushing noise. She stared at the place where her father had stood, her mind replaying the scene again and again within a matter of milliseconds. Was her father injured? Struck down by the falling glass? *No, it's impossible, how....?*

*What are you doing?* an inner voice screamed at her. *This is your chance—run!*

Automatically, clumsily, Sora turned and fled. For the moment, her father was out of commission; it was the perfect time to slip away. She was certain he would be fine; after all, he had more than 100 servants at his beck and call who were far better equipped to handle an injury than she was.

And so, boots crunching on glass, pandemonium ringing in her ears, she dove for the opening to the servants' hall. While the manor was vast with corridors branching out in several directions, she knew every nook and cranny. She sprinted into the hall and down the flagstone corridor.

As she ran, she ripped off what she could of her skirts, freeing up her legs. She used a strip of cloth to wipe off the face paint. This dress was an ugly garment, anyway. She headed down another narrow hallway that was barely lit by a few candles. It would lead her out the back door and into the freedom of the night.

Already Sora could see her travel bag up ahead, stashed in one of the servant alcoves. She had hidden it before the dance, on her way to the Blooming Hall. Her breath heavy in her lungs, she redoubled her pace. She could hear the servants stirring, alarmed by the calamity in the ballroom. *Just what caused the skylight to break like that, anyway?* she thought. *And what did I see before it fell?* It must have been someone on the rooftop. Was it possible her father had been attacked?

*Silly, of course not.* Now was not the time to scare herself with vague questions. Her father would be fine; she had to focus on escaping. Sora passed the alcove where her bag was and grabbed it without breaking her stride. She had to leave quickly before someone discovered her absence. The red carpet seemed to lead on forever, though it was only a few rooms away from the back door. *Gods, I'll never make it outside. Come on legs, move!*

Without warning, a door burst open ahead of her, and a crowd of servants flooded the hall. Sora barely contained a yelp of surprise. Flinging herself into a broom closet, she slipped deep into the shadows and prayed that nobody had seen her. Breathless, nervous and quivering, she scanned the hallway with wide eyes.

The entire kitchen staff rushed past, hurrying to reach the traumatized guests. Some carried lanterns, illuminating her hair and face momentarily, but no one noticed. No one looked. Sora let out a slow breath, then stripped off what remained of her dress and changed into her traveling clothes, doing her best to wipe off the rest of the face paint, even though she didn't have a mirror.

When the hallways were silent again, she allowed herself a long, slow sigh of relief. She kicked the ruined dress into the far reaches of the closet, shouldered her bag, and walked carefully to the stone corridor, checking in both directions. Nothing.

She launched herself onto the flagstone, gathered herself and turned.

*Wham!*

An unidentified something-or-other crashed into her, hard enough to send her sprawling to the floor. She hit hard and rolled several feet before slamming into the wall. A body was tangled on top of her. She felt the toe of a boot in her back.

Without thinking, Sora did what any sensible woman would do: she screamed.

Immediately whoever it was jumped off her. A hand grabbed her braid and yanked her to her feet. Sora screeched, but her cry was cut off by a smart slap to the face that stunned her to silence.

She looked at the man holding her—by her standards quite tall, around six feet. She was stunned by green eyes so vibrant that for a moment she thought they glowed.

Then she blinked and brought the rest of the man's features into focus. Black hair darker than a raven's wing swept across his brow in a short cut, exposing two neat ears. His skin was lightly tanned, but she could make out very little of his face. Most of his lower features were hidden behind a black veil. Once again, her eyes were riveted to his gaze, sharper than a knife, his expression terrifying.

Suddenly she felt her throat close. *Dear Goddess....*Was this the man who had destroyed the skylight? *With eyes like that, I wouldn't put it past him!*

Before her imagination could run away with her, he whipped out a knife and pressed it against her throat. "Make a noise and it'll be your last," he hissed. His voice was quiet and smooth, like a snake.

With a shudder, Sora thought it must be the voice of Death. She licked her dry lips, shaking with terror, her fingers curling up like dried leaves.

Somehow she found the will to speak. "Who are you?" she asked.

"No questions." The knife bit deeper.

"Please...." she shuddered, and the words slipped out like water. "Don't kill me. I-I won't tell anyone!"

"Tongues talk. I should take yours."

"N-no!" Sora's thoughts spun helplessly, trying to think of a way to stall him. "If you don't trust me, then...t-take me with you!"

Saying that shocked her. Her lips stayed parted, as though expecting more, her breath wheezing out in a hollow gasp. He gazed at her with those calculating serpentine eyes, traveling over her hair, her face, across her shoulders. Then his eyes lingered at her throat, close to where the knife pressed against her skin. Slowly he frowned, staring at the base of her neck. No reply.

At that moment, a commotion broke out down the hall. There was a distant flicker of light. His eyes looked up and focused behind her.

He grabbed her hand, turned and ran.

Sora was so stunned, she couldn't make her legs move. She found herself half-dragged, half-carried down the hallway. Then, with a surge of willpower, she forced her legs to work and launched into a sprint. Despite her fit condition, it was almost impossible to keep up with him.

*Dear Goddess, have I gone mad?* Was she actually running next to this man? She had no answer to that. His hand on her wrist was like solid steel, but the rest of him was a shadow, a ghost flickering in and out of the lantern light, existing between two worlds. He could have been a dream, a nightmare, some corporeal spirit...she almost half-believed it. *Who is he?*

They burst through a side door, one of the servants' entrances, and plunged into the freezing night. Sora felt that she'd been doused with ice water, suddenly awake. The stables were in the opposite direction and she still had her satchel. She could run for her horse...if this person would only let go of her hand.

"Enough," she grunted. She had joined him willingly, but she didn't intend to travel with him, not at all! When she tried to pull her hand away, his grip tightened.

Her fighting instincts kicked in. With a jerk, she yanked hard, trying to free her arm. His fingers clamped down like iron, shocking her with their strength. She winced. *That's going to bruise.*

"Hey! Let go!" she demanded, still pulling away from him, though it wasn't very effective. He moved her along at a rapid pace, half-lifting her from the ground, hardly sparing her a glance. "Where are you taking me?" She dug her feet into the gravel driveway, skidding across the loose shale.

His fingers gripped a little tighter, but other than that, he ignored her. There was no one around; no servants, no lawn workers, no maids. Everyone had gone to the ballroom. She was caught, helpless.

Then she had a terrible thought. Would anyone notice her disappearance? With all of the distraction inside the manor, she highly doubted it. The guests and servants would think she was hiding in her room, shamed by her deplorable performance. *Ha!* The Blooming hardly seemed like much of an ordeal now.

The man in black continued to drag her up the driveway and then into a thick outcropping of bushes. *He's going to take me to the middle of nowhere and kill me,* she thought, something like an icy fist seizing her chest. *I'm such a fool.* She should have died in the manor by letting him slit her throat; at least then her corpse wouldn't be ravaged by animals.

She dug her heels into the ground again, tossing herself to one side, almost yanking her arm out of its socket...but there was no way she could fight his strength. He adjusted easily. With a light tug, she was sent stumbling forward, completely off-balance.

Then, through the murky, leafy darkness, she saw a horse. An ugly, awkward animal by what she could make out; dull gray in color, like the gravel beneath them, and built only for speed. Before she could protest, a powerful arm snaked around her and forcefully threw her into the saddle. A yelp of shock and outrage came from her throat, but quickly stopped when he jumped up behind her, the knife still glinting in his hand.

Now Sora really began to panic. All her nerve disappeared. "Help!" she screamed desperately. "Help me! I'm being kidnapped! Help!" With wild abandon, she tried to throw herself from the horse, but the dark man grabbed her as she started to fall. He jerked her back against him and the knife was at her throat a second time. She winced. Her shoulder ached and throbbed from the struggle.

"Silence!" he growled, pressing the knife hard against her throat, enough to draw blood. "You can die now, if you'd like."

Sora could feel the sting of the blade. A thin, hot trickle of blood crept down her neck. She would have gulped, but she was afraid of splitting her throat.

The man pressed against the horse, which had been pawing the earth impatiently, and the beast leapt into a gallop. Sora couldn't see how fast they were going since she was surrounded by darkness. From the wind in her face and the feel of the steed beneath her, she figured it was a formidable pace. Her suspicions were confirmed when they passed the gates of the estate in under ten minutes.

The night was bitingly cold, sinking through Sora's clothes and into her skin. There was a cloak in her satchel, but no way to pull it out. Her captor was like a furnace behind her, she could feel his heat through the back of her thin shirt.

The man turned off the front drive into a wide, open field, scattered with ferns and small bushes. The ground changed, now soft and muffled beneath the horse's hooves. Sora squeaked in surprise as the horse stumbled over a hidden rock, but the man righted the beast immediately. She clutched her satchel desperately and sent a silent prayer to the Goddess. *How did this happen? I was supposed to be running away!*

And who was this intruder? A common thief? More than that—someone deadly. She thought back to Lord Fallcrest, lying wounded in the ballroom. Had the disaster been more than an accident? Had her Lord father been hurt intentionally?

Was he even...alive?

The thought sent her spiraling into panic. She had the sudden, horrible feeling that the birthday party had been sabotaged on purpose. Lord Fallcrest had been gone for quite a while at the City of Crowns. Who knew what enemies he had made...and in what kind of business he had been dabbling?

The knife blade was lowered, though it stayed in her peripheral vision. She swallowed hard, tamping down her fear. No, she was overreacting. Her father was still alive—only slightly injured, like several of the other guests. This man was a thief, a lowly criminal. *That's it. He just wants me for ransom!*

Her thoughts were strange, surreal. She felt oddly disconnected. Then a fragile calm settled over her, like fine mist.

She had to think logically. Whether Lord Fallcrest was alive or dead, nothing changed. If she ran back home, she would still have to take suits, marry, start a family. *Be realistic. You can't run an estate by yourself.* If anything, that thought terrified her even more than the man behind her. There was no avoiding that life, not after tonight.

No, she wasn't going home. She couldn't. Not after making it this far.

Which meant she would have to escape her captor.

She gripped the satchel before her, fingers cramped with anxiety. The ever-constant motion of the horse was almost soothing, the man behind her was momentarily silent.

*Well,* she finally figured, *I need a plan.* Sooner or later they would have to stop. *Simple is best.* When her captor dismounted, she could knee him in the groin and run into the woods. It was the most logical thing to do. Then she would continue on her way to town. She didn't know the road, but she could ask anyone for directions....

And she still had her satchel, her lifeline. She had enough money to buy a horse and be gone before anyone thought to look for her. She would leave this killer and her ill-fated manor in the dust. Then she would begin the hunt for her mother. Local house servants, newsboys, the county recorders might know something. A Lord's business was everyone's business, after all.

It was admittedly a flawed plan, but the best she could do for the moment.

She reached up and touched the necklace that dangled beneath her shirt. The stone felt warm, even through the thick linen.

A line of trees appeared in the distance, a forest. Sora felt a sliver of doubt. She had explored much of her father's lands, but had never gone this far out. They had been galloping for almost an hour. This proved that she was thoroughly lost. The horse whuffed and panted, a sheen of sweat on its thick gray neck.

They reached the treeline and entered the forest. It was dark and overgrown, menacing, far different from the acreage around her manor. The branches overhead blocked out the stars, obscuring all hint of light. Sora leaned forward in the saddle cautiously, hit by another wave of sickly terror.

Without warning, the man grabbed her head and forced it down below a branch, drawing a muffled shriek from her lips. She thought for sure she would be beheaded. When she sat back up, she was not only breathing hard, but trembling and flinching at every small shift the horse made. *Did he put the knife away?* she wondered, still regrouping.

Sora looked ahead, peering between the darkened trees, as though they held an unseen solution. She was determined to be prepared for whatever came next.

She squinted. It seemed that there was a slight flicker of light ahead, the telltale signs of a campfire. A nervous grin came to her lips. *What kind of idiot leaves a fire burning untended in the middle of a forest?* Maybe this would be easier than she had first thought.

They reached the fire quickly; her captor halted the horse just outside the circle of light. Then the man dismounted smoothly, then grabbed her with firm hands and lifted her down next to him.

Sora found herself standing on a soft cushion of pine needles. She looked up at her captor, trying to see him clearly in the darkness, though he was almost invisible. Finally, she made out his shadowy, intimidating face.

Gathering her wits—*here it is, my chance!*—she launched herself at him, trying to attack him as she had planned. She fumbled, attempting to knee his unprotected groin.

He caught her easily and held her hands up by the wrists, barely concerned by her sudden action. Her lips parted, the air taken out of her, shocked by a sudden sense of failure.

*That went well,* she thought sarcastically. All hope left her and Sora sagged in his grip. Her strength seemed to have drained out through the soles of her feet. She was lost.

Then she noticed the rope he was carrying. She watched numbly as he tied her hands in front of her. When he was finished tying her, he shoved her into the firelight without ceremony.

She looked around the camp, truly unsure of herself. The clearing was small and neat, a mere pocket of light and warmth amidst the trees. A rabbit was roasting over a modest fire, the delicious smell of cooking meat rich in the air. A heap of saddlebags rested to one side of the fire. She let out a breath. A dangerous-looking sword leaned against a tree, glinting in the firelight, and several other weapons were laid out alongside it. Next to that were two bedrolls.

Sora's breath caught. Two bedrolls?

Then her eyes saw a figure sitting on the opposite side of the fire, half-obscured by shadow. In this light, she wasn't sure if it was a man or a woman. The fire danced, casting peculiar shadows. The person's nose was small and pointed, the lips not overly generous; there was a thin jaw with wide, exaggerated cheeks. Feminine. Yet a thicker neck, muscular shoulders and a flat chest. To her mind, the stranger was completely androgynous. He or she looked youthful, only six or seven years older than herself, and yet the hair was at odds with the age. The locks were pure silver, pulled back in a thick braid that trailed to the ground. Sora had never seen such a brazen color, like concentrated starlight—not even on her most elderly servants.

The figure shifted, scratching its back against a tree, then said wryly, "Bringing home stray pets, Crash? You know we can't keep it."

"Quiet, Dorian," her captor said, still the voice of Death. "I ran into her in the halls...couldn't just let her go, could I?"

The silver-haired Dorian snorted in response. "Couldn't you have killed her?"

Her dark captor remained silent.

"I see," Dorian murmured. Sora guessed it was a man by the name and his wide shoulders, but the voice was evenly pitched and could have gone either way. There was a slight accent to the words. It reminded her of the North, thick and rounded. "I trust that the job went well?"

"It did...though unexpectedly," Crash murmured. Sora thought it was a strange name. Crash. Perhaps not his true name at all.

"So what are we going to do with her?" Dorian asked.

Crash left the fire to unsaddle his horse. Sora stood awkwardly, wondering if she should sit.

Dorian spoke again. "This doesn't make our position any better, you know. We should just cut her loose, let her go."

"Volcrian will find her," the dark man replied. "And...she might be of some use."

"Right," Dorian replied. A lopsided grin split his face. "But I don't share my women."

Crash cast a cold, pointed look at the silver-haired man. Sora shuddered, catching the gist of their conversation. She knew she was in a vulnerable position—they could do whatever they wanted to her, and she wouldn't be able to stop them.

Then Crash spoke again. "Her necklace," he grunted.

"What's that?" Dorian cocked his head to one side, then looked back to Sora, a curious glint in his eyes. His gaze fell to her neck. "Is it worth much? Let's see it, sweetness. Where is this necklace?"

Sora frowned. She was loath to pull the chain out into the open; what if they stole it? It was the only thing remaining of her mother. But one look at Crash changed her mind. Better her necklace than her throat. She pulled the piece of jewelry out of her shirt, dangling it in the open.

Dorian squinted for a moment, then his eyes widened. His brows shot up to his hairline. "Is that...?"

"Yes. I am almost certain of it."

"Ah."

And the two fell silent.

Sora dropped the piece of jewelry back into her shirt. She raised a hand to her neck self-consciously. She wanted to ask what they were talking about—demand that they explain themselves— but she was too terrified. They could still kill her. Why keep her alive, just for a necklace? *Just count your lucky stars,* she told herself, biting her lip. *At least they haven't disposed of you yet.*

"So...is that the plan?" Dorian asked again. "We just bring her along?"

Crash was staring at her. His face was hard and cold behind the black veil. All she could see were those cool green eyes, like flecked algae, oddly unblinking.

And yet there was a sudden, inexplicable connection, an almost-understanding. She was reminded of her words in the hallway, desperate, breathless. *Take me with you.*

With an abrupt move, the dark man crossed the campsite and grabbed her satchel, easily yanking it from her grasp. Sora practically dropped the bag, she was so surprised. He ripped it open, spilling the contents to the ground, and she gasped, looking down in despair.

A sudden flush of embarrassment crossed her cheeks—of all things! There lay her humble loaf of travel bread and a small lump of dried meat. Her shabby gray cloak, still fine next to her captor's grimy clothes. The coin purse and flute. She glanced up, quickly meeting Dorian's eyes, then looked away. A tension settled on the camp.

Sora gazed at her belongings, trying to remember all she had packed. Her knife? Where had her knife gone? Her eyes darted around in the shadows and she finally saw the glint of a blade, half-obscured by a gnarled tree root. She looked away quickly, trying not to think about it, to alert her captors.

But the two men were still staring at the spilled contents of the satchel.

"Well," Dorian said after a moment. "It seems that we have a runaway."

Sora's face paled, turning a stark white, humiliated to no end. Did he have to say it like that? Like she was a child sneaking off into the woods?

Crash picked up the bag of coins and tossed it to Dorian. It made a heavy sound in his hand. Then the assassin wordlessly sifted through her belongings, tucking away what he could use—

very little. When the satchel was passed back to her, all it contained were a change of clothes and her wooden flute.

"Quaint," Dorian murmured, raising an eyebrow. "But quite a bit of coin. Seems unlikely that a servant would carry this much. I doubt you are a commoner, my dear. And you don't appear a thief. By the way, what is that all over your face?"

It took Sora a moment to realize what he was talking about—and that he expected an answer. "M-My face?" she echoed. She raised a shaky hand to her cheek, then pulled it away, only to see smudges of red paint across her fingers. "Oh."

"Yes. Oh." Dorian echoed.

"It's...eh...well," Sora bit her lip. Should she tell them the truth? Who she really was? Or would that endanger her even further? She was nobility, after all, even if it was only Second Tier. She could be worth a hefty ransom....

Her eyes slid to the man in black. He had been in the manor, had witnessed the Blooming, or had at least known of it. Her identity was no secret. They were playing a game.

"Sora Fallcrest," she said, resisting the urge to raise her chin. It felt strange to say her name without the "Lady" attached, but she was leaving that life behind. For good.

"Hmph. Fallcrest, eh?" Dorian raised an eyebrow and looked at Crash. "Our new pet has a pedigree?"

The dark man didn't reply.

Dorian continued, looking back to Sora. He spoke mockingly. "Well, then...it was your birthday, was it not? Happy birthday, my dear."

Her eyes widened. In all of the panic, she had almost forgotten. "Oh. Yes."

"Did you perform the Blooming?"

Sora was surprised by his knowledge of her, and more than a little insulted by his tone. He spoke as though she were five years old. Her brow lowered. What else did they know about her? Had they watched her family for some time? She didn't know much about the ways of criminals. It was very unnerving.

Her mouth was clamped shut. If they knew this much already, she wouldn't tell these bastards anything more. For all she knew, they had conspired to harm Lord Fallcrest, and she could well be next.

Dorian grinned at her silence, a sly, terrible look. "Any chance of a rendition?" he asked wickedly. "I've never seen a Blooming, but I hear it is quite...*provocative*. About fertility, you know."

*Gross.* Sora glanced down, focusing on the fire. Her face turned even whiter with anger. The Blooming was a sacred ceremony. Young girls were prepped as early as eleven. They practiced for years...and here he was, scoffing at it like a jester's act.

Crash moved away from them, back to his horse. He finished removing the saddle and began brushing down the steed.

Dorian seemed to grow bored with her silence and let out a long yawn. "Sit down, girl. You're making my neck ache," he finally growled, and waved his hand.

Sora obeyed tightly, seething on the inside. *Better to sit,* she told herself firmly. Her legs were shaking from a mixture of fear and outrage, but she was trying to hide it. She sat as close to the hidden knife as possible. The dirt was cold and damp beneath the trees, and the chill crept straight through the seat of her pants. *Good thing I thought to bring a cloak.* She picked up the thick fabric from the ground, trying to drag it across her shoulders, though she was limited by her bound hands.

Dorian seemed to notice her discomfort, and another sneer pulled at his lips. "I suppose you're used to soft feather beds and warm meals, eh? Well, don't expect anything like that around here. You'll be sleeping on dirt until we find a way to get rid of you."

She ignored him, though the words circled around in her head. *Get rid of me.* Would they kill her? Dispose of the body? Or worse, sell her? She glanced again to the man in black, who had finished with his horse and was now sitting at her far left. He held a long, thin sword across his lap, and his fingers moved over it expertly, turning and flipping the blade in his hands as he polished it with an old rag. He worked deftly, silently.

"Ah, the meat's done," Dorian said, and leaned forward to poke at the rabbit with a wicked knife. His face finally came into full view, brightly illuminated by the orange fire.

Sora drew in a sharp gasp. Two long ears protruded from his hair, elegantly sloped, pointed. Ashen skin and brilliant blue eyes, the color of an arctic sky. Dorian caught her stare and cocked his head slightly to one side. Twitched one long ear. His large, pale eyes met hers.

Then he showed his teeth—no, not teeth. Fangs. The man had fangs. *Dear Goddess, fangs!*

He chuckled and speared the meat from the fire in a vicious movement. "What's the matter, sweetness?" he said, addressing her stare. "Never seen a Wolfy before?"

"A...a Wolfy?" Sora stuttered, eyes growing wider. Now she didn't know what to think. She would have laughed if he hadn't been holding a sharp knife. "A Wolfy! That's impossible. You're kidding...!"

His look made her fall silent. She glanced at Crash, who was still polishing the sword, ignoring the conversation. "But...the Wolfy race....They've been dead for centuries...."

"Obviously not, since you're looking at one," Dorian responded wryly.

Sora couldn't think of what to say.

"Rich and ignorant. Typical," he grunted, and went back to slicing meat.

Sora couldn't help herself. If there was one thing she had earned in life, it was an education. "I'm not ignorant!" She burst out. "I've...I've heard about your kind, but only as legends. Not even in history books," she tried to explain. There were countless mentions of Wolfies in the tales of Kaelyn the Wanderer, but those were stories from ages past, before magic had been lost, before the great War of the Races....

And could she truly believe this man? He was an outlaw, a common thief. He might be playing another game...but his ears, his unusual hair...his *fangs*....

Dorian turned away from her toward the menace in black. "Seems like she'll be very useful," he said, and offered Crash the first slice of meat. Sora heard the sarcasm.

Crash ignored the comment, as he seemed to ignore everything. His silence was not comforting. It caused a sense of foreboding, like a dark cloud hanging over their camp. Sora wished he would speak; she couldn't guess his thoughts. The lack of insight made her breath quiver. *I'm of no value to them.* Would they kill her after all? It was only a matter of time....

Crash lowered his cowl to eat. She stared in rapt attention, trying to glean some sense of the man. And again, she was surprised.

His features were almost pleasant to look upon. His face was clean, without a hint of stubble. A straight nose rested evenly above hard, unforgiving lips. A tight jaw, stern brows and deep-set eyes. She would have described him as a rogue fox or a wolf, ruffled from the wilderness yet strong and sleek. He appeared in his mid-20s, around the same age as Dorian. His skin was tanned by the road, creased by the sun. His form was lean and wiry, fit but not bulky, clothed in black leather and a well-used belt. She caught sight of a wide silver scar traveling down his jaw into his shirt. It looked like it had once been a ghastly wound. She shuddered.

He stared boldly back at her. She looked away quickly, only to give another jump of surprise. Hovering before her face was another slice of meat, proffered by the...the self-proclaimed Wolfy.

"Come now, sweetness," Dorian said, with a slight bite to it. "Plain meat not good enough for you?"

Sora glared at him, thinking all sorts of horrible things. She forcefully grabbed the piece of meat, though it was hard to hold with her tied wrists. She bit into it and chewed through, trying not to grimace at the burnt flavor, the stringy, tough sinews that caught between her teeth. It was, in a word, disgusting.

The man snorted and sat back, then took a healthy portion of the rabbit for himself. "'You're welcome,'" he said, mocking her once again.

Sora refused to rise to the bait. She concentrated on eating and kept to a stubborn silence. She didn't want their attention, so she wouldn't ask for it.

Eventually, her two captors finished their meals. They shared a glance, then stood up, moving away from the fire. They paused somewhere just beyond her line of sight, hidden by a thin curtain of foliage, conversing in quiet tones. She obviously wasn't supposed to overhear their conversation.

Sora glanced around, wondering if they had a clear view of her. She was absolutely certain that they were discussing her death. In that moment, she was ready for anything, especially the worst. *I won't sit here like a docile sheep!* She scooted to the side and curled up, as close to the thick tree roots as she could get. She sent a silent prayer to the Goddess. She waited for some sign that they were watching, but there was none. Carefully, she stretched out.

The knife was only a few inches from her hand.

Her fingers wrapped around the hilt.

She snatched the blade up into her palm, slipped it between her hands and started cutting one of the bonds. The rope was thick and tough, unexpectedly resistant. Her breath came in short, quick gasps, tight with the effort. She glanced up again, squinting against the glare of the fire, trying to glimpse the two figures between the leaves....

There was a blur before her eyes. A shadow flitted above her, a sudden rustle in the brush.

Then the knife was taken effortlessly from her fingers. Sora gasped. It was as though she had been holding a feather.

She sat up, shocked, to find Crash glaring down at her. The look made her heart stop.

"I don't make idle threats, girl," he hissed, and her blood turned to ice. "I spared you once. But we don't need you alive."

*Thud.* The knife struck the ground, less than a half-inch from her foot. Sora flinched. Her eyes widened. She looked from hilt to hand, to the hilt, then back to his hand. She hadn't even seen him move.

Crash turned and walked away. She watched his broad back, the ripple of muscle thinly veiled by his black shirt. His strength was shocking. The knife was fully embedded in the dirt, buried up to the hilt. She remembered how he had lifted her onto and off the horse, how he had effortlessly dragged her from the manor.

He crossed to the other side of the fire and sank back into the treeline, his sword once again in hand. Then he sat near the base of a tree, all but removed from her line of sight; so still that, after several moments, he seemed to blend into the woods behind him. The shadows rose up, licking at the edges of his body, ready to swallow him whole.

Sora didn't know how long she stared at that tree. The man wavered in and out of sight, like a ghost. Finally her eyes turned to Dorian, who had returned to his position across from the fire, sprawled in plain sight. He had a deck of worn yellow cards and was playing a game, throwing the cards down in a circular pattern, then occasionally flipping a few over. She was thankful when he didn't return her look. She had had enough threats for one evening.

She turned to her satchel and folded it, plumping up her change of clothes. Then she stretched out and laid her head against it, a makeshift pillow. If she pretended to sleep, maybe they would leave her alone.

*Well, at least I'm not dead,* she reminded herself, wrapping herself in the heavy cloak, trying to ignore the cold moisture seeping up from the ground. The forest sounds were loud and forceful, not soothing like she was used to hearing from her bedroom window. Bird calls seemed harsh and grating, the crickets like rusty violins. The fire snapped and crackled, eating at the air.

The wind clawed and hissed through the leaves, branches cracking together. There were strange rustlings in the underbrush, the heavy bodies of four-footed animals. She tried not to flinch at every sound, not to groan with fear. *Will we be attacked by wolves? A bear?* Dark terrors seemed to loom between the trees, staring down at her.

And every time she closed her eyes, she saw her father drop to his knees, heavy as stone.

# CHAPTER 3

It was the morning after the disastrous birthday. Lily stood on the wide grand foyer, thick sunlight spilling down the walls like syrup. Two large staircases stretched up behind her, starting on either side of the room and arching above her head. The floor was pure white granite, the walls were painted a deep navy blue with bright white crown molding. A set of carved, wooden double-doors stood open to her left, leading to the ruined ballroom. Servants ran in and out with brooms, dustbins and buckets of glass.

She kept twirling her apron, picking apart the seams, running over the hem. She looked at the white floor, the mud that had found its way between the tiles. She thought of the amount of time it would take to clean those tiles.

A rather tall, dark-haired man stood only a few feet away. He was dressed in a midnight-blue velvet suit trimmed in silver thread. He was young, traditionally handsome, yet his hair was flecked with gray. She knew from the other servants that he was in his prime, a desirable 28 years. There was a firmness around his mouth that spoke of heavy responsibility, which would explain the gray hairs.

She watched him shift in the sunlight. His hands rested on a tall, dark wood cane. His velvet suit was adorned with small tokens of the First Tier—a large gold pin in the shape of two unfurling wings and three badges carved from perfectly black onyx: military honors. And his House insignia, a rearing blue stallion on a field of silver thread. She knew the House colors, of course. Lord Gracen Seabourne, Captain of His Majesty's personal guard...one of the few military positions reserved for nobility.

"Lady Fallcrest is...gone?" he asked slowly. Lily didn't respond right away. It was a redundant question. She had already told him the news.

"My Lord," she bobbed a curtsy. "I went to check her room this morning. We all thought she was asleep last night. But when I looked in, it was the same as she had left it. No sign."

Lord Gracen nodded slowly again. He had a stern face, as intense as an eagle, with dark, unreadable eyes. "And you are her personal handmaid?"

Lily nodded. He knew this as well. He had spoken first to Housekeeper Grem, the thankless woman in charge of the staff.

"I must ask....Did the Lady speak of any...discontent? Was she upset with her father?"

Lily's lips paled, set in a firm, tight line. She certainly couldn't lie. He had only to ask another servant or any of the serfs to know the truth. "The Lady argued with her father, just as any young person would. But...she is gentle, my Lord. She couldn't have...."

"And they maintained a stark silence these past two years? No letters? No pleasantries?"

Lily let out a slow breath. She knew what it looked like. "There were letters about her schooling. Few of them, to be sure. Lord Fallcrest was a...a practical man, good at business, not the warm or sensitive sort. Not the type to raise a daughter...."

Lord Gracen glanced up the first set of stairs to a large, closed oak door. Two servants stood outside the door, trying to appear alert after a long, sleepless night. Lily winced at their shabby appearance, crooked uniforms and mussed hair.

Beyond that tightly shut door was a very cold body. With Lord Fallcrest dead, the servants were holding their breaths, praying for Lady Sora's return. All of their jobs—their very livelihoods—hung in the balance. Unless the Lady reappeared, the estate would be seized by the King. A probate would ensue, the assets passed off to distant relatives. The King would keep a hefty chunk of money, to be given as gifts to his favorite courtiers.

A small crowd of serfs had already formed on the back steps; many had brought copies of their land contracts and a few even had swords. Lily didn't know where to start with them. *My Lady!* she admonished in her mind. *Where could you have gone?* She felt as though her younger sister had disappeared. She had known Lady Sora almost since birth, and knew her better than anyone. Her mistress rarely had both feet on the ground. Had she fled the manor? Taken a fright? Or perhaps, more likely, run away from the humiliation? Lily chewed her lip, determinedly examining the situation. There were no horses missing from the stables, and no one had seen her outside....

But her dress was found last night, torn to pieces, shoved in a hallway closet. The servants were now in the process of turning the manor upside down, looking for more evidence—any evidence, really—of what had happened.

"I will see to it that she is found," Lord Gracen murmured. His tone was unexpectedly dark, not the least bit reassuring. Lily looked up to realize that the Lord was gazing at her with a cold expression.

"My Lord...?" she asked slowly.

"I will leave my footman with you, in case she returns to the manor," Lord Gracen continued. "You must alert me immediately if she makes an appearance."

He turned and strode across the foyer, his black cane tap-tapping. Lily hurried to keep up. It was considered rude to walk next to the First Tier, yet one didn't dare fall too far behind. Lord Gracen strode confidently across the white tile, through the wide open doors and into the shattered ballroom. He stepped around scurrying servants and piles of broken glass.

Lily recalled that he had been present at the dance last night. He had witnessed the catastrophe firsthand. He had even held a handkerchief to Lord Fallcrest's neck, until the man had finally stuttered and died.

She frowned, watching his broad shoulders encased in sleek velvet. It suddenly seemed strange. Why would someone as prestigious as the King's personal Captain attend the birthday? There were hundreds of country nobles, all similar to Lady Fallcrest in rank and station. Their manor was several weeks' journey from the City of Crowns. Had he truly come to offer suit?

"It is absolutely essential that you report to me, should she appear," he repeated, stepping around a particularly large pile of glass. "As of this instant, she is under warrant of arrest by royal decree."

"M-my Lord?" Lily stopped dead in her tracks.

Lord Gracen looked at her levelly, his eyes still hard, as dark as his military badges. "The guilty often flee the scene of the crime, my dear girl," he murmured. "Lord Fallcrest did not die innocently last night. What we have on our hands is a thinly guised murder. In the case of nobility, that usually points to a guilty relative."

"B-but, the glass!" Lily replied. "The skylight! The shard went straight through his neck! You can't imply, m-my Lord!"

Lord Gracen passed his hand through the air, dismissing her lapse in etiquette, her frantic tone of voice. "I inspected the wound thoroughly. The angle and force of the projectile do not make sense. The shard did not fall from above, but from the side." Lord Gracen glanced upward to the broken skylight, then to the chips of glass that littered the ballroom carpet.

Another breath squeezed out of her. Lily followed his eyes, pale and shaken. She knew that Lady Sora had been distant from her father...even resented him, perhaps. But her Lady was not a murderer!

Lord Gracen turned and retraced his steps, heading back toward the ballroom entrance. Lily followed on his heels, bobbing her head. "My Lord, with all due respect...Lady Fallcrest is not a murderer...she wouldn't know how!"

"She must be questioned." Lord Gracen turned one last time and slammed his cane down. The sound reverberated off the ballroom floor and echoed around the walls. Several servants stopped in their tracks, staring with wide eyes. "And if you, or any other members of this House, hide the Lady on purpose...you will be hanged for obstructing the King's justice. Have I made myself clear?"

Lily nodded shakily, her mouth as dry as parchment.

"Good." Lord Gracen turned on his heel and continued out of the ballroom to where his manservant awaited, stiff in his blue uniform and top hat. "I will be continuing to the town of Mayville, where I will alert the local guard and put them on the hunt. We will find her and discover exactly what happened last night. In the meantime, I will contact Lord Fallcrest's brother in the City. Your estate will be handled according to law."

Lord Gracen gave her a polite nod, unnecessary of the First Tier, and excused himself. His footman fell into step behind him, utterly ignoring Lily's presence. The servants of the First Tier acted superior to those of the Second, though it was all hierarchical nonsense. Lily wrinkled her nose at the manservant's back, wishing she could push him down the front steps. *Snooty servants for snooty nobles,* she thought angrily. No wonder Lady Sora didn't want to marry.

Lily turned away from the front door before another noble could flag her down. She had been on her feet since before dawn, sending off guests, loading chests of luggage and unopened birthday gifts aboard carriages. Shiny, expensive coaches were lined up almost a mile down the front drive, a river of polished wood and bright paint. An endless stream of horses were walking to and from the stables. Lord Gracen's accusations made her feel even more exhausted.

*A murder!* She sighed, her thoughts returning to last night. When the skylight caved in, the manor had been thrown into chaos. No one knew what was happening. At first, they blamed it on the condition of the ballroom...the skylight had stood for generations, hardly maintained, rained on and rusted.

Then, people said it was bad luck. Lady Sora's botched performance brought on the calamity, and the Goddess had a wry sense of humor.

When Lord Fallcrest died, with no way to stanch the bleeding, everyone sank into stunned silence.

*But who?* Lily ran the events over again in her mind. Who could orchestrate such a thing? And why? Lord Fallcrest had been gone for two years; letters had been consistent but vague, usually addressing estate matters. No one knew whom he had consorted with....

And what to do with the body? Lily felt quite over her head. Housekeeper Grem would have to contact Sora's uncle, the only remaining relative who could navigate the estate. The burial would be a stressful affair. They would need to hire a local Priestess to perform the necessary embalming and death rites. There would be no public ceremony, no eulogy, no tears.

In the meantime, the body of Lord Fallcrest lay stiff and silent behind closed oak doors, his glassy eyes wide open. The thin gash across his throat was hidden by an expensive scarf. Three small brass bells hung above the closed doors to his study, blessings for the spirit.

Lily was lost in thought when the smart tap of boots approached her. She recognized the steps before she raised her eyes. She sighed. Housekeeper Grem walked towards her, her face as rigid as a dead buzzard. The woman was tall, crane-like and suffocatingly proper.

She looked up into the matron's eyes.

"There is someone else asking questions," Grem snapped. "He requested to speak to you." She pointed an accusing finger at the ballroom. "Be quick about it. They need more help in the stables."

Lily curtsied politely. Housekeeper Grem gave her a discouraging look as though insulted, then stalked away. Lily rolled her eyes at the old woman's back. Perhaps losing her job wasn't such a bad thing.

Then her gaze traveled curiously to the ballroom doors. She hadn't seen anyone unusual enter...and yet, the manor was full of guests. Perhaps she had missed this new visitor.

Sick with anxiety, she turned and headed back to the ballroom, where Lord Gracen had paced just moments before. Was it a reporter from the local newspaper? A curious Lord from a neighboring estate? Certainly not anyone offering to help. She couldn't believe how quickly word had spread of the disaster. It would be the gossip of the county within another day.

She spotted the man immediately. The first thing she saw was his long silvery hair. Yet he didn't seem old. He stood several dozen yards away from the ballroom doors, inspecting an area of smudged white tiles where Lord Fallcrest's body had fallen the previous night. The servants had tried to clean up the blood, but there was so much, some had sunk into the cracks between the tiles, almost impossible to scrape out.

She approached him quickly, trying to hold herself a bit straighter. Thanks to Lord Gracen's attention, she had garnered some sort of authority. Since, as Lady Sora's handmaid, she had the most contact with the noble family, the lower servants regarded her with mild awe—second only to Housekeeper Grem.

"Excuse me," she said formally, and made another quick bow. The man didn't turn around immediately, but when he did, Lily felt like she had swallowed a walnut.

He was unlike any man she had ever seen before. He held himself with a regal air, yet she knew he wasn't royalty. He might have been a Lord of noble birth, a rich peasant, or something in-between. His clothes were certainly well-made, but stained by the road. He wore no gold, gemstones or medals.

Perhaps another woman might have found his exotic appearance attractive, but Lily found him chilling. His skin was noticeably pale, his hair woven strands of silver, and his eyes a piercingly cold blue. That wasn't what startled her, however. Lily found herself staring at the man's sloping ears, which drew back into pointed tips.

He smiled at her, as though enjoying her surprise, and then Lily got a second shock—fangs! *Fangs?* Truly, there was no other explanation. His canines were long, sharp and wicked.

The man—if it was a man—stepped forward and nodded to her. She could see a nervous tic begin around his mouth. He kept himself turned slightly away from her, one hand hidden beneath his cloak, but she caught a glimpse of what lay inside: warped fingers, bent inward like claws.

A cripple. *Bad luck.* It almost made her pull away, suddenly sick to her stomach. There were some who cared for cripples, who embraced them as victims to be pitied—yet she was country-raised. She believed in curses. In signs from the Goddess and the old ways.

Another eerie chill settled over her shoulders, like a frosty cloak. The hair on the back of her neck stiffened.

"M-may I help you?" she asked, steeling her nerve.

He responded in an equally soft voice. "I heard there was a murder last night. This will sound strange, but I would like to see the body."

Lily nodded, feeling more and more uneasy. "I'm not sure I understand. Who are you?"

"Someone you can trust. Not a Lord, not the King's men," the man replied. His voice was unsettling. "I am hunting a very dangerous man, an assassin, and his trail has led me to this place. I thought it was no coincidence when I heard of the accident."

"Oh." Lily's mind raced. Lord Gracen's suspicions came

suddenly to mind. Here, a complete stranger as good as confirmed the Lord's theory. He could clear Sora's name! She opened her mouth, then snapped it shut. But Lord Gracen had already left...and this man was...strange. She didn't trust him yet.

"Why do you want to see the body?" she asked, eyes narrowed.

The silver-haired man bowed his head, acquiescing. Lily watched him closely, but besides his eerie appearance, he didn't seem threatening. "I can recognize the assassin's work very easily. I have been trailing him for several years now. I have simply to see the wounds, and I'll know."

Lily thought on this. It didn't seem out of place, considering the last twenty-four hours. Since last night, her life had been one gut-wrenching surprise after another. In fact, this was perhaps a most normal thing to happen.

*Anything to help Sora.* "All right," she finally said. "This way. But we must respect the body."

She led him through the ballroom, stepping carefully around piles of glass shards, then entered the foyer and started up the first staircase. They had placed the body in her Lord's study, simply because it was close to the ballroom and fairly out of the way. Her upbringing had demanded that she hang ceremonial bells above the doorway to ensure that the body was blessed. Her Lord had been a strict man, not warm or loving; yet he, too, deserved to be carried on the Winds of the Goddess.

When they reached the doorway, the man hesitated for a minute. She noticed his hands quiver as he crossed the threshold.

This was a chamber she had cleaned and dusted many times. It was richly decorated with indoor plants in the corners, bookshelves along the walls, and a magnificent fireplace on one side, with a long couch in front. At this moment, the couch was occupied by a body shrouded in white linen. A hint of blood showed through the cloth. Lily frowned at this. They had done their best to dress the wound, but even after death, blood had seeped stubbornly down her Lord's neck.

Lily brought the strange man next to the body and carefully pulled back the sheet. She averted her gaze from the blue-tinted skin, the slightly bloated eyes, the flat jowls. "Here he is. We did nothing to the body but move it."

The man stiffened at the sight of the blood. She could only assume that put him off, though somehow she was not reassured. "I see," the man murmured, his voice thick. "And was there a blade?"

"Only a shard of glass. We thought it fell from the roof, but...."

"Yes?"

Lily swallowed. She could clearly hear Lord Gracen's voice in her head, and repeated his words almost by rote. "The force and angle of the projectile was different. It...it came from the side. As though someone had thrown it."

The man was standing icily still. The corner of his mouth lifted. His arctic-blue gaze remained trained on the body.

"Were there any witnesses?" he asked.

Lily let out a slow breath. "No," she paused, then bit her tongue. Should she tell him about Sora? Of course, and yet, she was still disturbed. His skin was too pale; his teeth were too long.

He was waiting. She could tell he could read her like a book; he knew she had more to say. Finally, she relented. "His daughter, Lady Sora, is missing." She licked her lips nervously. Something almost made sense about that, now that she said it aloud. No witnesses, and the Lady missing. Had Sora seen something...?

"And no idea where she might have gone?" The man's eyes sharpened.

"N-no," Lily bit her tongue again. The energy around him was decidedly cold. "But Lord Gracen, of the King's Private Guard, you know....He suspects that she arranged the murder."

The man nodded slowly. When his eyes met hers, there was a strange pity in them, as though he was gazing at a wounded animal. "And she might have," he spoke carefully, watching her reaction. "Assassins rarely kill on their own whim. This man had need of money...and your Lady had motive to kill, I take it?"

Lily felt her hopes plummet. This man wouldn't understand. Her mistress spent her time in the open fields, whittling wooden flutes and studying birds. She didn't have a vicious bone in her body.

But something had happened last night. Her gut twisted sickeningly again. Sora had witnessed something. Bumped into the killer, perhaps?

"Do you know what this assassin looks like, sir?" she asked. "Perhaps I could ask the servants if anyone else saw him...."

"Athletic build," the man replied idly, almost disinterestedly. "A little over six feet, perhaps. Young, barely in his prime." He stepped away from the couch, slowly touring the room, obviously finished with the body. Lily let the white sheet drop over the corpse, then watched the man closely.

He gazed at the Lord's bookshelves. Then he picked up a large crystal sphere, a decorative paperweight, from Lord Fallcrest's desk. He slowly turned it in his hand, watching the light play off the surface. "Black hair, green eyes," he continued thoughtfully. "And I expect—yes, I expect he'd be dressed in black." The man grinned, strange for such a conversation. "He has an immeasurable capacity for violence. To state it quite plainly, my dear, he is a very highly trained murderer. Some might even say his thirst for blood is...*inhuman*." Then he grinned wider, and his fangs flashed in the light.

Lily tried not to flinch. "Uhm," she said slowly, her mouth dry. "I will certainly ask around. Would you like to speak to Lord Gracen? He would be very interested in this. You might catch up with him in Mayville...."

"No," the traveler said shortly. "My investigation is private. It is of a personal nature, you see. And the killer is a cunning man. The less he hears of me, the better."

A personal nature? Lily wasn't sure what to say to that. She wanted to ask, but then didn't. She doubted this man was as good-intentioned as he seemed.

Finally, the man set the crystal back on the desk. "I have imposed on you long enough. Thank you for your help, miss, and..." his face pulled into a frown, "I am sorry. This is a tragedy. Lord Fallcrest was well respected by his serfs, by what I have heard."

Lily nodded slowly. "Yes. A tragedy." She wondered which serfs he had spoken to. Her Lord had been a businessman, concerned with trade and money, his sights set on the First Tier. He had governed with a strict, if consistent, hand, dealing harsh punishments in all disputes. But who knew? In the lawless countryside, perhaps that was necessary. The serfs did not love him...but they did respect him.

The traveler stood for a moment, eerily still like a frozen lake. Then he turned toward the door. "Your assistance has been invaluable. Never fear, child. The killer will be put down. Lord

Fallcrest will have justice."

Lily nodded again, still sick to her stomach. Justice? And who was this man? She had never seen him before, and she doubted he knew much of her Lord beyond a serf's conversation. She watched as he stepped swiftly toward the hallway, his blue cloak swirling around him, his crippled hand clutched against his body.

On impulse, she called out, almost choking on the words, "If you find the killer, could you see that Lady Sora is safe?" She doubted this man would do that. But she could easily imagine Sora's dead body lying in a ditch somewhere, cold and stiff after a night in the forest, perhaps gnawed by animals. It was not so uncommon. "I feel there might have been an accident...."

"Murder is never an accident," the man said harshly.

She opened her mouth to reply, but the door slammed in her face.

\* \* \*

A thin smile spread across Volcrian's lips as he walked out of the manor. He passed scurrying servants and pockets of guests on his way to the spindly tree where he had tethered his horse. The rush of excitement kept his thoughts optimistic and clear. Viper had been here. He could smell the assassin on the Lord's body, on the blood spilled in the ballroom. Death always left a memory of the killer, after all.

*And Viper is certainly a killer capable of this.* An entire ballroom of guests convinced it was an accident? Surely the work of a master. And yet, not quite the perfect crime. A Lady was missing.

As Volcrian mounted his horse and turned toward the forest,

he continued to ponder the strange situation. The girl had disappeared, but no body had been found. Had she gone with the assassin? The facts didn't add up. A creature like Viper was incapable of sparing life. He had no concept of innocence, of mercy. Lady Sora was most likely dead, her body stashed in a closet somewhere, to be discovered when the corpse began to rot.

He didn't feel sorry for the girl. Those who dealt with Viper could expect nothing less. If she had devised to murder her father—which was a common thing amongst the higher Tiers—then she deserved her own fate.

He had spoken to quite a few of the serfs mingling outside, and was all but convinced this was the case. There had been no love between father and daughter in the Fallcrest household. She was of questionable birth and had a decidedly stubborn demeanor. He could easily see the girl hiring an assassin as a last-ditch attempt to escape her nuptials. With a dead father and no husband, she would inherit the entire estate.

Volcrian clenched his fist suddenly—pain cramped his distorted muscles. His crippled hand convulsed, twitching in spasm. Just thinking of the girl's wickedness made his head throb. Killing her own father? With any luck, the assassin would use her and toss her to the roadside, a wasted shell of a woman. Better yet, the mage might stumble across her corpse within the next few days, perhaps while the blood was still fresh. Good enough to be used for his sorcery.

Volcrian shook his head slowly, leading his horse down the long gravel driveway toward the acres of fields and forest outside the gates. His own brother had been dead for two years now. Two years, and never a night's peace. Always nightmares and memories, shadows plaguing his dreams. He knew Etienne's spirit wouldn't rest until the assassin was dead. He knew, because in his dreams, that is what Etienne told him. *Avenge me,* his voice whispered. *Finish this, and I will sleep.*

At times, his brother told him other things, too...dark thoughts that played in his head, seethed within him, resurrected from beyond the grave. He had to push them away. He knew that his brother suffered, that his spirit writhed in the underworld. It followed him into the waking hours, drifting just beyond sight, the memory of those black dreams.

He finally passed through the wide iron gates and exited the Fallcrest manor. His nostrils flared, searching for a hint of a path. Now that he was certain of the assassin's presence, he knew what to look for. And he found it. The trail of a horse leaving the road, entering the tall grass. It was almost too easy.

Volcrian's smile stretched wide, his fangs gleaming in the light. Yes, Viper was in his grasp, only a day's ride away. Soon there would be justice. But Volcrian had been this close before; if he wasted too much time, the killer would slip through his fingers again. He needed to stall the travelers until he could catch up with them.

He wanted to feel Viper's blood running over his crippled hand. He needed to taste it dripping from his fangs....

He led his horse through a thicket of trees into a shallow meadow of bright green grass, nestled away from the main road. There was no movement but the gentle swish of wind. A lock of silver hair fell across his fine-boned face. He swept it aside absently, his eyes searching the underbrush. *I will need a spell to follow them...to keep them busy for a while....*To delay them while he caught up.

He dismounted from the horse and reached into his saddlebags, withdrawing an old journal. It had been his great-grandfather's, passed down by the men in his family, and once was Etienne's. A book of spells, of blood-magic. He knew each page, each flow of handwriting. Once upon a time, all Wolfy families had carried such spellbooks, handed down from parent to child, generation after generation, unique to each bloodline. The most practiced families had the most powerful spells.

That was hundreds of years ago, however. His own family's heritage had been destroyed long ago. This journal was a meager example of what could have been; the spells of only three generations were not very impressive. And it was always a challenge to pick the right recipe. Wolfy magic was perhaps the most powerful of the races, and the hardest to learn. There were many different means to reach the same end.

For any spell he needed a sacrifice, an offering to the Sea Goddess. It could be as simple and basic as putting out a bowl of saltwater and fish scales. But usually, curses and enchantments demanded something more. It could take days to find the right animal, or in rare cases, a human. Volcrian grimaced at that. Hardly ever did he need a human.

He and Etienne had learned from their father. Their mother died in childbirth, as was common to the Wolfy race. After his father's death from illness, Volcrian moved to the City of Crowns with Etienne. They opened an apothecary, the most obvious business for a pair of young Wolfy sorcerers. On the outside, they proved to be an honest herb shop, dealing cold remedies and aphrodisiacs to the common public. And yet, for wealthier patrons, they would do more than just sell tea. Working magic, taking that risk, cost precious money. Nobility had money.

Volcrian shook himself, trying to brush off the chill that had settled over him. He had to admit that after using so much magic, he felt...*different*. Cold. It was the mantle of a Wolfy bloodmage, *the badge of snow,* his father had called it. A certain indifference to life. A removal. Killing animals for sacrifices no longer bothered him. Once, a human sacrifice had seemed unthinkable, dirty, taboo. But even that had changed.

After practicing his craft so long, he was beginning to understand the true power of a Wolfy mage. There was more than enough life inhabiting the world, and it was all a source of magic, ready to mold to his will. Humans were especially disposable. *Selfish, festering creatures.* They bred like rabbits, dirtying the water, raping the fields. The weakest of the races was now spreading across the earth. Volcrian grimaced at the thought. The Wolfies should be in power now. The magic-wielders. Not the flat-footed humans, useless as pigs.

His mind turned toward the journal and which spell he would use to waylay the assassin. Something fast and simple that wouldn't take too much of a toll. Time was of the essence; he didn't have days to spend in recovery. Just a simple animal spell, enough to track down the killer and slow his pace.

He thumbed through the pages of the book, glancing over titles, recipes, causes-and-effects. A plan slowly began to form in his mind, and as it did, another twisted smile came to his lips. This time he was sure to succeed, and then?....And then Etienne would truly sleep.

# CHAPTER 4

Sora awoke with the toe of a boot jabbing her in the back.

"Wake up, girl. We're leaving."

She groaned. Every fiber of her body was in pain. When she sat up, she felt stiff as an old woman and twice as sore. A light mist hung above their camp, clinging to the lower branches like a fragile curtain.

She rubbed the sleep from her eyes and grimaced at the retreating figure of Crash. *What a rude awakening!* She didn't mind glaring at him—as long as his back was turned. She pulled her cloak about her shoulders and rubbed down her legs, trying to stave off the chill. It had been a cold, moist night, and although she had curled up close to the fire, she was too uncomfortable to sleep. Finally she drifted off close to dawn, but only for a few hours of true rest.

She brushed the leaves from her clothing, then paused, staring down at her hands. They were no longer tied. Her heart leapt—but quickly plummeted. Perhaps she wasn't tied up, but she was still a captive. Obviously they didn't think she could escape. She posed no threat at all.

But she would escape! She promised herself that.

Sora got awkwardly to her feet and lifted her satchel. Her stomach rumbled, but she didn't care to ask her captors for breakfast. *I'd rather starve!* She glanced around, suddenly uncertain. The camp seemed unusually quiet.

As though reading her thoughts, Dorian's voice drifted over to her: "Women are always more beautiful in the morning, especially after a night on the cold ground!" His words were sharp and crisp on the misty air.

Sora ignored the Wolfy as he entered the clearing. He was atop a pretty brown horse, which she assumed was stolen. She avoided making eye contact, even when he pulled up next to her. "Is our Lady ready to leave?" he said with a sneer.

Her cheeks flushed, but she refused to answer. Perhaps she had grown up with wealth, but she had never lorded her status above others, like so many noble-born. In fact, her only friends were servants. She gave him a stiff nod, biting the inside of her cheek.

Dorian abruptly reached down and offered her his gloved hand. She stared up at him, surprised.

"Well, sweetness? Get on!" he said impatiently. "Or do you need a footstool? Maybe a nice cushion to sit on?"

Sora could take no more. With a huff of anger, she shoved away his hand. "In case you're wondering," she spat out, "or in case you're deaf, my name is Sora, not sweetness, or sweetheart, or sweet-anything! And I'm not a pampered little princess! In fact, I'd rather *walk* than ride on your dirty horse!" She spat at his feet, though she wasn't very good at spitting.

The expression on Dorian's face made her words worth it, and Sora braced herself for the swing of a sword, or a kick from his boot. *At least I'll die happy.* Then, much to her surprise, the creature threw back his head and let out a barking laugh, his pointed ears twitching with mirth.

"So the girl has some spirit after all!" he shouted. Then he reached down, grabbed her forcefully by the arm, and dragged her onto the horse behind him—his strength made her gasp. She struggled into the saddle with little choice. "Dorian's the name, thieving is the trade, and perhaps this won't be such an agony after all."

She stared at the back of his head, still shocked. *Shouldn't he be trying to kill me now?* She thought of Crash's threats from the night before and the pink scratches along her neck.

"Uh, yes, perhaps," she said carefully.

He was still laughing. "I think we're going to get along just fine," he said. With that, he tugged on the reins and whirled the horse around, setting off through the trees. Sora had to grab his hips for balance; it was awkward, and she tried to touch him as little as possible.

He seemed to be in a good mood, though she couldn't imagine why. The Wolfy hummed to himself as they started through the forest, an old woodland tune known to the area. Sora had heard the yard workers sing it during long afternoons, while they were trimming the grass or weeding the flowerbeds. Its familiarity was soothing and reminded her of home.

After a few minutes, she cleared her throat. "Uh...thanks for untying my hands," she said. *Stupid.* She shouldn't speak to him; he was her enemy.

"It was the most practical thing to do," the thief replied. "Don't see how you could ride otherwise. But if you try anything stupid, Crash will have to put you down. I'd hate to lose such a pretty new pet."

His words were a sharp reminder of her position, as though she needed one. Sora shut her mouth, her sense of relief dissipating. *Pet?* she thought in disgust.

Still, perhaps it was a good sign that he kept talking to her. She wasn't as scared of Dorian as she was of Crash. She got the feeling that he was warming up to her, which could be used to her advantage.

*So he thinks I'm pretty, huh?* she thought with a little smirk. She glanced down at her stained shirt and felt the unexpected urge to laugh. How refreshing to be in day-old clothes! She hoped she would get dirtier before the day was done.

"Git!" Dorian clicked his tongue to the horse, who moved into a smooth, fast trot. Sora wasn't expecting the sudden change of pace, and held on tighter. The horse found a trail and they followed it through the woods, ducking under low branches, picking their way around rocks. She could only assume they were following Crash's lead, though she hadn't caught a glimpse of him since waking. With any luck, she wouldn't see the killer until nightfall.

Almost an hour passed in dull silence. The trail moved through dense forest and hidden meadows strung with wildflowers, yellow and blue petals scattered throughout the shade. Sora tried to entertain herself by bird-watching; she counted twenty-three species before losing track. There were dark-winged crows, skinny red robins and blue jays. A few plump yellow finches kept following the horse. They flitted quietly from branch to branch, waiting for seeds to fall, or crumbs.

Then the path opened up and joined with a main road. Golden wheat fields stretched out to their right while the dense forest stayed to their left. The trees fell away, as did the birds, leaving a broad, seamless sky and a hawk-like speck on the horizon. She wondered how far away she was from her father's house—*probably quite a ways*. She had never seen farmland like this before.

"Where are we?" she finally asked, her curiosity loosening her tongue.

"Don't you know?" Dorian sneered. "These are Fallcrest lands, all twenty-thousand acres...or thirty miles, if you're not a farmer. Your serfs work them and pay a seasonal tax."

Sora blushed, then glared at the back of his neck. "Of course I knew that!" she lied. "I just meant, where are we going?"

"A good ways from here, I can assure you," Dorian answered vaguely.

Sora gritted her teeth. She tried again. "There is a town on my father's land, is there not?"

"Oh, did your servants tell you that, too? My, my, you are clever." His voice trailed on, decidedly bored. "Yes, my girl, we are going to Mayville. A certain assassin needs to collect his payment."

Sora stiffened, her breath catching in her lungs. Assassin? Her fingers tightened on Dorian's waist. "W-what?"

The Wolfy stiffened as well, his shoulders going rigid. "Forget I said anything," he grunted.

Sora shook her head, trying to clear her thoughts. "No, wait, you can't just leave it at that! What assassin? What payment?" Her stomach had turned to rock. She suddenly felt sick and oddly deceived, even though Dorian was not her friend. Her heart pounded. *Assassin*. Suddenly her thoughts were racing, memories of the previous night, of her father falling to the ground, injured. Perhaps worse than injured. *Perhaps....*

"Lord Fallcrest is dead," she said numbly.

Her captor didn't answer immediately. Dorian sat as though stuffed with straw. He clicked to the horse, who then moved into a faster trot.

"It's Crash, isn't it?" she said, her words coming far too quickly. "He's the assassin. He's who you're talking about. Someone paid him to be in the manor. Oh, dear Goddess...." And her mouth went dry, realizing that the entire party had been a trap, that Lord Fallcrest had been a target. Her Lord father.

*Don't panic,* she thought, tears pressing their way to the surface. *Don't cry!*

"Who?" she demanded, forcing herself to stay composed. "Who hired him?"

"I've said too much, and you need to stop asking questions," Dorian said briefly.

"Who?" she repeated, the panic rearing up again. She grabbed the Wolfy's narrow shoulder, wrenching him around in the saddle. "*Who did this?*"

"Get off me!"

"Answer me!"

Dorian flung her aside, shoving her back. Sora lost her balance with a yelp. Struggling to stay on the trotting horse, she tumbled out of the saddle, landing gracelessly in the dirt. She winced; her hip and shoulder were bruised.

"Dammit!" Dorian yelled, and brought his steed to a skidding halt. He whirled on her, reining in the horse only a few feet away from her. With a strange expression on his face, he looked down at her. "Don't run!" he said. "If you run, I'll have to kill you."

Sora was still recovering from the fall. She sucked in a breath of air, then rolled to one side, climbing painfully to her feet. It had been a hard, unexpected impact. "Blast you," she cursed. "Murderers. The both of you. You deserve to be hanged!"

Dorian dismounted and stood next to his horse, who was upset, pawing at the earth and flicking its ears about. He ran a hand over the horse's nose, holding it firmly by the reins.

"Don't run," he repeated to Sora, watching her in alarm.

"Why not?" she balked, already moving back to the treeline. It would be better to run, truly. Even if she was to be taken by an arrow or a knife in the back, at least she wouldn't be traveling with this lying scum. And to think, she had been warming up to him. "You killed my...Lord Fallcrest," she grunted, her gut churning again. It was difficult to say "my father." He had been so little a father to her, more like a distant employer or a landlord. Still, the tears swelled up again, clogging her throat.

"I don't want to kill you," Dorian said. But suddenly she noticed the knife glinting in his hand. He held it up, following her gaze, as though trying to prove his good intentions. "You're not a bad sort, Sora. You're quite spirited, for a spoiled noble. Trust me, I'm not the one you have to be afraid of. Just don't run."

Sora glared. His words almost won a laugh from her. "Trust you?" she choked. "Trust *you?* After all you just said? No bloody chance!"

"There are worse people out there than an honest thief," Dorian replied earnestly. He actually looked concerned.

"You take me for a fool?" Sora demanded, almost to the treeline. Only a few more feet, and she could dash into the underbrush. "I'll report you to the nearest patrol and have you arrested! You'll be sent to the King's prisons! Murdering nobility is as good as treason!"

"Like I said, I'm not the one you should be afraid of," Dorian repeated. Why wasn't he following her into the forest?

"Oh? And who is that? My father's assassin?" she spat.

"Yes." The voice came from behind her, soft and lethal.

Sora gasped.

Arms grabbed her from behind, easily swooping under her shoulders and around the back of her neck. She was clamped against a tall body, lean and hard with muscle. Her arms were locked and a painful pressure was applied to her neck. Her eyes met Dorian's, full of fear, but she saw no pity on the Wolfy's face—only a solemn frown.

Sora opened her mouth, but fear choked her, like ice caught in the back of her throat. "Who hired you?" she managed.

But the assassin didn't answer—or at least, not in the way she wanted. "You may have something of great use to us," his dark voice murmured. *If the Night could speak....*"Until we know for sure, we can't let you go."

"Then take it!" Sora shrieked. She knew what they were talking about—her mother's necklace. She didn't know anything about it, and in that moment, she didn't care. She just wanted to be away from them. Far, far away. "Take the damned necklace! I don't want it!"

"We can't do that," Dorian said.

"Just let me go!"

His grip tightened sharply behind her neck, forcing her head forward and down. Tears squeezed out of her eyes and she gritted her teeth in pain. Dorian's arctic-blue eyes slid over her shoulder, sharing a look with the man behind her. She couldn't read the Wolfy's expression, but she caught the gist of his silence.

After a moment, Crash slipped his arms down the side of her body, grabbing her wrists, pulling her hands behind her. Again, she felt rough, thick ropes against her soft skin. They were drawn uncomfortably tight.

"She rides with me," the assassin said, his voice like steel. "You scout the road."

Dorian nodded, then went to mount his horse. Sora watched him speechlessly. That was it? One command and he turned his back?

She was dragged awkwardly into the shade of the trees. The assassin's gray steed was tethered to a low branch. It danced slightly to one side, disturbed by her fierce struggle.

Sora dug her heels into the soft dirt. She caught her foot on a jutting tree root, trying to resist the assassin. She no longer cared if he killed her. Anger surged. She tried to squirm free, but she was held fast by the hands of her father's murderer. It was...horrifying.

"You bastard," she choked, the words tumbling out of her mouth, half-hysterical. "You godless, disgusting bastard! They'll find you! I am noble-born—every soldier in the countryside will be looking for me! They'll flay you alive once they know what you are!"

He didn't reply. Instead, his hand went over her mouth. Suddenly she was gagging, a nasty, dirty cloth shoved between her teeth. It tasted bitter, strange. No smell. In fact, she couldn't smell anything, not even the musty scent of his leathers or the heavy pine trees. She felt as though her entire face was buzzing.

She kept yelling, choking incoherently. Finally, he released her. She spat out the rag immediately, then she spun, off-balance, unable to catch herself with her tied arms. She toppled sideways against a tree. Her mouth felt numb. Her tongue was swollen. Her ears were muffled. She looked up, trying to fight off a wave of dizziness. The assassin's serpent-green eyes gazed back at her, unflinching.

Then she sank to her knees, suddenly underwater, swimming into blackness....

* * *

Sora came to at nightfall. She was tied to the front of the saddle. She caught the bare edges of sunset, her vision blurry and her head throbbing. Then she leaned to one side and vomited onto the road.

Crash remained silent behind her, an eerie, lethal presence. She straightened up on the horse, her mouth tasting of acidic bile, her arms still roped behind her. The world swam, her balance faulty. She kept blinking, trying to clear her vision. Her head felt equally cloudy. Her thoughts were dim, muffled. She knew where she was and who she was with, but that was all she could reason.

They turned off the road and into the forest once again, where they set up camp amidst the trees. Dorian had already cleared a circle in the wilderness and started a fire. Crash dismounted from behind her, then lifted her easily from the saddle, setting her on her feet. Sora swayed back and forth. She felt distant, one foot caught in a dream.

Dorian came up to her and waved a hand in her face, watching for a response. "Poppy extract?" he muttered, glancing at Crash.

"That, and valerian root," the assassin replied.

"A bit strong, don't you think?" Dorian said. Then, with a signal from Crash, he stepped behind her and cut her bonds.

Sora was barely in control of her body. With her hands free, she sank back against a tree and slipped to the ground, rubbing her wrists, flexing her fingers. She put her head back against the bark, blinking her eyes repeatedly, trying to focus on the branches. She listened to her captors move about the camp. Pots and pans rattled. The horses were brushed down. Eventually, the assassin grabbed a shortbow from his saddle and entered the trees, hunting for dinner. Sora felt the tension loosen once he was gone and took a deep, slow breath.

Dorian glanced in her direction. He knelt by the fire, building a spit for the meat. She avoided his eyes.

"It's not that we don't like you," he started, clearing his throat awkwardly. "But we told you not to cause trouble."

Sora looked away coldly. She felt sick to her stomach—both from the drug and the situation.

He tried again. "Honestly, you're better off than you think."

"How?" Sora snapped. Her lips felt swollen, her words thick in her mouth. She had to chew on them before spitting them out. "How am I better off with a pair of murderers?"

Dorian rolled his eyes. "We're not murderers! Well, I'm not a murderer. I've never killed anyone in my life." He spread his hands open, as though proving his innocence. His words made her nauseous.

"Just a thief, then," she growled, her voice coated with disgust. "And a liar."

He didn't flinch at the accusations. Instead he grinned, his long teeth standing out against his lips, mocking her. "There are worse things than thieves and liars," he said.

"Like what?" she grumbled.

"Like rapists. Child abductors. Slavers." Dorian strode around the side of the fire and paused nearby, watching her carefully. Sora stared back, matching him look for look. Her mind was sharpening from the conversation, slowly regaining focus, though she was still in no condition to stand or run.

Dorian continued. "Crash and I might not be innocent, but we're not the worst. Trust me. The worst would have tied you up, beaten and raped you, and left you to die of exposure. Or they'd sell you into slavery. You'd fetch a high price on the black market, several golds at least. I know plenty of Lords who'd jump for a pretty blond bed-warmer."

"How dare you!" she exclaimed. "Pig!" She spat at his feet and glared, unable to do anything else.

"You know I have a point," he murmured.

"No, you don't. And you couldn't sell me into slavery! I am noble-born. My father's men would come for me. They're searching for me right now. It's just a matter of time."

Dorian's eyes glinted in amusement, but he didn't reply immediately. Instead he turned back to the fire and continued fussing with the logs. "And what about the noble-born?" he murmured. "You think nobility is incorruptible? You think your own father didn't own slaves? Didn't hire assassins? Didn't meddle in other's business?" He glanced at her. "Why do you think Crash was hired, hmm? Out of innocence? Dear old dad—just a victim?"

Sora raised her head a notch. His words were insulting, and yet they struck a terrible, off-note chord. She had heard the kitchen staff speak of her father's "pastimes," his curious business in the City of Crowns. They had said he enjoyed the young ones; that he might have bought and sold a few girls. *Innocents,* their old cook had said. *A damned selfish man.* Sora had barely understood the comments and had closed her ears, refusing to believe any gossip. Slavery wasn't illegal, but it was frowned upon by the King. Her father, a secret philanderer, a slave-buyer, all tucked away in the labyrinthine City of Crowns.

She glanced at Dorian, sick to her stomach. When she spoke, her voice had become just a murmur. "Who hired you? Who killed Lord Fallcrest?"

At that moment, Crash reappeared from the trees with two rabbits. He tossed them to Dorian, who caught them clumsily, taken off-guard. The assassin glanced between them, his eyes cold, then turned to one of the horses and lifted a hoof, picking out little rocks. For a killer, he certainly took good care of his horses. Sora wondered how much of the conversation he had heard.

Dorian set down the rabbits and took out his knife, beginning to skin them. Abruptly he unhooked his water flask from his belt, then threw the flask across the campfire. It landed with a dull thud next to Sora's foot.

"Might want to wash out your mouth," he said, and gave her a pointed look.

Sora glared in defiance, but drank the water anyway. She was horribly dehydrated after the drugs.

Dorian prepared the rabbits quickly and set them on a spit over the fire; the three of them sat back to wait for the food to cook. Sora kept staring at Crash between sips from the canteen, trying to imagine the mind of such a man.

He ignored her scrutiny and examined the next hoof, always busy, his hands always moving. Always silent.

"So can you play that flute, or is it just for decoration?" Dorian asked, interrupting her disturbed thoughts.

Sora looked at him, startled. "What?"

"That flute in your bag, dear," he sneered. "Or did my eyes deceive me? Was that just a twig?"

Sora glared. *So I'm their entertainment too, hm?* A puppet on a string. She wanted to refuse him, to lie and say that it was, indeed, just a useless twig—but then she noticed the assassin looking at her. His eyes were shadowed, impassive. An icy fist curled in her stomach. He was unpredictable. Unreadable.

With a jerky nod, she reached for her pack and brought out the plain wooden pipe, studying it from all angles. It was beaten up and scratched from countless hikes across her father's estate, but still playable. She had practiced most of her life. Young noblewomen were expected to play an instrument. She had tried the harp and the piano, but hadn't been very good at either.

"It's not some intricate machine," Dorian said as she continued to inspect the instrument.

"I know," she grunted indignantly. Truthfully, she had been stalling, trying to remember the most recent song she had learned. It all seemed fuzzy from the drugs. She thought of refusing him again, but...perhaps the music would give her a release, some sort of distraction. Maybe that was his intention.

With another glare in his direction, Sora raised the flute to her lips and paused. It took a moment to remember the notes, and she shifted her fingers several times before they settled into place. The only melody she could think of was a light springtime tune, although it didn't seem fitting to the mood. *Oh well;* she doubted they would care. She started off slowly, breathing lightly against the mouthpiece, the notes drifting hesitantly across the crackling fire.

She played for several minutes, gaining confidence, looping the melody around as she had been taught, with light improvisation. She found that the music was more soothing than she had expected. It gave her something to focus on, something that wasn't dangerous, unknown or terrifying. Slowly, the tension loosened from her shoulders and her stomach felt less sick. Her head cleared.

She lost track of time. If she closed her eyes, she could almost imagine her bedroom, the sound of workers outside, humming along. She imagined her windows open, a cool breeze brushing her cheeks, the scent of jasmine and pine....

Somewhere in her imagination, a faint jingling reached her ears. At first she thought it was part of her memories, the charms that swayed above her bed, or a carriage on the driveway. But the sound grew and grew. Finally, she frowned and lowered the flute, opening her eyes.

The sound stopped.

She stared at Dorian across the fire. He was leaning back against a tree, his arms behind his head, his legs crossed. He looked deeply relaxed. His eye opened to a slit, glancing at her.

She shrugged, suddenly self-conscious. Her frown deepened. *Strange, to have my imagination run away like that....*Dorian looked like he was about to ask her something, and she hurriedly raised the flute to her lips again before he could speak. She didn't want to hear his voice, didn't want to break the spell.

This time she had only reached the second measure when the bells started again, at first tickling her ears, then making a startling rush of sound. Sora came to another abrupt stop. The bells stopped just as fast.

She whirled to look around the darkness behind her, sure that she had heard something, perhaps a rustling in the underbrush. *I'm not losing my mind, I'm not!* Nothing stirred but the wind, but she continued to search the shadows, her heart pounding.

"What is it, Sora?" Dorian asked quietly. He sounded uncharacteristically serious. Her alarm must have been apparent.

She turned back toward him, hesitant to speak. "Do you...do you hear...bells?" she asked carefully. She didn't want to sound loony...though given the situation, it was probably unavoidable.

The wolf-man twitched his long ears, an almost comical sight, then shook his head. He sneered. "Unless you're referring to the crickets, no. Why?"

"I...." Sora saw the way he was looking at her, and decided it was best to say nothing. "No reason. Never mind."

She bent back over her flute and began playing again, but this time the music was filled with wrong notes. She concentrated much harder on the noises in the forest. The sense of peace had vanished from their camp, and it seemed that her two companions were also listening to the woods.

The crickets were hushed. The only sound was the brush of leaves and grass, perhaps the far-off jitter of a forest creature, certainly nothing larger than a raccoon. *Right?* For a long minute she played, doubt beginning to grow. Maybe her ears were ringing; maybe it was an aftereffect of the drugs. But just when she started to relax, the jingle started again, this time alarmingly loud.

It was too much. Sora leapt to her feet, spinning around and pointing dramatically at the trees. "There! Don't you hear it?" The woods were still, silent, but she could sense something just beyond the shadows, feel it moving around, like a worm under her skin. It made her want to squirm. The chinking, chiming noise was persistent, ever-growing in volume, louder and louder and louder....

"Sora!" Dorian stood up in alarm and jumped to her side, as though to restrain her. "What are you doing?"

"How can you *not* hear it?" she demanded, her voice panicked. "It's so loud!"

"I hear nothing; you're imagining it," Dorian said with conviction. "Really, sweetness, getting all worked up like this. It's probably just fatigue."

"No! You have to go look!" Suddenly Sora was scared. She knew she wasn't losing her sanity. For some reason they couldn't hear it.

"Sora...."

"Dorian, do what she says." The assassin's voice was soft with authority. "Put her worries to rest. It's probably the valerian root wearing off, but if not....You know who follows us."

Sora was caught off-guard. Truly? Did he believe her word? She turned to stare at the assassin, speechless.

Dorian nodded silently, though he didn't appear happy about it. He drew two long, wickedly curved knives from his belt and turned to the forest. It stood before him, a seemingly unbreachable dark wall, barely penetrated by the firelight. Then he moved swiftly over to the trees, soundless, a stealthy slink to his walk.

"Stay with her," Dorian spoke over his shoulder, his words directed at Crash. It was an unexpected command. Then he stepped beyond the treeline, vanishing almost instantly into the shadows.

Sora moistened her dry lips. The sound of bells still danced at the edges of her hearing, half out of her thoughts, as though manifesting from a dream. It unnerved her.

"Is there something in the forest?" she asked, turning to look at the assassin.

"Shhh," he hissed.

She bit her lip, trying not to groan as her heart raced. The dark forest was terrifying, and the strange noises only made her want to panic. *I'm still on Fallcrest lands, my lands,* she tried to remind herself, to take comfort in that, but she didn't feel like she owned this forest. No, this was a wild place, untamed, bound by its own whims and laws.

And she hardly felt safer standing next to Crash. He was probably more dangerous than whatever awaited in the forest...but that didn't mean he would protect her. She couldn't—*wouldn't*—trust him.

"Who follows you?" she whispered. Her anxiety forced her to speak. She couldn't look away from where Dorian had vanished into the trees. *What if something really is out there?*

"It's probably just a squirrel," Crash answered, his words short and clipped. "Even if it's a bear, not a lot of beasts can harm a Wolfy mage."

He neatly sidestepped her question. She wasn't surprised. "So he really is a Wolfy?" she asked instead, her voice soft.

"Of course."

"Then why not use his magic to protect us?"

"It's not that simple."

*Well, at least he didn't say no,* she thought.

Sora was suddenly distracted by the idea of magic; it was all but legend now, only found in the stories of the five races. Of course, her people had superstitions....Healers and Priestesses, blessings from the Goddess, omens, charms, bad luck...just not magic. She wondered what it looked like, if it was anything like her favorite stories or something completely different. *Dorian can use magic.* The thought left her hopelessly intrigued. Maybe he would give her a demonstration. She could easily imagine the Wolfy rising to the task, eager to show off.

"Magic is not something to romanticize," the assassin said quietly, watching her face. "It's dangerous and unnatural. The world is better without it."

If Sora could ignore his harsh tone, she could keep from trembling. "Magic is all but legend anyway," she said stiffly. "It's been extinct since the War of the Races...if the War even happened. Who cares about it?" She shrugged. "Some people say that the races never existed."

"And would you agree with them, after meeting Dorian?" the assassin asked. It was a rhetorical question. "There are scattered bands of the other races still running around, hiding their identities from humans. You've probably met several and didn't know it." He looked at her with a stern eye, eerily bright against the night. "Dorian is one of the very last of his kind."

Sora was shocked, but tried not to show it. She clasped her hands instead, turning away from the assassin, staring determinedly at the trees. The bells chinked softly against her ears. Besides that, the woods were uncomfortably quiet.

She knew that Dorian had to be a Wolfy; his fangs and silver hair proved it. But she had always thought the races were only a myth, no more than fantastic stories from a long-forgotten age. And even if they had existed once, they had died out hundreds of years ago; great civilizations turned to ash. There were hardly any relics of that time left, only the barest ruins of ancient cities, of old temples and shrines, whose origins were highly disputed. It was a different world now.

But Dorian was a Wolfy. A true Wolfy. *With magic, at that!*

Suddenly a howl split the air, causing the tiny blond hairs on Sora's arms to rise. She looked at the trees in alarm until her view was blocked by the assassin. He stepped in front of her, shielding her from whatever was coming. He was half-crouched, a thin sword in hand, prepared to lunge at a second's notice.

There was a thrashing noise in the trees and Dorian appeared, his hand clamped to a wound on his side. She could see blood oozing between his fingers. Concerned, she took a step forward but was pushed back by Crash.

Her eyes returned to the trees. She could feel that there was something else coming, thundering in her ears, a sickening clench in her gut—*sleighbells*. The campsite suddenly filled with a repugnant smell, like rotted flesh.

Crash leapt forward just as a creature burst from the shadows. It was tall and bulky, twice the height of the assassin, with dangling arms, wide hands, thin bony fingers, vicious claws and rust-red fur matted with blood. Long yellow fangs protruded past its jaw. The being walked on its hind legs with a lurching gait, bent into an unnatural posture. Its face, which slightly resembled a fox, appeared slightly concave, as though it had been clubbed over the head.

Sora stared in horror. It was unlike anything she had ever seen before—*a monster?* She lost her balance, collapsing in panic.

Everything became a blur. Dorian was flung aside by the beast's massive, distorted claw. It threw back its extended crooked neck and roared, shaking tree branches overhead; leaves rained down on them. Then it dove after the Wolfy with jaws the size of a bear trap.

Crash tried to deter the beast, swinging his narrow blade, but he, too, was easily swept aside by the giant claws. He narrowly dodged a blow, jumping and rolling, hitting the ground and then immediately recovering his stance. Sora thought Crash looked rather puny against the monster, which lumbered around their camp like a shaggy, red-fur mountain.

Suddenly, the assassin was by her side. She expected him to help her to her feet, to run—but instead, he grabbed her forcefully and hauled her up from the ground, pushing her in front of him like a shield. She gasped, her scream caught in her lungs, so panicked that she couldn't even order her limbs to obey.

The assassin shoved her, stumbling, straight into the path of the monster. Sora froze, off-balance, seeing only big, vicious teeth and hooked claws. The beast barreled toward her, a nightmare of red fur and blazing yellow eyes, its wide-open mouth dripping with thick, acrid saliva....

The sound of bells exploded, overpowering, an ocean of noise that swept up into her body, pounding in her ears.

Something rose inside her, warm and steady and fluid, starting at the soles of her feet and going straight up to her neck. It swept her thoughts away, taking control. Her legs and hands stopped shaking. Her mouth closed.

She faced the beast, her fear snuffed out like a candle, and raised her arms to bar the creature from passing—or perhaps, to grasp it in a powerful embrace. She was defenseless, fully exposed, no shield but the air in her lungs.

Then, there was a flash of light. Green. Brilliant. Dazzling.

It split the sky like lightning, illuminating the gaps between the trees, easily penetrating the forest for perhaps a hundred yards. A dome of energy fell over the three travelers like a broad tent. Bolts of yellow electricity crashed down around them, striking the ground, scorching patches of grass.

The creature hit the shield and let out a screech of pain. There was a startling *snap!* A sizzling *pop!* Then a final, shocking flash of green light. Stars danced. Sora was momentarily blinded.

She collapsed on the ground. The dome dissipated as quickly as it had appeared. Her cheek hit the dirt. She felt as though she had run five miles straight without stopping. It was hard to breathe, to pull in enough air. She tried to put her hand on her chest, to understand what had happened, but her limbs were shaky and useless, as heavy as sand.

Finally, finally her eyes cleared. She was able to drag herself upward, as though moving through cold water. She struggled into a sitting position, as slow and clumsy as a tortoise. Her head buzzed, her ears were sore and ringing. Dazedly, she looked around for the monster.

Several yards away, a steaming pile of flesh smoldered on the ground. The mangled, burning corpse was much smaller than the actual creature had been, and she glanced around again, wondering where the monster had disappeared to. The remains looked far more like those of a fox or a badger, half-skinned, its neck broken, matted with blood. She stared at the sizzling body, trying to make sense of it, then slowly swooned and leaned to one side. Caught herself with her hands. Gagged.

She stayed like that for several minutes, emptying the contents of her stomach onto the ground until she could only dry-heave. No one moved. No one spoke. Finally, she looked up, wondering what had happened to her captors.

Both Crash and Dorian were staring at her, eyes wide and unreadable, obviously just as alarmed as she was. Crash was slightly crouched, his arm raised halfway, as though he had been shielding his eyes. Dorian was sprawled on his back, half-propped on an elbow, blood staining his shirt. Her gaze fell to the bloody wound at his hip, unable to hide her confusion. She had no explanation. *Were we struck by lightning?* was her first thought, and yet, there had been no rain. She glanced at the sky just to make certain. No, there were only tiny stars, winking secretively.

From the expressions on her companions' faces, she felt somehow responsible. But she had done nothing fantastical; there was no secret weapon, there were no tricks up her sleeve. She waited for them to speak, wondering what they might say, if they could tell her what had happened.

Suddenly she reached up to touch her mother's necklace. It was warm and intact. A sense of relief filled her, and she let out a long, slow sigh. Good, it hadn't fallen off in the fight.

Then Crash crossed the campsite. His movements were swift and jerky. He reached down and grabbed her, his hand going to her neck with no warning. She abruptly remembered how he had thrown her into the fight, as good as monster chow, as a sacrifice in Dorian's place. *That bastard!* Was he going to strangle her now?

She opened her mouth to scream, but he caught the silver chain and pulled the necklace into the open.

"Then it's true," he murmured, his eyes dark.

Sora began to tremble, recoiling from his touch. She didn't like his hand on her necklace, although she wasn't sure why. She would have knocked him away if she hadn't been so terrified. The assassin stared at her, his expression unreadable, then turned to Dorian. "She wears a Cat's Eye," he said. "Just as I thought."

Dorian was still staring at her in shock. "A...a Cat's Eye?" he muttered, incredulous. "A real, authentic Cat's- Eye necklace? So then Volcrian sent that creature...."

"Yes. He's found our trail."

The two shared a meaningful look that Sora didn't understand. At that moment, she felt more alone than ever, completely excluded from their conversation. *What the hell is going on?* There were too many secrets.

"All right," she began, irritated. She got to her feet, crossing her arms. "I think I deserve an explanation. What are you two talking about? And what is *that?*" She pointed at the smoldering corpse with disgust.

"It's a dead animal," Crash said bluntly.

"I can see that," she snapped.

Dorian tried another answer. "It was transformed by blood-magic into a monster," he offered. "When you killed it, it reverted to its natural form."

"Oh," and she raised an eyebrow. That made about as much sense as anything else. "Fair enough," she said sarcastically. "And what about my necklace? What in hell just happened?"

The two looked at each other again. Neither seemed to want to speak. Finally, Dorian said, "It's a Cat's Eye."

"A what?"

He sighed irritably. "Come now, sweetness, did you knock your head? You've read stories about the War of the Races. You've never heard of the Cat's-Eye necklaces?"

She stared blankly, her ears starting to ring again.

He sighed. "I guess not. Well, haven't you ever wondered about the War? How the humans killed off the races?"

In truth, she had not. Sora had enjoyed the stories of Kaelyn the Wanderer, but she had never truly lingered there. They were just stories, after all, not true history. And what did any of that have to do with her mother's necklace? A Cat's Eye? She put one hand on her head to stop the world from spinning. "What are you talking about?" she repeated.

"The War of the Races," Dorian said, his voice uncharacteristically impatient. He was beginning to sound like Crash. "The beginning of the end. What, do you think the races just dispersed and died off? The humans exterminated them, one by one."

Sora was more than horrified. She could only believe him, considering he was one of the last of the Wolfies. "B-but how is that possible? Humans don't have magic."

"Exactly. So your kind used something else. A cheat." Dorian spoke bitterly. He went to reach for her necklace, but she yanked it away, guarding the jewel protectively. She didn't like the look on his face. She was suddenly afraid that they would try to take it away from her—the necklace, her only link to her mother.

"I still don't get it. What's a Cat's-Eye necklace?" Sora repeated. "And why does it matter?"

"It's a stone..." Crash answered brusquely. She turned to look at him. He pinned her with his stare, his eyes like gleaming daggers. "A stone that eats magic. It protects whoever wears it, a talisman of sorts. It was the undoing of the races, the only reason why humans won the War. While they were wearing these stones, humans became immune to magic and its effects...just like you've demonstrated tonight. The rest is history."

"Why haven't I heard about this before?" she asked.

"Ignorance?" Dorian offered.

She shot him a glare. The Wolfy glared right back. Sora could understand why he was being so defensive, why he greeted her necklace with so much hostility. If his words were true, then it was a devious weapon indeed. But she had never even heard of a Cat's Eye! It wasn't her fault that the humans had killed off the other races.

Then Sora's eyes widened. Had she just saved their lives? *That's what I did, right? Wasn't it?*

"Well, if this necklace is so important to you, just take it," she said, and went to remove the gemstone from her neck.

"No!" Dorian exclaimed, and lurched towards her, holding out his hands. "Stop! Put it back!"

She paused in alarm, the necklace halfway over her head. "Why?" She blinked in surprise.

"J-just do as I say," Dorian said, the hostility vanished. "Please."

She dropped the necklace back in place on her neck, then waited for an explanation. The Wolfy let out a very long sigh, then looked to Crash, obviously asking for help. But the assassin moved away and inspected the charred body of the fox, turning it over with his sword.

"You can't take off the necklace," Dorian murmured. "It will kill you."

Sora's mouth dropped open. "W-what!?"

They stared at each other, another awkward pause. Dorian licked his lips slowly, glancing up to his left, as though searching for the words.

Sora tried again. "I thought you said that the necklace will protect me from magic? What do you mean, it will also kill me?" She now had a full-blown headache.

When Dorian finally spoke, it was a little less confidently. "The Cat's Eye is more of a curse than a blessing," he said haltingly. "It...it's a parasite, a semi-living thing that feeds on magic. It uses the bearer, you see? As much as it protects you, it also uses you. It creates a psychic bond, and if you lose contact with the stone, then the bond is broken."

Sora nodded to show that she was following. The scene replayed over and over in her head, the monster in the darkness, the sound of sleighbells, her forced act of heroism. After Crash's firm shove, she had lost control of her own body, hadn't she? Yes, she remembered that. Something else had taken control, moving her feet, her limbs. But what? The necklace? *How is that possible?*

"What do you mean by that? I still don't understand," Sora repeated, waiting for Dorian to continue.

"The bond grows with time," Dorian explained. "Eventually, the bearer and the necklace become like one mind, inseparable. And, if the necklace is removed, the bond is broken. The bearer falls into a coma and dies."

Sora opened her mouth, then shut it. Her thoughts raced, whirling like a weathervane, round and round and round. She still hadn't let go of the necklace. It burned in her hand, buzzing with energy, hotter than ever before. And she had a strange feeling of fullness, as though she had just eaten bread after a month of nothing but carrots.

"This is why the Cat's Eyes are so rare these days," Crash spoke unexpectedly, breaking the hollow silence. She started, surprised by his voice. "Most were destroyed after the War, too dangerous to be kept as mere trinkets. A single touch can create a bond...and destroy a mind."

Sora's finger rubbed the surface of the small stone. It had the texture of smooth skin, as though she truly wore an eyeball on her neck. She frowned and started to unclasp the necklace, but Dorian's hand stopped her.

"Weren't you listening?" he snapped. "You can't take it off. Not now."

"Why? Because of some stupid legend?" Sora shook her head firmly, frightened but still stubborn. What if this was all superstition? "I don't believe a word of it. This necklace isn't going to kill me."

"Don't be a fool! If the races exist, then so do the Cat's Eyes," Dorian growled. His voice became surprisingly wolf-like, low and deep in his throat. "I'm not talking about silly stories, girl. The necklace is real. It has been bonding with you since you first put it on. How long have you worn it?"

Sora thought back, remembering her birthday, counting the hours. "A full day at least," she murmured.

"Then it's too late. Leave it."

"But...." her voice faded to silence. She had nothing left to say. She didn't know if Dorian's words were true, but she had seen the effects of the necklace only a few minutes ago. She had felt its burst of power, fiercer than a thunderstorm.

And worse than that, she had sensed in her mind a psychic

bond with the necklace. She turned to Crash suddenly, all of the pieces falling into place, realization dawning. "That's why you kidnapped me," she said, stunned. "That's why you won't let me go. You knew I had this necklace."

The assassin shrugged, meeting her eyes coldly. "I thought that's what it might be, but I wasn't sure," he murmured. "I had to see for myself."

Sora sat back, her thoughts still buzzing. She was sore and worn out, but she had to know the truth, the full story. She had heard a name pass between them twice now, a name that had stayed in her mind, hanging sharply like an icicle. "Who is Volcrian? Does he want the necklace?"

The assassin remained silent. Slowly, his brow furrowed.

Sora whirled around to look at Dorian. She was certain that she was onto something. She leaned forward, her words rushed. "Is he the one who hired you? Who wanted Lord Fallcrest dead?"

But Dorian was already shaking his head, his ears slightly drooping. He had ripped a piece of cloth from his shirt and was pressing it tightly against his wound, grimacing in pain. "No, no, not at all," he muttered through bared fangs. "He is a Wolfy mage, very skilled at magic, very practiced. He has been hunting Crash for years, killing anyone who comes near him. Now he's hunting both of us. And you, too, I expect."

"A Wolfy mage?" Sora murmured. Her eyes turned to the small corpse of the fox, which had once been a raging, ferocious demon-beast. "He...he made that?"

"Yes," Dorian said.

"With magic?"

"Yes."

"And he's...hunting you?"

"Again, yes."

"And my necklace...my necklace...." Sora's eyes opened wide. It all made sense. Crash and Dorian had a sorcerer on their trail, and her necklace could protect them. No wonder they wouldn't let her go. No wonder Crash had thrown her in front of the monster. He had wanted to test the necklace—to see if his suspicions were right. And perhaps he had known she would be protected.

Hatred burst in her chest. Crash hadn't cared about her safety in the least. There had to be other ways to test a Cat's Eye. Ways that didn't risk her life.

Sora shook her head, her headache growing worse. She had a lot to digest. A day ago, all of this magic business would have seemed impossible. But there was no other explanation for what she had just experienced. She suddenly wondered if she was awake and conscious, or if she had entered some strange delusion brought on by the valerian root.

No, no, the necklace was real, she knew it had to be true. She had felt odd pulls and nudges at her thoughts, intuitions that she couldn't quite explain, and now the sound of sleighbells. Communication? Warning bells? From a rock? A rock!? *Not just a rock...*she corrected herself, remembering Dorian's words. *A semi-living thing.*

Dear Goddess, what if the stone was conscious? What if it could hear her very thoughts? Share them? Influence them? She shuddered. *I will not scare myself!* No, it was just a dumb story. She had never heard of such a thing as a psychic bond, or a necklace that fed on magic, that lived off the bearer like a leech. And yet, now she didn't want to remove the necklace and find out the truth. Crash and Dorian's reactions had scared her, convinced her of the danger.

There were too many questions, too many unknowns. She would have to find out more, somehow. There had to be a jeweler somewhere in the world, perhaps in Mayville, or the City of Crowns, or any of the dozens of cities that graced the kingdom. A specialist on the matter....

*And my mother....*Who had she been, to have had such an extraordinary artifact? Was she still alive? And where? *How am I going to last long enough to find her?*

"Dorian, we're changing plans," the assassin said abruptly, startling Sora from her thoughts. Crash walked to the other side of the camp, kneeling next to the fallen Wolfy. He had ripped open Dorian's shirt and deftly cleaned his wounds, using water and a mixture of crushed leaves that Sora didn't recognize.

"Is that so?" the Wolfy replied, wincing, looking down at Crash's handiwork.

"We're going through the swamp," the assassin said.

The Wolfy blinked, alarmed. "But..."

"We have a Cat's Eye now. The spells won't harm us, and Volcrian won't be able to follow."

Sora leaned forward, holding up a hand, also concerned. "Wait a moment. You mean...Fennbog swamp? To the West?"

They ignored her. "We should consult Burn about this," Dorian said uneasily. "He might not like it. In fact, I know he won't." He winced as the assassin cleaned out his shallow wound. Despite the blood, it looked like the monster's claws had barely grazed the skin, catching mostly cloth.

"It's our best chance to escape the mage," the assassin

repeated darkly.

"Maybe you're right...but we should wait to consult with Burn."

They fell silent once more. Sora was completely bewildered. *Who's Burn?* She hadn't heard his name mentioned before. More people she didn't know about. And were these two really about to drag her through a swamp? Truly? *Over my dead body!* she thought fiercely. She had to escape! She would have tried to escape right then, but she was so tired after using the necklace, her legs couldn't bear her weight.

Fennbog was the only swamp she knew about. Her father's lands bordered on it, far, far to the West. If her servants were truthful at all, it was a horrid place, full of poisonous plants and mud pits that could swallow a horse. During the rainy season, the waters rose by fifteen feet, and half the landscape was completely submerged. Large patches of marshland would float on the tide, shifting landmarks and creating a terrain that was impossible to navigate.

Besides, Fennbog was rumored to be cursed. If one traveled too deep into it, compasses would fail and the traveler would be lost forever. No one knew for sure how large it was—certainly over a hundred miles. *A hundred miles.* And, assuming she survived the journey, there would be no road back to her manor.

Dorian sat up, his shirt fully removed, a bandage around his waist. Despite his small, pale frame, his chest was chiseled with hard-packed muscle. He leaned toward the fire. She watched the line of his abdominal muscles stretch and bulge.

Then he removed the meat and sliced it on a flat stone, passing the food around the campfire. Sora received her small share, cushioning the hot meat on her cloak. It was burnt almost completely black, forgotten in the brief skirmish. Honestly, she didn't have much of an appetite anymore. She was too worried to eat. But she knew she needed her strength, so she forced the charred bits into her mouth, chewing on the tough, dry chunks.

She didn't want to travel through Fennbog, and she didn't like this news of a Wolfy mage, of magic that could create monsters, and a necklace that could break her mind. *That name, Volcrian.* It made her think of vultures and wolves and frozen things.

Maybe she would have been better off in her manor. Maybe she had made a horrible, horrible mistake.

"Must I...must I travel with you?" she asked, her voice small.

"With that necklace? You can count on it," Dorian replied. He didn't sound happy for her. "So eat and rest. Tomorrow we reach Mayville."

She opened her mouth, wondering if it was worthwhile to plead, to beg them to let her go. But one glance at the assassin told her otherwise. He was sitting uncomfortably close, only a few feet away, slightly behind her, watching her. She knew he was thinking she would make a run for it.

She went back to eating her meat and tried not to think of the next day, or the past hour, or anything other than the mud on her boots. She could still escape, she told herself, trying to keep hope alive. Before they reached the swamp, somewhere in Mayville, she would slip away and buy a horse and flee. She could still find her mother. It wasn't too late for that.

The only alternative was to become a tool in the assassin's game. No choice, no freedom, just like her manor. Her eyes grew serious, her jaw clamped down on the tough meat. She was done with being a pawn.

She looked to the trees, to the night, to the stars above, distant and glinting. She had made it this far—she would make it out alive somehow.

# CHAPTER 5

Volcrian felt the shock run through him. It almost threw him from his horse.

His steed whinnied and bucked, sensitive to emotions. Volcrian wavered in the saddle, almost toppling backward, his crippled hand snagging in the reins and dragging sideways. He gasped in agony, then righted himself and regained control by pushing his weight down. He disentangled his hand and pulled firmly on the harness. The horse shied for a moment, dancing across the earth, then settled down.

Volcrian sat atop the still horse, breath heaving in his lungs, his crippled hand spasming from pain. *No.* He hadn't expected this.

Every blood-mage had a connection to his minions. They shared the same blood, after all. He had felt a shockwave crash over his body: a gust of wind and a firm shove from behind. His creation. His servant. Gone.

After all of the blood he had put into his sorcery, the hours spent catching the fox, a few failed attempts at creating other creatures, monsters that had all decomposed back into dirt—the beast had been destroyed. Obliterated in a matter of seconds.

There were very few explanations for this. His creations were supposed to be immortal, imperishable. It was not possible, unless his prey had stumbled upon very powerful magic. Ancient magic. Rare, indeed. As long as Volcrian had practiced the blood arts, he had never met another sorcerer than Etienne. Not in all the towns and cities they had visited.

Volcrian was not the type to guess in the dark. The fox-corpse should have been powerful enough, with stamina enough, to kill the bastard Dorian and bring Viper to heel. And yet, there had been something slightly different about this energy, this burst of static that had touched his body, reaching straight through the blood of his magic. It had been...green. Lush. He had heard...bells.

Female.

*The girl,* Volcrian suddenly thought, his eyes narrowing slightly. Could it be...that Lady Fallcrest was alive after all? *Ironic, that.* It was one explanation, but how could she conquer a Wolfy's spell? She was a pathetic human. *I must get to the bottom of this. Now.* He couldn't wait too long. He knew Viper well. True to his name, the assassin was as slippery as a snake in the grass.

In one smooth movement, he dismounted. He tied his steed to a nearby thistle bush and walked a brief distance away, glancing around. Eventually he found what he was looking for. A young sapling, just barely sprouted, about knee-high. The spell he would use was brief and simple, very basic.

In order to speak to the dead, one must exchange new life for old. Some would think this meant sacrificing a child or a kitten, but no, a young tree would work as well.

He uprooted the small sapling, its shallow roots pried free easily of the loose, moist dirt. Then Volcrian threw it on the ground, and struck a fire by rubbing flint on rock. In his native tongue, the tongue of his ancestors, he began the long and methodical chant of the dead.

Perhaps twenty minutes passed before a white, filmy shape appeared in the smoke. It was the silhouette of a female, the shade of some unnameable spirit, perhaps a woman who had died in this forest hundreds of years ago. Not all of the races believed the same things about spirits and the afterlife, and not all spirits could be contacted. Only the ones who were willing.

Some races believed that spirits were just as limited as their living counterparts. They only knew certain information, that which they were privy to in life, or else soon after death. But Wolfy lore believed that all things were connected, that all blood was of the same ocean. Once dead, the veil of the body was lifted, and one had full knowledge of all things.

"I am hunting an assassin," he said. The spirit wavered quietly. It was an eerie thing to watch, vaporous and misty, faceless but for the shallow indent of a mouth and a thin trail of hair. "He has a new weapon to aid him. What is it?"

The spirit's figure shuddered, flashed. For a moment, the woman's face was vaguely visible, her hands held up to her cheeks, her jaw drawn out in a long, silent howl. Voiceless words. The sudden vision made Volcrian flinch and move back, but then he held his ground, watching the white mist closely. The spirit spun, smeared, wavered....

"*A Cat's Eye,*" the voice breathed. There was fear in those words.

Volcrian's ears twitched. It was an otherworldly sound, incoherent to any other ear. "Explain," he murmured.

"*I have seen a girl traveling through these woods...a young girl who aids the Dark One. She carries a Cat's-Eye stone.*" The spirit swirled, her long, disfigured face spinning round towards him, her hair bleeding into the wind. The soft voice spoke one last time. "*A Cat's Eye, rich in souls.*"

Then, with a long eerie whine, the Spirit collapsed inward on itself. It was sucked back to the in-between, a dark forest where souls did not rest, but were not damned, simply watched and waited.

The mage took a deep, calming breath, and kept breathing until his mind was cold and clear. A young girl with a Cat's-Eye stone. *A Cat's Eye.* He had never dealt with such a thing before. In all of his years of practice, he had never come across one. He had heard of Cat's-Eye stones in stories of the races, a few vague mentions in his grandfather's script. Supposedly, the stones had all been destroyed shortly after the decimation of the races, tossed to the depths of the ocean from which they had originated.

Was it possible? *How does a child come across such a powerful artifact?* And yet...there was no other explanation for the green light, the jolt that had almost thrown him from his horse. He didn't like its ferocity, the way it had drained his blood-magic like so much water. It felt wild, raw. The girl couldn't possibly know how to use it. Not yet. He doubted she had a clue what she was doing.

Yet as an experienced magic user, he knew the danger of an untrained hand. She was vulnerable, susceptible to manipulation. The necklace was a loose cannon. Magic was not something to be used lightly, like a simple toy. It had consequences, side effects, moods and preferences...each and every spell had a price.

Volcrian turned back to his horse, glancing at the starry sky above him, the sliver of moon on the horizon just above the hills, perched like a wicked smile. He might as well make camp. With his blood-minion destroyed, he wouldn't be catching up with the three travelers tomorrow. They would continue on in the morning, and he would be too exhausted to keep up.

He led his horse to a separate clearing and built another small fire—a natural one. He unsaddled the steed and started setting up a small camp, unpacking his provisions, laying out a bedroll. His mind mulled over the new information.

He had to get rid of the necklace before it ruined his plans. Which meant killing the girl as soon as possible. Once the girl was dead, the problem would be solved. He doubted that the assassin or the Wolfies would try to wear the necklace; that would be risky, dangerous, especially for those who already wielded magic.

But killing her wouldn't be easy. His power would be next to useless. He would need to confront her in person, do the deed himself with his bare hands.

The thought was invigorating, making his heart pound; his hands clenched in anticipation as though they were already curling around her weak, skinny neck. The sooner she was out of the picture, the sooner he could achieve his revenge.

Hurrying to set camp, clearing a space between two low-bending birch trees, he removed a spare saddle blanket and stretched it across a branch as a makeshift tent. His thoughts were eagerly planning the next morning. Tomorrow, he would do a simple tracing spell to gauge their general direction. It shouldn't take more than a bird's egg. Then he could devise a shortcut, cut them off further down the road. The girl would slow down the assassin, enough for Volcrian to get ahead. It was always faster traveling alone.

* * *

Sora awoke in the gray dawn. It was slightly warmer than the previous morning, but she was still sore, her rump covered in bruises from the previous day's ride. She sat up with a yawn and stretched out her arms, rolling her shoulders and neck.

The camp appeared to be in order, except for a few scuffs in the dirt where the monster had appeared the night before. Dorian had thrown the corpse to the trees shortly before falling asleep. It had been mutilated almost beyond recognition. He had used a long stick to move the body, reluctant to touch it or get any blood on him. She hadn't asked why.

Her hand traveled to her necklace, touching the small, warm stone. The memories were fresh and vivid, and she shuddered. *A Cat's Eye, huh?*

It was strange to think that, for the last seven years, she had assumed it was merely a pretty bauble. Now she thought back to the strange stories Lily had told her, stories they had shared late at night, huddled under her bedsheets, the pale light of a candle illuminating their round young faces. *"She never wore it, but sometimes she would talk to the stone. I thought it was magic but...that's just silly."* Lily admitted that she was very young, only six or seven, when Sora's mother had lived in the manor, and wildly imaginative. And yet, she was the only witness to the necklace—or the only witness who would fess up.

So her mother had never worn it, although she must have known what it was. But why would she leave it behind, forgotten, in the nursery, with no warning about its powers? Sora was deep in thought. Maybe it hadn't been intentional. Maybe the necklace had simply been misplaced.

Or perhaps her mother had left in a hurry, with no time to

cunningly hide a letter. Maybe Sora wasn't supposed to have found the necklace; maybe it wasn't meant for her at all.

She sighed. There were no answers. The only option was to find the woman, if she ever could. And she wasn't about to tell her captors about her true quest. They might watch her more closely if they knew she had other plans—then she would forfeit all chance of escape.

Her eyes wandered around the camp to Dorian's resting form and the freshly lit fire. *Crash must be up*, she thought, watching the smoke blend with the fog. She had yet to see him sleep. He was always the first to take watch, the first up in the morning. She thought, briefly, of trying to run away, but she didn't trust the silence of the forest. The surrounding woods were hushed and subdued. She couldn't imagine an eerier place, the fog lingering between the trees, the dim hoot of an owl, the soft crunch of a squirrel in the leaves. The assassin's peculiar absence. She knew he was watching her. He always was.

She stretched one last time, rubbed her arms, then stood up and walked over to the sleeping Wolfy.

She reached out to touch his shoulder.

Immediately Dorian jolted awake. He shot upright and Sora jumped back, a shriek on her lips, but he grabbed her before she could scream and pulled her back down to the ground. Within a minute, she was lying on the dirt by his side, with a rock poking her back and pine needles stuck in her hair.

"Good morning," he said pleasantly.

She tried to contain her response, but a fit of giggles, partly hysterical, burst forth. *Goddess, my nerves are ruined!* It took her a moment to catch her breath. When he grabbed her, she fully imagined it was the monster from last night, howling out of the darkness, its great claws reaching for her....

Dorian sat up, unaware of her near-panic. Then he winced, putting his hand against his wounded hip. He stretched his right side where the monster had clawed him.

"No shirt?" Sora said, indicating his smooth, pale chest.

Dorian's ears twitched in response, and a wicked smile curved at his lips. "I didn't bring a spare," he winked. "Why? Do you like what you see?"

Sora felt her cheeks turn red, but she kept eye contact with him. She shrugged. "I don't court thieves," she said sharply, raising her head, hoping the barb would hit home.

But Dorian seemed immune to her in every way. He laughed instead, a short bark, just like he always did. "We wouldn't be 'courting,' my dear."

She glared, receiving the full gist of his words. She would have spat at him, but he spoke instead, catching her off-guard. "How did you sleep last night, by the way?" he asked.

Sora snorted. "Fine."

"Any nightmares? Monsters in your dreams?"

"No, surprisingly," she said. It was a lie. She barely slept a wink, flinching and starting at every rustle in the bushes. She muttered, "The only monster around here is Crash."

Dorian's eyes widened, then he grinned, looking at her strangely, as though uncertain whether to laugh. "Come now...he's not such a bad sort...."

"Bad sort? He's the worst sort! A murderer for hire, and he killed my...my Lord!"

Dorian seemed surprisingly thoughtful about it, though

perhaps it was just another game. "We've all done our share of bad things," he said evenly.

Sora balked. "He is a killer and should be hung!"

"Now that's a strong opinion for a child," came a soft voice from the trees.

Sora sat up. She turned, her eyes combing the deep shadows between the trunks. Crash stood in the deepest shade, his arms crossed and one boot propped up on a tree root, his black cloak shifting in the wind. Who knew how long he had been standing there? Perhaps since she had awakened. Had he heard their entire conversation? She felt another blush begin under the collar of her shirt and climb up to her forehead—the second blush of the morning.

He spoke to Dorian, ignoring her completely. "Mayville is only a short way off. I didn't see Burn."

Dorian cocked an eyebrow at this. "Probably because he didn't want to be seen."

"What?" Sora blurted, forcing herself into the conversation. "Who's Burn?"

No one answered her. On some silent cue, Dorian got up and started clearing their campsite. Bags were packed and ashes scattered from the fire. They threw pine needles and leaves around, arranging branches so it looked like no one had ever stopped there. Sora was reminded that they were being followed. Hunted. She remembered the name—*Volcrian*—and shuddered, suddenly afraid, glancing over her shoulder into the trees.

Finally they were ready to ride. Sora waited in the middle of the campsite, crossing her arms defiantly, her empty satchel slung over one shoulder. She would wait to be directed. It was a small rebellion, but the best she could manage.

Dorian climbed into his saddle with some difficulty, favoring his wounds, then shot her a pointed look. "You're being a nuisance, sweetheart," he said. Then he nodded over her shoulder. "Go with him."

Sora was puzzled at first. Not about being a nuisance, but the second part. "With Crash?" she asked, to clarify. Her heart sank even lower at the mention of his name. "Can't I just walk behind your horse?"

He grinned at her expression, ears twitching. "An opportunist! I like that. But no, sweetness, quite the opposite. You've already slowed us down too much. Volcrian is on our heels. And we can't have you running away...."

"What? I wouldn't!" Sora exclaimed. The lie was so transparent, she almost laughed at herself.

The thief raised an eyebrow. "You're riding with Crash today," he repeated, and she caught the wryness around his soft lips.

Sora let out a long, expressive sigh, definitely nonplussed.

Dorian nodded again to where Crash was saddling his steed a few yards away. "Go on now. *Be good.*"

She glared, ruffled by his words. Be good. She had never been condescended to before, not like this. It was even more infuriating than the sneers of the city nobility. This man was a common peasant and a thief at that! *How dare he....*

She turned, seething quietly, adjusting the cloak on her shoulders. Then she stalked towards Crash's horse, fists clenched, and stood waiting for him to finish with the saddle.

Her eyes traveled around the forest, counting pine cones, taking note of a few birds' nests. She wondered if they would be eating breakfast any time soon. She had a sudden longing for the manor's kitchen, for the warm tiles and smell of pastries. If there was one thing she missed, it was her usual thick slice of toast in the morning, smothered in butter. *Mmmm, butter.* Or a fresh bowl of porridge with blueberries. Or fruit from her orchard. Or scones and jam. *Yes, scones and jam, fresh from the oven!* The smell would drift from the kitchen through the whole bottom floor of the manor. She could remember being a small child, bent over her math book, thoroughly distracted by the smell of warm, sweet honey scones seeping under the door....

Sora snapped out of her reverie; had someone asked her a question?

Crash was staring at her with an annoyed frown.

"What?" she asked.

"*Get on,*" he said, as if he had repeated himself several times.

"Oh," Sora grunted, then wiped her mouth, surprised at a bit of drool on her lips. *Goddess!* Was she really so hungry?

She stepped up to the horse and put her foot in the stirrup, a little uncertain. She had expected to ride behind him, not in front of him. She wanted to protest, but she also didn't want to look the assassin in the eye. She mounted the horse after a slight hesitation, expecting him to whip out another cloth and try to drug her. But he made no move toward her.

In fact, he completely ignored her as he swung up into the saddle. She sat forward, her back rigid, loathe to touch the man in any way, but he reached his arms around her for the reins. She could feel the press of his thighs against hers. They were warm, firm with muscle. She closed her eyes and thought again of her manor, of the breakfast table, of a delicious fresh scone....

He turned the horse, steering almost completely with his legs, and they headed for the road. Sora's stomach growled but she pretended not to hear it. The sun was bright, although it was still early in the morning. They followed the road as it wandered to the right, where it dipped down the side of a steep hill covered in loose shale. The countryside had become notably more rocky since the previous day, the grass tough and dry, the dirt mixed with rocks and pebbles. It had a dull red sheen, rich with iron. They kicked up small clouds of the red dirt as they made their way forward.

The horse picked its way carefully down the hill, treading slowly over rocks. Sora had to lean back against Crash to keep her balance, and she hated the feeling of his chest against her shoulder blades. It reminded her of her birthday night and their panicked ride through the woods. She felt sick. Today was going to be very long and silent; she wasn't going to say one word to the killer. Not. One. Word.

"Ow!" Sora yelped as the horse stumbled over a rock.

"Pay attention," Crash growled.

Sora shot a glare over her shoulder. *There. Glaring doesn't count as speaking,* she thought. Then she winced as the horse stumbled over another rock; her back was still sore from the previous day's ride, and the stiff, awkward position wasn't helping. *I'd sell my soul for my own horse right about now,* she thought. She wondered if Crash felt the same way. He probably didn't like sharing his horse—or who knew, maybe he got a sick satisfaction out of torturing her. He didn't seem concerned that she was in any sort of discomfort. It occurred to her that perhaps he was jarring the horse on purpose.

"Ouch," Sora flinched again when the horse jolted beneath her, taking an uneven step. She was so sore!

"Try not to damage her, Crash," Dorian called. "I'll scout ahead!"

His little brown steed sped past them, having scaled the hill much faster with only one rider. They were left in a cloud of red dust. Dorian took the lead.

Crash didn't reply, but picked up the pace, rocking gently in the saddle. Sora kept waiting for the next surprising jolt, the next misstep, but it never came; now that they were on flat land, the dirt was firm and most of the rocks were pushed to the side of the road. The horse took off at a fast trot, and she was surprised by its smooth gait. She hardly felt the shift from trot to canter. *Well...this is much better,* she amended.

Over time, she grew accustomed to the motion of the horse and began to relax. Her shoulders slouched, the tension running out of her. The thin morning mist evaporated as the sun rose higher in the sky, but the spring weather stayed cool and refreshing with a brisk wind.

"Ugh, how much longer?" Sora groaned after a while, breaking her promise to herself. She spoke out of sheer boredom, more to herself than to the man behind her. The countryside was nothing but stubborn scrub grass and iron-rich dirt, and she was tired of thinking about her Cat's-Eye necklace and the terrifying Fennbog swamp.

Crash didn't reply until almost ten minutes later, when he finally said, "Burn is approaching. Mayville is just beyond that rise."

Sora felt the horse pick up speed; she was taken off-guard and wobbled in the saddle, close to falling. Crash grabbed her arm and jerked her upright. "You don't ride often, do you?" he sneered.

She recovered quickly from her slip. "Of course I ride!" she snapped back. "By myself! And on finer beasts than *this*."

"Well, obviously your 'fine' beasts make no difference. You're a terrible rider."

"How dare you!" Sora growled, half-turning in the saddle, fully rising to the occasion. "I'm an expert rider! I can jump any fence or wall! I was instructed by the finest of horsemasters, straight from the City of Crowns!"

"Ah, here's Burn."

Crash's dismissal was obvious. Sora's mouth snapped shut, and she turned to look ahead of them, her cheeks still hot with anger. *The nerve!* she thought, even more disgusted at the man behind her, if that was possible.

The steed trotted around a bend in the road and she was finally able to see the last member of their group—he was up ahead, talking to Dorian. Sora's breath caught in her throat. She hadn't truly known what to expect from a man named "Burn." Perhaps someone like the Wolfy mage: small and slender, with nimble hands.

But this man was huge, even at a distance; probably close to seven feet tall. He sat upon a giant Clydesdale, chestnut in color with a white blaze down its nose. Burn's hair trailed freely past his shoulders, a tawny golden-brown, and she could see two long, elegant ears protruding. Another Wolfy? Could it be? Sora stared in fascination at the strong, square jaw, the shoulders as wide as an oak. She couldn't see much else at this distance. He wore a dull, dented chestplate over his clothes, his only piece of armor, and a heavy scabbard across his back, as long as she was tall.

"Mayville is just ahead," she heard the man's voice boom. It was a deep baritone that carried easily over the countryside, like an avalanche of rocks. "Been waiting here for a day or more. What took you so long?"

She watched the man lean down to hear whatever Dorian was saying. Then that large, square head swung around. He was a distance away, but she could still see the gleam of his eyes, bright gold in the sun, and his long, long fangs. Longer than Dorian's, and broader; lion's teeth. She felt her mouth go dry.

Sora braced herself, but she couldn't prepare for the broad, welcoming smile that split his canine face. She fidgeted nervously in the saddle. Was it a good sign, or did she look more like a warm meal?

Finally Crash drew up alongside the two. It was difficult to judge Burn's age by his toughened appearance, but he definitely looked the oldest of the lot. He continued to gaze at her with close interest, not at all concerned with her discomfort. Yet his curiosity wasn't threatening. She felt more like a source of entertainment, like he couldn't quite believe his eyes.

"What vision is this?" he said, confirming her thoughts, and he glanced up at Crash. "A beautiful lady, in the arms of our assassin? A prize?"

"Her necklace." Crash ignored the comment. "A powerful tool against Volcrian."

"I can see that," Burn replied. His voice was several leagues deep, like the bottom of a great crater. Every time he spoke, she felt a cascade of water fall over her ears, echoing into a rocky basin. She couldn't imagine him speaking softly. His height, too, was overwhelming, and he was as wide and encompassing as a mountain.

"Your name, child?" he spoke.

"S-Sora," she introduced herself, wincing when she heard the tremor in her voice. She cleared her throat. "My name is Sora."

"Sora *Fallcrest*," Dorian mentioned, with a wink.

Burn took her hand unexpectedly, clasping it in a very large palm. Her hand was fully engulfed in his, and yet his hold was surprisingly delicate. She felt like he was trying very hard not to grip too tightly. His skin was so thick and calloused, she doubted she could puncture it with a needle.

"Well met," he said, and didn't make any mention of her family name. "I am Burn, mercenary by trade, at least for the time being." He leaned down and murmured, "Honestly, I prefer more mundane pursuits, like bookkeeping. Have you eaten breakfast yet? I'm starving."

Sora found herself smiling.

Crash maneuvered his horse, carrying her away from the gentle warrior. "No time for breakfast," he said shortly. "Did Dorian fill you in about last night? Volcrian has found us."

Burn nodded thoughtfully. "I've heard the important bits," he said. "And I hear you want to cross the swamp. That's a dangerous plan; we might risk more than it's worth. Can I see the necklace?"

Sora didn't get a chance to refuse. The assassin reached around and pulled the chain out of her shirt. The small stone glinted in the noontime sun. She flinched, repulsed by his touch, by the closeness of his hand to her face.

Burn's eyes lingered on the necklace, thoughtful, one ear slightly drooped. He shifted on the back of his horse and gripped the reins, running the leather through his fingers. Sora felt uncomfortable, awkward under such intense scrutiny from a stranger. He had seemed friendly at first, but friendly didn't mean much, she was coming to realize.

Burn finally whistled between his teeth. "Imagine that," he murmured, and he raised his hand as though to touch the stone, but then let it fall back onto the horse. "I've seen a lot of rare things in my life, but nothing like this. And it works?"

"Far better than one would expect," Crash confirmed.

"Oh, yes," Dorian grunted, and raised his hand to his wounded hip. "It vanquished Volcrian's spell like...like...." His voice trailed off, obviously unable to describe the event.

Sora didn't know how she would describe it, either. She shared a glance with the thief.

"Well, then, perhaps we should give it a try," Burn consented, nodding his great head. "The swamp is not far from this town. First things first, though. I have a reservation at an inn with no money to pay for it. They are about to knock down my door and confiscate our belongings. I expected your arrival last night...." He glanced at Crash. "Shall we collect your payment and be on our way?"

Sora felt the blood drain from her face. She wavered in the saddle. Somehow, she felt she had been slapped. How could the three of them conspire to kill Lord Fallcrest and then speak of that so casually in front of her? They knew her name—did they not think it rude or insensitive?

She felt a small twinge of guilt somewhere above her stomach. And who was she to suddenly defend the man? *You hated him,* she reminded herself, thinking of his small, gray eyes, deep and narrow above a long, sloping nose. The downward slant to his mouth, teeth yellowed from pipe smoke and, in more recent years, opium. *He didn't raise you. You were merely a horse waiting to be bred.*

And yet, there had been a time when she was younger...much younger, under ten...that she had desired his affection, had sought it out, time after time. Each attempt had been met with disapproval, annoyance or anger. Sora could remember his slaps across her face, his shouts for her maids to take her away. *"Take her out! Take the girl out!"* Never once calling her his daughter. An heiress, perhaps, for lack of a son as an heir. But never his daughter.

"I suppose, if we're going to cross the swamp, we'll need supplies." Dorian's voice shook Sora from her thoughts. She glanced up, her face unfurling from a tight frown. He was holding up her bag of coins, and he bounced it in his hand to show its weight.

Burn nodded again, this time thoughtful. He looked at Crash. "Why don't you pick up your payment?" he suggested. "Then we will buy supplies."

Crash shook his head slowly. "I can't until nightfall. That's the agreement."

Sora listened acutely, leaning forward, wondering who had hired him.

"Hm," Burn murmured. "Then we will split these coins; it should at least pacify the landlord. Dorian needs rest, and I need to pay for the room." He reached out, taking the bag from Dorian and opening it, then slipping out a few silver coins.

Sora watched, slightly annoyed. It didn't feel right, watching them take her money, as though they had every right in the world to it.

Burn handed the coin purse to Crash once he was done. "Why

don't you take the money and the girl to buy supplies?" he suggested. "If we are going to travel through the swamp, she will need weapons."

"Is that wise?" Dorian asked, wincing and placing his hand on his wound. Sora wondered if he was in more pain than he let on. Probably.

Burn shrugged. "She's a novice at best. She won't give us any trouble. But she needs to be able to defend herself." He cast a grim look at Dorian. "You know the dangers."

The young thief looked uncomfortable, then turned away.

Sora didn't like the exchange. A weapon sounded useful—it would be that much easier to escape—but she didn't like the ominous warning about Fennbog, the way Dorian's eyes looked down. Crash shifted behind her, seeming tense.

"What's in the swamp?" she asked.

Burn glanced at her. "Enemies," he said. "Dangerous beasts. Poisonous plants. Oh yes, we will need to stock up, indeed." Then he glanced at Crash. "You're a poisons expert, no? I trust you will buy all of the proper antidotes."

"I will see to the necessities," he nodded. "And we shall get her a weapon. Though I doubt she will learn to use it." His words hung in the air, tactless, factual.

Sora felt her neck cramp. But of course he would doubt her abilities. He thought she was just some spoiled noble brat. *I'll show him.* "Is that all?" she asked, breaking the silence. "If so, can we go now? I'm getting a sunburn."

Burn threw back his head and laughed—an avalanche of sound. It startled a nearby bird, which took off from a low bush, bolting into the sky. He waved his hand, still chuckling with mirth, though Sora didn't catch the full humor.

"Get on with you," he called. "We will expect you back at sundown. We're staying at The Oaken Door, top floor."

Crash might have nodded, she didn't know, but he shifted behind her, nudging the horse. It took off in a fast trot, leaving the two Wolfies behind, though the sound of laughter followed.

"Don't worry your sweet head about anything!" Dorian called to her from behind them. She turned and leaned to the side, trying to see around Crash's form, but she couldn't. Dorian's voice reached her again. "Just be happy he's the quiet type!"

Then the dirt trail took a sharp turn, rounding a small hill, and joined with the main thoroughfare. The road became wide, well-maintained, paved in brightly hued river stone. She looked up at the distance, down a half-mile of road and across a wide bridge, straight to the red-tiled rooftops of Mayville.

Suddenly, inexplicably, she was excited. She had never been in town before. Of course, she would have preferred to be here with Lily, or perhaps on her very own. But all things considered, she had something to look forward to.

Crash shifted behind her. "If you cause any trouble...." the assassin murmured.

"You'll kill me?" she asked, ready for the threat. She turned slightly to catch his eye. She knew she was challenging him, but she felt momentarily bold. He couldn't kill her, not now. He needed her necklace. And, she suspected, he was too cowardly to wear it himself.

He met her gaze; his eyes were flat, as green as venom, serpentine. She tried to hold out, to sustain the silent confrontation, but it was impossible. Her courage shuddered and wilted, like a dying mouse.

"Don't try me," he murmured. Then the assassin reached up and pulled his cloak over his head, a black shield against the noontime sun. Even in broad daylight, he looked menacing.

She turned back toward the town, unnerved.

# CHAPTER 6

Mayville was the only town on her father's lands. Populated by serfs, it wasn't fully in her father's jurisdiction, as it was half-sprawled on a neighboring Lord's estate. It resided on opposite sides of a trickling stream, a border of sorts, crossed over by tiny footbridges.

The Fallcrest side had red clay-tiled roofs and whitewashed buildings. The Sinclair side favored tin roofs and brick. The villagers and farmers were just as competitive as the two families, holding a yearly festival to prove which side was better. The Tin Roofs baked the best bread and shod the best horses, or so they claimed. The Red Roofs made fancier ceramics and sewed prettier quilts.

Needless to say, a long history of tension existed within the town. Every year, there were disputes over taxes and trade laws.

Sora had met Lady Sinclair once at a tea party about three years ago. The young Lady had been a perfect specimen of country nobility—that is to say, mimicking the First Tier in every way possible. She had worn her hair in a mountain of dark curls, her cheeks pinker than even the sunniest sunburn.

As they entered town, Sora entertained the dark, horrifying thought of bumping into Lady Sinclair and being recognized. *"Dressed as a peasant in day-old clothes,"* she could almost hear. *"I'm sure her mother would be proud."* Followed by shrieks of laughter, of course. But she shook her head, trying to clear it. If she were recognized, that would lead to her rescue, which would be more than welcomed. But her rescue would return her to noble life, which she dreaded. At that moment, she wasn't sure which she preferred—the life of a captive, or the life of a Lady. They felt much the same.

She and Crash followed the cobblestone road through town. It took some time to find an inconspicuous place to tie their horse, away from traffic and yet not so far as to be stolen. Then Sora followed the assassin on foot, carving their way deeper into the marketplace. He kept a subtle grip on her hand, as though they were old friends...or worse, lovers. Sora tried to pull away, but his grip tightened.

"It's too crowded," she muttered, narrowly avoiding a large woman in aprons, a tray of freshly baked bread in each hand.

"Stop dawdling," Crash said sharply, dragging her through another swarm of people. She had no choice but to follow, his hand solidly on hers. She was barely able to dodge the stampede of farmers, bakers, smiths, midwives and chickens. It seemed like everyone from the surrounding countryside was at market. *Well, she figured, thinking back on her estate studies, it is Spring and they are clearing their barns for new crops.* Countless serfs haggled over wares, buying livestock or spending well-earned coin.

Lily had described Mayville as a "mid-sized" town; until now Sora hadn't known what that meant. It seemed pretty big to her. The vendors' carts were numerous and there was more than enough to stare at. Baskets of flowers hung from windowsills, fountains decorated each market square, and sheepdogs ran back and forth, fighting over bones or chasing cats.

Crash led her past everything, stopping only to buy a few

biscuits, one of which he tossed in her direction. Sora caught the roll in midair, immediately popping it into her mouth, relieved to fill her stomach.

Then a voice burst out from her right-hand side, making her jump.

"Goddess here! Bells of the Goddess! Her Winds bring you good luck!" A skinny man leapt frantically around the crowd, a cluster of brass bells in his hand, charms of the Wind Goddess. There were several other bells of various shapes and sizes hanging from his booth.

His stand was full of miniature figurines, whittled from cheap wood. Sora glanced over them curiously. There were the two male gods, Fire and Light, and the rest were of the goddesses: Wind, Earth and Water. There was a final sixth god, that of Darkness, but it was considered bad luck to portray Him.

Each god or goddess had its own pose, its own fortune: good luck, good business, courage, wisdom, health. Their lore went back to the creation of the world and the different races. At one time, all of the gods and goddesses had been worshipped; each race had paid homage to a different deity. But now the races were gone, and the humans only worshiped their patron Goddess of the Wind.

Shrines to the other gods could still be found in rural areas, but they were small affairs, stone monuments found deep in the forest, overgrown with moss.

For a moment, she yearned for such a bell—maybe it would bring her luck on the road—but then Crash was by her side, tugging her into the crowd. He didn't seem impressed by the salesman.

They waded across to a store that read *Dried Goods* across the front window. Sora was stunned by the line of people out the door, so long it trailed into the street and around the corner. She thought Crash might try to enter anyway—barge his way to the front, step on a few toes—but no such luck. They followed the line to the end and got behind a withered old woman with two scabby children, both smudged with dirt.

Perhaps even more terrible was when the woman turned and said to them, "Did you hear?," pinning Crash with a milky-blue stare. "Lord Fallcrest is dead. And his own daughter, the culprit!"

Sora's mouth dropped open.

"Aye, missy," the woman said, nodding to Sora with an air of knowing. "I almost fainted meself when I heard the news. But the funeral was yesterday and the Lady gone missing. Why else would she run from the crime? The whole town is speculating—if not the whole countryside!" Then the woman laughed, a large, gap-toothed grin. "The nobility think they're above the King's laws! Well, this'll teach her!"

Sora was speechless, her mouth full of dust. *The culprit?* Had she heard correctly? No, it must be a mistake, perhaps she had misheard, or the woman had misspoken. *Killed my own father? Is that what they think?*

She glanced at Crash, still stunned. She should do something— tell the woman the truth, point to her dark companion and proclaim him a killer. But she had seen the knives gleaming at his belt, and even more blades concealed beneath his cloak. She would be dead in a heartbeat if she raised her voice.

She caught a look from the assassin and knew that was true.

"Right," she said, turning back to the woman. "That wretched nobility!"

The woman nodded agreement and turned back to her

children.

Sora spent the remainder of the time in brooding, contemplative silence. They left the store almost an hour later, her arms laden with brown bags and heavy packages. The crowds were larger and sweatier than before. It was mid-afternoon, bright and blazing hot. Sweat began to form at the base of her neck, trickling between her shoulder blades.

*A murderer.* That's truly what they thought. And the serfs believed whatever the manor's servants told them. It almost hurt worse, knowing what those servants must think of her. Now that Sora's ears had been alerted, she seemed to hear the same conversation everywhere, shouted from second-story balconies through open windows, from clotheslines to street corners: *"Lord Fallcrest is dead, and our Lady, a murderer!"*

*"We shall have to protest, to petition the King."*

*"They haven't found her yet. Where could she have gone? In the swamp, methinks. Nowhere else to hide...."*

*"The Sinclairs, I'd bet you two acres they did it. They're old enemies of the Fallcrest name."*

*"Of course a Red Roof would say that! The Sinclairs are good, honest, hardworking people...with any luck, the estate will go to them!"*

The Sinclairs. Now that she thought of it, it didn't seem so farfetched. They had connections in the City of Crowns; they could arrange an assassination. She glanced at Crash, again wondering who had hired him. The question was on the tip of her tongue. They were in Mayville, after all, the most likely place to collect payment if the Sinclairs were guilty. And Lord Sinclair could lay claim to their land in such a fragile situation...or at least, to the town, as he'd been trying to do since before she was born. It suddenly made too much sense.

The sound of laughter caught Sora's attention, distracting her from her dark thoughts. She looked up, curious. A whirl of bright colors appeared ahead of her, breaking through the crowd. Blues, greens and reds....

As she neared, she saw a street entertainer standing inside a large circle of people. He was dancing to a musicbox, whirling left and right, a rainbow-colored cape flowing around him, scarves and bells twirling in the air. He wore a lopsided hat; a crow was perched on the brim, maintaining its balance with a few awkward wing flaps.

Intrigued, Sora stopped, mesmerized by the flashing colors.

The music changed, and the street entertainer ran around the circle of spectators, pulling nuts and oddments out of children's ears, then trying to put things into their pockets that were too big to fit. Sora had never seen anything quite so ridiculous. The large crow flew above the crowd, snatching up coins that were flipped in the air. The street entertainer spun around amid roars of approval.

When he reached her side, he pulled out a long yellow lily from his sleeve. With a small bow, he offered her the flower. "A beautiful flower for a beautiful lady," he said.

Sora opened her mouth, surprised. She was momentarily reminded of her handmaid, who had loved lilies, her namesake. She found herself suddenly choked with emotion.

"Thank you!" she finally managed to say. She set down the heavy packages and took the flower.

The man laughed. He had twinkling, aqua-colored eyes, somewhere between blue and green. For a moment she had to wonder at those eyes, which seemed unnaturally bright and shiny, sort of like opals or sapphires.

Then the odd man danced away back to his audience. Sora sighed, wishing she had a coin to toss him. She would have given him an entire goldpiece. She glanced at Crash, thinking of her stolen purse.

But the assassin was not by her side, where she had expected him to be. She turned around, searching the crowd....

Gone.

She looked again, left and right.

Yes, gone.

Sora's heart began to pound. She couldn't quite believe it, and she turned around full circle, astounded. The assassin was nowhere to be seen. He'd lost her in the crush of people! *Now's my chance to escape.*

Sora turned on her heel and pushed her way through the swirling foot traffic. A few people shouted, pointing to her dropped packages, but she ignored them. No time to waste. The assassin would notice her absence at any moment, if he hadn't already. She remembered where Crash had tied his horse. She would take the steed and make a run for it. She wondered where Crash had got to....

Sora was so focused on her thoughts that she ran head-first into something very large and very solid. *Whumph!* She gasped, stopping dead in her tracks, and brought her hand up to her nose, her eyes tearing in pain. She glanced up....

"Well there, little thing. Don'cha have someplace to go?"

She had half expected the street entertainer again, but came face to face with a massive belly. Her mouth dropped open. She craned her head back quite a long ways, and found herself staring at a blunt, shaggy face, fat lips and an exaggerated nose. Mean little eyes stared back at her.

"I-I..." Sora was tongue-tied. She didn't know what to say. The man was as ripe as a pig barn and utterly gruesome.

"Ya know, it's dangerous in town these days, what with Lord Fallcrest gone," the giant man chortled. "Not much law on this side of Mayville. I'd be careful. Never know who you might...bump into." There were a few stifled laughs from behind him. It was only then that she noticed his friends, weasel-like cronies lurking in the background, grinning.

Sora backed away, horrified. She had no weapons, no means of defense. What could she possibly do—use her necklace? She touched the stone at her neck, wondering if it would work to protect her, but there was no murmur in response, no sense of energy, no movement.

Then she bumped into another body, this one behind her.

"She's with me," came a familiar voice.

Sora whirled around, her heart in her throat. She knew that voice, soft and lethal. She took one look at Crash and almost collapsed. *Blast!* Now she was right back where she had started. He held a bundle of rope in his hands; she recognized it from a nearby vendor's stall. So he hadn't been far away.

The assassin didn't even glance at her. Instead his eyes were locked on the giant. "Is there someplace you should be going?" he asked the man. His voice was as sharp as a knife and twice as deadly.

"Yer lucky there is, shrimp, or else I'd smash in your face," came the guttural response. They stared at each other for a long moment before the man lumbered off, parting the crowd effortlessly, cronies trailing in his wake.

Sora turned to Crash, wondering if he would kill her after all. She opened her mouth, ready to explain.

He shoved the bundle of rope into her hands. "Come on," he cut her off, then turned and stalked away.

She stared after him, surprised. He kept walking. She waited, wondering if he would disappear into the crowd again, but he stopped above the pile of their bags. She had only traveled about thirty feet; it had seemed much more with all of the people in the way.

He turned to look at her. The expression on his face was not encouraging.

She slung the rope over her shoulder and scurried to pick up their bags and packages, his gaze a whip at her heels. He started walking again as soon as she had picked up the last package. She wasn't used to carrying such a heavy load and, to be honest, felt absolutely humiliated. Not only was she being treated as his servant, but he had just bailed her out of a very awkward, potentially dangerous situation. What if he hadn't arrived? She hated to think that he had actually *helped* her.

They walked for a few minutes and suddenly the crowds parted before them, leaving them in front of a small shop. It was low to the sidewalk, with smudged windows and chipped paint. A sign with a sword on it hung above the faded green door. Sora figured this was some sort of weapons dealer.

Crash swept her into the shop before she could say anything. The door closed behind them with the small ring of a bell. *Ding-ding.*

She paused and looked around, hesitant to set foot in the gloomy darkness; the shop was not very big, from what she could tell; most of it was shrouded in shadows and dust. The air was musty, like a bedroom that hadn't been used for a long time. A row of old candles spewed thick smoke but hardly shed any light.

She glanced uneasily at Crash. At first, her eyes passed right over him; he was barely visible in his black clothes. He seemed to belong in the musty store, snug on a shelf somewhere, with all of his daggers and swords and road dust.

Suddenly, from her left, a voice drifted through the gloom —"May I help you?"

Startled, Sora pivoted sideways and landed on Crash's foot. He grunted and caught her shoulders, steadying her for the hundredth time that day. *All of those nights spent sleeping in the woods must be getting to me,* she thought, brushing herself off, trying to regain her dignity. Then she peered into the shadows, her eyes narrowed, trying to determine where the voice had come from.

After a few moments, the darkness seemed to form into a man. He was tall, thinly built, with very pale skin like alabaster—the last kind of person she would expect to see in a weapons shop. As he stepped toward them, she could see that he had soft, delicate features, pale hair that wafted across his forehead and wide, sensitive eyes of a peculiarly glassy color.

He paused a few feet away and clasped his long, bony hands in front of him. He coughed lightly into them as if hiding a smile, and Sora felt a sense of disbelief, as though she were talking to a ghost.

"So sorry," came his sweet voice again; his words were gentle and airy, pleasing to the ear. "I didn't mean to startle you. Are you looking for anything specific?"

"A good blade—if you carry any," Crash sneered.

Sora glanced at the assassin and raised an eyebrow. She wasn't truly surprised; as far as she knew, he was always rude. Turning back to the store clerk, she witnessed the man's expression change from warm to cold; his face hardened and he glared straight back at Crash. The dislike between them was so intense, Sora wondered if they knew each other. But how could they?

Then the clerk pointed a pale, elegant hand past her into the shadows. "Our blades are toward the back of the store," he drawled. "I hope you find what you're looking for. If you are in need of assistance, don't hesitate to ask." He smiled tightly at her. Then he turned away, as though carried by a slight wind, and disappeared into the gloomy shadows.

With an impatient tug on the back of her cloak, Crash led her toward the rear of the store, his pace swift. Soon Sora found herself at the opening of a narrow aisle. Her eyes had grown accustomed to the lack of sunlight, and revealed a sight she had never expected to see.

Both sides of the aisle were lined with blades: swords, sabers, cutlasses, and other weapons that she had never before imagined. Sora doubted that she would be able to lift even the smallest one. She kept to the center of the aisle, holding her arms to her sides, hugging the meat packages close.

To her relief, Crash didn't stop at the sword section, but continued to walk until they were looking at a row of daggers, each laid with explicit delicacy upon the shelf. They didn't look particularly sharp. In fact, they looked downright *old*, as if they had been rummaged from attics and basements, abandoned houses, or —perhaps—crypts.

She decided to mention that.

"What are these—butter knives? You couldn't slice cheese with them," she said loudly.

"A whetstone should do the trick," Crash murmured, and plucked two long, curved knives from the shelf. "And we don't want you cutting off a finger."

Sora opened her mouth to respond, but was distracted by the flick of his wrists. The blades spun in his hands, smooth as windmills. He flipped one dagger and caught it deftly, spinning it again between his fingers.

After a moment, he set the pair back on the shelf. Then he moved to the next.

He repeated this process several times with many other knives. They all looked the same to Sora, who stood a safe distance away, but she didn't ask what he was looking for. After a while, she stopped watching. Every flip of the knife reminded her of his deadly hands.

Finally he turned to her and offered two docile-looking daggers, almost twice as long as her hand. They looked blunt and bulky, but when she picked them up, she was surprised to find them almost weightless. She had never held anything bigger than a steak knife before, but somehow the grip felt natural; she could feel the dagger's balance and shifted her hands easily. She saw, or rather thought she saw, a hint of a smile pass over Crash's face. Then he asked, "Have you ever handled a knife before?"

"No," was her only answer.

"You'll work with them well," he murmured. "Though you'll need a larger weapon."

"Larger...?" Sora echoed in surprise. Weren't these wicked

blades enough?

He nodded, then turned, striding into the darkness. Sora half-jogged to catch up to him. He made his way down the center aisle, checking the shelves on either side. They passed spears, ropes, archery, hooks, maces, and other rows of weapons that Sora couldn't identify. Still he didn't stop. She was now striding just behind him, thoroughly puzzled about what he was looking for.

Finally, he stopped at the very back of the store, where the shadows were the murkiest. Sora hesitated to follow him into the gloom; she could hardly see. She stepped up to the nearest shelf and timidly ran her hands over it, then blinked in surprise. Both sides of the aisle were lined with wooden staffs in different shapes and sizes.

"Pick one," came Crash's voice from in front of her.

"What?"

"You need a larger weapon. I doubt you can lift a sword, and it takes too long to learn archery."

"Why not a spear?" she asked.

"You need to learn the staff first. Trust me."

Sora glared at him; he raised a dark eyebrow. She stiffened indignantly—then looked back at the shelves, rows upon rows of silent wood. There were no hints, no signs indicating what she should do. Finally, she shrugged. "I don't know anything about weapons. How am I supposed to pick one?"

"Well, I can't help you," Crash's tone was scornful. "I don't know what will balance for you. You're quite...short."

"Petite," she corrected him in annoyance.

He just stared at her. With another sigh, Sora gave up and turned back to the shelves, a peculiar sinking sensation in her stomach. "How will I know if it balances for me or not? I know nothing of testing for balance." It made her anxious. *What if I pick the wrong one?* And what good would a large stick do in defending herself?

"You'll know," was his only response. "It will feel natural."

Sora nodded in defeat. Well, there was a first time for everything...but she was pretty sure this would be hard, and she would probably pick the wrong one. Tentatively, she reached for the first to her left, a stout oak staff. Sora gripped it and turned to look at Crash to see if she was doing the right thing.

He nodded. "Hurry up."

Sora turned away from his scrutinizing gaze and lifted the staff off the shelf. It was so heavy, she almost dropped it. After fumbling for a moment, she placed it back on its perch. That definitely wasn't it. The next one was made out of willow, and she was attracted to its classy sheen, but it proved too tall for her to wield easily. She tried one made of pine that turned out to be slightly heavier on one end. With a small smile, she felt her confidence grow. Maybe this would be easier than she had originally thought.

She repeated this process several more times, trying woods that she was familiar with and a few she had never heard of before. Most were either too heavy or too tall. Finally, when she was just about to give up, her hand bumped into a staff that was placed far back on the shelf, barely noticeable. Its wood was a dark, dusty gray, almost blue. Lifting the staff from the shelf, she found it had a sturdy weight to it, though not too much to tire her hand. It reached eye level, and the letters KW were carved into the top, most likely the initials of some loving past owner. She gripped it in the middle and laid it crosswise. It felt comfortable. Familiar.

Turning to Crash, she said, "This is it; I found one." She did her best to give him a smile, though smiling at the assassin seemed odd. "We can go now."

He nodded and took the staff from her, feeling it in his own grasp. He seemed satisfied, and without a word, turned back down the aisle. Sora had to rush again to match his strides. Sometimes she hated being so petite.

When she caught up to him, he was standing at a front counter that she hadn't noticed before. As soon as Crash reached for the service bell, the strange man appeared again.

"I hope you found everything you needed," he said in his musical voice. Sora wanted to lean in closer. Though she couldn't explain why, she could listen to that voice for days. His voice was truly like honey to the ears. She almost asked him to sing.

"Yes, fine," Crash said, his own voice like brass.

The man nodded and then smiled charmingly at her. He took their items and checked them over, assessing the price. He stopped when he saw the initials on the staff and glanced up at her, his eyes searching. "Are you sure you want this one? There are several other good staffs back there," he said.

Crash snorted his opinion, but Sora ignored him. She was intrigued by the question. "Of course I want that one," she said. "Why?"

"I'm not one to argue with a customer, but this is witch wood," he said, as though expecting her to know what that meant. She waited for him to explain. "It's...for professionals. You know, trained soldiers or the King's Wanderers...." He paused, looking back and forth between them. Neither spoke. Finally, the man sighed. "I was holding it for another customer, but he is long overdue and I fear he won't come for it. So I'll sell it to you...for a bit more. The wood has special properties. It's excellent as a weapon, harder than normal wood, and can't be broken by a sword."

"How much does it cost?" came Crash's annoyed voice. He dropped Sora's coin purse onto the table.

Sora held up her hand to stop him, engrossed in the man's story. "Wait. What do you mean, witch wood? You say it's unbreakable?"

The clerk frowned, pursing his lips. "Well, it's all but extinct. It comes from The Bracken, a land far to the east of here. Very rare. The wood is unbreakable, and some say it has magical properties, but I can't vouch for that. This one was found floating off the coast."

"Enough with the lesson," Crash cut in. He shot Sora a glare when she tried to interject again. "What's the price?"

Sora wanted to scream in frustration. Here was another man who acted as though magic was more than just a myth, who might even know something about her Cat's-Eye necklace, and now she couldn't even speak! She opened and then shut her mouth, wondering if it was worth fighting with the assassin; she didn't doubt that he would lift her up and carry her from the store if she provoked him. And she had already tested his anger once today. It felt like he was growing more and more annoyed with her by the minute—and that wasn't good for her health.

With an angry sigh, she turned away from the store clerk and stormed toward the door, eager to leave the assassin's company and run back out into the daylight.

Crash bought the weapons and followed her swiftly. He

overtook her at the doorway and grabbed her wrist with enough force to hurt her, dragging her from the store. The clerk's eyes followed them.

Outside, Crash shoved her into the alley next to the building that was shielded by a small sapling tree. Then he stood in front of her, eyes narrowed, lips curled.

"Dorian might find your ignorance charming, but I don't," he hissed. "I am not your friend, nor your footman. Silence yourself, or I will. *Don't test me.*" Flashes of heat swept through her; she felt fiery and cold all at once. Furious that he had threatened her. Powerless to defend herself. It overtook her suddenly, a strange need to cower, to hide her face. *I'm a coward,* she thought, realizing it for the first time. *Without my father's name, I'm nothing.*

If anything, this infuriated her even more.

Crash turned away, looking for a sound in the alley; so he didn't see the confusing mess of emotions pass over Sora's face. *Evil bastard!* she thought, watching him. She blinked back hot tears, regaining her self-control, angry for letting in that moment of weakness. Her teeth dug into her lip, showing her stab at willpower.

Then she followed Crash back into the crowded streets. She was glad that she had the bags to carry because they hid her shaking hands.

The two visited several more shops. Sora stayed silent, as she'd been told. The sun started to set, smearing a gory mess across the sky. The crowds thinned to a few scattered people. Even as she watched, they seemed to slowly melt into the surrounding streets. As though by magic, the square was empty by just past 4 o'clock, draining with the sinking sun.

She looked around in wonder at the wide-open cobblestone streets scattered with scraps of cloth and paper, the only remnants of the busy market. There was a large fountain in the middle of the square with water splashing quietly down its sides; she wondered if it had been there before. The buildings around the square were closed, the windows dark, already shut down for the day.

Then she noticed Crash counting on his fingers, ticking off items on a mental list. "All we need now is a map," he muttered to himself.

Sora sighed; one more item to add to her already sore arms. Even an extra piece of paper sounded too heavy to carry. All she wanted to do was sit down and rest.

"Girl," he beckoned to her unexpectedly. *I have a name, you know.* Then he turned and walked away, obviously expecting her to follow.

Sora stared after him, speechless. She thought of dropping the packages and making a run for it, but she knew she wouldn't get far. Finally, she started after him, juggling the bags in her arms. The packages teetered precariously. "A map of Fennbog swamp?" she called. "But no one has ever crossed it."

"That remains to be seen," Crash replied, and turned down another street.

*Of course.* Sora followed, still skeptical. *What good is a map when the landmarks float around?* She had heard stories of Fennbog. More than just stories. Facts. Each rainy season completely rearranged the territory. Hundreds of miles of muck.

It was beginning to get cold. The wind picked up and the sun sank lower on the horizon, now just a blurry rim of light. The stars had crept into the sky. Several twinkled right at her, winking merrily as though laughing at her predicament, telling her all of her worries were just a big joke. She picked out the constellation of Kaelyn the Wanderer and wondered if the lady warrior was looking down at her, somehow sharing her troubles.

She smiled softly at the thought, still staring at the stars. Her astronomy teacher once told her that all of the world's stories could be found in the heavens. Each constellation had a history, a piece of lore. If one listened closely, the stars would share their stories, telling of years long past, of places long lost to the world, of secrets long forgotten by man.

Fanciful, perhaps. But the stars were still pretty to look at.

The streets they were walking through now were lined with shabby shops and pubs set low to the ground. She could hear muffled noises from the alleys they passed, grunts and hoots and bottles breaking; she quickened her step. She still did not feel safe with the assassin. He seemed to fit in with the shadows, into the odd sounds from the alleys, as though he came from a place of murky smoke and darkness.

He stopped in front of a small shop with a large domed roof. Light glowed from inside like a giant paper lantern, illuminating the streets in the immediate vicinity. Sora stared at the strange building until Crash yanked her toward the door and opened it. He took her bags, then motioned to her to go inside, a very chivalrous act for a man like him.

Sora stepped inside. With a small click, the door swung shut and Crash paused next to her. She immediately reveled in the warmth that flooded her senses, and looked around the room in wonder. Cheery lanterns graced the walls on either side of the shop.

She had never seen anything quite like this, not even in Lord Fallcrest's library, which was one of her favorite places.

The small circular room was jammed full of bookshelves, which were crammed with all sorts of books. She could see the twinkle of a thousand stars through the large domed roof. Tables set up like a maze throughout the tiny shop were stacked with piles of dusty scrolls, yellowed books and wrinkled parchments. The air was heavy with the scent of paper. Sora had the sudden, intense urge to curl up in an armchair with an old book and maybe a nice cup of tea.

Crash didn't make any attempt to find the storekeeper; instead, he circled a nearby table, leafing through old papers and books. Sora waited, glancing around, until she grew impatient. "Hello?" she called. "Is anybody here?"

"A second! Just a second! Hold your horses!" was the immediate response, closely followed by the unmistakable sound of a book closing. A small cloud of dust rose above a tall stack of papers somewhere to her left. A sneeze issued from behind the table. "Hearing ain't what it used to be," muttered an ancient, scratchy voice.

Sora looked around, wondering where the owner of the voice was hiding; suddenly she saw a weathered brown hat (obviously with a person underneath it) wandering through the maze of tables. *I thought that was a decoration!* she thought in surprise.

Then out came an old man, stooped and worn, with stiff gray hair that stuck out from under the hat like the bristles of a broom. He sneezed once more and looked up at her with vivid blue eyes. Sora thought he looked like a crafty badger or a gray fox. He wiggled a thick white mustache at her and scratched his stubbly chin.

"Well, what d'ya want? Eh? I wouldn't be out this late if I were a pretty young girl like you. Getting dark these nights—darker than usual, even with a full moon, and all of those ruffians out on the streets...." He trailed off, blinking at her. Sora was too tired to reply. She shifted on her sore feet.

"But of course, I'm not a pretty young lady like you, am I? Ha ha! And I certainly don't have my own bodyguard—eh, young man?" he called over her shoulder. "I'm sorry, are you looking for something? I'm a bit scattered at the moment. Age catches up with you, you know—doesn't matter how far you travel. Just the other day I almost set this whole place on fire, spilled a candle. Not very good for business...anyway, what is it you need?"

Crash didn't answer.

"A—a map," Sora said. The man's rambling was a little hard to follow. Now that she was in a warm room, the full force of her exhaustion hit her; she wanted to take a nap right there on the floor.

The storekeeper turned away and threw up his arms, making a loud sound of annoyance. He stalked off toward one of the back tables. "'A map,' she says, 'I need a map!' Well that's certainly a big request! A map of what, exactly? The world? Hasn't been made yet. The oceans? Mostly uncharted, except for the coasts. How about further inland? The City of Crowns? A grand sight, to be sure. The Temple of the North Wind? You'll need to join their discipleship to go there. Sorry if that spoils your plans." He paused and looked her over. Sora knew she looked a mess—her hair was relatively straight, but her clothes were muddy and wrinkled from her nights spent in the woods. The storekeeper, however, seemed to look right past all the stains. "You seem like a well-off patron," he said, and eyed their bags by the door. "Are you taking a vacation? A little getaway? I know of some great spots."

Sora couldn't answer the strange old man. Her mouth was dry; she was overwhelmed by the possibilities. The silence stretched— *get a hold of yourself!* She swallowed with a force of will.

Then Crash spoke up, saving her from further embarrassment. "A map of Fennbog," he said pointedly. "The *full* swamp."

The man frowned at him, appearing genuinely concerned. "Have you lost your wits, man? Fennbog swamp has never been traveled, let alone mapped. The geography changes each season, anyhow. You can't map the weather!" And then he laughed, throwing back his head, spittle flying from his lips. Sora didn't think the joke was that funny. The man calmed down, wiping a tear of mirth from his eye. "Besides," he finished, "They say that swamp is cursed."

Sora gave Crash a pointed look. She had tried to warn the men days ago, but of course, no one had listened.

"Right," Crash said, and took an unexpected step toward her. "But we have this." And he nudged Sora with his shoulder. She stumbled forward, her mouth opening in surprise.

The old man stared at her, his eyes narrowing, then his gaze slowly traveled down her face, to her neck, to the chain that wound under her shirt. With a huff of annoyance, Sora pulled the Cat's Eye into the open. She knew this was what Crash wanted, though she wasn't sure why. She didn't see how a magical necklace would help in the swamp.

The man gazed at the stone. His eyebrows rising almost into the rim of his hat, he took a steady step toward her. "Is that...." he murmured, still staring. "Is that...."

"A Cat's Eye," Crash said bluntly.

"But...I haven't seen one since I was a lad. Where...where would you get such a thing?"

Sora opened her mouth to speak, but Crash cut her off again. "No matter," he grunted. "But to my understanding, you are a specialist on such things, are you not? How might it lead us through the swamp?"

"'Lead us through the swamp?'" Sora balked, turning to stare at Crash in horror. Was she to be responsible for navigating Fennbog? Ludicrous!

The old man saw the look on her face and grinned again, displaying the gaps between his yellowed teeth. "Why, yes, my girl," he said, and nodded once again to her necklace. Sora let it slip back under her shirt, disliking the way his eyes lingered on the artifact. "Yes, indeed. The Cat's Eye works as a compass of sorts. It leads you...to where you want to go." Then he held up a finger. "To where you *truly* want to go."

Sora hadn't been expecting that. She turned to glance at Crash, her eyebrow raised skeptically. The assassin didn't meet her gaze; he was propped up against a wall, arms crossed, distinctly unimpressed.

"How do you mean?" she asked, turning back to the mapmaker.

"I mean...that you can ask it to lead you through the swamp. You can ask it to direct you. But the Cat's Eye has whims of its own. If it senses that you want to be somewhere else...well, then it might just take you there instead."

Sora paled at this, a myriad of possibilities running through her head. She touched the stone subconsciously under her shirt, wishing that it was more familiar to her, that it didn't feel so mischievous and unpredictable.

She turned back to the storekeeper to see a small, stormy cloud of dust rising in the air. He was scuffling from table to table, shuffling through parchment like a madman, stacking and unstacking. Finally from a table at the back of the room he pulled a large book, almost too heavy to lift, bound in wood and string. He opened it wide, the pages crackling.

"Ah, here we are," he muttered. Sora stepped around the tables and paused behind him, peering over his shoulder, trying to see around his wide hat. "An older tome, to be sure, but I can't imagine much has changed. This is a history of sorts. It speaks of the War of the Races. Bought it quite a few decades ago while I was mapping the changes in land formations...." His voice petered off as he caught a cold glance from Crash. "Right. This section here tells of the Cat's Eye, perhaps on a brief page. Not much is known of them anymore, you know. Nor ever, I suspect. But here it is, here it is...yes." Sora saw a small drawing of an orb that looked similar to the Cat's-Eye stone. She recognized the smooth swirl at its center, the black lines highlighting its glow. The letters were heavy and ornate, drawn with an artist's hand.

"The stones were used to lead armies through dense mist, across stormy oceans and treacherous terrain," he quoted. "They were essential in the Battle of Aerobourne, when the humans fought against the Harpies....The Harpy ships flew above-ground, powered by sunstones that were mined from the ocean...."

Crash snorted. Sora blinked, realizing she had been holding her breath, spellbound. She had already been imagining the sweeping masts, billowing sails and great gusts of wind that had lifted the flying ships into the air, up through the clouds, powered by shining white sunstones. She had read stories of the Battle of Aerobourne before.

"A bearer had to keep firm control of his thoughts and desires while leading a legion. He had to be completely loyal to the cause. Any thoughts of doubt or deceit, or a desire to run from battle, could lead the entire army into aimless circles. Above all, the bearer must be disciplined."

*Disciplined.* The word fell on Sora's ears like a heavy stone. *Am I?* She quickly recounted several times she had refused an extra scone at breakfast, or had waited patiently through her morning studies for an afternoon ride. And yet, traveling with Crash and Dorian had showed her a different kind of discipline. A whole new world of hardship, where one had to hunt each night, wait an hour or more for a warm meal, constantly cover one's trail, and take good care of the horses.

"How much discipline?" Sora asked. Her voice wavered only slightly.

"Never mind that," Crash snapped. "How does one direct the Cat's Eye? Need she visualize her destination? Or simply wish it?"

The old man turned away from the book. "I haven't the slightest," he said, his mustache bristling. He gave Crash a pointed look. "I've never worn a Cat's Eye, and I wouldn't know. You would have to be stupidly desperate to travel through the swamp, either way." And then his eyes narrowed, darting back and forth between Crash and Sora. He gave them a second look, perhaps wondering why they were so anxious to travel into Fennbog swamp....

Crash seemed to pick up on the same thought, flipping the

storekeeper a silver coin. The old man caught it in mid-air with a practiced hand.

"For your trouble," Crash said. He turned away, motioning for Sora to follow. She quickly picked up their bags, giving the mapmaker a slight nod for courtesy's sake, then hustled from the room.

The storekeeper watched them leave with quiet, thoughtful eyes.

Crash and Sora walked for a brisk twenty minutes until they were in a completely different district of Mayville, though still on the Fallcrest side. Crash finally paused in the dim glow of a window and waited for her to catch up. Sora reached his side and awkwardly met his eyes, firmly resisting the urge to look away.

"This is The Oaken Door," he said, indicating the building next to them. True to its name, there was a solid oak door painted a deep, rich red under a hanging lantern. It looked as though it had been built for giants. The doorknob was a large brass ring, dangling at Sora's eye level. "Burn and Dorian will be waiting for you in the common room, downstairs."

"You're leaving?" she asked sharply. She knew what that meant. Collecting payment. Her thoughts began to race, spinning about in her head. Her eyes darted around the shadowy streets, wondering which way he was headed, where his contact awaited. Or perhaps there was no middleman, and he was meeting directly with his employer. She could suddenly envision Lord Sinclair riding up in a polished carriage of burnt cherrywood, with the sheen of four gray thoroughbred horses prancing through the night. A heavy sack of coins dangled from his ringed hand, thrust elegantly through the carriage window. "How much?" she blurted, her eyes still focused on that imaginary carriage. "How much are you being paid?" she boldly asked Crash. "I will pay you more—double—triple —if you'll tell me who hired you!"

The assassin gave her a smooth, blank stare, like a pane of glass. "I was given no name," he finally consented to say. Sora was surprised by the direct answer. "And I have seen no faces. I work in complete anonymity."

"Then take me with you!" Sora repeated. "I'll hide in the shadows, I'll try to identify...."

"Go inside," he ordered icily.

Sora flinched at those words. She searched his eyes but saw only hardness, the coldblooded gaze of a snake. She turned to the door, simultaneously juggling the packages and trying to turn the knob.

"Is it far?" she said, still struggling with the door. "How soon will you return?" She finally got the knob to turn, and shoved the solid, heavy door open. Despite its size, the door swung easily on its hinges.

Suddenly she was engulfed by a wave of light and sound.

When she glanced up, Crash was gone.

# CHAPTER 7

Sora entered the building. Her first thought was to drop the packages and head straight back out the door, but then Burn's golden eyes gleaming across the room met hers.

He and Dorian sat at a low table toward the back of the inn. Upon seeing her, the giant Wolfy nudged his companion, and the silver-haired thief looked up. Grinned. Fangs. He set down his cards and slipped out of his chair, smoothly navigating the room to her side.

"You look no worse for wear, sweetness," he said, taking her by the elbow. But he didn't offer to help her with the packages, which was irritating, since she felt like her arms were made of strained rope. "Did Crash say when he will be back?"

"No," she muttered. She wondered how many times they had done this before—sat in some smoky rundown tavern while the assassin did his dirty work.

"Ah, then it should be soon. Come sit by us. Your hands are like ice." Finally he took the bags from her and slipped his hand into her cold grasp. She glanced sideways at him, shock briefly passing over her face.

He grinned, a wicked look that made her wonder at his thoughts. Then he leaned in close to her ear. "Come now, sweetness. Everyone in the room is staring. At least act amiable toward me."

Now Sora noticed quite a few sets of eyes glancing in her

direction. Perhaps it was because of her many packages, or maybe it was unusual to see a young woman here. The room was mostly filled with farm types, grizzly old men and weathered merchants relaxing after a long day at market. The few women in the room looked lush and bawdy, wearing low-cut blouses and frayed skirts.

She caught sight of a familiar man, and her eyes widened. It was the ugly, bulbous giant from the market. He sat opposite them, close to the door, creating an uproar with his shouting, drunken companions. They laughed and sang, thunking their tankards on the table. He caught her eye and raised his mug to her, ale sloshing over the side, a rosy tint on his cheeks. She grimaced and turned away.

Dorian led her across the room. Sora kept her head bowed, avoiding the side glances she got from different tables. When they reached Burn's corner, she piled all her stuff under his chair, then sat down on an empty stool, relieved to give her legs a rest. Her feet were ridiculously sore, her toes rubbed raw by her leather boots.

Three other travelers sat at their table—an older serf in a worn linen shirt, a man who was perhaps his son, and a narrow, dark-eyed fellow with a blackened front tooth. Burn shuffled the cards as the men guzzled their drinks. None of them attempted to make conversation beyond the card game.

Then Burn put a massive hand on her shoulder, as if he was a warm, solid rock. "Have you eaten?" he rumbled, giving her a lion-fanged grin. Sora was momentarily startled by his long canines, which protruded past his lip. She shook her head numbly, and he signaled for a waitress to come over. "A bowl of stew for the lass," he called, and patted her shoulder again. Sora felt a small earthquake pass through her body. Then he turned back to the game, dealing the cards swiftly around the table. His hands were surprisingly dexterous.

Sora couldn't stop thinking about Crash and his mysterious payment. She had to find out who this middleman was...and if he was connected somehow to Lord Sinclair.

"I need to use the privy," she said suddenly. She looked up, meeting Burn's and Dorian's eyes, and a few disinterested glances from the other card players. "I'll be right back. Is it down that hall?" She pointed to a hallway just beyond their table, which might or might not lead to the rear of the building.

Dorian's ear twitched. He regarded her sternly. "Aye," he finally said. Then he glanced back at his drink. "I take it you can handle yourself, sweetness?" he muttered. "This game just started warming up...."

Burn looked at his smaller companion. "You should go with her, keep an eye on her," he grumbled.

Sora studied the two men, sizing up their body language and the number of empty glasses on the table. Well into their third or fourth drinks, she guessed neither of them would want to trundle through the packed common room just to stand in the cold hallway, waiting for a girl to finish her business.

She gave them a fierce look. "If I'm not back in a minute, you can tie me to the chair for the rest of the night."

The thief and the mercenary glanced at each other. Dorian sighed, leaning back. "I can see down the hallway from here," he grumbled. "Be fast about it, sweetness. If you're not back in a minute, I'll do more than just tie you down."

His words were slightly slurred. Sora knew what drunkenness looked like, even if she herself had never been drunk. In fact, she didn't like the taste of wine.

"I'll be right back," she said, trying to look appropriately cowed. Then she slipped from her chair and darted away from the table before the men could change their mind.

She entered the dark hallway only a few yards to their left. She could feel Dorian's eyes on her as she stepped into the shadows, barely illuminated by a smoky candle high up on a shelf. The privy was marked by a half-moon carved into the door. She glanced over her shoulder; at this angle, Dorian could barely glimpse her.

Sora entered the small, dank closet, holding her hand to her nose. She didn't close the door completely behind her. Instead, she gazed through the slight crack, waiting for Dorian to look away; that didn't take long. The smaller thief laughed and looked down, distracted by his cards. She quickly slipped out of the privy and down the hallway, as quickly as her sore legs would carry her.

*An exit. I have to find an exit!* She would steal a horse from the rear of the inn and be on the road in minutes, riding bareback if she had to. She would return to her manor, call the King's guard and have Lord Sinclair firmly interrogated for murder....

*Whumph!* Something was pulled over her head.

Sora struggled, her hands flying to her neck, where a cord tightened. Someone had pulled a bag over her head! She tried to scream, to suck air into her lungs, but the nasty cloth firmly smothered her mouth. Then her arms were twisted behind her, and a large body—a juggernaut, for sure—lifted her clear off her feet. She was aggressively shoved forward, slammed against the sharp edge of a door-frame and then out into the coldness of the night.

There was the crunch of gravel. Horses snorting and whuffing. Jingling harnesses. Rough hands throwing her over a high saddle.

She tried to kick her feet and roll back onto the ground, but a heavy fist knocked her upside the head—*wham!*—and she went silent, stunned.

A minute later, they were galloping down the street.

* * *

Sora awakened with her hands tied. She was seated in a hardwood chair, the sack still over her head. She didn't know how much time had passed.

There was the sound of footsteps, a door opening and closing. And then....

"Really, Gunter! Take that blasted bag off her head! She is a Lady!"

"'pologies, My Lord," came the guttural response. Sora recognized the voice, having heard it once before, as belonging to the large man from the market.

There was another scuffle. The drawstring was loosened from around her neck and the bag was slipped off her head. She blinked; one of her eyes was swollen almost shut. The side of her face throbbed where she had been struck. Even the brush of air felt like fingers going across her cheek.

When she looked up, her first sight was of a narrow window with a glimpse of a red-tiled rooftop. She was in an attic, she guessed, or perhaps a second story. They were still on the Fallcrest side of town. She didn't know how much time had passed, but it couldn't have been more than an hour. The moon was full and heavy, bright stars fanning out like a silver skirt.

Her good eye combed the room, taking in corners with dust

and cobwebs, old boxes and crates, a half-covered painting. She spotted Gunter's shadow in the corner, holding the black bag in his massive paw. She would have glared at him, but it hurt too much to frown. There was another man, slight of build, in the corner, sitting on a short stool with a piece of paper in his hand.

Then a tall figure appeared. He shifted, blocking out the pearlescent light of the moon. Sora turned to stare at him. He wore a very expensive blue cloak. Though the room was in shadow, he still looked dimly familiar; had he been at her Blooming? Remembering her clumsy performance, she paled at the thought. His hair, falling around his ears in wispy layers, was dark, yet flecks of gray glinted in the moonlight—he had been carrying too many burdens for his age.

"Jerith, light the candles, will you?" he said, irritated.

The small man in the corner stood up and shuffled to a tall candelabra. He struck a match and quickly lit the four white candles at the top. Sora's nose wrinkled as heavy smoke spewed into the air.

When she looked again at the man in front of her, she saw the silver emblem on his breast pocket, glinting in the candlelight. "A Seabourne," she murmured, surprised.

"Lord Gracen Seabourne, of His Majesty's Royal Guard," the man corrected. As he moved and blocked the window, his cloak fluttered about him like the great wings of a raven. When he looked down at her, she saw his gaze flicker over her swollen eye. He grimaced. "That was not intentional; my apologies," he said. "And I am very sorry about the death of your father, Lord Fallcrest."

Sora winced painfully at that, but said nothing. The death of her father seemed almost trivial compared to everything else she had been through: the abduction, the Cat's Eye, the monster in the forest, and soon, a trip through Fennbog swamp....

She let out a sigh of relief, some of her tension loosening. Well, at least now the madness would come to an end. She was amongst nobility again, people who knew and respected her title. It was time to set things straight. "My Lord, I have reason to suspect that my father was murdered," she said, raising her chin slightly.

"As do I," Lord Gracen replied.

Sora frowned, wondering what he meant. "Then you know of the assassin?" she asked, confused.

"I suspected there was an assassin, yes. Would you agree?" the Lord murmured. His dark eyes were unreadable. Sora opened her mouth to speak, then paused, suddenly suspicious. She didn't like his tone of voice. Just why had she been abducted from the back of an inn? If she had been rescued, then why was she tied to a chair—and why hadn't her captors been arrested?

Her eyes traveled to the giant man in the corner, Gunter. His massive, hairy forearms dangled almost to his knees, like heavy tree limbs. She guessed he was the one who had recognized her and brought her in. There was a large sack at his belt that bulged with coins. Her thoughts began to race, arranging and rearranging all of the little pieces of the puzzle.

"What's this about?" she finally asked.

"You don't know?" Lord Gracen replied, raising one dark, smooth eyebrow. "Or perhaps you are very good at playing dumb. There is a warrant out for your arrest."

"*My* arrest?" Sora shouted incredulously.

"Yes," Lord Gracen nodded, his voice grave. "On suspicion of murder."

"*Murder?* Whose murder?"

"Your father's."

Sora's jaw dropped almost to her chest. She stared up at Lord Gracen, too shocked to think.

At her stunned silence, the Lord began to pace. A long cane made of polished black wood emerged from his cloak. It clip-clipped against the hollow floor. "Where were you on the night of the murder?"

"A-at my father's house. It was my birthday. My Blooming," Sora said directly. Suddenly she recognized him and his broad, barrel chest. He had been sitting in the front row and had caught her scarf during the dance. "You saw me!"

"And afterward? After the skylight broke? Where were you the rest of the night and the following morning?" he asked aggressively.

"I was...I was kidnapped!" she exclaimed, sitting forward, straining against her bonds.

"By the murderer?"

"Yes!"

"Why? For ransom?" he barked.

"No...." Sora's voice trailed off, suddenly doubtful.

"For what, then?" he pressed.

"I...uh...." Sora tried to formulate her spinning thoughts. How could she describe the Wolfy mage, the Cat's-Eye necklace, the magic? These were figments of lore and legend, impossible....

"There was an assassin," she started to explain again. "He kidnapped me in the hallway!"

"What assassin? Who is he?"

"I-I don't know! Crash, his name is Crash!"

Lord Gracen nodded to the corner where the young man sat

with the roll of parchment. Sora saw him withdraw a long, fluffy quill. The young man bent over the paper on his knee and began jotting down her words.

She stared at the wiggling quill in horror, suddenly aware that she was in a confessional—that they were interrogating her for the murder of her own father. Here. Now. Every word recorded by the King's guard.

"The assassin came here to collect payment!" she blurted out. "He's planning to flee into Fennbog swamp!"

Lord Gracen gave her a sharp look. "Payment from whom?" he asked.

"I-I don't know...." Sora stuttered, her voice growing weak. Her story sounded terrible, full of holes. "He said it was anonymous. I...." She did something desperate, because she couldn't think of what else to do. "I suspect Lord Sinclair. He has never been fond of our family. He intends to acquire the whole of Mayville!"

"Indeed." Lord Gracen turned away from her and continued pacing around the room, his cane clack-clacking at a furious pace, his cloak swirling around his boots in a river of blue fabric. He appeared to consider her words. "It is quite a serious matter, to accuse another noble of murder. Have you any evidence, besides hearsay?"

Sora's eyebrows shot up. Evidence? "The assassin...maybe he'll lead us to his employer...."

"Or he might lead us in a big circle, right back to you," Lord Gracen muttered. "I've heard the serfs speculate about Lord Sinclair. But he is currently residing in the City of Crowns. Quite a ways away to plan an elaborate murder...."

Sora tightened up. She should have known Lord Gracen

wouldn't believe her. He seemed set on believing her guilty of murder.

He paused, looking down, meeting her eyes, echoing her thoughts. "You want me to believe that Lord Sinclair orchestrated a murder from over a hundred miles away. That you were abducted, but for no ransom. And that now the killer has come to Mayville, the only village on your father's lands, to collect payment. With you in tow?" He paused, but Sora stayed silent. "I am no fool, Lady. I have come to learn that the simplest explanation is often the truth. All indicators point to you. Let's try another story."

Then Lord Gracen cleared his throat, perhaps enjoying the drama of the moment. "You became used to having your father gone in the City. When he decided to take suits and wed you off, you became threatened. You wanted the entire estate to yourself. So you arranged an assassination, and you planned to pay the killer here, in Mayville. That is why you fled from the manor so quickly after the Blooming. Sadly, you didn't expect me to be here, did you? Looks like your plans have fallen through." He knelt down in front of her, inches away, eye to eye. "Come now," he said quietly. "It is cold up here and the night wears on. Do you plead guilty?"

Sora paled. She shook her head wordlessly.

Lord Gracen harrumphed, his skepticism clear. "Well, I believe part of what you say. There is an assassin somewhere in this town, perhaps traveling to meet you right now." He paused, watching her closely for a response. "And perhaps you do plan to take a risky venture through Fennbog. Only the guilty would devise such a plan."

Sora opened her mouth and quickly closed it, like a suffocating fish. Abruptly Lord Gracen turned, slamming his cane into the floor. The whole room jumped, including the juggernaut in the corner. "Why? Why did you do it?" he demanded, his eyes cold. "So you wouldn't have to marry? To inherit the full estate? The manor servants told me of your strained relationship with Lord Fallcrest. I mention his name, and you don't even flinch. Was there no love between father and daughter?"

Sora steeled herself. She felt as though her intestines were being slowly drawn out through her mouth. She wanted to cry, but she couldn't, not in front of his man, this interrogator from the King. "Love?" she murmured, and stared at the floor, blinking her dry eyes. "No, my father did not love me."

"A lie. What father couldn't love his own child? Even if it was a rigid love...."

"There was no love," Sora gritted her teeth tightly. "He wanted me gone. Married off. He hated me." She finally closed her eyes, pain wrapping around her heart like a fierce vine. She could barely speak. "I was no daughter to him."

Lord Gracen nodded, coming to a halt in front of her, his cane tapping into silence. "We have a motive. Write that down, Jerith." He nodded to the scribe in the corner. The quill continued to scratch.

Sora looked up, her eyes wide. "What?" she exclaimed.

"No love of your father, no remorse over his death, and an entire estate to inherit," Lord Gracen said coldly. "Gone missing the day after his death. Talk of an assassin that only you've seen." His eyes were like granite. "What do you expect me to believe?"

Sora took a deep breath. Her tears welled up frighteningly close to the surface of her eyes. *They hang murderers*, she thought, suddenly re-envisioning her future. She would be imprisoned.

Taken to the royal court. Tried in front of a committee of the First Tier, where there would be no sympathy—a peasant-born noble with blood on her hands. And what could she tell the court that she hadn't already told Lord Gracen? She could show them the Cat's Eye, but with no magic to provoke it, the necklace would remain a simple bauble, a worthless stone worn on her neck.

"I'm not guilty," she said hoarsely.

Lord Gracen bowed his head and said nothing.

At that moment, there was a flicker of movement outside the window. Sora turned, squinting at the darkness. Was it a bird?

An earsplitting *crash!* shook the air. Lord Gracen threw himself to one side, away from the window. Glass exploded inward as a brick went flying across the room, thudding solidly against the wall.

Sora stared, shocked. Lord Gracen acted swiftly, lunging in front of her, swinging his cane at some unforeseen foe.

Then a familiar figure leapt into the building through the broken window.

A long, silver braid whipped over Dorian's shoulder; a knife was in his hand. He landed on the floor and turned to Lord Gracen, giving him a short once-over.

"'ello," he said cheerfully. He ducked the cane smoothly, then punched Lord Gracen in the face, laying him out flat.

The giant Gunter lunged at Dorian, trying to grab him from behind, but a second shadow flickered at the window. Crash entered the room, a long, thin blade in his hand. As Sora watched, the blade whizzed through the air and straight through Gunter's thick arm, slicing it like a loaf of bread.

Gunter roared and stumbled backward, dropping the purse of

coins, blood spurting from his half-severed arm. Sora gazed in shock, unable to believe the horrible sight. Blood spilled across the floor in every direction, shooting out of the giant's arm in short, swift bursts, spattering halfway across the room. Sora had to lift her feet so the blood wouldn't reach her boots.

Crash darted into the corner where the scribe cowered. He smashed him back against the wall, then let the unconscious man slide to the ground. Next he grabbed the parchment from the scribe's hands and glanced over it briefly, a look of distaste on his face. He held the parchment over the candelabra. With a crackle and a long stream of smoke, it slowly dissolved into ash and air.

Sora stared at her two captors, sinking in a conflicting swamp of emotions: relief, dread, and the sudden sour realization that she was being rescued. She couldn't stay here, not with the King's Guard, whom she had believed was her only hope. No, she had to go with the ones who had caused this mess in the first place.

*I'm wanted by the Royal Guard*, she thought numbly, her entire world suddenly turned on its head. *I'm a criminal*. A criminal!

"Th-they want me for murder," she gasped as Dorian started to untie her. Her hands were shaking, even though they were tied to the chair, and her knees were trembling uncontrollably. "Th-they think I killed my father!"

"We know, sweetness," Dorian said, a surprisingly gentle lilt to his voice. "Word's spread around town—or haven't you heard? One thousand gold pieces on your head. We should've known someone would recognize you."

It was a very small amount—some criminals had bounties as high as fifty-thousand gold pieces. Still, it was a considerable amount to the serfs. Sora thought of the giant, Gunter. Her eyes traveled to him, over in the corner. He was sitting silently, gripping his wounded arm, his eyes wide and glassy in shock. From the way the arm was bleeding, he seemed likely he would topple over soon, dead.

"We need to help him," she blurted out.

"Wrong, sweetness," Dorian said, taking her hands in his. "We need to get out of here before anyone comes looking."

"But...." It was cruel and heartless, but what could she expect from these two?

"Men like him are the worst kind," Crash said suddenly. "You're lucky there was a bounty on your head. I'm sure he would have done much worse." He stared at her from across the room, his eyes roving over her face. Then he looked at Dorian. "You should have watched her more closely."

"Oh? Are we pointing fingers now?" Dorian sneered.

Crash gave him a dark look. Then the assassin turned back to the fallen giant. A strange expression passed over his face. "Dorian, take her. I'll meet you on the road."

Dorian grabbed her arm lightly and touched her cheek, running a gentle hand over her black eye. "Follow me, sweetness. Let's get out of here."

"Wait," Sora said as Dorian led her toward the window. She glanced over her shoulder. "What are you going to do to him?"

"Never mind that, sweetness," Dorian cajoled. Then he picked her up, lifting her out the window onto the roof. Sora didn't have the strength to fight back. She followed Dorian across the red tiles, allowing him to clasp her tightly while he mounted the rope. He shimmied down expertly, her weight hardly a burden.

"What's he going to do?" she asked again, once they had reached the ground.

Dorian gave her a perplexed look. "Crash might not be an easy man to trust," he said slowly. "But he takes care of his own."

Sora nodded numbly. Suddenly she didn't want to know the details.

They slipped quietly through the night, circling around the side of the building to a narrow alley at the rear. Sora didn't recognize the house they had been in, although the emblem of the King hung above the doorway—a golden shield with a red boar's head at its center. A guardhouse, perhaps. A place for the King's men. She could hear them shouting and rummaging inside, and wondered how many soldiers were in there, and how long it would be until they found Lord Gracen's unconscious body in the bloody attic.

Burn waited for them about two streets away, their steeds in hand. Except now there was an extra steed, a white-and-brown spotted mare. By the emblem on its saddle, it belonged to the King's Guard.

"We can't just...steal one of the King's horses!" Sora exclaimed as they dragged her up onto the dappled steed. It was tied fast to the rear of Burn's saddle and given just enough tether to gallop. "That's a crime against the Crown!"

"Aren't you wanted for murder?" Dorian quipped, pulling himself up onto his own brown steed. "Stop caring so much about your precious Crown!" Then he kicked his steed into a gallop, taking off through the abandoned streets.

Burn's and Sora's horses followed suit, albeit a bit slower, tied together as they were. She wasn't sure exactly when Crash joined their party. Suddenly he was at the rear, following them closely. She wondered what he had done in that dark room. Wondered if his dagger was slick with blood.

There was a loud clanging at their backs, harsh and clamorous on the night air. A warning bell from the guardhouse tower.

Dorian's words sank into her, making Sora feel empty and despairing. *He's right, you know,* her inner voice said. Now she was wanted for murder. In the eyes of the law, she was no better than the band she traveled with. The King's Court would be no more merciful to her than the assassin riding behind her. *Truly?* she thought, bile and revulsion rising in her throat.

They passed under the city gates, galloping wildly, thundering past a second guardhouse. A soldier ran out to stop them, half-dressed, his torso bare, but he was too late and the horses were too fast. He screamed something at their backs, but Sora could only hear hooves on cobblestone. They continued down the road and into the forest, at full tilt.

About fifteen minutes later, they reached a fork in the road. The main thoroughfare broke off onto a smaller dirt trail, overgrown by blackberry bushes and low, bristly oak trees. Burn led them down the path, slowing his steed only slightly.

They entered the dense woods, splashing through a shallow stream that split the path. It was the border of the Fallcrest lands.

\* \* \*

Volcrian led his horse through the last stretch of brush and onto the cobblestone road. Ahead of him, he could see the glowing town of Mayville—candlelight flickering in second-story windows, warm hearths lit after dark. He was bent over the saddle, weary from a full day's ride, though relieved that he had made such excellent time.

With any luck, his prey would still be in the town. He had cut through the forest and found their ill-fated campsite, then surveyed the markings in the dirt, searching for blood, for a trail. Their tracks were well-hidden, but not by Wolfy standards—his keen eyes and ears noted everything.

Now, closer to town, he could see more tracks, scarcely a half-day old. Two horses had converged with a third—the mercenary Burn's—then diverged again, taking slightly different paths into Mayville. Knowing the ways of the assassin and his companions, they were most likely in a tavern somewhere, drinking and gambling with the money from their most recent kill.

Volcrian paused as he neared the town and narrowed his eyes. There was some sort of commotion around the gatehouse. An unusual flurry of activity. Horses stamped and snorted; the shadowy forms of soldiers ran back and forth, gathering weapons and strapping on shields.

Then a large, impressive black steed rode up to the gatehouse, parting the chaos like an arrow. Volcrian watched with interest. After a moment, he led his horse to the side of the road, tying his beast behind a series of tall bushes, fully obscured from view.

The black stallion was immediately recognizable, the dark sheen of its coat, the subtle hint of dun markings. The majestic man atop the saddle was just as familiar, a dark blue cloak swirling around his proud figure. Volcrian pursed his lips. He had seen this same man back at the Fallcrest Manor. It was no other than Lord Seabourne—Captain of His Majesty's personal guard. It was unusual for such a high-ranking officer to be in a place like this.

His interest piqued, Volcrian dismounted and approached the guardhouse on foot, carefully traveling off to the side of the road, keeping to the deep shadows. He easily passed by the disordered guards; they were far too busy strapping on armor and clambering onto their horses. Lord Seabourne went into the gatehouse proper, and Volcrian slunk around back, a nervous tilt to his lips. Suddenly he was certain that this had something to do with his prey. Had they caught the assassin? No, impossible, 'twas not so easy. Perhaps they had caught the girl. Or knew of their whereabouts....

Pausing beneath the rear window of the small gatehouse, he twitched his long ears, adjusting to the sounds from inside. To a normal human, this noise would have seemed like muffled nonsense. But keen Wolfy ears could pick out each individual set of footsteps, each distinct voice.

Loud boots confidently crossed the floorboards, accompanied by the sturdy thunk-thunk of a cane. Lord Seabourne, to be certain. Volcrian sneered. That cane was useless. The First Tier put style before practicality, a sure indication of too much wealth.

If Volcrian remembered correctly, the Captain was typically involved with matters that concerned the King. Why would he come out here, to the middle of the country, where the bumpkin nobility held sway? Surely, there were much more pressing matters in the City? *What does the King's guard-dog have to say?*

"They passed through the gates just an hour ago," he heard. This was perhaps a soldier's voice. "My Lord, your head...."

"Is fine," Lord Seabourne snapped. He was in a nasty mood. "They are traveling to Fennbog swamp. Organize a garrison and give chase immediately!"

"My Lord," there was a brief click of heels, and Volcrian imagined a guard saluting. "But...are you quite sure? Fennbog is impassable. Perhaps the Lady was trying to mislead us."

"No, she's not smart enough for that," Seabourne grunted.

Volcrian had to agree with him. The girl was hardly a threat. The assassin, on the other hand, was quite a bit more tricky. A frown curved his thin lips and a vein throbbed in his temple. They were headed into Fennbog. *Nasty, cunning creature,* he thought, imagining his prey. Of course the killer would go there. It was the most immediate path of escape, especially with a Cat's Eye.

He was deep in thought. If Lady Sora was skilled enough, she could put the stone to use as a compass. He had heard of such things in tales of the War. But he doubted she had that kind of discipline. At the very least, it would offer protection from the magic of the swamp and also the dangers within it. Fennbog was the one place where he could not follow them. At least, not on foot.

"Seek out their trail while it's still fresh," Lord Seabourne snapped, continuing his orders. "You'll find them soon enough. You must catch them before they reach the marshlands. It's too dangerous to enter the swamp, though I expect a few men will die trying."

"Suicide, Milord, with all due respect," another older, wizened voice chimed in, closer to the window. "And a waste of manpower. Mayhap we should leave them to their fate. They'll never survive Fennbog. The place is cursed...."

*Crack!* The cane snapped against the floor, splitting the air, and Volcrian flinched, his ears ringing at the sound. A tense silence followed.

"Superstitious nonsense," Lord Seabourne finally growled. He had the voice of command, loud and striking. "You will follow them and arrest them. They will be tried by the King's court and, if I do say so, hanged by the King's law. We do not tolerate murder, especially amongst the First and Second Tiers."

The silence that followed was wrought with doubt. Volcrian could imagine what was going through the soldiers' minds. Fennbog was a horrid place, full of sink-sand, sulfurous gases, poisonous plants and ravenous, reptilian beasts....

"What of your Lordship?" the first voice spoke up. "Will you accompany us?"

"No."

*Typical nobility.* Volcrian grimaced. *Why dirty your boots when you have an entire garrison at your command?* He glanced toward the road, peering through the thick bushes and leaves. The soldiers were calm now, organizing a line of horses, preparing to leave. The light from the guardhouse glinted against their heavy armor. *That will certainly help them sink faster,* Volcrian thought, and pictured them running headfirst into the mud. Fennbog had a hundred miles of it. And yet all twenty-five soldiers looked as eager as their prancing steeds. They must not have heard their assignment. *A waste of blood, to be sure.*

"I have business in the City of Crowns," Lord Seabourne spoke. Volcrian's ears twitched, and he looked up at the windowsill with renewed interest. "I thought, perhaps, that Lord Fallcrest's murder was of greater import. But it is just a family feud, nothing more. The King has requested my return, and I haven't the time to dally around in the swamp. I will expect news once you have captured the girl. Try to bring her back alive—I have more questions about her father's doings." There was a pause. Lord Seabourne resumed pacing. He seemed to be an awfully tense man. "Head out now, before they pull further ahead. Knowing how a Lady travels, overtaking them should be no trouble at all. Especially for the King's guard." His voice ended on a dire note, threatening. Volcrian could imagine the cold glint in Seabourne's iron-gray eyes.

Heels clicked again, more saluting. This was followed by a chorus of "Sir!" and "Yes, Milord!"

Then he listened to Lord Seabourne's unmistakable walk, step-tap-step, go across the room. The door to the guardhouse opened and closed. There was a series of salutes from the soldiers outside, barely visible beyond the corner of the house. Then Lord Seabourne took his leave, his great black stallion charging down the road, back into Mayville and perhaps further into the lands beyond. Two soldiers departed with him. The rest stayed in rank.

Volcrian remained hunched behind the building as the commanding officers filed out of the gatehouse. They muttered amongst each other, groaning about the swamp, about the peculiar ways of nobility and the "sad state" of the Fallcrest lands. Then they called orders to their troops, mounted their horses, and took off down the road at a formidable pace. The ground trembled beneath them. Pebbles skittered and shook with the sound of over four dozen thundering hooves.

As soon as they left, Volcrian mounted his horse and moved onto the cobblestone road. His eyes followed the soldiers' trail, his thoughts whirring and whistling at this new information. So there would be no respite—no relief in Mayville. He had to continue traveling. He almost wanted to turn around, head back into town and find a nice, warm cot for the night.

Yet he didn't have that luxury. No, he had to catch up with the assassin, preferably before the soldiers did. But how to follow him into the swamp? Volcrian was no fool. Perhaps the assassin hoped to kill him by luring him into Fennbog. Considering the location, he was likely to succeed. Volcrian would have to be smarter than his prey.

His eyes abruptly lit up, and his hand slipped to his pouch; he withdrew a small glass vial. A clump of dirt matted with old blood lingered at the base. If he couldn't follow his prey physically, he would use other ways. *Yes, there are other ways.*

With an abrupt change of direction, Volcrian headed back to the gatehouse. All of the soldiers were either on patrol or had joined the hunting party. With a few quick flicks of his dagger, he picked the lock and kicked open the heavy oak door.

The guardhouse was a small affair, two sitting rooms and a closet of a kitchen, which was really just a pantry and a wood-burning stove. He crossed to the cupboards and immediately found what he was looking for—a brown package of salt. Moving swiftly, he emptied his water flask into a wide pan, dumped in a cup of salt, and then added the old blood. He had used this spell several times in his life, especially as an adolescent, to spy on women in the bathhouses.

The dirt held a remnant of Dorian's blood from their last battle, when he had sent the fox-corpse to attack. However, even a teaspoon of blood held powerful properties. Using this, he could find a way into the thief's mind. Observe without being seen. Monitor their progress. Perhaps even assert his influence.

As old and diluted as it was, the spell wouldn't be terribly effective, but it was the only thing he had. For now.

Volcrian heated the salt water. At times it could be substituted for blood, especially in simpler spells. It was not nearly as potent as the real thing, but it would boost the spell's effects. That was really all he needed.

He emptied the bloody dirt into the water, letting it boil for several minutes and included several sprigs of herbs that he found hanging in a dark closet. They were purely for taste. This spell was one of the most basic tricks and only required the victim's blood and a few choice words of power.

Once the tea was ready, Volcrian poured it into a large jug and left the gatehouse as swiftly as he had arrived. The entire spell had taken no more than ten minutes. His sensitive ears picked up the approach of more soldiers as he ducked into the woods.

Once there, he found a quiet, secluded place to sit down. He drank the jug of tea as quickly as possible, gulping down the salty, gritty mixture, forcing himself not to gag. Then he repeated a fierce chant under his breath, speaking in the Old Tongue, the original language of the world.

When he was done, he leaned back, closed his eyes and sank deep into meditation, as only a master could. Then, in the expanded darkness of his mind, he reached out for the thin silver light that was Dorian....

# CHAPTER 8

They rode at a breakneck pace for several hours, until the rim of dawn seeped across the sky. Sora could barely cling to her horse. She felt more like a saddlebag than a rider. Her steed was tethered to the back of Burn's saddle; she didn't even need to use the reins.

They dashed down forest paths, through winding streams and deep brush, then plunged past muddy meadows and giant ferns. The forest was rich and deep, the air moist; the only illumination was the moon. Sora couldn't believe how long they traveled on. Would they ever rest?

When they finally slowed the horses, it was a half-hour before sunrise. Birds were waking in the trees, fluttering across the ground. They came to a halt and dismounted.

"Half an hour," Burn said, his voice like a thundercloud. "A half-hour's rest and we go on."

Sora slid from the saddle, stiff and weary. They distributed food from their bags and sat under the trees, allowing the horses to graze in the small clearing. A stream of clear water trickled nearby; she splashed some on her face, trying to stay alert, then leaned back in the cold morning dew and closed her eyes, the fringes of sleep pulling at her, coaxing her to lie down on the wet grass.

"So how does it feel to be an outlaw?" Dorian asked. His ears twitched cheekily.

Sora opened her eyes and glared at him. She couldn't seem to lift her head from the soft grass, and was too exhausted to care.

"I'm innocent, and you all deserved to be hanged," she said.

"Hanged?" Dorian repeated with mock offense. He sank down next her, only a few feet away. "We just saved you from a long, cold trip to prison! You should be thanking us!"

"For what? Killing my father? Abducting me?" Sora almost choked on her outrage, wishing she could fling a knife right between his eyes. "You just want my necklace. You're disgusting."

"I'm sorry you feel that way, sweetness." Dorian munched for a moment on his travel bread, then frowned, putting his hand to his head. He blinked his eyes strangely.

"What?" Sora asked, wondering if there was something wrong with the food.

"Nothing," he said, "just a headache. Not enough sleep." Then he glanced over her, his eyes lingering on her face. "I daresay, your cheek is turning a glorious shade of purple. How is your eye?"

Sora didn't respond. She was too angry, and the reminder of her injuries only made them hurt worse. The swelling had gone down and she could see better now, but touching the side of her face brought a throb of pain through her nose and teeth.

"Leave the girl alone, Dorian," Burn said quietly. "I think she's been through enough."

Sora looked at the giant Wolfy, surprised. There was a softness on his face, unexpected kindness. After a moment, she said, "Thank you."

Burn cocked his head thoughtfully, gazing at her with gentle, warm eyes. Something about his expression beckoned her to talk. She bit her lip, the words pressing to come out of her mouth.

"I can't go back now," she finally said. "I can never be seen in my manor again." That thought wrenched her heart. She had wanted to run away, to leave her life behind...but not in ruins. Not with such finality. She would always be remembered as a murderer. A complete disgrace.

Burn edged closer and reached out a long, long arm. He patted her shoulder, a friendly gesture, though it only served to make her head throb.

"Come with us," he said quietly.

"I *am* coming with you," she sniffed, and gave him another angry glance.

"No, my dear," Burn said softly. His gentleness was disarming, and Sora wondered who he really was, how he had come into league with someone as evil and terrible as Crash. "We have dragged you with us. But you don't have to be a captive. You could *join* us."

It was an unexpected offer—so clear and straightforward. She was an exile now; returning home meant committing herself to the noose. She had no friends in court. Her arrest and execution would be a quick matter indeed.

And now Burn was offering her a different option. A better option, perhaps. Something more than threats and coercion. Yet the thought made her ill. This entire mess was their fault. She couldn't forget that. Some deeds were unforgivable—like murder and kidnapping.

"Never," she snapped.

"Think on it, then," Burn said, his voice deep and smooth. She didn't want to be persuaded, yet his show of kindness was incredibly alluring, especially after so much tension. "Why be alone, when you can have friends like us?"

Sora snorted, unable to help herself. She was choked by

bitterness. *With friends like these, who needs enemies?* "That's a laugh."

"This isn't the end of the world, you know. Though it might seem like it," Burn continued, unperturbed by her reaction. "Tomorrow is a new day. Surely there is something more you want? Something worth traveling for?"

Sora looked away and stared at a tall birch tree, smooth and white in the pale morning. The horses snorted softly in the gray dawn, roaming across the grass, their noses to the ground. The stream's trickle was almost peaceful. *What do I have worth traveling for?* Her thoughts went back to her birthday, to the evening sunset and the musicbox. The mystery of the Cat's Eye. *My mother.* It was her original quest...and perhaps now her only direction.

But she couldn't tell them that. She couldn't let them take it away. Even if Burn was trustworthy—a small chance of that—her other captors were not. She could see Crash out of the corner of her eye, lingering in the shadows beneath the trees, tending his horse. He looked like he wasn't listening, but she knew he was.

"No," she said softly. "I have nothing."

Burn frowned, his yellow-hued eyes searching her face. His brow furrowed. Was it sympathy?

"All the more reason to come with us!" Dorian cut in. His small, soft hand landed on her other shoulder, in vast contrast to Burn's rough palm. "What have you left to lose? And it's mighty inconvenient, always having to keep an eye on you. It won't do in the swamp. We need to be able to trust each other. Look, we even bought you weapons." Dorian nodded to his saddlebags, where her staff and daggers rested, tied to the side of the horse. "If that's not a show of good faith, I don't know what is."

Sora glared at him, his almost offensive words ringing in her head. *What have I left to lose?* As though, just because she had no other option, she should willingly and thankfully join their party? She thought of her manor, her ruined family name. *How can I join them? They're despicable.* She had more honor than that, and she raised her chin stiffly, her jaw so tight she couldn't speak. She saw Burn cast a mean glance over her head at Dorian.

Dorian raised an eyebrow, one ear flicking upward like a confused dog.

"Enough," Crash said, breaking into their conversation. He crossed the small clearing quickly, pausing above them, his black cloak swirling to a stop. "Volcrian is behind us and Fennbog ahead. Soldiers scour the woods while we speak. We must learn to use the necklace while there is still time."

Sora looked up at the hard angles of his face, the sharpness of his jaw, the way his black hair swept across his forehead. He seemed tireless, full of strength, despite another sleepless night.Her anger was renewed. "And what if I don't? What if I refuse?"

Crash raised an eyebrow. He didn't need to reach for the knives at his belt; the blades glinted dangerously in the thin morning light. She thought she already knew his answer, but when he spoke, it was unexpected. "The King's guard is after you. Not us. You." He nodded to the necklace concealed beneath her shirt. "I think you need to consider who your true allies are."

Sora snorted in surprise. "Now that's rich! You kidnap me, threaten me, drag me around the countryside against my will—and you are supposed to be my allies?" She looked around at the

Wolfies incredulously. "You're all insane!"

"Think what you want," Dorian said. "But we have a squad of soldiers and a blood-mage on our trail. Whatever you decide, sweetness—do so quickly."

Sora blinked and looked at the three men. She hated them—but they had a point. So far, they were the only ones who hadn't tried to kill her or throw her in jail. She let out a sigh of annoyance. "And how am I supposed to use the necklace?" she snapped. "I didn't even believe in magic until yesterday! I don't know anything about it. I'm useless."

Crash gave her a cold stare. "Then make yourself *not* useless," he said bluntly.

Sora stared at him, her mouth dry. She waited, half-hoping that one of the Wolfies would stand up in her defense, but they just watched the silent confrontation. She couldn't believe it. They were using logic against her—and it was working.

She thought of the King's prisons, of her own beheading. Then she thought of Volcrian and the monster in the forest. She cleared her throat. "Right," she finally said. "I'll try."

Dorian approached her, reaching out with a gentle hand, but she stepped back, not wanting to be touched just then. The Wolfy gave her a slow smile instead. "Hurry, love. We don't have much time."

She nodded and put a shaky hand on her necklace. And then, slowly, realization dawned. It was strange to think about, almost out-of-body, but what if...what if this was just another day to them? Another day trying to survive? She looked around the group, reading that message in their eyes.

"We need you, Sora," Burn said, breaking the silence.

Sora nodded again. She knew what Burn meant. Her captors were in a far worse predicament, and now she was in it with them.

With a breath of resignation, she gripped the necklace and closed her eyes, thinking back to what the mapmaker had said. *A bearer need keep firm control of their thoughts and desires. He must be completely loyal to the cause. Any thoughts of doubt or deceit, or a desire to run from battle, can lead the entire army in aimless circles. Above all, the bearer must be disciplined.*

Disciplined.

She let out a deeper breath and tried to forget the three men around her, the soldiers on their trail, the looming threat of Volcrian. There were plenty of reasons to panic...but she couldn't let panic disrupt her concentration. She had to communicate with the necklace. She wasn't sure how, but as she thought back on the encounter with the fox-corpse, she started to form a few ideas. The necklace seemed to exist entirely within her mind; it would nudge her thoughts, however fleetingly.

When she sat down next to the stream, it was unexpectedly easy to slip into a meditative state. Sora had only meditated a few times before, when a tutor suggested that meditation would help her studies. But she was blessedly close to falling asleep, so her mind quickly relaxed. She let the tension flow from her shoulders, down her neck and spine and into the ground.

She spent several minutes like that, breathing calmly, allowing herself to be still. Then she ran her smooth finger over the surface of the stone. *Help me*, she thought, quelling the sense of foolishness that arose with her words. *We need to pass through Fennbog to the other side.* She tried to envision the other side of the swamp, the warmer climate of the lowlands, the fields of grass and the merciless winds. She focused on her message as clearly as possible, trying to make it pointed and precise. *Take me to the other side of the swamp.*

But it was difficult to control her thoughts, and worries and concerns slipped through the message. She thought of her mother, wondering where she might live, or if she was even still alive. She thought of her own death, of the terrible creatures that lived in Fennbog, of the coming nights in the wilderness. She thought of Lord Seabourne and her arrest. And...she thought of Crash.Abruptly, there was a murmur from the necklace. A slight movement of thought. But when she focused, it whisked away like a passing cloud.

"Hey!" a voice disrupted her meditation. "Did you see that?"

Sora blinked, coming out of her relaxed state. She glanced up, noticing that her companions were now all standing around her, looking at her with strange, surprised expressions. Except for Crash. He had his arms crossed, watching her closely, observant.

When she looked down at her hand, she saw the Cat's-Eye stone glowing through the cracks of her fingers. As she watched, the green light slowly dimmed and disappeared. But it left something in its wake—a warm feeling, like honey drizzled on her chest.

When she looked back to the three men, she wasn't afraid anymore, but rather filled with a sense of strength and confidence. She met each of their gazes head-on.

"Well?" Dorian asked. "Did it work?"

Sora nodded. Honestly, she didn't know what had changed. There had been no words, no instructions, no bells. But the glowing green light seemed an indicator. "Yes," she said simply. And then she looked up, her head turning toward the forest, a sense of urgency passing through her. "Wait, I think...I think they're coming."

At that moment, a long, wailing howl split the morning silence. A hound. It was still at a distance, but as they listened, several other hounds picked up the call. An entire pack...had found their trail.

"Move," Burn said. "Hurry!" They quickly packed away the food and climbed back up on the horses. For a moment the four hesitated, pacing about the small clearing, uncertain of which direction to travel. But suddenly Sora felt a nudge inside her—like a finger prodding her back. *That way.*

She pointed to a deer path to their right. No need for words. Burn leapt onto the trail and Sora followed suit, her small pinto charging into the woods. Dorian and Crash brought up the rear. With hardly a backward glance, they raced through the forest, the horses leaping nimbly over ferns and rocks.

*It worked,* Sora thought, amazed at herself, at the necklace, at the whole damned thing. *By Goddess, it worked!* A small, satisfied grin came to her lips. The necklace wasn't as hard to control as she had thought. Perhaps she wasn't useless after all.

* * *

As they rode, the ground became noticeably less and less firm. The morning stretched on, but the sky didn't grow lighter. Sora felt like it was late evening, as though night had never truly left. Heavy clouds the color of wet stone hung above them, close to the ground. The air was thick with moisture that saturated their clothes. Bursts of drizzle fell, but never full rain. The clouds withheld their downpour, content to sit heavily on top of the trees, watching the mad race below.

The four travelers stayed true to the deer trails and woodland paths. The land off the path was soft and muddy, and sucked heavily at the horses' hooves. Plants thrived in this part of the forest, growing thick and lush, bright emerald against dark wood. The foliage was clumped together, covered in moss and ivy. She saw more and more pools of stagnant water. Trickling streams wended through ditches, overgrown by tall ferns.

"Have we entered the swamp already?" she called out.

"No, but we are at its border. Mayville isn't far from the fringes of Fennbog," Burn explained. "These lands are a giant river basin. The rain flows into the Crown's Rush."

Sora nodded at that. The Crown's Rush was the longest river this side of the royal city. She had studied a bit of geography; if one followed the Rush, it would lead straight to the City of Crowns. She also knew that the Rush disappeared into the sludgy mire of Fennbog swamp, nigh impassible. It had never been traveled to the ocean. Boats had a way of vanishing into the bog.

Close to mid-morning, Burn finally eased up on his horse, bringing the small party to a stop. The barks and yelps of the hounds sounded occasionally, a reminder that they were still being hunted. Speed was of the essence. Only a fool would follow them into the swamp. *Only a fool would go there in the first place.*

Burn brought them up short, raising his hand. Then he sat atop his horse, half-obscured by a ridge of thick blackberry bushes. Dorian trotted up to his side, nudging past Sora's horse. Crash followed him, treading carefully across the soft ground.

Sora could tell that their steeds didn't like the mud. They kept shifting their weight, lifting one hoof and then another, uncomfortable.

"Why have we stopped?" Crash called.

"An obstruction," Dorian said sarcastically. "However minor."

Sora frowned at this. Curious, she led her horse through the remaining bramble to Dorian's side. The trees fell behind them. She looked up, her view no longer obscured by leaves and branches. Her jaw dropped.

A river.

No, worse than a river. A slough. The land dipped down into a wide stretch of brackish water, interrupted by lumps of rust-brown wetland covered in cattails, weeds and Goddess-only-knew-what. Far, far away, on the very edges of her vision, she could see the smooth, towering eucalyptus trees of Fennbog swamp, partially shrouded in a veil of gray mist. Several birds flew back and forth across the open stretch of land, large creatures with long, wide beaks and dangling yellow legs.

"That's not so bad," she said, looking across the flatland to the tall trees, several miles away. "At least there's no roughage. We should be able to cross in no time." She shifted her hips and urged her horse down the hill, but Burn reached out and grabbed her reins, stopping her.

"That's not land," he said, indicating the broad basin.

"No," Dorian chimed in. "It's mud, the likes of which you have never seen. Enough to swallow our horses and everything else." The silver-haired man turned to look at her, his brows drawn low. "Nice work, sweetness. That Cat's Eye is certainly useful. We've only reached a dead end." Then he looked at Crash. "This was a brilliant idea...."

"Quiet, Wolfy," Crash said darkly. He didn't seem disturbed by the stretch of wetland, but watched coolly from atop his steed, gazing into the distance. The calls of the hounds were growing closer, lighting up the air with eager yelps. Sora felt the hair on the back of her neck rise. They didn't have long to make a decision.

Finally, Crash turned to look at her. "Girl," he said, "you take the lead." Then he withdrew a dagger from his belt. He cut the rope connecting her horse to Burn's.

"What?" Sora demanded. She felt as though she had swallowed a handful of dirt.

"You heard me," he said, sheathing the dagger. "Quickly, use the necklace to get us across this bog. There is no time for doubt." He watched her with that same cold look, as though she was already disappointing him. Strangely, it reminded her of her father. And even stranger, it lit a small fire inside of her, one of radiant defiance.

"Fine," Sora snapped, and touched her necklace, hoping it could read her intentions. When she looked out across the wetland, she only felt numb. "Follow me!"

She kicked her steed a little harder than intended. The horse leapt into action, skidding down the hill with a frightened whinny. On its first step into the slough, it plunged knee-deep into the mud. Sora let out a short scream, barely staying in the saddle. She could see the truth of the swamp now. Everything that she had thought was grass—solid ground—was really a soupy, putrid substance that sucked down like quicksand.

"Hyyah!" she shouted, and urged her horse forward. It maneuvered sideways, away from the deep mud. She touched her necklace again. Perhaps it was her adrenaline or the sudden urgency of the situation, but the Cat's Eye responded immediately, nudged by her thoughts.

Sora directed her horse to the right, where the ground was more solid, clumped together by grassroots and shrubbery. Her steed regained its footing, and then they were off, charging across the slough, weaving along a route of long grass, reeds and rotted logs, her Cat's Eye their only guide. Crash and the Wolfies stayed close behind, following her step for step, turn for turn. Countless times she almost lost her footing, but Sora was a keen rider, well-studied, and was able to right her horse.

Perhaps a half-hour into the wetlands, the hounds burst from the forest, howling and yapping in victory, their prey finally in sight. They were big dogs, wolfhounds or larger. Some might have been mutts, mixed with shaggy herding dogs, almost the size of ponies. Sora glanced over her shoulder in horror. The fleeting gray shapes flew down the hill and entered the mire. She hoped that the dogs would plunge straight into the bog.

The pack leader did just that, falling into a well-disguised sinkhole. But a new leader took its place, snapping and snarling, and the hounds quickly regrouped. They followed Sora's trail perfectly. They weren't faster than the horses, but they could certainly keep pace, and the terrain was unpredictable. Her heart sank. She urged her horse faster, praying they didn't plunge into the mud.

Then a hollow, moaning sound floated eerily across the marsh, blending with the mist. A horn. More riders appeared at the hilltop, red uniforms starkly visible against the low, gray clouds. They paused, their horses dancing back and forth, and Sora could imagine their conversation. Doubtless they were looking at the muck, wondering how to cross.

"Follow the hounds!" she heard. The voice was distant and muffled, carried by the empty wind. "Step only where they step! Careful now! Cautious!" A team broke off to follow, albeit at a slower pace. A small group stayed on top of the hill.

Sora smirked at that. Cowards. Their captains had kept to the woods, scared of getting their boots wet. She wondered if Lord Seabourne was among them.

"Watch your backs!" Crash yelled, shaking her from her thoughts. He was several dozen yards behind her, farthest in the rear. "Lean down! Close to your horses!"

"What?" Sora exclaimed, confused. But she saw Dorian and Burn obey. She bent across the saddle, pressing herself to her horse's neck, not a moment too soon. With a quick *fffttttp!*, a black arrow flew past her head, quicker than a bolting sparrow. A shriek escaped her lips despite the warning.

"Blast!" Dorian cried. "They have archers!"

"Run!" Crash's voice reached them. "Faster!"

Sora pressed her horse again, though it was already at its limit. A rain of arrows followed them. Their only hope was to outdistance the archers, but with the ground growing ever softer, it was difficult to maintain her pace. The Cat's Eye's directions came in short bursts and prompts, and she could barely lead her horse, first one way, then the other. Twice she almost plunged into the mire, barely correcting her steed in time. They needed to slow down, step more carefully—but that was far too great a risk.

Then, suddenly, there was no more ground. Sora's horse came to a skidding halt, snorting and whuffing, digging its hooves into the soft earth. She leaned backward, struggling to control her mount. When they finally stopped, she could only stare at the sight before her, mouth slightly open, helpless.

The slough dissolved into an outright river—the Crown's Rush, she assumed. It moved at a sluggish pace, perhaps a half-mile across. Sora had the feeling that this river wasn't normally so wide, but it was the rainy season. The slough was swollen with water from the recently melted snow.

And there, slightly to their left, was a rotted, broken bridge. The water had risen so much that the bridge floated on the river's surface, pieces of it completely submerged. Large stakes protruded from the river every couple of paces, but to Sora's eyes, they looked half-rotted and the ropes well-worn. She doubted any maintenance had been done in the last few years. It was a wonder that thing still stood.

It also appeared to be the only way to cross the river. A coincidence? Or had the Cat's Eye led her straight to it?

*If the necklace led me here, then it must be passable,* she thought, gripping the stone. But that was a long shot. She didn't know if that was true; she wasn't experienced enough.

But it was too late to turn back and search for a better route. She could hear the baying of the hounds on their trail, frantic wails and vicious snarls. And the soldiers hadn't given up yet. She leapt from her steed just as another series of arrows rained down upon them, speckling the ground, narrowly missing their horses. Luckily, the arrows were losing their accuracy because of the distance.

Dorian and Burn arrived next to her, immediately fanning out, jumping from their horses and ducking low to the brush. They were both breathing hard, full of adrenaline. The howling had grown to a fever pitch; the dogs could sense they were close to their prey. The horses pawed the ground, panicked, the whites of their eyes showing. Sora knew her mare was one second from bolting. She held on firmly to its reins, staying to one side so she wouldn't get kicked.

She wasn't normally afraid of dogs, but hearing the primitive, brutal snarls struck terror in her heart. These animals weren't just dogs anymore. No, they were hunters fully consumed by the chase. Who knew what a frenzied pack would do?

Crash arrived a second later, leaping from his horse while still in canter. He landed smoothly, running toward them, his sword drawn.

"Should we cross the bridge?" Sora asked, wincing. It sounded more like, *Can I go home now?*

"Yes," Burn said. The response was grim and immediate. "I'll go first. I'm the heaviest. If the supports give, then it'll be under my weight."

Sora's mouth gaped. "But you'll fall into the river!"

"Sweetness, he's a warrior," Dorian cut her off. "And a Wolfy at that. Do you really think mud will swallow him?"

Sora pushed Dorian away from her, shaking her head. "You'll need the Cat's Eye," she tried again.

"I doubt I'll get lost on a bridge," Burn said, humor in his eyes. "I've crossed more treacherous rivers than this." He turned back to the sludgy water, feet planted on firm earth, tall and strong. Sora gazed at his muscular back, as wide as a bear, the greatsword reaching almost down to his knees. She raised an eyebrow.

Dorian spoke up, his tone sharp and urgent. "Hurry, Burn, I feel a dog gnawing at my ankle...."

As though summoned by his words, a giant, black wolfhound

jumped from the bushes to their right, its coat matted with mud and reeds. Sora gasped, stumbling backwards. The hound turned and snapped at her, its vicious fangs glinting with saliva. It lunged, mouth wide open, flying at her throat.

The *shing!* of steel pierced the air, the glint of a blade. The assassin dodged in front of her, an unexpectedly valiant move, and his blade caught the hound's jaw. It cleaved halfway through its muzzle before lodging into the bone. Crash pulled the hound toward him and rammed a knife into its throat, then tossed the body to one side, dumping it into the slough.

Sora stared in horror, unable to believe the swiftness of the battle. More hounds leapt from the bushes, perhaps over a dozen, though some hung back, obscured by clots of grass. They kept their distance, circling and snapping from just beyond Crash's reach. The assassin faced the pack in a half-circle, his sword in one hand, a short knife in the other. Every time one got too close, he lunged forward, slashing with his blade.

When Sora turned back to the bridge, she saw that Burn had mounted the first planks and was starting across, coaxing his horse behind him. The horse trod gingerly on the half-submerged planks, its ears back. Sora marveled at the horse's training, following its master into such dire straits. The bridge swayed and jerked in the heavy, sluggish water.

Dorian followed with his horse, but stopped just before the bridge. He waited until Burn had reached almost midway across the planks. But by that point, Sora could hear the shouts of human voices, the squish of unseen hooves. The soldiers would be upon them soon.

"Dorian, take my horse," Crash called, and indicated the tall gray steed. Dorian nodded and caught the reins, then tied it to the back of his horse.

Crash turned back to the hounds, swinging his sword several times to back them off.

Dorian turned to Sora and nodded curtly. "You're next," he said. "Should anything happen, just call my name." And he winked, a terribly roguish look. "I'll come back for you."

Sora balked at that. Come back for her? Unlikely, especially if the bridge collapsed. She was about to say something, but the thief had already started across the expanse, the two horses stepping lightly after him. They were smaller steeds with long, delicate legs. The ropes strained. The boards creaked. So far, the bridge held.

Another hound leapt from the brush, drawing her attention. Crash hacked it down with his sword just as quickly. The dog whined pathetically, writhing on the ground, blood spurting from a wound at its neck. The other dogs paced back and forth, even more excited by the scent of blood, then skittered away to avoid Crash's blade. They paced just beyond the fringe of grass, looking for an opening.

Sora waited for Dorian to make some headway across the bridge. She felt a nervous knot form in her stomach. *I'm next.* She looked back across the drizzling wetland to the distant shapes on the hill. The clouds had moved lower, if that was possible, and the soldiers were filmy on the horizon.

"They've stopped shooting," she said, relief in her voice. "Maybe they'll give up...?"

"No," Crash replied darkly. "The other soldiers are too close. They won't risk hitting their own men." Then he turned and started moving her toward the bridge, one eye on the dogs, his sword still at the ready. Sora led her horse toward the platform, following Crash's direction, unable to protest. She tried to hide the tremor in her knees. The river might appear slow and sluggish, but she was certain that it had a nasty undertow, and that the water might be too thick to swim against.

"Prepare yourself," Crash said. Then he headed her onto the bridge.

Sora started across carefully. Burn was almost to the other side, and this gave her hope. Dorian was just past the halfway point. The smaller Wolfy shouted back to her occasionally, pointing out rotted beams or loose ropes, but she could barely concentrate. She was too busy gripping her necklace in one hand and the horse's reins in the other, her eyes trained on her feet.

Burn reached the other side. Dorian was two-thirds of the way across. Where he stood, the water was shallow and the bridge was supported by thick mud, much more secure. Sora felt a bit of tension loosen. With less weight on the bridge, she was certain it would hold. She started stepping more boldly, leading her horse as quickly as she could. The water flowed over her boots, icy cold, seeping through the leather and freezing her toes. At times, the bridge dipped downward, submerged. She was almost waist-deep in water, her clothes soaked. Her horse balked, and she had to pause for a moment, coaxing it forward, cautiously testing each beam before putting weight on it. It was painfully slow going.

Finally Dorian made it to the other side. After securing his two horses, he returned to the bridge and waited for her, standing lightly on the planks, watching her progress. Sora, grateful for his vigilance, felt more secure.

"Here they come," Crash called. He was only a few paces

behind her.

Sora glanced back and spotted the shiny helmets through the tall grass. The dogs had noticeably calmed. Her heart lurched. The soldiers were right behind them and would probably try to cross the bridge too....*What can we do?*

Crash raised his shortbow and fired a few arrows into the brush. One of them caught flesh and a gurgling scream split the air, along with the howl of a few dogs. Her horse paused at the sound, legs  stiff, ears back. *No!* Sora tried to coax the mare forward, clicking her tongue, pulling on the reins. But her steed would not budge.

"Ugh, stupid horse," Sora snapped, trying to drag it forward. She could sense Crash's impatience. He fired off an arrow, striking yet another soldier. She cursed the steed and hoped that the soldiers didn't return fire. She and her steed were helplessly exposed in the center of the bridge.

Then a sudden, terrible snapping sound reached her ears. Distracted, she looked down at her foot. The planks were bound by a frayed rope, and as she watched, the last strands split apart. The bridge sagged abruptly under her weight. Then, with several twists and snaps, the ropes broke apart in a chain reaction, one plank after the next.

"Dorian!" she cried, suddenly sick. She looked up to see him a few dozen feet away, lingering on the bridge, watching her. He could make it to her side if he moved fast. "Dorian! Help! The bridge!"

She waited for him to rush to her, or at least reply. But when she met his eyes, they were strangely dark. He watched her blankly, inquisitively, and for a moment...just a moment...she thought his face looked different. Like someone else.

Then the center of the bridge dissolved under her feet. The water leapt up to claim her. Sludgy and thick, it felt like falling into ice-cold porridge. Rocks and twigs propelled by the vicious current snagged her skin, cutting and bruising it. Her horse screamed in terror, sinking up to its saddle, hooves buried in the muddy bottom of the slough.

The horse bucked and kicked, dancing to one side. Its harness became entangled with a fallen tree branch, knocking Sora even further into the water. The current rushed up to grab her, twisting her away from the bridge and the ropes, dragging her downstream mercilessly. The river was much stronger than she had thought. Before she knew it, she was fully submerged, the water swallowing her whole.

She fought her way back up to the surface, struggling against the current. "Help!" she screamed, kicking her legs and propelling her arms, trying to stay afloat. The water was impossibly deep, with no sense of a bottom, and she was quickly swept downstream. She grabbed hold of the rope that had once held the bridge, hoping it was tied to something at the other end.

Luckily, the rope caught, and she tried to pull her way back. But the current was powerful and the rope tenuous, and her head kept going underwater. She was far away from the bridge, with no way back. She opened her mouth and inhaled mud, choking. She couldn't stop coughing, with the water splashing up in her face.

The water was so cold, her fingers became numb. Her hands tired and slipped. Her head went under again, and this time the river yanked her downward, catching her foot in an undertow. She couldn't hold on anymore. She didn't even know if the rope was still in her hands.

Then suddenly, strong, rough fingers snagged her shirt.

She was dragged upward against a strong, toned body. Held tightly against a broad chest as the water rushed against her, trying to press her down. A rope was looped around her wrist, binding her tightly to her rescuer's belt. He started pulling her back to the bridge, fighting the fierce current and lots of debris.

Relief surged through her. *Dorian, it has to be!* He had been paralyzed back there on the riverbank, perhaps by panic or fear. But he had come for her, just like he had promised.

Her head broke the surface of the water and Sora gasped brokenly, weak and drained. She clung to Dorian's hard torso like a squirrel to a branch, digging her fingers into his skin, wrapping her legs around his waist, half-squeezing the breath out of him, terrified. A second rope was tossed to them; he grabbed it in two firm hands. Arm-length by arm-length, she was pulled toward the opposite side of the river, where Burn and the horses were gathered. It was all she could do to keep her head above water. Dirt muddied her eyes and mouth, twigs were caught in her hair, her clothes were heavy and tangled.

It seemed to take an hour to reach solid land. Finally she felt the soft bank beneath her, but didn't have the strength to use her limbs. She was pushed and lifted through the water, propelling herself clumsily with her legs, too numb and weak to do much else.

Once the water was shallow enough, her rescuer cut the rope between them and stood, lifting her into his arms, settling her partway over his shoulder. Then he carried her through the waist-deep water much as one might carry a child, her legs around his waist, her arms tight at his neck.

She hugged Dorian tightly, still choking, spitting out sludge from the back of her throat. She wiped her face across his shoulder, blinking the grit from her eyes, then buried herself against his wet black hair.

Wait! Black hair?

"Burn! Bring a saddle blanket!" her rescuer called. It was not Dorian's voice, but deeper, stronger, carrying the weight of authority.

Crash!

Sora wanted to care, but she was too exhausted. She hadn't the strength to thrust him away. All she could do was cling and shiver.

She was carried a short ways from the riverbank behind a thin copse of trees, then easily maneuvered to the ground. Although it was soft and sludgy, it was solid, not the quicksand of the slough. She wanted to stand up, but her limbs shook. Her teeth chattered uncontrollably. And, she suddenly realized, it was raining.

When she looked up, the assassin knelt above her, his eyes the color of moss, his black hair bristling with water. He briefly checked her for injuries, silently and efficiently, his hands running over her body in a brusque manner. She tried to protest by pushing him away, but he deftly avoided her attempts.

"Do you feel pain?" he asked, stretching out her arms and legs, pressing at her ribs.

"No," she gasped, then coughed again, spitting out a shard of leaf.

"Good." Then he reached up and took the saddle blanket that Burn offered. "We have to continue for a ways, but not far, just out of range of the soldiers. Can you stand?"

Sora nodded and pulled the saddle blanket around her. It was rough and heavy, and not immediately warm. She couldn't stop shivering. Still, she managed to climb to her feet and pull her wet hair away from her face. She was surprised that Crash stayed there by her side, assisting with her balance. She slowly tugged off her leather boots and dumped out the icy water. He didn't release her arm until she was able to stand on her own.

Dorian appeared, leading their horses. Somehow, they had managed to rescue her mare. They had lost several bags of supplies to the river, but the majority was still intact, if a bit damp. Sora looked at Dorian strangely, but he avoided her eyes, focusing solely on the beasts.

"I called for you," she said, thinking back to the sinking bridge. "Did you ignore me?"

Dorian still didn't meet her eyes. It seemed as if he hadn't even heard her words. He acted very interested in the saddlebags, untying a few to check their contents. Sora watched him, her hands tight on the rough blanket, speechless. *It's like he doesn't even care!* She would have expected this from the assassin, but not Dorian. He, at least, had acted like a friend.

When she turned back to Crash, he was watching the Wolfy with a searching gaze. From the set of his jaw, he was definitely tense. His eyes flickered over Dorian's lean form, from his face to his boots.

"You left her to drown," he said shortly, then grabbed the reins of his gray steed, pulling the horse away from the Wolfy. "You left *both of us* to drown."

Dorian raised an eyebrow, unable to avoid the assassin. "I froze up! I didn't know what to do," he said irritatedly. "I don't know what happened. I mean, I heard her...." He glanced to Sora, then looked away again, glaring at the horses.

Burn took his steed as well, his gaze full of concern. Then he glanced to Crash, and the two shared a strained look that Sora couldn't interpret. "How are your wounds, Dorian?" Burn asked suddenly. It seemed like an odd question, given the context. "From the attack in the woods?"

"They're healing," Dorian grunted, and briefly lifted his shirt, showing the long red scabs. Then he winced. "Another week and they'll be gone."

Burn nodded slowly, thoughtfully. Then he looked to Sora. "Whatever just happened," he said, "we can discuss it later. Come, let's find a place to set up camp and dry our things. I think a big fire is in order."

For once, no one argued. The rain became an honest downpour. Everyone took charge of their mounts and started into the swamp proper, eager to find shelter from the storm. The ground was much firmer between the massive tree roots, and the horses were able to walk easily. Sora looked up at the tall eucalyptus trees, the naked trunks that wove in and out of each other like thick tendons. The trees had wide, high branches, fanning out into a perfect canopy. The air was dense with noise: pattering raindrops, croaks and bird calls, rustles in the underbrush, chirping crickets.

Sora gazed into the depths of Fennbog. She wondered what other surprises—what other horrors—awaited.

* * *

Volcrian looked up at the sound of bodies crashing through the underbrush. Bold and confident footsteps, perhaps a party of three, careless about whether they were being overheard.

But why should they care? They were deep in the forest and evening was closing in. The woods were damp and slick with rain, glittering in the fragile twilight. In a sense, it was exactly what he had been waiting for.

The spell using Dorian's blood was almost a complete failure, but at least he knew that the three travelers had entered the swamp. And that following them would have been a waste of time. His power over the Wolfy was dismally weak. He had been able to slip into Dorian's thoughts during a moment of distraction and panic, but he couldn't keep his hold and had caused only a slight hesitation in Dorian's actions, nothing more.

He would need a new plan. Something stronger. Some sort of magic that could resist the Cat's Eye. Perhaps something that wasn't entirely magic at all.

There was only one spell like that he could think of. But it was a dark spell, black-blooded. Forbidden magic, or so his great-grandfather's journal said. But what other choice did he have? He faced an entire journey across the mountains, a year before he could catch his prey on the other side, if they didn't make it to the coast before he did. No, he would need something to track and catch them—something more powerful than fox-corpses or sleight-of-hand.

Which is why the footsteps in the underbrush attracted his attention.

Next, he heard people speaking.

"Twelve men, gone. Swept up by the river when the bridge broke. It's a shame. Too many rookies; they should've been better trained."

"They needed a Captain," a deeper voice grunted. "They had no one to give them orders. It was a mistake."

"Is that what the King's army has come to? Mindless imbeciles waiting for orders?" the first voice demanded.

"Well, that's how we train them."

There was a pause. The voices sounded familiar. Volcrian remembered the brief conversation in the guardhouse between Lord Seabourne and his commanding officers.

"What are we going to say in our report? That we abandoned our men to the swamp?" the first voice asked.

There was a brief, derisive snort. "Well, Lord Seabourne recommended that a few men die in the chase. He must be expecting this."

"Perhaps. But still it's our jobs on the line."

Volcrian slipped behind the three men, leaving his horse tethered to the bushes. It was easy to approach them, since they were making enough noise to drown out the crickets and evening owls. He followed the three captains a short distance until they came to a halt, bickering in the woods.

"Since you're the senior officer, you should file the report," one was saying.

"We should all file separate reports, as regulations dictate," the older one growled.

"Then we need to decide on a story!"

"Honesty, lads," the third man broke in. "Honesty is always best when dealing with the Crown."

"Says the Captain with the lowest salary," the first muttered.

Volcrian slid through the underbrush like an eel. He was now close enough to see their boots, their red tunics through the underbrush. He watched them closely.

"Damn," the older man said. "It's starting to rain."

The third one sighed. "Lads, let's set up camp and eat a hot meal. The answer will come to us."

"Right," the first one said.

They rummaged about in a small area between the trees, clearing the ground of sticks and rocks. Volcrian waited. He was good at waiting. He didn't move until the camp was set up, a fire struck, and rations passed around the circle.

The night deepened. Rain drenched his clothes. A low mist rose from the ground, but Volcrian didn't mind. Rarely did such an excellent opportunity present itself.

He waited until the soldiers had constructed three tiny tents and stretched out their bedrolls, relatively sheltered from the rain. A half-hour later, he heard deep breaths rise and fall, soft grunts and snores. One of the officers was on watch, but he wasn't watching very closely. He stretched out on the ground with a book, reading close to the firelight.

Volcrian whipped out a knife. He ran his tongue along it, senses heightened, eager for the taste of blood. His eyes dilated in excitement.

Then he launched himself onto the watchman. Plunged the knife into his back, through the kidneys. With a loud, piercing wail, the man rolled on the ground, screaming in pain.

Volcrian was prepared for the next man. Another officer jumped from his bedroll, entangled in his sleeping tents. The Wolfy leapt on the man, plunging his dagger straight through his heart. Or at least, that was his intention. He missed a few times before he struck it exactly.

Then he scooped up a pool of blood into his hands, whispered a word of power, and threw it onto the last officer. The blood struck the old man in the face, burning and hissing like potent acid. His screams lit up the night, filtering through the darkness like music. The man died in pain. Horrible, blistering pain.

The mage stood still for a moment, panting, staring at the bodies. He had his sacrifices. There was no time to lose. Now he would work his spell.

Volcrian was up for hours afterward. He removed his clothes so as not to get them dirty, preparing the bodies by the light of the fire. He ran his knife smoothly under each man's skin, stripping it piece by piece, then spread the blood across his arms and chest, letting it dribble over his tight stomach. It was warm. Thick.

He pressed his hands against their quivering organs, the bloated mounds of stomach and intestines, down to the various muscles weeping fat. One by one, he cut out their hearts, still slippery, jittery in his grasp, a mimicry of life.

It was a three-day ritual, one for each of the wraiths, one for each of the spirits he would tie to his will. Using ceremonial herbs, the bodies would be burned, each at a different hour of the day; the skin would be sewn into cloaks and new suits, ready for the use of magic. There were countless spells he would have to chant, ensuring that the soul did not remember its previous identity, or its own autonomy.

It would take a large toll on him, but in the end, he would create minions that were all but invincible. Then he would send them after the assassin and his companions. He doubted the Cat's Eye would be able to affect them, not with the amount of blood and physical matter that they were comprised of. Spirits rode in the magical shells, ghosts were made flesh, solid and real—and they were at his complete command.

Volcrian began building a bonfire, his crippled hand clamped tight against the cold.

# CHAPTER 9

"Don't listen to your head, sweetness! Listen to your gut!"

*Swoosh!*

*Clack!*

*Goddess! I think I'm going to die!*

"Yes, like that, good...don't wipe your eyes; it leaves you open."

"I can't see!"

"You don't have to see."

Dorian was a strange instructor. At times, she couldn't tell if he was teaching her or just teasing. She ducked as he took a swing at her head, the staff hurtling through the air, connecting solidly with the tree behind her. *Crack!*

She gasped, desperate for air, too tired to appreciate the small victory.

They had been traveling for a week through the swamp, following wherever the Cat's Eye directed them, which was seldom in a straight line. She tried to stay as focused as possible on their direction, but it was a challenge. Most days were given to hacking and slashing at the underbrush, clearing a pathway for the horses. Fennbog was a mysterious place, veiled in thin mist, bitterly cold and wet. Everything smelled of damp earth and mold. There was a definite sense of being enclosed, lost in the wilderness. At times it seemed like they weren't even walking on land, but on shallow lakes of grass, full of exotic fungi and large, white mushrooms. They had passed through fields and fields of well-disguised sinkholes, smothered with giant lily-pads as wide as she was tall.

Now they had entered the thick of the forest. Giant, moss-covered trees exploded from the ground, so tall that Sora lost sight of the canopy overhead. Their roots were so vast and wide, it wasn't clear where one tree ended and another began. Vines sprawled across every surface, falling like curtains from the sky. Vibrant flowers speckled the landscape, some larger than her head, blooming bright purples and yellows. She had seen more species of frogs than she could count, and almost as many birds.

She trained a few hours with her new weapons each morning, when it was easiest to see.

"Good, sweetness," Dorian murmured. Then he started speeding up his attacks, mock-jabbing at her ribs, her face, her legs. Sora practiced blocking, using the top and bottom of the staff, trying to think three-dimensionally. It was very different from how she imagined a sword. She had two ends to work with, not just one.

"Excellent; now jump!" Dorian instructed, and went low for her legs. Sora gave a tired, halfhearted leap in the air. The staff passed under her—barely.

She stumbled when she landed, staggering to one side. She clumsily dodged another blow and caught herself on a tree, her shoulders aching and her hands numb; her feet had been rubbed raw by her leather boots. Her arms were covered in bruises and her nails chipped down to the pink.

"Give me a moment," she panted, taking deep breaths, trying to suppress the stitch in her side. With a dirty sleeve, she wiped the sweat from her eyes. This was, without a doubt, the most physically challenging activity she had ever experienced: dancing across the tree-roots, trying not to slip on the damp wood. Yet despite her bruises, her staff remained in pristine condition. It was neither chipped nor dented. Dorian had gone through several different poles by this point, carving a new one each night.

Sora gazed at her staff in admiration. Apparently the salesman in Mayville hadn't been exaggerating. Witch wood—it made a difference. She wondered if it could even be chipped by a sword.

Sora groaned; she could feel the pulled muscles only too well in her calves and arms. Quick as lightning, she brought up her staff and heard a sharp *crack!* She smiled in grim satisfaction. Dorian's blow was deflected.

"And she shows potential!" the thief cried, grinning at her fiercely. Sora flushed, trying not to look too pleased with herself. She could hear Burn applauding in the background. The two other members of their camp were lingering near the horses, tending to the beast's hooves. Crash didn't spare her a glance.

Then Dorian swooped down. He picked up her daggers and tossed them to her. "Let's finish with a bit of knife-fighting, shall we?" He dropped his makeshift staff and pulled out his knives, his weapon of choice. Sora sighed and picked up her daggers reluctantly. She liked the staff because it had a longer range. Knife-fighting was a bit riskier.

"Can we find more even ground?" she asked, wiping sweat from her eyes. Daggers required more concentration and she didn't want to watch her feet.

Dorian nodded and pointed off to their left, through the trees. "There's a circle of grass that way. Let's move over there. We'll be back in a few minutes," he called over his shoulder. Burn waved a distracted hand, busy repacking his saddlebags.

Sora followed her instructor through a brief stretch of ferns, pushing through the hanging vines. When she reached the small circle of grass, she found that the ground was soft and spongy, definitely not what she had hoped for. She sighed, then leveled her daggers in front of her, readying herself for the fight.

Dorian lashed out unexpectedly. She barely dodged his blow, leaping out of range. She gasped. "What are you trying to do? Stab me?" she laughed, taking a few steps back and shaking out her arms.

Dorian remained quiet. His eyes glinted in the pale morning light.

The smile faded from her lips and she looked at him uneasily. He had the same empty, solemn expression he had back at the river, when he had watched her almost drown. Sora frowned. She hadn't thought about the incident for a week or more; they had been too busy struggling against the difficult terrain of the swamp.

Dorian lunged forward again, swiping at her with both knives in a butterfly pattern. She jumped back nimbly, deflecting one blade out of pure instinct. He backed her around the clearing.

"Dorian?" she asked quietly. "What are you doing?" The change had come over him so suddenly, she couldn't tell if he was testing her or if he had somehow become another person. It felt like he was trying to push her deeper into the woods. She wanted to head back to camp, suddenly unnerved, but she couldn't tell from which direction they had come.

He lunged at her again, using moves that he hadn't taught her, combining dagger swipes with kicks and punches. Sora dodged desperately, her knives forgotten. She threw herself to one side, tumbling across the wet ground, then tried to roll back to her feet. She slipped in the grass and went down. Dorian was directly behind her, and he plunged the dagger into the ground, an inch from her arm. She rolled again, scrambling to her feet. When she looked into Dorian's face, he stared back at her blankly, stoically, like a sleepwalker.

He lifted his knives again. Sora screamed.

She kept screaming as she deflected two more blows with the flat of her blade. His knife caught her shoulder, ripping through her shirt with ease, puncturing flesh, although she had no idea how deep. Her adrenaline pounded and she couldn't feel the wound.

Instinct took over. Sora threw herself on the Wolfy, trying to dislodge his knives. She clawed at his face, kicking him in the ribs. He grabbed her easily and threw her off, picking up his knives from the ground. Sora scuttled backwards on her hands and legs, like a crab.

"Dorian!" she screamed. "Dorian, it's me! What's gotten into you?" But her companion did not reply.

She finally regained her footing at the edge of the clearing. She paused, watching Dorian come at her. He charged across the muddy ground, his boots sucking and slipping.

At that moment, a black shadow shot across the grass, fast as a wildcat. Crash threw himself on the Wolfy, slamming Dorian face-first into the ground. The thief howled, an inhuman sound, and turned on Crash, the daggers forgotten. The two men wrestled, rolling back and forth. Sora tried to avoid the chaos, but they tumbled directly into her legs. She leapt backwards, out of the way, into the forest...except suddenly, there was no more ground. She put her foot down—on air.

"Aaah!" With a short, sharp yelp, Sora pitched backwards, falling down a steep slope. The two men spilled after her, carried by the momentum of their fight. She grabbed at a bush, but uprooted it. Grass whipped her face, thorns tore at her clothes. When she landed at the base of the steep slope, she found herself staring up at the overcast sky, dazed, the trees and foliage slowly spinning around her. She imagined that the clouds were so low, she could reach up and touch them.

Crash and Dorian landed a second later. The assassin, on top, smashed the air from the Wolfy's lungs. Then he grabbed the thief, heaving him effortlessly off the ground, and slammed him into a tree. The assassin's knife was out, the blade shoved against Dorian's stomach, his other hand tight on his throat.

"You fool!" Crash yelled. "You fool of a thief!"

Dorian blinked, his eyes slowly refocusing. Sora sat up and watched, her lips dry and parted. Speechless.

"W-what?" Dorian started.

Crash shoved him back against the tree again. "You idiot. You could have killed her!"

"Wait!" another voice broke through the panic. Burn skidded down the steep slope, far more balanced and controlled than when Sora fell. He reached them a moment later, sinking into the soft earth. "Hold your blade, Crash! Dorian didn't know! He wasn't in control!"

"And what about next time?" Crash snapped. "We might as well be traveling with Volcrian in our midst. Dorian's a danger to all of us. I say kill him and be done with it."

"You are quick to use a blade," Burn said steadily. Then he nodded to Dorian. "Let the man speak."

Sora didn't know what was going on. She watched as Crash let go of Dorian. The Wolfy slid back to the ground, shaking. When he looked at her, his eyes were full of fear.

"I-I don't know what happened," he said. "I blacked out. I can't remember anything."

"Dorian," Burn said slowly, steadily. "Did you bleed a lot from that cut on your hip? Could Volcrian have gotten hold of it?"

"I think it's obvious that he has," Crash grunted.

Wordlessly, Dorian raised his shirt, inspecting the thin strip of pink flesh. It was almost completely healed. When he looked up again, there was more than just fear in his eyes. There was despair. "What do we do?" he asked quietly.

"Wait," Sora said, holding up her hand. "What happened? What does Volcrian have to do with this?"

Crash turned to her, surprise registering on his face, if only for a moment. Then he let out a short breath. "I forget that you don't know these things," he muttered.

Burn cut in. "Volcrian has somehow gotten his hands on Dorian's blood," he explained. "He's worked a spell with it. He's...uh...influencing Dorian's behavior, you could say." Burn frowned. "Not sure of all the details, I'm not a mage myself. But my guess is that he didn't have enough of Dorian's blood to work the full spell. It looks like his influence is only minor."

Sora nodded slowly. It was the first she had ever heard of this —and more than a little worrisome. She looked at Dorian, catching his eye, but the Wolfy thief glanced away quickly. She wondered if he was ashamed of what he had done.

"We've been trying to avoid this from happening again," Crash murmured.

"Again?" Sora asked, surprised.

None of the men would meet her gaze this time. Burn finally

said, "We had a fourth companion very briefly, about a year ago. Volcrian got hold of his blood. Needless to say, he didn't last long."

"We had to kill him," Dorian said.

Sora shuddered. It hadn't occurred to her that more people might have been involved with Crash's party. She wondered what kind of men would fall into league with him. Cutthroats and kidnappers, she was certain.

"Twice this has happened around me," Sora said slowly. "Do you think that Volcrian is...targeting me? Through Dorian?" She hated to ask, and the words almost caught in her throat. The men looked at her, and she read the truth in their eyes. "It's the Cat's Eye, isn't it? He knows about it."

"If he didn't before, he does now," Dorian confirmed. "Using this spell, who knows what he has seen through my eyes?"

Sora paled. "So he is following us into the swamp?"

"The only way he can," Crash confirmed. "By invading Dorian's thoughts."

A brief silence fell. Sora winced, touching her sore shoulder, pulling back her bloody hand. It was disturbing to think about. Dorian hadn't just been playing rough—he had been earnestly trying to kill her. She had escaped by pure luck. If she had been just a little clumsier, he could have stabbed her through the heart, or pierced a lung, or cut the artery under her arm. She would have bled to death....

She looked back at Dorian, unable to hide her distrust.

He watched her with large, regretful eyes. "Sorry, sweetness," he murmured.

"My Cat's Eye," Sora said suddenly, realization dawning. "Maybe it can counteract the spell somehow. Like that monster in the forest, remember?"

"You're not going anywhere near him." Crash glared at the thief. "It's too dangerous. He's out of control."

"Careful, Crash," Dorian sneered. "You almost sound concerned."

The assassin stepped up to the thief, intimidating him with his presence, pushing him back. "I have reason to be," he said darkly.

Sora saw the fear in Dorian's face. The smaller man backed away.

"Enough!" Burn yelled, forcing himself between them. "Sora's suggestion might be our only option. We can't fight amongst ourselves. That is exactly what Volcrian wants!"

Sora watched the men, shaken by the confrontation between Crash to Dorian. She was unsure of what to say.

Burn spoke again. "Before we do anything, we have to get back to the horses. Sora, are you all right to stand?"

"Of course," she said, climbing to her feet and running a careful hand over her cut shoulder. She caught Burn's worried look. "It's not deep," she reassured him. It had already stopped bleeding. She glanced around the trees, searching for the best way back up the hill,. Then she paused and frowned.

"What is that?" she asked, pointing to an odd structure in the branches. It hung a few yards away amidst a thick tangle of bramble, obscured by leaves. She stepped boldly up to the nest of bushes, grabbed hold of a stick and pulled. After a short struggle, she dislodged it from the tree.

It might have been a scarecrow at one time, but it was missing a head. The pole was perhaps eight feet in length, and another branch had been tied to it crosswise. Old, rotted cloth, what might have been a shirt or a cloak, was draped over it. As she looked closer, Sora could make out a string of bones and teeth around the wooden neck. There was a pile of junk scattered at the roots of the tree: beads, feathers, chips of glass, old teeth and more bones. She couldn't tell if they were animal or human, perhaps both.

A cold wind gusted past them, slightly moving the damp cloth. The string of bones clinked softly in the breeze. Sora felt a chill run across her skin. She threw the pole down, suddenly loathe to touch it. Her eyes roved over the pile of scraps, tangled in the overgrown brush.

"What is this?" she asked again.

"A marker," Crash answered her. He shared a look with Burn. "Catlin territory."

"This must be the border," Dorian echoed.

"Catlins?" Sora asked, raising a skeptical eyebrow.

Dorian sighed and gave her a patient look. "Another one of the five races, dearest...."

"I know that!" Sora snapped. Catlins had also been mentioned in the stories of Kaelyn the Wanderer. Giant, savage beasts with the bodies of men but the heads of giant cats. They were thought to be the most ferocious and brutal of the races. But no one had told her they still existed. She struggled with that for a moment. "They live here? Truly? Why didn't anyone tell me?" She glanced around at their serious faces, but she already knew the answer. These men never told her anything. "This isn't just some cheap trick?"

"Far from it. It's a warning," Burn said. His hand landed on her shoulder, and Sora blinked her eyes, as though shaken from a daydream. "Travelers aren't welcome here. We'd best continue moving. From here on out, we should keep in mind that we are not alone. The Catlins could be anywhere among these trees. Let's try not to draw attention to ourselves."

"Right," Dorian agreed. Then he added after a brief pause, "No more snoring, Sora."

She turned to him, surprised, the solemn atmosphere broken, and glared. "I don't snore!"

"Like a bear," Burn nodded. He grinned at Dorian over her head.

"What? That's not funny!" Sora exclaimed, though she knew they were only teasing her. Well, maybe. Her maids had certainly never mentioned it. "I'm as quiet as a whisper! Burn is the one who snores!"

"Nonsense!" Burn rumbled.

"Quiet," Crash snapped. All three turned to look at him. "Your voices could wake up the trees, you're so loud. No more meaningless banter. Only speak when necessary."

The Wolfies nodded. Sora rolled her eyes, wishing he would quit being so serious. The swamp appeared to be a dead place, deserted; she hadn't seen a sign of life in days, except for giant snails and bright red frogs. The silence of the swamp was deafening; she felt as though she were drowning in it, like someone had put a heavy blanket over her head. Perhaps Catlins had lived here once, but who knew how long ago that was? They might have all died off, or moved territories, or whatever it was that Catlins did. *I hope so.* The headless scarecrow certainly looked old and forgotten.

"We should go back for the horses. Staying in one place too long is dangerous on this ground," Crash said. Then he turned back to the hill and started upward, grabbing onto saplings and vines as he went.

Back at camp, they packed up swiftly and saddled their horses. Burn discarded a few pots and pans, saying they would clank together and cause too much noise. Dorian followed suit, though they carried very little metal other than their weapons. They muffled their saddles as best as they could with old cloth, then continued on their way.

* * *

Volcrian looked at the three muddy pools of blood before him, his nose discerning each one clearly. His great-grandfather's book sat at his side, pages spread wide open, dog-eared and stained with dirt and blood.

It had taken days to chant the various spells, to enact the strange rituals and drawings that would summon the wraiths. He had lost track of time amidst his chanting, oblivious to day or night, storm or sun. He had done nothing more than drink water. The magical energy had nourished his body, along with the spell.

Today, he would raise the dead.

Would they remember their past identities once they were reawakened as wraiths? The thought nagged at the back of his mind, but, thumbing through his great-grandfather's journal, he couldn't find any word he had skipped, any symbol out of sequence. He had chanted countless spells over the last several days, hoping to erase the spirits' memories. They shouldn't remember their human life at all. They would arise as emotionless, thoughtless servants, following his commands.

It was one of the oldest spells, manipulating the very life force that tied the soul to the body. His great-grandfather's writing had hinted to its origin, back before the War of the Races, a spell that had survived their family's destruction. It was dangerous to use, black-blooded. The book had warned him of the consequences. A weak-willed and inexperienced sorcerer might be manipulated by the bond, become as dumb and soulless as the wraiths themselves, a servant to his own creations. The magic could burrow into one's mind, change one's thoughts.

But Volcrian's bloodlust was pure, his thoughts clean, his purpose clear.

Drawing a knife, the mage muttered a few words of power under his breath to concentrate his energy. He frowned, focusing on his hunt, on the assassin, his prey. Then he held his arm above the first pool of blood and slit his own skin, spilling a few precious drops of his lifeblood into the mix. It sizzled and bubbled. He allowed a small smile. The wound stung at first, but it was soon covered by a rush of energy. Of pleasure. His veins began to sing, his entire body vibrated with strength and vitality. Magic.

Steam began to rise from the first pool, a sign that the spell was working. He moved to the second, then the third, offering his blood and murmuring the few words of power. A dull wind picked up, slowly swirling around the fields where he had began the ritual, as though awakened by the magic.

Such power flooded Volcrian's veins, he could barely contain it. Fueled by a clear sense of purpose, the magic flowed much more strongly, thrumming down his arms, his legs. He could feel the spirits gathering. The shades of the dead men were thick in the air, practically solid, a tangible vapor.

"Rise," he whispered. "*Rise* and bond to me."

The steam rose faster, the blood swiftly dissipating into a dense mist, clouding thicker and darker. Soon the woods were consumed by it. The sun's rays grew dull, the air heavy with charged energy. Volcrian's eyes watched the fog sharply, waiting, unsure of what might happen next. This was the most uncertain time in the spell—one wrong word or move and the spirits could slip the noose, return to the dark forest between life and death.

But the blood was fresh and the bodies newly dead; the spirits would miss their physical forms and be drawn to the heaps of skin and organs next to each pool. He was confident that they would respond to his call.

Dimly, shapes began to appear in the mist, as though built from the air itself. The three figures began to solidify, turning darker, until Volcrian could make out humanoid forms, shaky and insubstantial as shadows. Then the piles of flesh began to tremble. The mist closed around them as though sucked inward, creating a whirlwind that brushed through Volcrian's hair, teasing it, tempting him. Finally the mist fully dispersed.

Three beings stood before him, shrouded in cloaks of darkest black. The cloaks seemed to dissolve into the air, as though made of smoke. Volcrian was not fooled—these were powerful beings, magic that reached beyond the veil of life and death. He took in their figures, neither feminine nor masculine, neither tall nor short, neither heavy nor thin. In fact, getting a good look at each creature was difficult. They seemed to constantly shift, blurring over before reappearing, each moment subtly different.

Volcrian grinned and licked his lips. The wraiths were perfect. "Minions," he murmured. "Do you know your master?"

The center wraith, who was slightly more substantial than the other two, raised one dark sleeve toward Volcrian, then pointed a skeletal finger. The Wolfy mage nodded, still smiling. It was the only answer he needed.

"Correct. I will give you your first task. Find the four that evade me: Viper, Sora, and two Wolfies. Kill them. Do not return until your task is finished."

The figures looked at him for a moment longer, or at least, Volcrian assumed they could see. He could make out no eyes in their empty black hoods. Then they shimmered in the air. There was an eerie wail, so faint it might have been an echo of the wind— and they were gone.

*Perhaps you have put some distance between us,* the mage thought to his prey. *But you're not free of me yet.*

The hunt would be over soon. He wanted to laugh, to kick up his heels in giddy exhilaration—but suddenly he staggered. Volcrian was hit with a wave of exhaustion.

He felt he had been punched in the stomach. He collapsed to the ground, shaking, sweat pouring out of his body. It was impossible to remain upright. The cut on his arm burned, his muscles were cramped—he could have sworn his crippled hand was on fire. He clutched the limb, gritting his teeth, willing himself not to cry out.

The exhaustion increased until he felt as though he would be sucked into the earth. A massive boulder weighed down on his chest. The effect of using so much magic was immediate and intense. Each breath became a laborious undertaking—even keeping his eyes opened drained him of energy. He wanted to scream, but couldn't drag enough air into his lungs.

For each wraith created, two years of life were sucked from the mage. He had read as much in the journal. But he hadn't actually thought he'd *experience* it.

He was weary—drained to his very bones. He finally gave in and laid his head down, unable to move his body. It felt as though the hands of death were pulling him into sleep, as though he would never wake up, and he could do nothing to fight against it. Perhaps he would die from this spell, and meet his gentle Etienne on the other side of eternity. It wouldn't be such a bad thing.

Volcrian sank into a deep sleep.

# CHAPTER 10

Several weeks passed as the swamp became more and more dense, the trees larger, the ground softer, until it was like wading through the slough all over again. Sora tried several times to help Dorian, usually at night by the campfire, putting her hands on his temples and trying to vanquish the spell. But the Cat's Eye remained dormant, as though it didn't sense any magic.

She asked Burn about it, and he could only shake his head. "That is the true power of a Wolfy mage," he murmured. "Blood magic is physical, not purely energy. Perhaps the necklace can't detect any magic inside of Dorian. Or perhaps it is too weak a spell."

Dorian didn't experience any more episodes. Still, she wasn't allowed to practice with him anymore. Crash took over her instruction. Surprisingly, it became a welcome change. He was a much different teacher than Dorian—strict and logical. He hardly ever spoke unless he was teaching her a new technique. He corrected several things, forcing her to relearn her staff, her daggers, her footwork. For the first week, she did nothing but push-ups and basic exercises, over and over again. "Repetition is key," he said brusquely. "No sparring until you master the forms."

The beasts grew thinner and weaker over the days, and had to rest more frequently. Grass was harder to find, and the horses were reluctant to eat moss or any of the other roughage in the swamp. The group was running low on feed, and the beasts would sink into the mud if they stood in one place too long. Sora began to wonder why they had brought the horses in the first place, and more than once, Dorian mentioned eating them. There was no other sign of game or wildlife. She didn't like the idea of killing their steeds, but a slow death by starvation sounded even worse. She was worried about taking the animals much farther into the swamp.

The trees continued to change, thickening and growing despite the soft earth, or perhaps because of it. Their bark became grayish-white and they leaned at odd angles, split at the trunk. They appeared like large, sinewy hands reaching for the sky, thick and ancient, wider than houses, growing into a shadowy mess above their heads. The clouds became thicker and thicker until they were like a solid roof.

As far as Sora was concerned, this was a place that should exist only in her nightmares. She could easily see how travelers could get lost there, with or without a curse. Thick vines hung down from the branches, like the bodies of giant snakes. Silence enveloped the four travelers, and she felt a vague depression come over her, a sadness that she couldn't explain. She wanted to go home, she wanted to sleep, she missed sunlight, and she longed desperately for a soft chair and a warm fireplace.

*But I don't have a home anymore,* she thought. That thought sat in her gut like a rock.

They continued through the damp gray world, sleeping in trees at night so as not to sink into the soft ground, eating handfuls of berries and a rare strip of dried meat. Her beautiful mansion seemed like a dream now, although it couldn't have been more than a month since she had last seen it. It seemed as unreal and nonexistent as the once legendary races.

"Block! Now, while I move like this. Raise your staff—there! Again! Again!"

Crash was seldom this vocal during their sparring. But he wanted her to get better at anticipating blows. Sora felt like she was being attacked by a thunderstorm. She barely raised her staff on time. *Clack! Crack!*

"Excellent!" Burn called from a nearby tree branch. Sora barely heard him, nor Dorian's light applause. It was nighttime, a fire crackling nearby, contained by a circle of rocks in the crook of an ancient trunk.

They sparred above ground, high up in the canopy. The trees had grown so old and thick that they became like a second highway far above the soft, sludgy earth. The branches were so large and the trunk so huge, Sora felt as though they stood on a wooden deck, on the balcony of an exotic palace.

Crash came back at her, leaping across the thick branches. Sora braced herself for another impact. He lunged, forcing his staff down on hers until she felt the strain in her arms. Using what little strength she had left, she threw him off and leapt over a low swing aimed at her knees. Whirling, she went for his chest and head, but found that no matter which way she tried, she was blocked. It was still a mystery to her how someone could fight so well with a large branch. *I doubt I'll ever be that good!*

With that thought, Sora wavered from her strict concentration. Then a blow from Crash came out of nowhere, catching her hard in the ribs.

With a cry of pain, she stumbled back against a tree. Her head cracked against a wide branch. She slid to the ground, clutching her ribcage, white-hot stars bursting against her eyelids.

When she refocused, Crash was above her, blocking out the firelight, his face in shadow.

"Foul, oh, foul!" she heard Dorian shouting, along with Burn's soft complaints. It might have been her imagination, though—her ears were still ringing from the blow.

"Quiet!" Crash snapped over his shoulder. Then he turned back to her, kneeling down. His hands searched her ribs, traveling gently yet firmly over her shirt. *Wow, gently?* She hadn't thought he knew how.

"Nothing broken," he murmured, his hands pausing just beneath her breasts, where the staff had hit. Sora felt her cheeks flush in embarrassment, and she tried to ignore the awkward position. She looked away from his face, focusing on the tall trees and wide, waxy leaves.

"My head," she said briefly. "It's a little tender." She wondered if he truly cared. By his businesslike approach, she doubted it.

"A slight bruise," he confirmed.

She nodded, still unable to make eye contact, his hands cradling her ribs. "Right," she muttered. She tried not to wince as she moved her head. She didn't want to show weakness in front of these warriors; she was beginning to understand just how skilled they were.

"You're improving," the assassin said abruptly. Then he was standing again, offering a hand to help her to her feet. "But you are not yet prepared. The Catlins could attack at any moment. You'll need to be able to defend yourself."

Sora couldn't believe her ears. Improvement? "Thanks," she muttered, partly sarcastic.

Crash frowned. She wondered if the sarcasm bothered him somehow. *Not bloody likely.* Why was he looking at her like that?

"Oh, come now!" Dorian protested. The Wolfy jumped up from where he had been sitting, his words directed at Crash. "Give the sweetheart a break. She's doing fantastic! She will be a seasoned warrior by the time we get through the swamp."

*If we get through,* Sora thought, but she didn't mention that part. Honestly, her Cat's-Eye necklace had been disturbingly quiet as of late, and she wondered if they were still on a good path. Or any path.

"Take a break," Burn agreed evenly. "It's late. Let's relax."

"Fine," Crash said.

Sora sighed. Hardly as much encouragement as she was used to. Back at the manor, her tutors would fawn over her, drenching her in praise every time she wrote an essay or balanced an equation.

"That brings up a good question," she said, walking back to her bedroll, which she had tied between two branches like a hammock. She moved gingerly on her tired feet, wincing with discomfort. "We've been in this swamp almost a month. I'm sure we will be out soon. What happens next?"

The three men fell silent. They shifted, looking at each other, several expressions passing between them. It seemed that they were deciding who should speak first. Sora put her staff down and waited, raising an eyebrow.

"The coast," Burn finally said.

"The coast?" she asked, surprised.

"Aye," Dorian agreed. "Leave the mainland, start a new life. Volcrian has always followed us, no matter where we've gone. At first we thought we could find a way to kill him, you know...off with his head, that sort of thing, but...." He trailed off, scratching his ear, a frown coming over his face. Sora was reminded of the blood spell, of the fragile influence that Volcrian had over Dorian's mind. She wondered if it was a good idea to discuss their plans in front of him. How much control did Volcrian actually have—assuming that the spell was real?

"Our best chance is to head overseas," Burn explained. "We can use our money to buy passage on a ship. Start over on some foreign coast, where Volcrian won't find us."

Sora frowned, gazing at Burn's soft-gold eyes. Their plan seemed...empty, somehow. Hopeless. *Is that it?* Their master plan was to catch a boat overseas?

"Seems a little cowardly," she mentioned.

Dorian snorted. "No one here denies it. We're not heroes, love. Just survivors."

She glanced at him, then at Burn, who didn't say anything. But the look on his face spoke volumes. She wondered what Volcrian had done to them, since it seemed obvious that they were afraid of him. She cleared her throat. "So you're running? That's it?"

They shuffled, looking at one another again. Then Dorian said, "Not without good cause, love. What about you? Where are you going?"

"Excuse me?" Sora asked, taken aback.

"Aye," Burn agreed. "Just where are you going after the swamp?"

Sora was surprised. She snorted in wry humor. "Are you saying that I'll be free to do as I wish?" she asked.

It was an uncomfortable question, met by a strange silence. They had grown closer since entering Fennbog, that was for certain. They relied on each other more, and—perhaps—had been forced to trust each other. But Sora wasn't one to forget the past. She knew who these men were. She hadn't come here by choice.

"Assuming we did," Dorian finally said. "Where would you go?"

She frowned, subconsciously touching the necklace under her shirt. She had tried not to think of the future too much. No use making plans if she wouldn't have her freedom, and no use planning to escape while they were still trapped in the swamp. But her necklace was a constant reminder of her true quest. *My mother.*

She was searching for a woman who might be dead, whom she had no true connection with. Yet what else did she have? Where else could she go?

She looked at the three men lingering around the fire. Their dirt-streaked clothes and matted hair. The only thing clean about them were their weapons. Certainly not their consciences. How could she tell them the truth? Her eyes roved to the assassin, who stood quiet and stoic in the shadow of a tree, cleaning his blades again. He was listening, of course. And she would rather he not know anything about her. He had killed Lord Fallcrest—a thought that still haunted her, especially on the fringes of sleep, when she could still see her father's body falling to the ground. What if he had killed her mother too? She had a powerful weapon on her neck —what would he do to keep it?

"Nowhere," she murmured, looking down at the thick tree

trunk. "I don't have anywhere to go."

Burn nodded sympathetically, as he always did. "All that matters now is survival," he said gently. He handed her a water flask, nodding to the trees around them. "No use making plans if we might not even survive."

"Right," Sora said. "I guess that's the truth of it, isn't it?" Then she looked at Crash, unexpectedly catching his eye. Survival— because he had put them all in danger. All of them, running blindly from a mad sorcerer, only focused on getting away, not reaching a destination. And now she was trapped, dragged into his mess, her fate irrevocably changed by a murderer.

And he had nothing to say. Crash turned and slid from the branches toward the ground, where the horses were tethered. He was the only one who hadn't spoken, despite having brought them here.

She had to wonder about it. The entire situation was his fault. Perhaps that was why he always walked away.

* * *

"It's quiet tonight," Sora murmured.

Crash didn't even glance at her.

The two Wolfies were fast asleep, snoring softly, nestled in the crook of a tree. The night had fully enclosed them with shadows in all directions. Crash was on watch, sitting out on a lone branch, suspended hundreds of feet above the swamp.

Sora was unable to sleep.

Her thoughts lingered on her father's death. It felt strange. Now that Lord Fallcrest was dead, she had more questions than ever. Who had he been, far off in the City of Crowns? What sort of miserable business had he fallen into, trying to worm his way into the First Tier? Would she ever discover his true murderer—and why? It became such a confusing mess of conspiracies and emotions that she had to put a hand on her stomach, wincing in pain. If she had been eating regularly, she might have felt sick.

And only one man had the answers—the assassin who had brought her here.

"Thanks, by the way," she offered, trying to warm him up a bit. She moved carefully out onto the branch next to him, balancing on the rough bark, "for saving my life back at the bridge, and for fending off Dorian. You didn't have to do that."

"Actually, I did," Crash murmured. But he moved to the side, allowing her enough room to sit down.

She perched on the branch next to him, their legs swinging out over infinite darkness. She looked down cautiously, her balance not quite mastered. This was a bad idea. She doubted the assassin would have much to say to her. But still she had to try.

"I've learned a lot since entering Fennbog," she started again. "Especially the weapons. It feels good to defend myself." She waited, matching him minute for minute, wondering how long he would let the silence stretch.

Finally, the assassin cleared his throat. "You're my first student," he said.

She glanced at him, curious. "Student?"

"Yes."

She frowned. His comment was unexpected. Is that who she was now—a student?

Crash continued after a moment. "What I know, I learned

from…very *long traditions.*" He cast a sideways glance at her, then looked away.

Sora pondered this. Long traditions. He instructed her much differently than Dorian. The Wolfy thief fought in an offhand manner, as though he had gained his skill from the streets, fending for his life. But Crash's instruction was different. Disciplined. Methodical. Intentional.

"A student, huh?" she said ironically. "I thought I was your captive." She couldn't keep the bite from her voice.

Crash raised a dark eyebrow. "You asked to come with me."

"I was desperate," Sora admitted.

"Yes. You were."

The blunt agreement left her slightly offended. *Patience,* her inner voice soothed. *He's not a friend, remember?* "Fine," she grunted. "Maybe I was. But that doesn't change the facts. You killed my father and kidnapped me."

He didn't reply to that, just kept looking out at the night, listening.

Sora sighed in frustration. "Who hired you?" she asked. "You can tell me now, can't you? We're in the middle of Fennbog and we might die tomorrow. I deserve an answer, don't I?"

He glanced at her. "I don't know how you imagine my work," he said, his voice sharp. "But your assumptions are that of a child. I am a professional. I work discreetly, I do not take names, money is left in designated locations by anonymous messengers. I don't know who hired me. I only know the weight of their coin."

Sora's mouth snapped shut, her jaw rigid. That was a cold, unfeeling speech. She raised her head a notch. A child? Is that how he saw her? Some whimsical spoiled brat?

"Where were you hired, then?" she asked instead, her words tight.

"In the City of Crowns," he replied shortly. She waited for more of an answer, and eventually he added, "in a tavern on the riverfront. It was handled by the tavern keeper. Letters exchanged hands. I received half of my payment in the City, and the second half in Mayville. Are you satisfied?"

Sora glared hard at him, trying to see through his cool, impassive facade. She wanted to give him a piece of her mind—explain how horrible he was, a blight on the world, scum of the earth. She imagined pushing him off the tree branch, watching him plummet into the shadows—but she knew it wouldn't work. He was too skilled for that, and probably expected it.

She grimaced instead, turning her gaze to the darkness of the swamp. "You destroyed my life," she said angrily.

When he replied, his words were surprisingly soft. "I know," he said. "And I've told you everything I can about your father."

She digested that, trying to calm down. The flicker of sympathy only made her hate him more. She didn't understand him at all. Did he truly see himself? His own wrongdoings? Or was he too jaded and cold to care?

"So who am I, then?" she asked instead. "Your student, or just a prisoner? Are you ever going to let me go?"

He watched her carefully with venom-green eyes. The question hung between them, naked and vulnerable. Finally, he said "No."

Sora stared at him, her mouth wide open. The answer was so brief, so permanent, that she couldn't organize her thoughts.

"Why?" she finally whispered, having lost her voice.

He continued to watch her, his eyes glowing like a nocturnal animal. A chilling sensation crossed her skin. She had the sudden sense that he was somehow more than his body. A dark aura lingered in the air. She wrapped her arms around herself, shivering.

"You haven't been our prisoner since entering Fennbog," Crash murmured. "But we cannot let you go. We have given you weapons and taken you under our wing. Be content with that." Then, after a slight hesitation, he added, "It is safer to travel with us than alone. Volcrian knows your name."

And Sora realized, despite her hatred for him, that it made sense. He was not a threat to her. At least, not anymore. She had worse things to worry about.

Suddenly, Crash stiffened. He sat upright, his head turned to one side, listening intently. Then he stood up, leaping smoothly from the branch to the main trunk, drawing his weapons. He was invisible within seconds.

Sora's heart pounded. She listened desperately, blind but for her own ears. Finally, she heard it. A strange scratching in the trees. She reached for her belt where she kept her daggers. Was it an animal of some kind? She couldn't imagine. She stood up carefully and headed back to the crook of the tree, where they had set up camp.

Crash awakened the Wolfies. She could see Burn's eyes glowing eerily in the darkness, a familiar gold. Dorian stirred slightly, his weapons clinking in the shadows. Using only her hands for guidance, she found her hammock and grabbed her staff, nervously waiting for a signal. What was going on? She wanted to ask, but also didn't want to make a sound.

*Scrrrtch. Scrrrtch.* She listened breathlessly. Dull scraping noises, like the scurrying of clawed feet. Her stomach clenched. She whirled around, looking left and right, prepared for an attack.

The warning wasn't a moment too soon. A blurry shape whizzed past her, narrowly missing her head. It looked like a rope, or a giant snake, thick and green. It was...a vine?

Completely autonomous, several other vines shot out of the darkness, like the tentacles of some giant sea creature. The largest group went for Burn, who was still drawing his longsword. He was bowled over into the tree branches.

Everything began to speed up. Sora looked around wildly for Dorian but couldn't find him anywhere, and there was no time to search. She shouldered her staff and drew her daggers, nestling the blades in her hands. She already felt clumsy, inadequate.

A vine whipped out of the branches nearby, attempting to coil around her neck. Sora shrieked and lashed out wildly with her daggers, cutting off its tip. Another vine tied itself around her ankle. She stabbed at it fiercely; frothy green acid spurted out, burning her skin. She screamed again, this time from pain.

The noise seemed to attract more vines. Another one bowled right into her, slamming her into the branches, almost impaling her. Her head spun from the blow and she teetered precariously on her back, trying not to plummet from the tree. The giant vine reared over her like a hungry snake, poison dripping from its thorns. On instinct, Sora whipped out her dagger and sliced through its length, cutting it in half, acid spewing everywhere. Her arm was drenched in the stinging liquid. It burned like fire, and she screamed again.

More vines flew at her, wrapping around her ankles, her arms. She was dragged backwards, into the darkness.

Then—*shing!* A blade cut through the air, but it wasn't hers.

Crash leapt next to her, sword in hand, slashing and hacking faster than she could see. His voice carried through the sound of ringing steel. "Where is Dorian?" he called.

"I don't know!" she cried back, panicked. She couldn't see either of the Wolfies, and the darkness was too thick to search far.

The vines were everywhere, moving in, surrounding them. Thick and slimy, curved with menace. She tried to raise her knife to defend herself against the vicious plants, but suddenly she couldn't move her arm. In shock, she looked down. Her skin was red and blistered from the green acid, her limb was fast becoming numb. She tried to move her fingers, but couldn't.

Her heart pounded in terror. The poison spread quickly. Now her entire left side had turned stiff and heavy. She looked at Crash, who was fighting a short distance away, hacking back the weeds. She tried to call out to him to tell him what was happening, but her throat was closed. It was becoming hard to breathe. *Dear Goddess....*

Then the sound of bells disrupted her thoughts. At first she thought her ears were ringing, perhaps from the poison. She couldn't believe it. Her hand flew to her Cat's Eye. The necklace was warm to the touch. Of course. Magic.

She gripped the necklace, falling back against one of the branches, barely able to stand. *Help me!* she thought, unable to do anything else.

The jingling increased, and she felt a sudden wave come over her, consuming her thoughts, pushing her almost out-of-body. And then—*flash!* A brilliant burst of green and yellow light, followed by several other flashes, like a miniature lightning storm. The vines immediately started to fall, writhing and twitching as the magic was sucked out of them.

Her Cat's Eye absorbed the energy quickly, ravenously, like a starving hound. Soon the tree branches were littered with limp, sagging vines. She saw Crash some distance away, across the giant tree, fighting doggedly on. She reached out her hand, wincing with the effort.

"Over there..." she muttered, feeling the air thicken. The Cat's Eye responded to her words like a well-trained animal. *Zzzzap!* The vines fell to the ground one by one, empty and lifeless, like tangled ropes. Within seconds the air was clear.

The battle was over. There was only silence. Sora sank back against the branches, slowly succumbing to the poison, no longer able to stand.

Then, unexpectedly, some things far larger and more dangerous dropped down from the branches, landing with a heavy thud. Graceful and catlike, several creatures entered their camp. They surrounded Crash, spears held threateningly, speaking in some muttered, growling tongue. The assassin tossed his knives to the ground, outnumbered.

Sora could barely see them in the darkness. She watched as though in a dream. More creatures arrived, prowling toward her, feline eyes flickering. She was defenseless against them. The poison burned through her veins, each heartbeat like a stab to the chest, and she had to wonder if she was hallucinating.

The creatures paused, staring down at her prone form.

"Don't touch her!" came Crash's voice, muffled and distant.

*Where are the Wolfies?* Sora thought blearily. She tried to look around, but her neck was stiffening, her muscles cramping and contorting. Then she couldn't focus anymore and lay quietly, wondering if this was the end, if her lungs would seize and her heart stop. Her head swam. She struggled to focus her eyes....

# CHAPTER 11

Volcrian perched on the hard bench of the coach.

Women and children surged in behind him, scrambling onto the wooden seats. A few farmers and clerks followed. Soon they were all packed together like a tightly rolled bale of hay. He watched the peasants and serfs arrange themselves. Already the coach was beginning to smell like a pig barn.

He wrinkled his nose. When he and his brother ran the apothecary, they owned a personal carriage, a beautiful creation of oak wood and finished seats. He had sold it shortly after his brother's death, exchanging it for a fast horse and a bag full of coins.

He hadn't ridden on a public coach since his childhood days. This particular specimen was designed for rough travel across the country. A mud wagon, the locals called it. He did not relish the name.

Somewhere nearby, a child began coughing. Volcrian pressed a handkerchief over his mouth and sucked in a breath.

Traveling by stagecoach was the fastest way to bypass the swamp. He would have to change in the next town, and again, near the City of Crowns. Once they passed there, he would make his solitary way over the mountains. Luckily, they were the lower mountains, more like foothills compared to the snow-covered monstrosities of the far North. The journey could take an entire year, depending on his timing and the weather, but he anticipated his wraiths would make short work of the four travelers. Perhaps by the time he reached the coast, they would all be dead.

That thought was the only thing that brought a smile to his lips.

"Last call!" he heard the stage conductor cry out. There was another shout from outside, and a few more people squeezed on-board. Volcrian grimaced. How many peasants could a mud wagon hold?

The final passengers settled in place. There was a thump from the rear of the coach. The boot was closed, their luggage secured. The door was shut.

The driver cracked his whip and yelled to his team, the sound muffled by wooden walls. The horses surged forward, the coach rocking precariously forward. Volcrian let out a slow breath. This was going to be a long trip.

* * *

Sora blinked woozily.

Her head pounded, like the morning after too much wine the night before. Her mouth was dry, her thoughts fuzzy. She stared at the smooth wooden ceiling above her. For a long moment, that's all she did, feeling the blood rush through her veins. Her body felt weak—like she was stuffed with cotton.

*Where am I?* Vaguely, she remembered the attacking vines. Her head pounded and her right arm was in agony. She wanted to roll over and go back to sleep; she was all too ready to slip back into unconsciousness. At least the bed was soft.

Bed?

The sound of voices disturbed her thoughts. She looked toward the noise and found herself staring at a wooden archway, set flawlessly in the side of a room that could have been carved from a tree. She blinked at the smooth walls—no boards or panels, no brick or mortar. Just seamless wood.

She looked back at the archway. At first it seemed completely open, but if she squinted, she noticed strange glints of light stretching across it, a near-invisible curtain. It took her a moment to realize what they must be. Spider webs?

It was enough effort for her to sit up. The room spun and she put her hand to her head, her stomach twisting. She waited for her eyes to focus. Then she glanced around, looking for any signs of spiders or bugs or other threats. But the room was clean and empty, except for her soft cot and a porthole window, too small to climb through.

The sound of voices drifted to her again, this time closer. It was like no language she had ever heard before. At times, it sounded more like two beasts growling and chirping at one another. She stared through the archway, trying to see into the corridor beyond, but her gaze was met by a plain wooden wall.

Sora swung her legs off the cot and grimaced, then leaned over the side of the bed, gagging. She heaved several times, trying to vomit, but nothing came out. *Saved by an empty stomach. Goddess!* She had never felt sicker!

Trying to lift her arm, she discovered it was wrapped in thick bandages from elbow to wrist, which tightly constricted her movement. She could remember the nasty, burning acid. Her blistered skin. *How long have I been here?* She put her hand on her pounding head and wondered how she could still be alive.

The sound of footsteps and muttering voices drew closer. Sora tried to stay calm. She looked around again for a place to hide, but there was nowhere except behind the cot, and she had more dignity than that. She licked her dry lips, her fingers tapping nervously on the bed.

A shadow lumbered outside the doorway. A hand reached up, gently touching the thin spider webs. Sora stared at the massive palm. It was unlike any hand she had seen before—long, thick fingers covered by thin orange fur. Nails hooked into long, powerful talons.

There was a brief shimmer of light. The spider webs fell away, curling back on their own accord. Sora heard the slight chime of bells. Her Cat's Eye. Magic.

Then a creature stepped in. It only slightly resembled a human.

She never could have prepared herself for the beast who entered the room. It wore sandals and a white robe, cinched at the waist with a wide tan belt. She stared at its feet—his feet?—which were more like giant paws.

His face terrified her. She had to stifle a gasp, her eyes wide in disbelief and horror. The creature's head was that of a tiger, long teeth protruding past his lip. Thick, clawed hands hung at his sides. By what she could see under the robe, his entire body was covered in orange and black fur, down to the tip of his tail. He was huge, towering almost a foot taller than Burn, completely filling the small bedroom. This beast made the Wolfy mercenary look average.

*So this is a Catlin,* Sora thought, trying to stay calm and reasonable. It was the only explanation.

The beast either grimaced at her or smiled—she couldn't tell, with those huge fangs. She hoped it was a smile.

"Human," he said in a low, grunting voice, more of a growl. "Can you walk?"

"Uh...." Sora didn't really know how to respond. She felt terrible. She didn't want to stand up and collapse on this fellow—*he'd probably eat me*. Then again, she didn't want to sit around staring at him, either.

Rather than answering, Sora decided to stall for time. If she was about to be eaten, she might as well get some answers.

"Where is this place?" she demanded boldly. Her voice came out dry and small. Her mouth was still slightly numb from the poison and her throat muscles resisted the effort it took to talk. "What have you done to my friends?"

The Catlin stared at her through slitted eyes. His teeth were pulled back into a snarl. Sora sat back despite herself—*maybe that was a mistake.*

"You *can* walk," he confirmed. She couldn't read his expression; he had a cat's head, after all.

"Well?" she heard her voice squeak, then cleared her throat. "What about my friends?"

He continued to look at her, as though considering her for a snack. "You are in our *shriekal*, our colony," he finally answered. "The others are here too. The...the trespassers are in con-con-" the Catlin paused, licking his lips awkwardly.

Sora felt unimpressed. *He certainly doesn't sound smart.* Then she realized that his mouth wouldn't allow him to sound the words properly.

"Con-tain-ment," he finally managed.

"Containment?"

"Yes, and your pro-tec-tor is in the cells."

"My what?"

The Catlin looked rather flustered and made several yowling sounds under his breath before continuing. "The dark one, the one who threatens without words." *Oh, Crash.* "You are lucky to have such a pro-tec-tor."

*Lucky he's locked up, maybe.* "Protector, that's what you mean." Sora nodded to herself. "So they're alive?"

"Yes."

She almost cried in relief. She wanted to be with Burn, or Dorian, or maybe back home where she could run into the woods and scream until the world made sense again. Instead, she looked calmly toward the doorway, retaining her composure. Another Catlin stood there, this one equally terrifying, though the pattern of his fur was different. Tan with brown spots.

The Catlins yowled at each other, a guttural language that sounded more like two lions fighting in the woods.

"Our Panthera is ready to see you,” the first guard finally said, turning back to her. “Don't keep him waiting."

"Panthera?"

"Our warlord."

Sora nodded. She didn't have much of a choice, but she was still terrified. *Nothing else for it.* She slid off the cot and swayed on her feet, woozy from the poison. The room kept moving, fluctuating in and out, as though the walls were breathing. She had to put out an arm to steady herself. *Come on, walk like a warrior!* her inner voice spoke up. *Chin up, foot down!*

The two Catlins escorted her from the room. They both carried long spears with feathers and beads tied around the top, just beneath the spearheads. Their belts contained several knives. The blades were longer than daggers, thin and curved. Some appeared to be carved from bone.

They took her into the short hall, past another room barred by spiderwebs. It looked like a storage room, full of wooden crates and knapsacks. She caught a glimpse of her saddlebags and weapons laying in a pile on the floor. The Catlins didn't seem too concerned with security.

They left the building through a broad archway. The exit was enclosed by a thick wall of vines, densely woven together, blocking any light from outside. She watched as one of the guards lifted a clawed finger and touched the net of plants. He traced strange patterns in the air, perhaps symbols.

The Cat's Eye murmured again, stirring in her mind. *Magic.*

Then, with the sound of scattering leaves, the vines all pulled to one side, revealing the world beyond. The guards prodded her forward. Sora was led into daylight. A fresh breeze hit her face and she looked up, her eyes wide.

The Catlin colony was at the heart of the swamp, deep in the forest—yet not on the ground. Her foot landed on a wooden balcony. As she looked up, she could see massive trees on every side of her, as wide as mansions, stretching high into the sky. The trunks disappeared into thick gray fog. She couldn't imagine their peaks, or the dense canopy that must exist overhead, far out of sight. Their branches were as large as streets, their leaves as wide as wagons. Holes speckled their trunks, hollowed windows blazed with golden light, doorways sheltered with vines, dwellings and stores and who-knew-what- else. Plant life was everywhere, thriving in every nook and cranny of the giant trees, purple-hued moss and hanging flowers, stamens like lamp posts, petals big enough for her to climb on.

No trees like this could possibly be natural; they would have to be millions of years old. Sora instinctively touched the necklace under her shirt. The Cat's Eye was humming quietly at her neck, as though charged by the very air. *Magic,* though she couldn't fathom how.

Wooden platforms encircled each tree, providing wide balconies and market squares. Rope bridges, some as wide as boulevards, crisscrossed the colony on several different levels. The city spread upward as much as downward. They paused next to the railing of a balcony, and Sora looked down upon countless Catlin heads: vendors and shoppers, hunters, merchants, all bustling about their lives. *It's far more crowded than Mayville!* Perhaps larger, even, than the City of Crowns.

Rope elevators moved among the different levels of the colony. As she watched, a crate of vegetables swung into the air on a flat wooden platform, directed by an intricate system of ropes and pulleys. A few of the elevators hung off in the mist, abandoned or in disuse. Her eyes grew wide, watching the platform's ascent into the fog.

Her guards clunked their spears on the ground and showed their teeth threateningly. Sora didn't need more prompting. She continued to walk. The bridge in front of her was narrow, built of sturdy wood, tied together with thick vines. Their level was mostly deserted. A few Catlins passed in the distance, wearing identical white robes. She wondered if they were some sort of elite guard. She really couldn't imagine who they were.

She peeked over the side of the bridge again, watching the

bustling city life. Then she stared beyond at the endless pit of mist. She was unnerved by the drop; there was no sign of any ground below.

"I wouldn't jump," came a higher-pitched voice from the second guard. She wondered if it was a female, since it stood slightly shorter than the first guard. "'Tis a long, long drop."

Sora shivered and moved to the center of the bridge. Only an idiot would try that—it was sure suicide.

They walked for some time. The colony was vast, stretching on and on. They boarded one of the elevators and descended a level, vines and wood creaking under their weight. The next floor down was a center of shopping and trading. It was much more crowded than the area she had started in. The guards stayed at her side, snarling at anyone who got too close.

The regular Catlin population did not wear white robes, but were almost completely nude. Or as nude as one could be when covered in fur. They walked around in different states of undress, exposing breasts, bellies and other parts. Some females had piercings through their ears and noses, decorated with hoops and beads, or long feathers hanging down the sides of their faces. The males were scarred and gruesome. The only article worn in abundance were knives. The Catlins all looked very different, no two coats the same, every color from albino white to blue-black.

Most avoided looking at her. Sora was reminded of several house cats sitting side by side, swishing their tails. If she accidentally made eye contact, a Catlin would curl its lip in a silent snarl, or press its ears back in a distinctly feline way. She wondered if it was rude to stare, or if she was issuing an unknown challenge.

Before long, she had a group of Catlin younglings behind her, jumping across bridges and ropes. They were as agile as squirrels, with giant fuzzy paws and huge eyes. Several times the guards tried to chase the children away, but they always came back. They gurgled and cooed to each other, which she thought might be laughter, but she couldn't understand a word of it. She had to work hard not to touch them, or snatch them up like stuffed dolls. These were not kittens, and she would probably get her hand bitten off.

Toward the end of the marketplace, they boarded another elevator. This one shot into the air at a startling pace, up and up, to the very top of the colony. When it finally came to a stop, they got off at a deserted walkway, not a Catlin in sight. Silent mist swirled around the giant branches.

In the distance stood an exceptionally large tree. Sora could see a door of vines standing out from the trunk, accented with exotic orange flowers. She could smell their pollen at this distance, pungent and thick, like overripe fruit. She licked her lips, suddenly nervous. A thousand fears rampaged through her mind. Her hands started to shake, so she clenched them into fists.

The archway was several dozen feet tall, formed out of the tree as though it had originally grown that way. They headed toward it. Nervous prickles rolled over her skin, and she began to feel a peculiar energy, a vibration in the air. A steady throb started behind her eyes. The Cat's Eye? She touched the necklace under her shirt, surprised. It vibrated and buzzed at her chest like an enraged bee. She glanced at the Catlins surrounding her, but they gave no sign of noticing. *What's wrong with it?* she wondered, unsure what the stone was responding to.

They paused outside the massive vines. Sora waited, fidgeting slightly from foot to foot. The Catlins' tails swished through the air, ears slightly back, and she realized—were they scared? *Really?*

A curious tingle slowly crawled up her body, from her toes to her hair. She felt as though invisible hands were running over her, searching her, trying to find her secrets. Her Cat's Eye jingled softly —some kind of magic. She felt exposed, vulnerable. She wasn't sure if the necklace could shield her or not.

Then the thick vines slowly pulled back. Tendril by tendril they unfurled, revealing the corridor beyond.

The guards gave her a hard shove through the doorway; otherwise, she never would have gone through. She stumbled forward with a yelp as they pushed her with their spears, stuffing her into the room like a stubborn horse.

The vines coiled shut behind her, sealing out all light. Alone in the dark room, she felt full-blown panic consume her. Her heart raced until she thought she would faint. Images of wild beasts and deformed monsters rose in her mind. *I need to calm down!* she thought desperately, forcing herself to breathe, to think clearly. She had trained with Crash and Dorian; she could defend herself. She wasn't helpless. Of course, she had no weapons at hand.

She listened intently, trying to hear beyond the pounding of her heart. There was a raspy, heavy sound somewhere nearby. Breathing.

Suddenly light poured into the room. Sora gasped. At first she thought a lantern had been struck, but now she could see that several holes had opened along the wall. Portholes. Windows grown out of the very tree.

The Cat's Eye stirred again.

Sora could only stare. One after the other, windows appeared along the walls, allowing soft gray light to cascade across the floor.

What manner of magic was this? The Catlins were somehow controlling the trees. She couldn't fathom such power. Had they created their colony purely out of magic? Were the trees natural at all, or planted by some otherworldly energy? With merely a touch of their fingers, the Catlins were able to manipulate the wood, command the vines. Who knew what else they were capable of....?

Now that the room was illumined, Sora could see that it wasn't as big as she had expected. A small conference chamber, perhaps as large as her bedroom back at the manor. A grassy, matted carpet split the floor, running toward the far end of the room. Her eyes followed the rug to its end, where a tall throne sat, a massive chair grown out of the tree, supported by woven branches. Feathers, leaves, and beautiful stones decorated the chair. And sitting on a cushion of moss and fur...was a *ferocious* Catlin.

Sora's mouth dropped. Sitting down, the beast was as tall as she was standing. He had a dark pelt, the color of rich soil, crossed with thin black stripes. White markings accented his jowls and chest. Her eyes traveled lower, to his long, faded green pants, his only article of clothing. A weapon of some kind rested against the throne. It was long enough to be a sword, but looked like it had been carved from a giant rib bone.

He watched her with two feline-yellow eyes. A gnarled gold tooth protruded from his lip.

Sora approached the Panthera and stopped a respectful distance away, turning to her long-hated court manners. *I guess they're good for something.* Who knew that she would actually need them in the swamp? She made an elegant bow—a curtsy would be a bit hard without skirts. She finished it with a flourish and clasped her hands before her, waiting expectantly. She didn't know whether to make eye contact or not. On one hand, it was a sign of her own heritage as a noblewoman. On the other hand, the Catlins didn't seem to respond well to direct stares.

The warlord gave a dry chuckle and motioned for her to step closer. His yellow claws, as long as an eagle's talons, looked threatening in the dim gray light.

"Welcome to my domain." The voice was deep and croaky. The accent was clearer than the guard's. "This is the last Catlin colony, and you are the only human to have seen it in a hundred years."

He paused, as though waiting for Sora to say something. She couldn't think of anything appropriate. Her heart was hammering—she was, quite honestly, terrified. How did one speak to a Panthera? Her words could make the difference between freedom or execution. She thought she might faint, but the outcome of that would be far worse.

After a few moments of awkward silence, the Panthera said, "Our colony was founded centuries ago. We sought refuge from the human world. Humans have since defiled the land of our ancestors. What is the phrase? *You breed like rats.*" The warlord looked her over again. "We want no dealings with humans, yet now you are here. I'd like to know why. And how."

Sora still didn't know what to say. Breed like rats? She supposed it might be true, but she still felt insulted. Humans weren't so bad. The Catlins appeared far more barbaric—and the Wolfies, the only other race she had met, were deranged by blood-magic.

The warlord spoke again before she could. "Answer me, human! The dark one and the Wolfies were far more entertaining than this! Say *something,* or your presence is of no use here!"

*No use?* So they were going to kill her if she didn't answer. Sora swallowed, organized her thoughts, and found the courage to look the beast in the eye. "We're not here to trespass," she said, and winced. "Or attack you, or anything like that. We're just trying to get through the swamp, that's all." She hoped that was good enough.

The Panthera narrowed those great, slitted eyes. "Is that so? But how have you found our colony? We are countless miles from the fringes of the swamp, no matter which way you travel." His gold tooth gleamed. "You are an explorer looking to build a town."

"No!" Sora said, alarmed. "No, not at all! We're just passing through. Once we leave, we'll never return, I swear."

"I don't take the word of humans," the Panthera sneered, displaying more teeth. "How did you make it this deep into Fennbog? We have warding spells that alert us to trespassers. There has been no such warning."

Warding spells. It suddenly made perfect sense why no one returned from the swamp. Even if someone was an expert navigator, the Catlins would find him and kill him. How many explorers had perished in this colony? She suddenly thought of the old scarecrow they had stumbled across, the bones littered at its base.

"How did you bypass our spells?" the Panthera repeated.

Sora stared. Her Cat's Eye had shielded them, of course. She opened her mouth to speak, but couldn't. The alien presence of the necklace asserted itself, more awake than ever. She was suddenly, irrevocably convinced that she could not tell the Panthera about the necklace. What if he tried to take it?

"What are you planning to do with us?" she demanded instead.

The giant Catlin was silent. The atmosphere grew fragile. One wrong word, and the peace would shatter like glass.

Then the warlord bared his teeth. "Boldness is greatly respected by my race," he growled. "You are a warrior, small human, though I did not think so at first. I shall answer your question. The Wolfies will be taken to the Grandmother Tree, where we shall sacrifice them to the Earth Goddess. The Tree has been dry for decades, and Wolfy blood is rare indeed."

Sora wondered if she looked as horrified as she felt.

The Panthera chuckled at her expression, and made a strange gurgling sound. "But I am not unreasonable. Tell me how you bypassed our wards, and you and your mate shall be set free...as long as you do not return."

Sora's eyes opened in alarm and fear. *They can't kill Burn and Dorian!* Then she paused, struck by the second half of the Panthera's sentence. "What?"

The Panthera frowned at her, a terrifying sight, and shifted in his chair. "Is the dark one not your protector?"

Sora was silenced by confusion. Her mind turned full circle, mulling over his statement, taking it apart one piece at a time. The guards had mentioned her "protector" before in reference to Crash. *As I recall, the guard also called me "lucky,"* she thought with some humor. Ironic, to be sure. Protector must mean something different to the Catlins. Something more...intimate.

"Sure," Sora stuttered. "I mean, yes."

The Panthera stared at her. She wished she could read his expression—he looked hungry, maybe. "Perhaps you don't know the meaning of the word?" he finally murmured. "The dark one implied that he was your protector, but perhaps I was mistaken.

When males and females become bonded, we call them protectors and providers. It is a sacred bond, respected by our species. It is unholy and cruel to separate a protector from his provider."

Sora didn't know what Crash was playing at, but if he had implied as much to the Panthera, then he probably had a good reason. "Right," she muttered. "I understand now. Yes, he is my protector."

The Catlin warlord seemed satisfied by this, and nodded. "Now answer my questions—how did you get past the spell?"

Sora swallowed and searched for a good excuse. She couldn't say anything about her Cat's Eye; the necklace had somehow planted the thought firmly in her mind. It felt like a very bad idea.

Suddenly, the warlord leaned forward in his chair. It seemed his patience was running thin. He withdrew a hand, hooked his finger, and suddenly the wood rippled beneath her feet like water. With a shriek, Sora fell to the ground. The wood thrust forward in an unnatural wave, carrying her down the grassy carpet to the base of the throne. She sat there, shaking, staring up at the massive warlord. His clawed feet were as long as her forearms.

He spoke quietly, a low growl in his throat. "If you will not tell me, then I will force it out," he hissed. Then, with another wave of his massive paws, the floor thrust upward.

Sora screamed. Vines fell from the ceiling, grabbing her arms. One went tight around her throat, cutting off her air. She was held up by the vines, suspended in mid-air, hovering helplessly above the ground.

The Panthera stood up, a terrifying height of perhaps ten feet. Silence filled the room. The only sound was of rustling foliage. More and more plants spread along the ground. Vines uncurled from the ceiling, dripping with venomous thorns. Toxic fungi thrust up from the wood and spores billowed into the air, creating noxious fumes. The vines loosened at her neck and she gasped, desperate to breathe, unwittingly inhaling the spores.

She immediately felt dizzy, as though she had drank three cups of wine. Her head spun, her tongue loosened.

"What are you hiding?" the Panthera asked. "How did you bypass our wards?"

A strange euphoria gushed through Sora's body, starting at her feet and overtaking her head within seconds. She suddenly felt light as a cloud.

"Tell me, young girl," the Panthera growled. "Who led you through the swamp?"

"Nothing," Sora mumbled, her lips thick. "No one."

"Don't lie to me. Do you work magic? Are you a sorcerer?"

*Humans can't use magic,* she wanted to say, but she didn't have the chance. The Panthera lost his temper. The giant cat reached for her and grabbed her arm. He slowly dragged his nails down her forearm, across the acid burns. Sora's eyes widened as pleasure quickly turned to pain—her body felt a hundred times more sensitized. She threw back her head and screamed in agony so intense she could have vomited.

"Tell me," the Panthera roared. "Tell me your secrets!"

Sora stuttered, still reeling from the pain. Secrets? Oh yes, she had those, perhaps too many. Selfish motives. Lies. She found herself seeing all that had happened since leaving her manor. She could see Lord Fallcrest stumbling to his knees, the skylight shattering into a million twinkling lights.

And suddenly she herself was falling, stars passing her,

whizzing at unknown speeds. She had never fallen so fast before. The lights were bright, dazzling—but there was also sound. Music? No, a dull chatter. The stars seemed to be talking to her, snatches of speech. *You have to listen. Listen to the stars, and they will tell you all of the secrets.*...Their voices were getting louder and louder, ringing in her ears, trying to get her attention. She thought she recognized some of them: kitchen maids, yard workers, servants she had passed in the hall...her handmaid, Lily. Her father's booming voice as he sat at his desk, his eyes dark and hard, screaming at the maids to take his daughter Sora away, out from underfoot, lock her in her room, such a useless child....The roaring grew and grew until it consumed her.

Bells.

Sora blinked her eyes.

The Cat's Eye sprang to life, jingling madly like a fistful of sleighbells. It eagerly consumed the magical energy around her. *Zzzzap! Zzzzzap!* Bursts of light flickered through the air like exploding fireflies. *Zap!* The vines fell to the ground, the fungi curled in on itself and melted back into the wood, leaving dark stains. Green light crackled around Sora's necklace. The vines dropped her, and she landed clumsily on the ground, reeling from the toxins she had inhaled.

The warlord took a step back, jaw agape, eyes wide. Then his expression melted into fury. "A Cat's Eye!" he roared. "The bane of our race! A tool of evil!" His tail lashed back and forth. He stepped forward and Sora scrambled back, trying to keep a distance between them.

He snarled at her, baring his vicious teeth. When he spoke, it sounded like a lion's roar. "You have brought this cursed stone into our colony! It must be destroyed! Give me the necklace!"

"No!" Sora screamed, recoiling.

He lunged, moving too fast for her to react. He smashed into her, slamming her into the ground, his full weight upon her. The beast hissed and frothed at the mouth. "Where is it? Give it to me now! Give it to me or I shall kill you!" Those giant hands tore at her, ripping her shirt, scraping her skin. "Where do you hide it? *Where does it hide?*" Finally, the Panthera's claws ripped open the front of her shirt and the necklace came into view. The warlord's eyes caught on it, his mouth open, heaving. Spittle dripped onto her body. Eyes wide, he reached for the stone....

But the Cat's Eye didn't want to be touched. As the Panthera's claws neared the necklace, she felt the stone buzz angrily. It crackled with energy.

With a hiss, the Panthera drew back, but the Cat's Eye wasn't done. Strands of yellow light shot through the air, followed by a brilliant green flash. There was a silent clap of power.

*Wham!* The warlord was thrown back. He skidded across the floor, tearing up clumps of grassy carpet as he went. When he had stopped tumbling, the Panthera crouched on all fours, looking more like a jungle beast than ever before. Pure rage lit his eyes. Then he smiled—a feral look, dangerous and wild.

"Hah!" he growled. "You think you have bested me?"

Sora crawled along the floor, dragging herself toward the exit, one hand pressed against the shallow wound on her hip.

"Oh no, you aren't leaving," the Panthera roared. "You will make a fine sacrifice to our Goddess. GUARDS!"

A sacrifice to their Goddess. The Grandmother Tree. Sentenced to the same fate as the Wolfies.

Sora opened her mouth, but there was no time to formulate words. The door opened behind her, the vines twisting to one side. The white-robed guards scrambled in, grabbed her by the waist and hoisted her off the floor.

She reached for the Cat's-Eye stone, trying to activate it again, to lash out and protect herself—but the stone only hummed quietly, content for the moment. She couldn't understand it.

"I want all four killed tomorrow evening!" the Panthera roared after them, enraged. "Skinned and tied to the Grandmother Tree!" Then he continued to scream orders in his native tongue, yowling and grunting, obviously enraged.

The guards flipped their tails in a strange salute. They didn't make eye contact with the Panthera, but kept their faces respectfully turned away. Then they escorted Sora out roughly.

She was dragged over a series of narrow bridges, shrouded in mist. They boarded a different elevator from the first one, a large basket woven of thick, dry reeds that moved slowly, creakily. The ride lasted much longer this time.

Sora didn't like the sensation of being suspended over space, the ground hidden by dense fog. It was impossible to tell how high up they were. She sank into a corner of the basket and crouched there, wrapping her arms around herself. Her acid wounds were raw and sore. The Panthera's claws had left long rents in her shirt, and in some places, had pierced her skin. She kept a hand clamped tight to her side, trying to stanch the bleeding. She felt dizzy, shocked, pain stabbing through her with each breath.

The guards took her back to the original tree, which she assumed was their prison. They escorted her through the vine-locked entrance, down the narrow hallway, past her room and down a flight of steps, deeper into the tree.

They passed by a series of cells, all empty except for one. Sora could see inside, since the cells were barred by spider thread. Burn and Dorian sat resolutely, neither looking at the other. She started to call out to the Wolfies but stopped herself, wary of the guards.

Dorian glanced up at their approach and smiled slightly, despite a black eye and a cut lip. Both Wolfies looked like they had been roughed up. Burn's arm bled heavily, stanched with a piece of cloth torn from his shirt. His eyes were closed, his face tight with pain. He didn't look up as they passed, and that worried her.

At first she thought that the guards would deposit her into the next cell, but they continued down the hallway. At the end of the corridor, the wall was blocked off by dense vines, similar to the entrance of the tree. One guard raised his hand, brushing a long claw across the vines, drawing out some sort of symbol, either a picture or a letter.

The leaves glowed briefly, then withdrew, coiling into themselves like snakes. Sora watched, still fascinated by the magic.

As soon as the vines parted, she was thrown inside. She hit the wall with a loud *thud* and fell to the hard ground. The vines closed up behind her, blocking out all light. Unlike her original cell, this room had no windows, no cot, no plausible exits. Her eyes would have to adjust to the gloom. The Panthera wanted to make sure she couldn't escape.

With a groan, she pulled herself to her feet, her head spinning. She hobbled over to the corner, nauseous, barely able to stand upright. Her stomach lurched. A moment later she threw up, both from fear and leftover poison.

Sora heaved a few last times, but there wasn't a lot in her

stomach, mostly bile. *Classy.* She wiped her mouth and wished for a glass of water.

Then, without warning, her body started to tremble. She backed away from the corner, suddenly cold. Fear flooded her, filling her veins with ice. *We're going to be executed.* Killed and sacrificed to the Grandmother Tree, whatever that was. And it was all her fault. She was too clumsy, too naive. If she had just kept her mouth shut...or come up with a convincing story, a believable lie, perhaps they would be free by now. *I'm so stupid!* She really, truly hated herself. *I have to do something. I have to fix this!*

Sora felt along the wall for the tightly woven vines. Her fingers found the leaves. She picked at them, trying to tear open a hole in the door, but the vines were unnaturally strong. Her nails couldn't even break their outer layer.

There was no escape, no way out. How was she supposed to tell her companions? How could she warn them? She smashed her fist against the vines, tears threatening to leak out of her eyes. "This is all my fault," she muttered to the darkness. "You're so stupid, Sora! Useless. Idiot. Fool!" She kept slamming her fist against the vines, ripping at the leaves, scratching at the thick plants.

Suddenly a hand landed on her shoulder. She yelped in surprise, jumping into the air.

A quiet voice said, "Be calm."

She whirled around. Crash stood behind her, a dim outline in the room; she only recognized his voice. How long had he been standing there, listening to her sobs and inane muttering? She was too distraught to be embarrassed. Before she could think about it, she blurted out, "We're all going to die because of me."

She could sense his frown in the darkness, the thoughtful

pause before he spoke. "What do you mean?"

Sora felt like she was going to cry. She took a deep breath, trying to contain herself. "My Cat's Eye!" she managed, speaking past the lump in her throat. "The Panthera thought you were my protector, so he had decided to let us go. Then he saw the necklace...and now...now we're all going to die!" She put a hand to her face, struggling to maintain her composure. She really, really didn't want to cry in front of the assassin. "We're all going to be sacrificed to the Grandmother Tree! And it's all my fault!"

Crash's hand remained on her shoulder. She wasn't sure if he was trying to be comforting, or had just forgotten it was there. He seemed deep in thought. "When?" he finally asked. "When are they coming for us?"

Sora's heart sank. "Soon. The Panthera wants the ceremony tomorrow night."

"The full moon," Crash murmured.

She frowned. "Huh?"

"Tomorrow is the full moon. Catlins live by the lunar calendar. That's why they're waiting." His voice was quiet and confident.

Sora nodded, somehow calmed by his tone. She had expected him to be mad, to yell or to lash out at her. She wondered where he had learned so much about Catlins.

"I...I didn't mean to cause more trouble." she whispered, still wallowing in guilt.

"Never mind that," he caught her off-guard. "We have the advantage."

Sora blinked. "What?"

"Your necklace."

She frowned, looking up at his dark face, wishing to see his expression. How was her necklace supposed to help? It had been no use against either the guards or their spears.

"You can break us out," he assured her, as though reading her mind.

She took a step away, shrugging off his hand. "It didn't open the door of the Panthera's chambers," she hedged. Then again, she hadn't directly asked it to.

"The Cat's Eye is a magical tool," he gritted out. "Try."

She could clearly hear his irritation. Unexpectedly, she grew annoyed in return. It was all well and good for him to contrive theories about the necklace—he wasn't the one wearing it!

She turned back to the doorway with an angry sigh. Her hands searched blindly until she felt the tightly woven vines. "Why did they put us in this cell?" she asked, feeling her way along the plants. "Why not use spider webs, like Dorian and Burn's cell?"

Crash replied, "Some prisoners require more restraint."

She snorted. "What can you do that the Wolfies can't?"

"More than you'd think," he quipped. "Focus on the vines, will you? We don't have a lot of time."

Sora rolled her eyes at the darkness. Then she put her hands back to the wall, trying to remember the symbol that the Catlins had traced, if it was even relevant. *Oh come now,* her inner voice chided. *Just use the necklace and get it over with.*

She frowned, concentrating, reaching into the depths of her mind where the Cat's Eye resided. It was easier this time. The necklace felt more alive, somehow. As though draining the Panthera's magic had made it stronger, heavier in her thoughts, more tangible.

*Open the door,* she thought.

The jingling of bells met her ears, loud and clear. The Cat's Eye responded immediately. It sensed the magical wall beneath her fingers. It seemed to be prodding the vines, testing them, sampling this new magic.

Then—*flash!*

Green light sparked, dancing around the enclosed cell, dazzling her eyes. It absorbed the magic eagerly. Sora gasped. The energy flooded her solar plexus like a sudden breath of air.

The vines fell to the ground, limp and dead. Light flowed into the enclosed cell. Sora was momentarily blinded, caught off-guard. She blinked and looked up, trying to clear her vision.

The hallway stretched before them. Then she heard the sound of voices, a language of short yowls, purrs and growls. A second later, two Catlin guards turned into the hallway, spears in hand, tails lashing. They paused abruptly, looking up at her. They both stared, mouths agape. Apparently the expression of surprise was consistent across races.

Immediately Crash lurched past her and sprinted down the corridor, directly at the Catlins. One let out a loud, high-pitched shriek, and the assassin rammed into him full force. He smashed his fist into the first Catlin's neck, breaking its windpipe. The guard collapsed to the floor, writhing and wheezing in pain, his spear falling to one side. Crash picked up the weapon and thrust it forcefully into the next guard's stomach, ripping a large hole through his gut. Blood and intestines spilled across the ground. The guard staggered back, screaming and hissing, toppling into an adjacent hallway.

Sora stared in disbelief. She felt sick.

Then she heard noises in the distance. Catlin voices and the sound of scrambling feet.

"Come on!" Crash motioned for her to follow, as though he hadn't just killed two seven-foot guards. Sora was still in shock. Her body moved automatically, stiff and awkward at the sight of so much blood.

"Hurry!" he insisted.

The sounds of pursuit were coming on fast. Still, Sora couldn't seem to organize her limbs. The assassin didn't hesitate. He dashed back to her side, grabbed her and dragged her down the hallway, past the massacred bodies and the Wolfies' cell. Sora gasped, catching Dorian's eye as they ran past. She dug in her feet, skidding across the blood.

"Crash!" she exclaimed. "We can't leave them!"

"Go!" Dorian yelled, signaling for them to keep running. "The guards are coming. We'll slow you down. Go!"

Crash pulled at her arm. "We can't help them if we're dead," he said harshly, and hauled her forward. "We'll come back."

Sora wasn't completely convinced, but she didn't have a choice. Dorian's eyes pleaded with her, his hands pointing desperately down the hallway. She could hear the guards approaching. Soon, they would block off any chance of escape.

Somehow, she found the strength to run. She leapt next to Crash and they sprinted down the hall, not looking back. They reeled around a corner, turning haphazardly down a network of corridors and stairs. She hoped that Crash knew where he was going—and apparently he did, because a minute later they reached the exit. It was blocked by thick, heavy vines.

"Quickly!" he yelled, and pushed her at the doorway.

This time, Sora only had to touch the wall. *Flash!* The green light blazed and the Cat's Eye eagerly drank in the magic. Her head spun briefly. The vines dropped to the ground, limp.

Crash grabbed her. They barreled through the exit, jumping over piles of loose vines and foliage. Outside, the colony was strangely quiet. Sora could hear distant sounds below them, chattering voices and the general bustle of the market. But on the prison level, there was hardly any foot traffic at all.

They took off running. Crash led her to a bridge on their left.

"Do you know where we're going?" Sora gasped. Her wounds ached with each step. She could feel blood dripping down her ribs.

"Maybe," Crash replied.

Sora wanted to roll her eyes, but she was too focused on running. *Well, "maybe" is better than "no."*

Then she heard the shouts of Catlin guards. A dozen or so converged from the mist, leaping from different bridges and ropes, trying to cut them off. She forced her legs to run faster, pain piercing her side. Adrenaline fueled her steps.

Crash took a sudden turn, cutting to a bridge that dangled off through the mist, separate from the thick tree branches that supported the colony. Sora followed him, worried that the bridge seemed old and decrepit, not well-maintained. It swung and bowed under their weight. But when she looked ahead past Crash, through the spinning veil of mist—she saw dense leaves and vines. Open, untamed foliage. The end of the colony and the beginnings of the swamp.

Hope bloomed. If they could just make it across, they might escape....

A series of yowls erupted in the air. More Catlins joined the chase, thundering onto the bridge, bounding from rope to log like fierce, giant squirrels. Then a Catlin dropped onto the bridge in front of them, swinging down on a large vine. Sora screamed. Crash ran headlong into the beast and tackled it, toppling across the wooden planks.

"Crash!" she yelled, skidding to a halt. They were blocked by the Catlin's massive body. The two struggled, wrestling with each other, a match of pure strength. The bridge rocked and creaked violently. Sora grabbed the ropes, holding on for dear life, fear choking her. When she looked back, she could see dozens of Catlins crowding the entrance to the bridge. A few were coming up behind her, spears held threateningly.

She turned back to Crash. Surprisingly, he was holding his own. As she watched, he threw the Catlin back and kicked the guard firmly in the chest. The guard stumbled away, half-off the bridge, struggling to reclaim his balance.

When Crash turned back to her, he held the Catlin's long, curved knife in his hand. His eyes met hers. "Can you swim?" he asked.

"Yes," she replied, frowning. She didn't like his expression. "Wait...." she murmured. He raised the knife. "Don't!"

Too late. The assassin swung the blade down with both hands. It passed cleanly through the ropes of the bridge. Sora's mouth dropped. She was too shocked to react, even as the planks started to pull apart beneath her. The ropes snapped, fraying under so much weight. The Catlin guards on either side started yowling in terror, fleeing from the bridge as quickly as possible.

"Wait!" she yelled, fear constricting her chest. Her voice was cut off by a sickening *crack!* The bridge started to cave in. She wanted to throw herself forward and grab onto the assassin—but she couldn't; there was no time. She thought she might have screamed. Her mouth opened. Her hands reached. Grasped. Useless.

Crash disappeared, plummeting into the mist.

Just as suddenly, the bridge tilted to one side and Sora's feet slipped. With a shriek of surprise, she jolted downward toward the endless drop. She grabbed onto a piece of rope just before the mist claimed her.

She clung there, suspended at an unknowable height, and tried not to look down. If she did, she would fall. Her heart pounded, her hands shook wildly. If she could just pull herself up, she could still escape. Climb across the damaged bridge, reach the other side. It wasn't too far now. *If I can just pull...a bit harder....*

Her hand slipped. The slick rope burned her skin.

Then the world gave way.

# CHAPTER 12

Lily sighed, watching Housekeeper Grem flounce about the room, dusting tables, straightening vases. The old woman hovered in the background like a vulture, casting malicious glances in her direction. She understood her anger. It was quite an honor, to be promoted at such a young age to a full Housekeeper. She wasn't entirely certain that she was qualified for the task. But if it would get her away from Grem's nasty claws, she would take it, no questions asked.

"Sit down, my dear," said The Honourable Dustin Fallcrest.

Lily hesitated. It was a breach of protocol, but she couldn't refuse him. She took a stiff perch at the edge of the chair opposite him.

The Honourable Dustin Fallcrest sat before her with a warm cup of tea. He was a stork of a man, tall and gangly, with a pronounced nose similar to his older brother's. She guessed him to be around forty, perhaps a little younger, with a thick head of brown hair, his sideburns turned a distinguished gray. His eyes were softer than his brother's, his tone less sharp. He took up the end of the couch, the armrest too low for him, but that was to be expected. They sat in Lady Sora's outer chamber, at the front of her compartments.

He nodded politely to Lily. "It's a simple townhouse, smaller than you're used to, I'd imagine," he said. "But our last Housekeeper has retired and we are looking for someone new." He cast a side-glance at Grem. "And fresh."

Lily saw Housekeeper Grem cast a vicious look at Dustin Fallcrest's back. *Lord Fallcrest,* she corrected her thoughts. For lack of an heir, the title passed to the brother, though the lands were still held by the King's court until Lady Sora could be confirmed dead. Lily hoped that never happened.

Lily held tightly to her handkerchief, her thoughts returning to her mistress. She still held on to a shred of hope that Lady Sora might return. She often lingered in her Lady's bedroom, gazing down at the gravel drive, wondering if her friend would appear some day, a little older and a lot wiser.

But it had been almost two months since her disappearance, and the odds of her return grew slimmer by the day. The countryside still talked about her, but less frequently. Few serfs cared about the matters of the estate as long as they were able to work there. The farmers were more concerned with planting crops.

The women were a different story. Midwives and farm girls still speculated about Lady Sora's whereabouts, chatting out of windows and over clotheslines. There had been several flurries of rumors. Some said she was dead, others said she was still in the manor, hiding in the attic or the basement.

Lady Sinclair claimed to have seen her on the streets of the City of Crowns. Lily remembered the conversation darkly. She had run across the noble Lady and her companions at the marketplace. Pretending to buy fruit, Lily had lingered nearby, listening to their chatter.

*"Hiding in plain sight,"* Lady Sinclair had put it. *"Albeit in a despicable district."* She winked knowingly to her friends, who burst into a chorus of laughter. The point was clear. Lady Sora was

now a woman of the night, a harlot begging on the streets. *"Takes after her mother, I suppose,"* Sinclair had snickered.

But Lily didn't believe that. She also didn't believe the story that ran in the papers stating that Lady Sora was now living in Fennbog swamp, hiding from the law. She couldn't imagine her delicate friend surrounded by wild animals, living on berries.

No, Lady Sora was somewhere safe and well-hidden, Lily was certain of it. She didn't know where. But she refused to believe the worst.

Dustin Fallcrest sneezed heavily into his handkerchief, drawing her attention. The new Lord had arrived three weeks earlier to put the estate in order. He hadn't been able to balance the accounts, so he'd hired a bookkeeper and steward. Tomorrow, he would be returning to the City of Crowns. He didn't take well to country life, or so he had explained. He had too many allergies.

His invitation to be his Housekeeper had come as somewhat of a surprise. Honestly, she had expected to be laid off, just like the kitchen staff.

*I suppose I should be grateful,* Lily thought, and smiled politely. "I would love to accompany you, My Lord," she said, once he was done blowing his nose. "It has been a pleasure to serve the Fallcrest family."

Dustin Fallcrest nodded, a wide smile coming over his face. At least he seemed friendlier than his brother. A shame that Lady Sora had never met him. Lily was certain they would have become fast friends.

"You'll have your bags packed in the morning?" Lord Fallcrest prompted, sipping on his tea.

"Gladly, Milord," Lily replied, and stood up, then dipping into an elegant curtsy. "I will see you tomorrow." She stepped lightly from the small sitting room, thankful when the door closed. For the next twenty-four hours, she would have to avoid Housekeeper Grem. She was certain the old crone would find countless ways to punish her before tomorrow.

Perhaps Lily would enjoy a final walk across the lawns, revisiting her favorite spots. A bit of sadness tugged at her heart. A shame that she would have to do it alone.

* * *

Sora seemed to plummet forever. The fog was so dense that she could see nothing but white; as far as she knew, she could have been falling up. Her stomach churned sickeningly. The wind whistled past her. The fall seemed to take a horribly long time, but then again, falling was better than landing.

*Wham!*

Icy water engulfed her, as hard as rock. She was immediately stunned. The air rushed from her lungs, her muscles cramped and convulsed. Her eyes closed tight, and for a brief moment, she blacked out.

The freezing water brought her back almost immediately. She writhed against it, as clumsy as a newborn child, fighting to organize her limbs, moving on instinct alone. She couldn't tell if she was facing up or down, but there was no time to decide. With the desperation of a drowning beast, she picked a direction and kicked her legs as hard as she could, propelling her numb arms, her lungs screaming for oxygen.

Luckily, she picked the right direction. A few seconds later,

Sora exploded through the surface of the lake, her mouth wide open, like a caught fish. She was too numb to feel any sort of pain; too overwhelmed by adrenaline. She looked around wildly, her eyes keen with panic, expecting an attack.

But nothing happened. Besides the smooth, swirling mist and rippling gray water, nothing moved.

It took a long minute to regain her thoughts. *I'm alive, I'm alive,* she kept thinking as she treaded water; a mantra of survival. Still, she couldn't quite believe it. The mist seemed to hint at an afterlife; a thin veil between her bruised body and the underworld. Any minute now, she expected the North Wind to appear in all of His dark glory, a herald of the Goddess, to escort her into the beyond.

She focused intently on the deep fog. She tried to regain her breath, though it seemed impossible to use her lungs. She kept choking on air, her body shaking uncontrollably, succumbing to fits and starts. Then, unexpectedly, she saw a shape drift into sight, obscured by mist. Her heart stuttered.

A low, flat object bobbed into view. It took a moment for her to recognize it. A fragile wooden platform, perhaps a long-forgotten elevator, floated along the surface of the lake.

Sora couldn't believe her luck. Still fueled by adrenaline, she surged toward the floating boards, swimming as fast as possible. She reached their side in under a minute. Desperate, she dragged herself on top of the slippery wood, sinking her fingers into the spongy dry rot, clawing her way up like a wet cat.

Once fully on-board the platform, she collapsed, shivering and shaking, absolutely exhausted. Her thoughts spun wildly. She wondered if the Catlins would follow her down to the water. Should she try to paddle her way to the forest, escape...? It was the most immediate choice.

Then she sat bolt upright. Crash!

Finally her thoughts cleared, her shock dissipating. *By the Goddess, where is he?* Had he survived the fall? Was he somewhere on the lake? He must have landed nearby.

She put her hand to her chest, trying to calm her heart. He might be dead. The thought didn't truly upset her—but he was her only chance of survival. She wouldn't last a day in the swamp, with no supplies and no weapons. And how was she supposed to rescue the Wolfies by herself?

Her eyes searched the water desperately, her vision obscured by fog. He *had* to be somewhere around here—she was certain of it. Spotting him should be easy. If he was still on the surface. Alive.

*Of course he's alive!* she thought. He *had* to be. Crash was the most capable person she had ever met—even if he was an evil bastard. And if he was dead...well, that didn't bode well for her, either.

She gazed at the water, still ruffled by her violent landing. Another shape loomed out of the mist—a giant, contorted pile of ropes and wood, the remnants of the bridge. Luckily, it had fallen quite a ways from where she had landed. She put her arms in the water and propelled her little raft towards the wreckage. Crash was probably nearby.

She examined the murky depths, her vision obscured by clots of dirt and grass, mud and branches. Shards of wood floated past, drifting away from the main wreckage. She thought she saw a peculiar amount of ripples towards one end of the bridge. Small bubbles breaking the surface.

She couldn't wait any longer on her raft. Crash might be caught under the ropes, drowning. Or perhaps he had been knocked unconscious by the fall. She hated the thought of entering that icy cold water, but she didn't see any other choice.

She stripped off her boots, then leapt from the raft, diving smoothly as a swan.

The water bit into her body, making her wounds burn. It was shockingly cold, close to freezing, as though the sun had never warmed its surface. She forced her limbs to move and dove downward, under the water, beneath the collapsed bridge.

Underwater, she could make out vague, lumbering shapes; wooden planks and ropes, all tangled together. A large bulk floated up in front of her, emerging from the cloudy depths, and Sora almost screamed. It was the body of a giant, dead Catlin, its glassy eyes wide in terror, a snarl frozen on its face.

She swam past it. She had to find Crash. He had already been submerged for too long. Then she saw another humanoid form floating in the distance, caught beneath a large pile of wood. *There.*

She kicked her legs, propelling herself further down. Her lungs burned, but she didn't have much further to go. She used her hands to navigate the sinking bridge, pushing beams of wood out of the way.

Finally, a piece of black cloth floated before her eyes. She snatched at it in slow motion, her fingers thick and numb. She gave it a tug and pulled Crash's shoulder into view, followed shortly by a head of black hair. Relief flooded her. Wrapping one frozen arm around him, she started up to the surface, her lungs aching.

She didn't know if she could make it. Crash's body was heavy and she was almost out of strength. *A little further,* she told herself.

The surface was visible, only a few more yards....

Then a rope suddenly drifted in front of her. It was knotted to a series of boards that still floated above the lake. She grabbed it, desperate, and started dragging herself upward. Crash was impossibly heavy, and more than once she almost lost her grip. She hooked him firmly under the armpits and continued to climb. The rope tore at her hand with each pull, but it was her only lifeline, a solitary route back to the surface—she thanked the Goddess for every inch.

A moment later, Sora broke the surface of the water. Her hair, having come undone from its braid, was a heavy mass against her back. She took a deep, aching breath before the assassin's body pulled her back into the water. With the remainder of her strength, she slung Crash's unconscious form over the remnants of the bridge, using the driftwood to help move the assassin to her makeshift raft. Gasping and shivering, her teeth chattering uncontrollably, she hauled him onto the wooden platform. She dragged herself after him with her last ounce of strength.

Panting and wheezing, Sora lay Crash on the narrow raft. She shook uncontrollably, her body numb. Exhaustion crept forward, clouding her thoughts.

*No.* She had to make sure that Crash was still alive. Dragging herself to her hands and knees, she turned towards the unconscious assassin.

He was stark white except that his lips were blue.

Her breath caught. She leaned over him and rested her fingers against his nose and mouth. He wasn't breathing.

Sora forced herself to remain calm. She thought back to last summer, when she and Lily spent almost every day at a nearby river that bordered her father's lands. They tied ropes to trees and swung out over the lazy green depths, falling into the gentle currents.

Once, she dove in and struck her head on an unseen rock. Lily dragged her from the water. Her handmaid had saved her life by breathing air back into her lungs. After that, Sora had learned the trick herself, determined to be prepared should it ever happen again. She tried to remember the steps Lily had demonstrated, every little detail.

Sora opened Crash's mouth to see if anything obstructed his throat. Nothing.

She tipped his head back and closed his nostrils, then firmly set her mouth against his.

At first his lips were freezing, as cold as a corpse. She continued to breathe into him, counting silently between intervals. She had to repeat the process quite a few times before she felt him start to move with her. She was flooded with relief a second time.

He stirred beneath her. Abruptly Sora sat up, wiping her mouth off on her sleeve. *I hope I don't get a disease,* she thought wryly.

Crash sat up unexpectedly. Sora gasped, leaning back. He didn't spare her a glance, but turned over and heaved. He coughed violently, water gushing from his mouth, over and over again. It looked like he was vomiting up half the lake. Then he collapsed backward, gasping, his breath wheezing in and out of his lungs.

"Crash!" She leaned over him in concern, then put a hand to his face. His skin was still dead cold. His eyes fluttered briefly, but he didn't respond. She checked his pulse at his neck—it was strong, steady. This, she assumed, was a good sign. But he was definitely unconscious again.

Sora suddenly wanted to laugh. She stuck her tongue out at the sleeping man. *Not so useless now, am I?* she thought.

But it was a useless victory. They couldn't stay on the raft forever. It was too cold on the lake; they would both catch pneumonia, or even worse, freeze to death. She had to get them to safety.

As she peered through the fog, she was finally able to make out the gigantic trunks of trees around her; huge, lumbering shadows stretching into the mist, giant sentinels, a reminder of the Catlin magic above. Would the beasts follow her down to the lake? She would have no way of defending herself.

Abruptly a light caught her eye. She stared, shocked. As she drifted around the trunks of the trees, she saw bright light glinting off the surface of the lake. She leaned down and paddled toward it with her hands.

Finally, she rounded the massive trunk. A harsh glow dazzled her eyes. Sticking out of the tree were two torches, burning quietly with unnaturally white fire. Perhaps even more shocking was the door between them. Barely discernible in the gloom, it blended perfectly with the curve of the tree trunk. She paddled closer until she could tentatively touch the rough surface.

*A trap?* Sora gnawed her lip, worried, but she didn't have a lot of options. She rested her hands against the curved surface of the door. She swallowed nervously, then gave a cautious push. The raft rocked gently at the force, and for a few perilous seconds, she thought it would tip over. But when she looked back at the door, she found that it had opened a few inches. *Well, better than nothing.*

Balancing precariously on the raft, Sora pushed the door open all the way. A small, dark space resided beyond. Based on the meager light, she judged it to be the size of a servant's bedroom, roughly ten by twelve feet. It looked abandoned, dusty, forgotten.

She leapt from the raft to the tree, then turned and dragged the assassin's heavy body after her—*dear Goddess, he's like a stone!* It took countless minutes of tugging and grunting before she had him fully inside the crawlspace.

There was no time to marvel at her good luck. She needed to make a fire as quickly as possible. She went back to the door, dragging a few pieces of driftwood from the water. She was so tired that she could have collapsed, but she threw them into a pile in the center of the floor. Then she grabbed one of the torches from outside, wiggling it out of the stubborn embrace of the sconce. Her Cat's Eye murmured quietly when she got close to the white light. Magic.

The wood lit immediately with the unnatural white flames, and Sora sent another silent prayer of thanks to the Goddess. She then laid Crash out and pulled off his wet boots, gloves, cloak and shirt, leaving only his pants, for the sake of decency. With the last of her strength, she pulled the wooden door shut, closing them in the small space.

The fire heated up the room in a matter of minutes. It was warmer than a normal fire, and it had a light, metallic scent, irritating her Cat's Eye senses. The smokeless flames unnerved her.

Sora tried to remember if there was anything else she was supposed to do—secure the raft, bank the fire, anything to that effect—but her eyes were already closing. Exhaustion crashed down on her like a lead quilt. Darkness claimed her, and she fell into a deep slumber.

* * *

Sora awoke to the sound of movement nearby.

She reached for the dagger at her belt, but it was gone. She berated herself silently—how many times had Dorian warned her about forgetting her knife? It was an amateur mistake!

*Why is the air so musty?* she thought groggily.

With a shock, Sora was brought back to the present. All of her aches and pains rushed back to life. She sat up, immediately alert, and looked around the small room.

Crash stood with his back to her, adjusting his belt, his shirt slung over one shoulder. She stared at him, breathing deeply until she was able to calm her heart. No need to panic. He was the only living thing in the room—unless one counted dust mites.

Firelight flickered across his back. It was impossible not to notice his broad, powerful shoulders, his sleek muscles and tanned skin. His back, like the rest of him, was covered in small nicks and scars, imperfections made obvious by the white light.

Realizing her thoughts were more than a little odd—this was Crash, after all, *the man I hate*—she averted her eyes and poked at the fire with a piece of wood. The white flames burned steadily, with no need for assistance. Strangely enough, there was no ash. The wood pyre didn't seem burned at all, despite countless hours having passed. She wasn't sure what to make of that.

Crash turned around at the sound, a strange expression on his face. He looked down at her.

Sora met his gaze, but her eyes caught on his jaw and her

breath lodged in her throat. A long, gruesome scar traveled down the length of his torso, starting at his collarbone and trailing to his navel. It must have been a gruesome wound—she wondered how he had survived it.

"A lesson learned," Crash murmured.

She looked up, startled, to see that his eyes had followed hers. "What happened?" she asked, wondering if he would answer the question.

"Bad timing," he said coldly. Then he turned away and pulled on his shirt.

Sora was somewhat stung by his words. She wasn't sure if he was referring to the accident or to her question. But she recovered quickly.

"So what are we going to do?" she asked instead.

"About what?" he grunted.

"The Wolfies."

"Rescue them." Crash finished dressing and turned to her, his eyes shadowed. He bowed his head in thought, then started pacing. "Do you know where those stairs lead?"

Sora frowned. Stairs? She glanced around the room, then noticed them. They were almost invisible, far back from the door, shrouded in darkness, covered in dust. The stairway appeared to have been carved out of the tree, just like the room itself. It disappeared upwards, into the trunk.

She shook her head wordlessly.

"Then we need to find out." He started toward the staircase.

Sora watched him, surprised. That was it? No comment on how they had arrived inside the tree in the first place? The icy lake or his inability to swim? She frowned. "We should rest for a while longer," she ventured. "That was quite a fall."

"We don't have time. The Catlins will kill Burn and Dorian soon. We have a day left, at most." His eyes were trained on the dark staircase.

Sora followed his gaze. She wondered where the stairs led. Perhaps a dead end? Exploring could be a greater waste of time, but Crash wasn't the kind of person to argue with.

She let out a long, strained sigh, then started to stand up. A sharp pain made her stop. She winced and sucked in a breath. Her side began to throb just below the ribcage. She hadn't felt it before because of all the adrenaline and ice water, but now that things were calm, she could remember the Panthera's claws digging into her.

Crash paused at the base of the stairs. His eyes flicked to her shirt. He hesitated, staring, then started towards her.

"W-what are you doing?" Sora asked, backing up. He wasn't looking at her face, but at her torso. She wanted to look down too, but her eyes were glued to his intense expression.

He stooped before her, his broad shoulders blocking out the light of the fire. His hand went to her waist where the pain ate at her side—he touched the spot with surprising gentleness. Sora stared down at the top of his head, too shocked to do anything else. She watched as he inspected the wound. She could see now that there was a bloodstain on her shirt, left over from yesterday. But she didn't think the wound was still bleeding.

"The Panthera did this to you?" Crash asked quietly.

Sora swallowed, "Yeah."

Crash grabbed the base of his shirt and ripped a long strip from it. "It's not too deep," he said. "All we need to do is bind it."

Then he tied the cloth securely around the wound. He met her eyes. "You cleaned it out when we went for that swim earlier."

The words hung between them, silent, a shade awkward. He frowned, still staring at her, as though she was not quite what he had expected. He cleared his throat. "I...well, thank you."

She was speechless. Gratitude? From this assassin? *Not bloody likely,* she thought, and yet there it was. Loud and clear.

"Of course," she said solemnly. Then she couldn't help it. She cracked a smile.

To her surprise, Crash let out a quiet chuckle. He stood and gave her a hand up, helping her to her feet. He picked up her cloak and threw it around her shoulders. "Come on."

With that he started up the steps, not waiting for her to follow. Sora blinked after him, still surprised, momentarily frozen in place. Then she hurried to catch up. *Some things never change.*

# CHAPTER 13

It wasn't long before Sora could feel the strain on her legs, despite the fact that they were fit from traveling. The staircase seemed to stretch on forever. It was barely the width of a broom closet, and the stairs were not evenly cut. Each step was either shorter or higher than the step they were on. She tripped several times.

Every couple of turns, a white torch was mounted on the wall to light the way. Being magic, it was able to light quite a distance. Crash had to move sideways to get past them, and more than once Sora almost knocked one over. One torch actually fell on top of her, but as soon as it touched her, the Cat's Eye let out a fierce chime. The fire was snuffed out like a candle, no sign of ashes or sparks.

As she climbed, she wondered what kind of power had created such a passage. *Nature magic,* some part of her whispered, and she quickened her step.

The two kept silent, neither in the mood to converse. Sora pushed herself mindlessly forward. She forced her way up the stairs, her legs moving without conscious effort. She didn't even look where she was going, keeping her eyes on her feet so she didn't trip. Her breath grew heavy in her lungs. *These stairs go on forever,* she thought. *When will they end? It's been an eternity since we were at the bottom.*

Her question was answered abruptly by her head hitting the ceiling. *Thunk!* She yelped and sat down, rubbing her bruised crown, looking up in surprise.

The stairs leveled off abruptly. She was at a dead end: no doors, no windows, no corridors, no ladders to climb, just a solid wooden ceiling. She had to sit down so she didn't bump her head again.

Crash already knelt in the small crawlspace, not making a sound. Sora shuddered, trying to keep some space between them. His presence lent her a newfound security—as long as he was at her back, she would be safe. But something about him still deeply frightened her. His uncanny stealth. His unusual aura.

"Dead end," she whispered.

Then she heard the sound of footsteps, not directly above her but a few feet in front. Crash put a finger to his lips. He slowly reached up and placed his hands on the roof, where Sora noticed something odd flickering in the firelight. A latch. A trapdoor.

She stared at it, watching in fascination. Stretching upward, Crash placed his ear to the door and listened, then opened it up a few inches. Sora could hear voices, but they were speaking in another language. *Catlins.* Anxiety curled in her stomach. What if, at this very moment, they were discussing the best way to trap them? Perhaps they had heard her head thunk against the wood? Her eyes flickered to the assassin nervously. Then she was hit by a realization.

He knew what they were saying!

She wanted to ask him what was going on, but she bit her lip instead, waiting. The minutes stretched on and her knees began to ache from her cramped position. Finally the footsteps left, and she heard the familiar crinkle of leaves—vines opening and closing.

He set down the door, carefully latching it again, then turned to look at her. He actually appeared pleased. "Seems like the whole colony is talking about us. They seem to think we died in the fall," he told her. "They've sent a search party to scan the area, but Catlins are horribly afraid of water. That's why they put lakes beneath their colonies, to protect them from other tribes. I doubt they'll look very hard." Crash smiled faintly, but that expression quickly melted. "They've already taken the Wolfies to the Grandmother Tree."

Sora's mouth went dry. Her heart raced once again. "What do we do?" she asked.

Crash nodded to the trap door. "We need to recover our weapons," he whispered. "It's still early in the morning; the colony won't be too crowded."

Sora gave him a pointed look. "That's a terrible idea! Let's just steal a few spears."

"I need my sword," Crash murmured. "And my dagger."

Sora frowned. His eyes grew cold, and she knew he had made his decision.

"Fine," she said. "What's your plan?"

Crash turned back to the trapdoor, lifting it once again, this time slightly higher. He peered outside, scanning whatever room lay beyond. "Don't get caught," he said.

"That's it?" Sora replied, incredulous.

He was already climbing through the opening into the world beyond. She let out a long, slow sigh. Perhaps it would be in her best interest to go back downstairs, return to the raft, sail to shore and disappear....

But she followed the assassin anyway.

They were in a mid-sized room. Boxes upon boxes of goods

were stacked alongside each wall: tubers, dried flowers, a myriad of vegetables that she didn't recognize, buckets of mushrooms and strips of dried meat. A small table stretched to one side. It held an old, dusty book, made from dried leaves. Sora took it all in with interest. A ledger, perhaps? They must be inside a store.

She could see a doorway leading outside, blocked by familiar magic vines. Several portholes decorated the far wall, flooded by ample morning light. Crash slunk up to one and peered through, then gave her a sharp nod. He motioned to the doorway. It took her a moment to realize what he wanted. Apparently, she was the master key.

Sora crept up to the door, standing slightly to one side so she wouldn't be caught in the open. Then she touched the vines, sending a silent command to her Cat's Eye. *Zzzzt!* With a jolt of energy, the necklace absorbed the magic and the vines fell to the ground.

Outside, the colony was strangely silent. Sora glanced around from left to right. Morning light filtered through the mist. She wasn't sure what time it was, but she guessed it was too early for the Catlins to be up and about. They must still be asleep. Far off in the distance, she saw a feline shape dash across a bridge, but that was all.

"This way," Crash murmured, his voice hushed.

They ran out of the building, crouching low to the ground. They were on the second level, the marketplace. It was easy to find cover between the stalls, ducking from empty tables to low benches, overshadowed by grassy canopies and cloth banners. They only ran across two Catlins, who were carrying heavy crates to some unknown destination. Sora and Crash paused behind a series of stacked barrels as the merchants passed. One of them sniffed the air, turned its head and glanced back and forth...but after a brief hesitation, continued on its way.

Sora let out a silent breath of relief. They waited several minutes after the Catlins had disappeared, then started off again, moving as fast as possible.

Although she was thoroughly lost, Crash seemed to recognize where they were. More than once he turned in a full circle, gauging their position, then continued across the giant branch. They turned onto a smaller bridge to the next thoroughfare. There, he ushered her onto an elevator and grabbed the levers, tugging experimentally at the ropes until the platform budged upwards. The mechanisms turned and grated as they rocked into the air.

"How do you know where we are?" Sora asked in a hushed voice. They sat low on the elevator, obscured by shallow walls.

He pointed to one side, over her shoulder. "Landmarks. The pattern of that bark looks like an arrow. And the stamen of that flower is bent."

Sora shifted, suddenly uncomfortable. She stared at the dark patches of the tree, turning her head slightly. *I suppose it looks like an arrow. A bit.* "You're observant," she muttered. Once again, she felt inadequate. She had been busy running for her life—she hadn't thought to pay attention to her surroundings.

They reached the prison tree without further complications. Sora had the sense that the colony was slowly waking up. Sounds could be heard from below—voices calling to each other, though she didn't know what was being said. The elevator arrived on the prison floor, rocking gently into place. Thankfully, no one was there to meet them. A pair of guards lingered at the doorway where the vines were still limp and lifeless, as they had left them.

Crash slunk up behind them. Sora averted her eyes, knowing what he was about to do. The assassin slipped a knife from one guard's belt and quietly slit its neck, toppling the body backwards behind a large flower. He dealt with the other guard just as silently. Soon, the passage was all clear.

They passed through the doorway unnoticed. Sora wondered how long it would take for the Catlins to resurrect a door.

Once inside the tree, they slunk down a narrow corridor, listening intently for footsteps. All was silent. The jail didn't have any other prisoners that she could see—there were not many travelers through the swamp. Then she paused, recognizing the hallway they were in, and pointed to an alcove to their left. "That's the room," she murmured, keeping her voice as soft as possible. "They put our weapons in there."

They dashed to the cobweb door. Crash stood to one side and motioned for her to get to work. She felt horribly exposed in the hallway, and moved as fast as possible, tapping the thin spiderwebs with her finger. This time, she almost didn't need to think. *Ching.* With a slight chime, the webs fell away, and the Cat's Eye drank in the energy. She wondered if it was wise to use the necklace so much. It felt much stronger than before. Almost alive.

They entered the room. Their weapons and bags were piled in the middle of the floor, just as Sora had first seen them. *At least this part is easy.* She shouldered her staff and buckled on her daggers, letting out a slow breath of relief. She might not be the most skilled fighter, but it certainly felt better than being unarmed.

Crash grabbed the rest of their bags. Sora took what she could, slipping their knapsacks onto her back. She would have to drop them fast if they got into a fight.

When they entered the hall again, Crash turned to their left—deeper into the tree—and started walking.

"Wait! Wrong way!" Sora hissed.

He glanced over his shoulder at her, then motioned with his hand. For some people, this might have been enough, but Sora wasn't convinced. "Have you lost your wits?" she growled. "The exit is behind us!"

Crash glared at her. It was enough to shut her mouth. "We can't go back through the colony," the assassin murmured, his voice as soft as a shadow. "There is another stairway in this tree. I think I know where it is."

Sora wanted to protest. It might be dangerous to tromp through the colony again, but going deeper into the prison tree was even more ludicrous. They would have no chance at escaping if everything went wrong.

But Crash was moving down the hallway again, and she couldn't go back without him. She would be lost and defenseless. *Damn it all,* she thought. *If I get out of this alive, I'm going to learn to fight on my own.*

They walked quickly and quietly down the hallway, barely pausing to check a corridor before dashing down it. Twice Crash turned and changed direction, going back to use a different hallway, or jumping down a few stairs. They passed two rooms that were occupied by Catlins. Sora recognized the sound of snoring. She glanced inside and saw rows of hammocks swaying softly, full of sleeping guards. Sora and Crash continued on swiftly.

Then suddenly they were passing by the Wolfies' old cells, from which they had escaped the day before. Sora looked at the empty alcove in horror. It was true, then. The Wolfies had been taken to the Grandmother Tree. Perhaps they were dead already.

The thought almost made her cry. Somewhere along the journey, Burn and Dorian had become close to her, people she could trust. She couldn't imagine leaving the swamp without them. She was consumed with dread.

They passed the final hallway of cells and reached an open doorway. It led into a storage room much like the one they had originally arrived in. Sora was shocked, to say the least. She stared at Crash, wondering how he had known this was here. *Perhaps he "observed" it.* The assassin scrutinized the floor, searching for the trapdoor that would lead them outside.

Suddenly, Sora heard voices from behind. Grunts and growls, the Catlin language. It occurred to her that they were in a room full of food—boxes of roots, eggs and other edibles. Breakfast?

She almost panicked.

Just then, Crash found the trapdoor. He dug a knife into its crevice and popped the door upward. Sora scrambled over, dropping her bags through the opening.

Crash shoved her in before she could lower herself down. She fell, biting her lip so she wouldn't scream. It was pitch black inside the stairwell. She couldn't see the ground, and it was impossible to brace herself for landing. *Thunk!* She fell hard on her wrist. The impact stunned her briefly, and she lay there, shaking. What if there had been no stairs? What if she had just kept falling? She couldn't clear the image from her head.

Crash slid in behind her and gently lowered the trapdoor. No sooner had it touched the floor than footsteps could be heard. Loud, heavy paws. A few boxes and crates scraped across the floor, and she heard something that sounded like a chuckle. She and Crash slowly drew their weapons, listening intently, prepared for the worst.

The guards kept talking. Eventually they left.

Finally, Sora could breathe. Then she turned on Crash and shoved him, unable to contain herself. "Bastard!" she hissed. "They could have caught us!"

She couldn't see the assassin's face in the darkness. He remained silent. She started to regret her words....

"But they didn't," he finally said. Then he sheathed his thin sword and shouldered his bags. Sora watched him, stunned, focusing the best she could on his shadow. She couldn't understand why he didn't worry more. It had been a close call—far too close for comfort. And they still had to find the Grandmother Tree and save the Wolfies.

Crash started down the stairwell, the white flames of a torch flickering around the bend.

After a long, seething hesitation, Sora shouldered her bags and followed suit.

# CHAPTER 14

Once they reached the bottom of the stairs, Crash signaled for her to wait. It was a welcome relief. Sora's legs were shaking from the long, steep staircase. This corridor had been darker and dustier than the last one, perhaps a passage through an older tree.

Turning his back to her, Crash started to take off his shirt. Sora's mouth dropped open, then she quickly averted her eyes. She turned toward the wall of the tree, staring resolutely at the wood grain, waiting as he undressed himself. "W-what are you doing?" she stuttered. It was silly, really. She had already seen him shirtless. But it was different when he was awake. *You know, not drowning.*

"I'll be back," he murmured.

"What do you mean?" she asked. She waited a moment longer, but curiosity finally made her turn her head. When she looked, the assassin was gone, as though he had vanished into thin air. Only his clothes remained.

She stared at the heap of black leather and linen. Shirt, gloves, cloak...pants. Her eyes widened. Then she ran to the doorway, gazing out at the cold, gray lake. She saw a ripple of water near the base of the tree, thin rings spreading outward. He had barely made a splash.

Her eyes searched the mist, wondering where he had gone. *He could have at least warned me.* With a breath of annoyance, she sat down against the wall of the tree and stretched out her legs. She winced. Her muscles were terribly stiff and sore. She rubbed them as she waited.

Her thoughts turned to the Cat's Eye, to the manor. She wondered what Lily was doing—whether or not the maid had found employment, or if life somehow carried on, unaffected by Lord Fallcrest's passing. She had the sudden, terrible urge to write a letter, though it was impossible. Her fingers itched to put pen to paper.

Then she thought of the Wolfies and their impending death. It was pathetic, really. She was drained from the panic and excitement, but somehow, she still shed a few tears. First her father, and now this. Given the seclusion of the moment, Sora pressed her face against her knees and allowed herself a few exhausted sobs.

Perhaps ten minutes later, Crash returned with another raft. If she hadn't been watching for him, she never would have heard him approach. The assassin swam behind an abandoned elevator, his arms holding on to the edge, pushing with his legs. She watched his powerful shoulders flex. They were broad and heavily layered with muscle. A few nicks and scars stood out against his wet skin.

Sora wondered how many elevators had fallen over the years, plunging unwary passengers to their deaths. The thought made her shudder. She could remember the Catlin's body clearly, drowned beneath the lake.

She turned away before Crash got too close. He was in the nude, after all. She waited for him to dress, focusing on her muddy knees. She had never been remotely close to a naked man before, nix the previous day. *It was only a matter of time,* she told herself. Even her thoughts sounded awkward. They had been traveling together for over a month now. Nudity was bound to happen.

Once he was dressed again, they loaded their supplies onto the makeshift raft. She still found it difficult to look Crash in the eye. She wondered if he noticed. Probably.

The raft was barely big enough for both of them. At first, she was afraid it would sink. It bobbed threateningly low in the water, but somehow held. Crash handed her a broad piece of driftwood to use as a paddle. She was careful to match his rhythm; she didn't want to overturn the boat.

They passed several abandoned elevators and lumps of driftwood, lost relics of the Catlin colony. Trees loomed out of the mist, blocking the route forward, and several times they had to change direction. The air above the lake was icy cold, and her nose turned numb before long. She listened for any signs of a search party, but there were none. The lake stretched on and on, with no shore in sight.

"Where are we going?" she finally asked. They had kept a stealthy silence, but she no longer saw the point. They hadn't seen another living thing in almost a mile.

"To shore," he said shortly.

"Right. That wasn't my question," Sora replied. "Well, not really."

"We're going to find the Wolfies," Crash said. "I'll track them once we are on land." He paused. "Or rather, in shallower water."

Sora raised an eyebrow. She hadn't thought of that. They were deep in the swamp—what if the lake never truly ended? They would have to make their way back into the trees. She couldn't fathom how he could track the Wolfies above ground. They could be anywhere, and tree bark didn't hold footprints.

As though reading her mind, the raft suddenly ran up against an embankment. She could see black mud beneath them. Clumps of reeds and ferns grew from the thick paste, clotted with decomposing leaves. She wrinkled her nose. It smelled like rotten eggs.

Crash leapt to shore...or rather, a nearby fern, then grabbed onto a series of thick vines that dangled to the ground. "I'll be back," he said. "Stay here. Don't make any noise."

He shimmied up the vines like a squirrel. Sora watched, trying not to be impressed. Then he was gone.

She pulled her cloak closer around her and took out a dagger, holding it in her lap, looking around at the thick underbrush. Her view was obscured by wide, flat leaves and silky mist. She tried to listen for anyone's approach, but all she heard was the gentle lap of the lake and the call of birds.

* * *

Sora wasn't sure how long Crash was gone. Only that by the time he reappeared, she was half-crazy with worry.

"Well?" she asked, as he slid down the vines, appearing out of the mist like a panther from the dark. "Did you find them? Where are they?" She twisted her hands around her dagger. Were they already dead?

"This way," Crash said shortly. "Grab the bags, we have to hurry."

He led her up into the trees. If it had been a month ago, the climb would have been hard. But Sora was used to the swamp by now, clambering through branches and swinging on vines. She followed his lead into the canopy.

They found an old tree trunk that was hollowed out inside, and hid their bags there. Then they continued on their way. Crash moved at a relentless pace, jumping from one branch to the next, using vines to swing across wide gaps. Sora followed as best she could. It was hard going. The wilderness was thick with foliage and they had to cut their way through more than once.

After about ten minutes, she heard a faint pounding sound in the distance. Drums? She frowned, staring at Crash's back. She wanted to ask what it was, but she sensed that it was better to remain silent. If Catlins were nearby, she didn't want to be overheard.

"Here," Crash whispered, showing her a gap in the leaves. They perched on the large branch, gazing out through the thick foliage. Surprise jolted through her.

Before her stood a giant tree, stretching well up into the sky. It glowed faintly with a strange, green light, clearly visible against the dark forest. The trunk was covered in moss and fungi so rich that it was hard to see the bark.

At one time, it appeared that two great trees had grown together, meeting countless yards above ground and tangling upwards. The tree stretched up and up into the sky, disappearing through the canopy, dwarfing the trees around it. The space between the two trunks was shaped like a lopsided heart. The tree's roots arched into the air like coiling snakes, dozens of feet above the ground. She guessed this was the Grandmother Tree.

Directly beneath the conjoined trunks, two poles had been erected with pyres beneath them. The poles were decorated with skulls and feathers.

At the base of the tree was a circular clearing. She could see bones littering the ground, even at this distance. The circle was lit by white torches, planted in even intervals around its border. And beyond the ring of light—hundreds of Catlin eyes. The first row sat on the ground, large drums between their legs, pounding out a uniform rhythm. The rest of the colony stood behind them, yowling and hissing, jumping in excitement.

Crash pointed. Far back in the shadows of the roots, she could see the two Wolfies bound and gagged, close to the central arch of the tree.

The drums leapt to a roaring pitch. Then, from the shadows, the Panthera leapt into the center of the ring. She recognized him by his sleek black fur and great height; he was far larger than the other Catlins. A wooden mask shielded his face. The Panthera continued to prowl and leap to the beat of the drums. It took Sora a moment to realize that it was a dance. He looked more like a great cat stuck in a pit, clawing its way to the air.

Then three other Catlin warriors leapt into the fray, dancing and spinning, crouching and leaping. They whirled alongside him, mimicking some sort of battle. Each of their masks was ornately painted in bright red and yellow. The teeth of various animals had been hammered into the wood, warped into terrifying faces.

As they watched, the Panthera bowled into one of the warriors. There was a great cry, the crowd was worked into a frenzy. The Panthera grabbed the head of the warrior and twisted it to one side, killing him in one blow. Then, he threw the body to the onlookers, who tore it to pieces.

She and Crash stared. Sora was completely horrified.

"What do we do?" she breathed. After the vicious

demonstration, she felt utterly powerless. There were far too many Catlins to fight, even with the assassin's excellent skills. She doubted she would be much help. Besides one-on-one battle, she was inexperienced.

"Go around," he nodded. "Under the tree. Free the Wolfies. I'll distract the rest."

Sora was incredulous. "Distract them? How do you propose to do that?"

"There are ways."

"You'll be killed!" Sora stopped there. She sounded terribly close to caring, and she didn't. Or at least, she told herself that she didn't. So what if the assassin was killed? *Dammit, this is a matter of survival!*

"The Wolfies will be dead soon. We can't hesitate much longer. Now go!"

"But what about afterward?"

"Run back to our supplies. If I'm not there, leave without me. I'll find you."

She shook her head, still disbelieving his words. But when she turned to speak to the assassin, he was already slinking off into the brush toward the circle of ravenous beasts. She stared for a moment, wondering if she should chase after him, try to change his mind. But no matter how fast her thoughts raced, she couldn't think of any other plan. There were simply too many frenzied Catlins.

*I have to hurry,* she thought. Soon they would move the Wolfies into the open, and then there would be no chance of a rescue.

Using what grace she had, Sora dove in the opposite direction, shimmying down the trunk to the lower branches, then moving as quietly as she could around the opposite side of the circle. She kept the firelight in sight, avoiding the crowds of Catlins that huddled on the ground. Luckily, the great beasts were distracted by the Panthera's dance, and none of them looked up or even seemed to hear her pass.

Once on the opposite side of the circle, she dropped to the ground and dashed into the cover of the massive roots. This close, the tree was impossibly large; she could have built a city amongst its branches.

She wove her way through the giant roots, using hanging fungi to shield herself. Finally, she was almost to the heart of the tree. Two Catlin guards watched the Wolfies. They crouched on either side of the prisoners, ready to pounce, their sleek arms heaving with muscle. They both carried spears wrapped with twine and beads. Ceremonial masks covered their faces.

Sora paused, just out of the firelight, slightly behind a large root. She wondered how much they could see through those masks. *No time, make your move,* her inner voice urged. She clutched her knife. No, too small. Shifting quietly, she sheathed the dagger and pulled her staff from her back.

Suddenly, a great roar split the air, and the drums stumbled to a stop. Sora didn't waste time looking. She surged forward and hammered the first guard over the head, hitting him so hard that her elbows jarred. Then she turned to the next guard and smashed him in the face, the mask shattering. The Catlin fell back, stunned by the blow. She kept hitting him, unsure if it was enough, until she heard a sickening crack. Blood poured from the Catlin's nose. She stared, heaving, only a little horrified. *I think that did the trick.*

Sweaty and shaking, she turned to the two Wolfies. Dorian's head sagged forward, unconscious. Burn watched her through wide amber eyes.

"Well done," he choked.

She nodded, already reaching for the bone knife strapped to the dead Catlin's chest, and yanked it into her grasp. Then she turned and crouched behind Burn, working on his bonds. His wrists were tied by tough, old vines. The vegetation was thick and stringy, difficult to slice through.

Finally, Burn was released. He grabbed the knife and dealt with Dorian's bonds much more quickly. Then he picked up the unconscious thief and put him over his shoulder.

"But Crash...." she started, turning back to the ceremonial circle. Her view was blocked by tree roots. She couldn't see what was going on.

"He'll find us. Let's go!" Burn said, and grabbed her arm. He dragged her back into the swamp. As soon as they cleared the firelight, she turned away from the Grandmother Tree, matching his steps, taking the lead. They had to go back for their supplies. And then...she touched her Cat's Eye, worry creasing her brow. She would have to find another direction.

But her thoughts kept returning to the assassin. *I'm not worried,* she told herself.

Yet she kept turning back, checking over her shoulder, hoping Crash was right behind them.

\* \* \*

The drums came to a stuttering halt. Silence fell over the arena like a dark cloud.

Crash stood in the circle of firelight, his eyes keen in the shadows. He could see almost as well in the darkness as in the daylight. The white fire danced to either side, crackling with unnatural intensity.

He held his dagger in his hand. He doubted he would need his sword.

The ground was already littered with dead bodies. The Panthera had killed the second warrior, an integral part of the dance. The blood of the warriors would go to strengthen the Grandmother Tree, and the Earth Goddess who supposedly slept beneath it. According to Catlin lore, the right sacrifice would satisfy the tree and awaken Her. *But not today.*

The third warrior backed quickly away from the Panthera, aligning himself with the crowd. He hissed, his tail lashing viciously. Crash ignored him. His main concern was the giant warlord that stood in the center of the circle, slightly crouched, staring through the slits of the mask.

"You," the Panthera hissed, raising a clawed finger. His voice was muffled by the painted wood. "You've tarnished our ceremony. The wrath of the Goddess will destroy you!"

Crash didn't flinch.

Then the Panthera grimaced, lifting the mask above his head, his eyes glowing bright in the darkness. "You've returned for the Wolfies," he sneered. "Strange, for your kind."

Crash couldn't see beneath the roots of the tree, not with all of the fire in the way, but he was certain that the Wolfies were gone. Sora had done her work. *Better than expected, perhaps.*

The Panthera snarled again, enraged by Crash's silence. "What do you want, Dark One? Have you come to bargain?" the great cat asked, standing up taller. His height dwarfed the assassin; the Panthera was almost twice his size.

The entire colony watched, hundreds of Catlin eyes staring from the shadows. A low rumble shook the trees—countless growls, low in the throat.

"I've come to challenge you," Crash said.

"What?" the Panthera grunted.

The assassin raised his knife slightly. "Fight me."

The Panthera's lips cracked into a wicked grin, saliva dripping from his yellow teeth. "You make this easy for me," he growled.

But Crash saw something else glimmering in the Panthera's eyes. Hesitation? Fear? He hoped so. It was hard to tell with Catlins; they were more bestial than humans. But fear would be a wise response.

Then, abruptly, the Panthera yowled with laughter. An act, performed in front of the colony. The beast wouldn't back down. Of that, Crash was certain.

"If you wish to die, so be it," the Panthera said. Then he pulled the mask back down over his face.

The drums started again, first one, then ten, then fifty, pounding out a fast, syncopated rhythm. The Catlins began to yowl in excitement, shifting from paw to paw, climbing on top of each other or taking to the trees, to get a better view. Crash fervently hoped that Sora and the Wolfies were long gone. He had given them as much time as he could.

The Panthera leapt towards him, like a charging bear. Crash waited, watching the beast's momentum, the roll of its paws in the dirt. At the last second, he leapt forward, rolling beneath the warlord's legs, missing his claws by fractions of an inch. The assassin regained his footing on the other side, behind his opponent. Then he leapt up on the Panthera's back.

The crowd of Catlins began wailing and shrieking. Their high-pitched keens split the night. The drums grew louder. He knew the spectators would not intervene. He had initiated a challenge, and the Catlins were bound by their own laws. The Panthera would defend his rank—or be killed. It was their way.

The warlord tossed himself to one side, rolling in the dirt, but not before Crash buried his dagger in the beast's back. His wooden mask flew off, tumbling across the ground. The Panthera crushed him backwards, but Crash held on, clamping his hands around the creature's throat.

The Panthera leapt to his feet and twisted, throwing Crash off with a mighty heave. But not before Crash could reclaim his dagger, dragging it out of the beast's back, causing as much damage on the exit wound as on the entrance wound.

The Panthera let out a ferocious roar, seething in pain. He shook himself, blood spattering to the ground, matting his fur. Then he stooped down and picked up a spear from the ground, whirling to face the assassin.

"A worthy opponent," the Panthera growled. "I would expect nothing less, Dark One." Then the giant lunged at him. The spear whirled and jabbed, left and right.

Crash recoiled like a snake. He deflected the spear with his dagger, sparks flying in the air. Then he grabbed the shaft and pulled the Panthera towards him. The beast let go of his weapon, stumbling backward, off-balance. Crash swung the length of the spear into the Panthera's head, connecting with his left cheek.

The Panthera staggered for a moment, shaking off the blow. Crash was somewhat surprised by the beast's endurance; he was certainly formidable.

Then the Panthera leapt at him again, lashing out with his claws, trying to rip the assassin in half. Crash dodged the giant paws, blocking with the spear. It would have been easier to just kill the beast, but he was trying to buy more time. Sora and the Wolfies needed to get as far away as possible—at least back to where they had stashed their supplies.

The Panthera's claws gouged his shoulder, a lucky blow. Crash hissed in a sharp breath, leaping away from his opponent, breaking off the close combat. They circled each other briefly, regaining their breath. The Panthera's tail lashed back and forth. He showed his teeth, growling low in his throat.

"I have killed creatures three times your size," the Panthera hissed. "To me, you are a darting gnat."

Crash smiled slowly. He didn't waste words while fighting. It was useless to taunt the dead.

"I'll kill you," the Panthera groaned. "And I'll flay the bodies of your companions, drain them of blood and burn them before the eyes of our wrathful Goddess...."

*Enough of this.* Crash's grip tightened on his weapon. He had stalled long enough.

The assassin charged the Panthera, the spear held in front of him. He feinted left, then jabbed to the right. He struck the Panthera in the face, plunging the spear into his eye.

With a yowl, the beast fell back, stumbling around the circle, his hands clamped to his face. Crash approached his opponent methodically, backing him into the corner of the ring, against one of the torches. The Panthera screamed in rage, clawing the air, unable to anticipate the assassin's moves.

Crash picked up a second spear from the ground. Taking full advantage, he plunged the weapon deep into the Panthera's chest, snapping through bone, puncturing the heart. Blood spurted around the shaft, gushing to the ground, turning the dirt to mud.

He released the spear and stepped back, allowing the Panthera's body to fall, gurgling, to the dark earth.

The drums stopped.

Crash didn't hesitate—he could sense the shock that ran through the colony like a lightning strike. The Catlins stood in silence, staring at their fallen leader.

He didn't give them time to respond. With a few swift steps, he launched into the roots of the Grandmother Tree, immediately swallowed up by shadows, then dashed to the other side, leaping onto a curtain of hanging fungi, pulling himself up into the tree. He jumped from branch to branch, moving as swiftly as possible, careful not to catch his clothes on any twigs.

Within seconds, he was gone.

# CHAPTER 15

Sora ran all night, stepping from branch to branch, swinging across vines, climbing up and down tree trunks. After returning for their bags, she had stopped briefly to regain her bearings. *Away,* she had thought, touching the Cat's Eye. *Away, through the swamp, to safety.*

Surprisingly, the necklace had surged in response, filling her with energy, almost toppling her from her feet. Its message was a thousand times stronger now. She felt as though it had burrowed deeper into her mind, planted its roots firmly in her thoughts. The Cat's Eye knew exactly what she wanted.

She nodded to Burn, turned and continued through the trees.

Close to morning, the three travelers collapsed. Burn was exhausted from carrying Dorian's unconscious body. Sora had checked the head wound twice; it wasn't bleeding anymore. They didn't know when the thief would wake up. She asked Burn about it, but he only shook his head.

They lay down for a brief rest. Sora shut her eyes, her body dragging her right into sleep.

About two hours later, she awoke to an unfamiliar noise. She sat up, her heart quickening, looking around in the dim morning light.

Crash hovered next to her, crouching low in the branches.

Sora's mouth was open; she was shocked. "Y-you're here!" she exclaimed, and was flooded by an unexpected wave of relief. She didn't linger on it. "How did you find us so quickly?"

"You left a clear trail," Crash said. "Come, we must continue. The Catlins might be following us. And if the ground is any indication, we are nearing the edges of the swamp."

Sora glanced over him, surprised again. His clothes were spattered in mud and leaves, his face scratched by branches. "Aren't you tired?" she asked. "You've been running all night!"

The assassin only stared at her.

"The end of the swamp?" Burn asked, sitting up from his roost in the tree. He was nestled slightly above them, closer to the trunk. He picked a leaf from his hair. "That's strangely optimistic of you. I hope you're right. What I would give for a mug of ale," he muttered. Then he shook his head slowly. "This is a nightmare."

"Yes, a nightmare," Sora murmured, staring at the trees. Dawn could barely be seen through the branches, but most of the forest was still in darkness. The canopy was so dense, sunlight usually wasn't visible until midday.

She had to admit that, in the filtered morning light, the trees appeared smaller and more widely spaced than the growth surrounding the Catlin colony. *We must have covered a lot of ground,* she thought, remembering the night before. Judging by the pain in her legs, she believed it.

"How is Dorian?" she suddenly asked, remembering her fallen friend. She turned, her eyes searching for him amidst the tree. He was curled up behind Burn, slightly higher in the branches, tied by a thick rope so he wouldn't fall off, still unconscious. She gazed at him in worry.

"He'll wake up," Burn said, giving her a soft look. It wasn't very comforting, given the thief's condition. Then he climbed up to the higher branches and started to untie him. "Let's go before those beasts catch up with us."

Sora couldn't agree more. They picked up camp and continued quickly through the trees. She was clumsier than the day before, her muscles sore and strained. Her eyes kept wandering to the ground far below them; the drop would certainly kill her. In her weakened state, she worried that she might miss a step.

Eventually, Crash stopped and turned to her. "Get on my back," he said bluntly.

"What?" Sora asked, panting and sweaty, slightly horrified by the idea.

"You're too slow. We're moving at a snail's pace compared to the Catlins." He knelt slightly on a large branch. "Get on."

Burn nodded to her.

Sora looked from one to the other, then let out an irritated breath. She was outnumbered. Stiff and hesitant, she climbed onto Crash's back and gripped him around the shoulders, wrapping her legs around his waist. She was suddenly self-conscious about how muddy their clothes were. She winced. She probably smelled like a mule.

They continued at a much faster pace, practically flying through the foliage. She couldn't believe the endurance of the two men. Burn, she could understand. But Crash...he was just an assassin, a regular human. Right?

* * *

That night, they stopped at the edge of a small stream. They were definitely approaching the border of Fennbog. There had been no streams in the swamp—just sinkholes and wetlands. They'd had to boil their water before drinking it.

The travelers set a small fire next to the stream and made a thin soup of tubers and wild onions. Burn found a nest of birds' eggs that they added to the mix.

At some point while they were eating, Dorian awakened.

"Ugh," the thief groaned, his eyes slitting open. He put a hand to his head. "What happened?" He glanced around their camp, squinting against the firelight, taking in their surroundings. "I suppose we're not dead, at least," he muttered.

Sora almost dropped her tin cup. She leapt to her feet and ran to the thief's side, kneeling close. "Are you all right? How do you feel?" she asked, the words rushing out before she could stop them.

"You took a nasty blow to the back of the skull," Burn rumbled.

"I vaguely remember," Dorian replied, his voice weak.

Sora put a hand behind the thief's shoulders and helped him to sit up. "Gently now," she murmured. She tried to quench the worry inside of her. She didn't like thinking that the thief could have died —and how much that scared her.

Dorian blinked, a bemused expression crossing his face. Then he winced. "I should get hit on the head more often. You almost seem concerned, sweetness."

Sora paused, the thief halfway in a sitting position, and almost dropped him back to the ground. *What am I doing?* she thought. Before their interlude with the Catlins, she had made a point of hating the three men, reminding herself again and again that they were evil, heartless scum. But now, after so much had happened, she couldn't summon her anger anymore. Somewhere along the line, her guard had fallen. She had risked her life for these men.

And...they had risked their lives for her.

"Don't mention it," she grunted, and settled him back against a log. She held out a cup of soup for him. "It's mostly water," she said.

"Ah, grass soup, my favorite," the thief mumbled, but downed the meal anyway. He moved slowly and stiffly, resettling his head against the hard log. "What I wouldn't give for a pot roast right now," he murmured. "Or a loaf of bread."

"A big, thick wedge of cheese," Burn added from across the fire. "A warm bottle of wine."

"I'd do with a soft bed," Sora replied, grinning slightly. She looked up to see the three men gazing at her, their expressions something like surprise. She glanced away, self-conscious.

The evening stretched on. Burn lay down to sleep while Crash took to the trees, keeping watch. Sora sat next to Dorian for a while, staring into the fire, keeping him company. They didn't speak, but shared the same exhausted silence. Then she let out a loud yawn. She stood up, thinking she would get some much needed sleep.

Dorian's hand grabbed her wrist. He was surprisingly strong. "Wait," he murmured. "Just a minute."

She turned to him, wondering what this was about.

"Can you...check my head?" He gazed up at her, a peculiar expression in his eyes. Vulnerability?

Sora didn't know what to make of it. She sighed. "Dorian, I'm not a Healer...."

"No, that's not what I mean."

She frowned, looking down at him. His effeminate features had grown on her; the sharp jaw, pointed nose and wide blue eyes. But his expression gave her pause. He looked...scared.

"Then what?" she asked, keeping her voice low. She sensed that Dorian didn't want to be overheard.

"With your Cat's Eye...can you...see if Volcrian's spell is still present?"

*Oh.* In all the excitement, she had almost forgotten about the mage. She glanced at Burn's sleeping form, the regular rise and fall of his breaths. Then she looked up to the trees, wondering if Crash was watching them, if he could hear what Dorian was saying. The thief's request made her nervous. She could remember his attack in the swamp, the way he had come after her, trying to take her life. It left a cold feeling in her gut. He suddenly seemed much more dangerous than just a wounded friend.

But perhaps she was worrying for no reason. Burn said the spell was weak. Volcrian hadn't used much of Dorian's blood. Perhaps it had worn off.

"Well, what do you want me to do?" she asked, curious.

"I don't know...I think you need to touch me."

"What?" Sora balked.

"Shhh!" Dorian glanced around, but Burn was still sleeping, and Crash was nowhere to be seen. He met her gaze and raised a finger to his head. "Touch my head. I don't know if it'll do anything, but...can you tell me if...if your Cat's Eye senses anything wrong?"

Sora let out a long breath, considering the request. "Well, I don't know if it works like that...." she said slowly. She had already tried this method once, and it hadn't been very effective. "But I guess I can try again," she murmured. Maybe things would be different now that her bond was stronger.

Dorian seemed relieved. He settled back against the log, waiting.

Sora wasn't sure how to begin. She wasn't very skilled at using her Cat's Eye—half of the time, she felt like it was using her instead. Finally, she decided to mimic what she had done last time. That is, set her fingers lightly on Dorian's temples and see what might happen. She did so, waiting for some sort of shock or revelation.

His skin was smooth and slightly clammy beneath the pads of her fingers, but Sora tried to concentrate past that, past the intensity of his eyes. She had to figure out what she was looking for, which was hard to do since she hadn't a clue.

Just as the thought crossed her mind, she felt something stir in the depths of her consciousness. The alien presence unwound itself, pressing into her thoughts, flowing down her body and into her fingers. The sensation was strange, electrifying. Dimly she saw Dorian's eyes widen in wonder.

The Cat's Eye searched, casting around for a sign of...well...anything. No, too broad; she had to narrow it down. *Wolfy magic,* she thought, hoping the Cat's Eye would understand. This necklace had been created back in the time of the races, right? It had to know what Wolfy magic felt like. *Blood,* she thought, trying to help it along. *Something unnatural.*

She waited for several minutes, the Cat's Eye stirring through Dorian's mind like an eel in a dark pond. But there was no sense of discovery, no magic, except for the dormant power that flowed through the Wolfy's veins. *And yet—yet I sense something....* It was a mere flicker, there and gone. Like a shadow hovering over his mind, an unknown shade.

She couldn't take it anymore. The sensation was beginning to border on something like pain, and she felt a bead of sweat slip down her brow.

"Nothing," she said, dropping her hands, though she felt like that was a lie. There was a residue of sorts. Something vague and lingering.

Dorian let out a sigh of relief, but still looked troubled. "Thanks, love," he said. She waited for some witty remark, a teasing word. But there was none.

"Sorry," she murmured. "I don't know everything about the necklace. At least, not yet."

Dorian grinned at this, the worry melting from his face. "Look at you, taking charge," he remarked. "You'll be an expert in no time."

Sora allowed herself a small smile, but it felt empty. She wished that were true...but she had a feeling it would take a long time to learn all of the necklace's secrets. Perhaps an entire lifetime.

"You should get some sleep," she said quietly, and moved away to the fire, stretching out on the hard ground. She wished she still had her bedroll, or at least something clean to wrap herself in, but only her tattered cloak protected her against the cold.

"No," Dorian said quietly. "*You* should get some sleep, love. I'll stay awake for a while yet. I've been sleeping long enough."

She nodded, giving him another slight smile. She must have looked as tired as she felt.

Sora cushioned her head in her arms, wishing she could relax. But every snap of the fire made her jolt back awake, every subtle movement in the woods. The Catlins seemed to lurk just beyond her line of sight. She kept listening for a sign from the darkness, like the telltale shift of leaves. She couldn't quite believe that they were safe, even with Crash watching over them. They had been running for a long, long time.

But her body was exhausted. There was no fighting it. Eventually, she slipped into troubled dreams, falling through dense gray clouds, plunging into an ice-cold sleep....

* * *

Several more days passed this way. The four travelers were exhausted, Sora especially. She didn't know where the men got their endurance. Food was scarce, though as the ground grew more solid and the trees smaller, they were able to find rabbits and wild hens. Finally, the swamp seemed to have turned into a genuine forest, interrupted by brief patches of wetland.

They walked long distances, stopping for brief rests, eating what they could find, special kinds of flowers or weeds or tubers. The occasional rodent. They slept in short, tense spurts, unable to fully relax; stopping was dangerous and left them open for attack.

She didn't know if the Catlins were following. At first, she had been certain that the beasts were only a league behind them. Her Cat's Eye had tingled occasionally, warning her of unseen magic, though she hadn't bothered to warn her friends. The magic would sweep over them, casting about like a net, and she always touched the necklace, certain of its protection. Each day, its presence grew stronger in her mind.

Now that they were out of the swamp proper, she felt more confident. She doubted the wild beasts would risk discovery. If she had learned one thing, it's that Catlins valued their privacy.

Almost a week later, four figures stumbled wearily out of the woods bordering the swamp. If a passerby had seen them, it would have seemed that four amazingly human-shaped rocks had appeared next to the road. They were covered in so much mud and dirt, they were almost unrecognizable. Luckily, no one was on the road to see them. The sun had almost set behind the hills and the countryside was deserted.

Sora sat with her head in the crook of Burn's arm, somewhere between dozing and sleeping. Crash, sitting next to her, had his eyes closed and seemed to be in a meditative state. On the other side of him was Dorian, his sweaty forehead resting against his knees. All four travelers were exhausted, on the verge of sleep.

After a few minutes, Burn looked off into the distance and squinted, his eyes narrowed against the glare of the setting sun.

"Crash?" The Wolfy glanced at his smaller companion. "Do you see that town?"

"Hmmm?"

"That town, over there across the field."

Crash opened his eyes. "Yes, I see it."

Sora listened with half an ear.

"We can make it by nightfall, get a room at an inn," the Wolfy mercenary suggested. "It looks about three miles away."

"Too far," Dorian said. "We'll never make it."

Sora grinned at the irony. She was surprised that she could still smile.

"You're welcome to stay here," Crash replied.

Dorian sighed and rose slowly to his feet, picking up one of their bags. Sora didn't know why they had kept the satchels—they were almost all empty. "The sooner we start, the sooner we get there," he said.

Burn stood up as well, disrupting Sora's resting place. Then the mercenary reached down and pulled her to her feet. He gave her a slight grin, then turned toward town, Dorian by his side. "We'll take the lead," he said. "No rush now—save your energy."

Sora nodded, too tired to care, and watched the two Wolfies set off across the fields: Burn, his hair flaring gold with the light of the setting sun, Dorian trotting along next to him. They were speaking to each other but she couldn't hear what was being said, and they walked quickly. The town was still some ways in the distance. She knew they were as eager for a soft bed and a warm meal as she was.

Crash hung back, lifting the other bags. Sora fell into step next to him, an uneasy silence between them. She had saved his life twice now, but she still had mixed feelings about it. What happened when they reached the town? Would he release her? Volcrian was far behind them—they didn't need her anymore, right?

She didn't want to bring that up quite yet; it seemed like bad timing. Reminding the assassin of her captive state might cause more problems than it would solve.

With each step they took away from the woods, Sora felt her heart lighten slightly. *We made it,* she finally thought in relief. That phrase kept repeating over and over in her mind until she smiled. She had survived her first journey, her first venture into peril. She couldn't believe how far she had come, how much she had learned.

Her thoughts drifted back to Mayville, to her father's manor, to the price on her head. Lord Seabourne would never find her this far away, and she doubted the King's men were still looking for her. It had to have been over a month. A year from now, they might have forgotten everything.

*What now?* she thought. She hoped fervently that they would let her go. Given their journey together, the Wolfies seemed to look at her more like a friend. Crash was the only one she had to convince. She glanced sideways at him, wondering if he was considering the same thing. Perhaps she would bring it up tomorrow, after a warm meal and a good night's sleep. Then maybe...she could begin her quest to find her mother.

* * *

Volcrian woke up with a start. He was wedged between an old widow and a greasy farmer who smoked incessantly on a corncob pipe. Falling asleep had been a problem in the cramped carriage, so he brewed a sleeping tonic at the last home station, preparing his own herbs, hoping it would make the hours go by faster. He had just dozed off...but waking up was far worse.

The mage gritted his teeth as a rush of pain shot through his crippled hand. He groaned, trying to ease his fingers open, to loosen the cramped muscles. Then another shock of pain ripped through him. He almost cried out.

Outside, early evening light rolled past, the sunset dotted with vague clouds. The woodland was dense and wild, with low scrub oaks and dense boysenberries. They were miles past the Sinclair lands, far from the Fallcrest estate, heading steadily Northwest. He checked his pocketwatch. It was a little after four.

He had switched carriages at the last home station, boarding a coach to the City of Crowns, disgruntled to learn that it would take them almost a month to arrive. That was the driver's best estimate, trusting that the mud wagon didn't fall apart, that the horses stayed in good shape, and that thieves didn't attack them on the road.

He hadn't expected the pain. It rolled around his body like a ball of fire, coming to rest somewhere deep in his gut.

Volcrian frowned, placing a hand on his chest. The ache grew and dimmed like an ocean wave. A horrible suspicion crept into his thoughts. The pain nestled there for a moment, then seemed to fade away, leaving him cold and shaky.

He grimaced. This was no ordinary ache.

He closed his eyes again, his forehead throbbing, sweat sprouting above his brow. Somewhere beneath the pain, he felt a strange sensation. A certain darkness, like a gaping hole splitting his stomach open, draining him of life. *What is happening?* he thought, trying not to panic.

He was suddenly certain that this pain had something to do with his spell. He wondered about the four travelers lost in the swamp. Had the wraiths found them? Somehow, this pain stemmed from his magic. It left a dark residue on his thoughts. He needed to know what was happening.

Trying to stay calm, Volcrian took deep breaths and closed his eyes, seeking the quiet place in his mind where he could access his creations. Usually, a Wolfy mage was tied to his minions through blood, and so sinking into their minds was relatively easy. But this time, it was different. The bond was strange, unstable, like trying to grasp a snake. He received no clear picture of what the wraiths were doing. They seemed far more autonomous than his other creations. A moment of doubt entered his thoughts. Perhaps they would not be so easy to control.

Volcrian shifted, adjusting his back against the hard seat. His nose wrinkled from the smoke of the corncob pipe. *Focus,* he told himself. He had other ways of spying on his prey. Better ways, perhaps.

He tried again, sinking deeper into his meditation until the pain subsided, until the smoke was gone and his mind was filled with cold mist. Then he cast out, searching for Dorian, for a brief glimpse through his eyes. But there was nothing.

Nothing? He searched again.

Only blackness.

Another wave of pain struck him, and Volcrian smashed his hand down on the seat. The farmer next to him jumped, gave him a queer look, then turned back to the window.

Volcrian glared at the man, as though this was all his fault. The blood bond had been weak from the beginning. Perhaps it had worn off. *Blast it all,* he thought viciously. *The Winds take you!* His bond with the thief was broken. He would be unable to spy on them, to learn what his prey was doing.

The assassin had outfoxed him again, and there was nothing he could do.

The carriage rolled onward, up a slight hill, then down into rougher terrain. The seats jolted and rocked. The floorboards quivered. The wheels squeaked. Somewhere up ahead, he heard the driver call to the horses, slowing the team, moving steadily over the uneven ground. The inside of the carriage became suffocatingly hot, filled with the stench of human bodies.

Volcrian could do no more than seethe in anger, the pain rolling and subsiding like an ocean wave.

# CHAPTER 16

Sora looked at the distant box-like shapes of the houses, the sloping roofs, barely a few lumps on the horizon. She could already feel the soft feather mattress against her sore muscles. And fresh food! Warm bread, thick stew, vegetables, apples dipped in sugar, oranges and cream....

She had never before appreciated true hunger. She was practically drooling on her shirt. She couldn't wait to stuff her face.

She sighed in longing, her mind full of warm butter and scones. They were still a mile from town. The field stretched before her, the sun sinking slowly. Peaceful silence lay over the grass, only disturbed by a slight wind. She had never been on this side of the swamp before. It was drier and warmer than she remembered by her manor.

"Sora! Get down!"

Abruptly Crash tackled her to the ground.

A black shape whizzed over their heads. Sora, who was lying face down in the tall grass, looked up in surprise. *What?* At first she thought it was a large bird. She scanned the field desperately, trying to figure out had happened. Why was Crash so alarmed?

Distantly, she could see a flying object hurtling toward the two Wolfies. It was far too big to be a bird or a rock. A horse? She squinted, unable to see its legs. It wasn't shaped like any animals she knew....

Then the shape paused a short distance from her Wolfy

friends. Now that she could see it more clearly, she could hardly believe her eyes. The shape was...floating?

An insubstantial black cloak drifted around the dark figure, blurring and blending like smoke. She couldn't see it clearly no matter how long she stared—her eyes seemed to slide over it, unable to focus. It shifted and flickered, forever subtly different, changing shape over and over again.

The wind gusted across the clearing, picking up force. The figure shimmered and appeared in a new position. There was a glint of light. A blade emerged out of the mist-like clothing, long and thin, like a sword—no, narrower—almost like a giant needle. Sora recognized it from her old fencing lessons. A rapier.

Then the creature threw back its head and screamed into the twilight. It was a bone-chilling sound, racing over her skin, shooting down her spine.

Crash leapt from the ground a second later, sprinting toward the Wolfies, his sword drawn. Sora watched, dumbstruck. Then she scrambled to her feet and dashed after him.

Dorian and Burn were more than a hundred feet ahead of her. She charged at full speed. Whatever this thing was, it was definitely no Catlin, and it definitely meant them harm. She was so tired though—exhausted—it felt like she was running through thick water.

Light glinted as Burn drew his massive sword. The steel was thick, sharp and easily visible, almost as long as he was tall. Burn launched himself at the apparition, the blade whirling through the air, creating a sound like a wind tunnel.

The wraith screamed again and raised its skinny rapier. The two clashed together, tendrils of fire leaping up from the blades.

Sora's mouth was wide open and she almost came to a stop. There was no way the rapier could last against such a huge sword. And yet it held. Magic, it had to be. She touched her necklace, but no sound came from her Cat's Eye, no alarm.

Sora could see Dorian behind Burn, his silver hair whipping back and forth. The wind picked up again, blowing stronger and stronger, as though engaging in the fight. The smaller Wolfy dodged around to the other side of the creature, daggers out. He tried to take a knife to the apparition, slashing at its cloak, but to no effect. The wraith screamed again in outrage, turning to swat at the thief with its sword.

Sora wished she knew what was happening, how she could help, but she could only watch uselessly. She wasn't as skilled as the men and knew that she would get in the way—or get her head cleaved off by Burn's sword.

Finally the Cat's Eye woke up. She heard a faint jingle at the edge of her hearing, like wind chimes—but the necklace seemed confused. The sound faded in and out with the wind. Magic, but something else, something different. The necklace sampled the creature's energy, and she could feel a strange resistance, like a rock against sand, a dark cloud in an empty sky, or...or a drop of blood in water.

*Blood.*

Information flooded her, sudden knowledge. The core of this magic was blood. Only Wolfies used blood. This was Volcrian's creation. The very thought made her heart stop.

Crash flung himself into the fray ahead of her. The assassin leapt out of the grass almost as suddenly as the wraith had. Three against one, and still the creature was holding its own.

The assassin attacked from behind, his sword slashing through the air. The mercenary blocked from the front, meeting the phantom blow for blow...and yet...nothing happened. The apparition seemed as inconsistent as air, fading and reappearing, like smoke in the wind. Crash's blade swung left and right, striking nothing.

The creature's sword, however, was solid and real, deadly sharp.

Burn blocked a jab and swung in riposte, coming from an unexpected angle. The Wolfy's giant blade plunged through the cloak and into the creature, a killing blow—except that the sword passed through the phantom as though slicing fog. A creature of mist. Nothing more.

Sora was stunned. It was magic, it had to be—and yet it seemed a part of nature, a figment of their minds.

There was an unearthly scream that arose from the ground, shaking through the grass. The creature struck out with some sort of energy force, like a gust of darkness; it knocked Burn from his feet. *Whooompphh!* The giant Wolfy tumbled backwards as easily as a child, landing in the grass.

Crash dove to his side, seeking to shield the mercenary. But as the assassin moved, the wraith's sword swung down. It was perfectly aimed, too fast to dodge. Inescapable....

"No!" Dorian threw himself in front of Crash and Burn, taking the blow head on. His two daggers crossed above his head to block the sword. Sora watched helplessly. Two puny daggers couldn't contend with a strike like that....

It happened too fast for her to scream. The wraith's sword fell downward in a perfect arc, slicing Dorian's daggers in half as though they were made of paper. She couldn't look away. The sword pierced the thief, striking him clean across the chest. Blood sprayed the air.

Then Sora was moving, though she didn't know it at the time. No sound reached her ears and she couldn't feel the ground. She charged forward, an inhuman sound ripping from her throat. Her Cat's Eye jingled madly in her ears, interrupted by the pounding of her heart. She sped across the grass in a blur, her staff forgotten.

"Dorian!" she screamed, a millisecond before she hit him. Her small body tackled the Wolfy with amazing force and sent him flying limply away from the wraith—she didn't know if he was alive or dead. Almost immediately there was a blinding flash. When Sora's eyes cleared, she found herself standing with arms outstretched, a dome of light around her, the Cat's Eye's shield. It engulfed both her body and her friends, who were lying in the grass at her back, unable to do anything.

This time, however, the shield wasn't perfect. The wraith screamed in rage and slammed its weapon down. The blow bounced back, energy crackling in the air. The shield trembled and shook.

The wraith kept pounding against it. *Clang! Clang! Clang!* The sword rang out in the chill air. Every time the weapons collided, a flash of brilliant light burst around them. Sora flinched with every blow. Fear lurched inside of her. Somehow, the wraith was breaking through.

She gripped the necklace in her hand desperately, focusing all of her mind on it.

The wraith drew its sword back, let out a terrifying scream, then plunged the blade down in a two-handed swing. The rapier struck the barrier of energy and pressed into it, denting it. The dome flickered around her dangerously. *No!*

The Cat's Eye made a static popping sound.

*Crack!*

The shield popped. A ripple of energy moved outward, like a small explosion.

Sora tried to throw herself out of the way—too late.

Her upper body exposed, the wraith jammed its sword deep between her ribs. The air left her in a sudden rush. Pain. Silence.

Then a dull whining in her ears. An enraged ringing from the Cat's Eye....

Energy surged forward, shooting from her body up through the blade, into the creature before her. The wraith screamed.

For a moment, the sound of clanging bells was heard by all of her companions. Then the Cat's Eye erupted in a whirlwind of green and yellow light, attacking the wraith with the fury of a tempest. The creature continued to scream, its voice carrying unnaturally across the fields, on and on and on. The wind whipped Sora's hair around her face. The necklace drained the phantom of life; it flickered like a dying fire. The black robes seemed to break apart, turning to dust, blown away piece by piece.

Finally, there was nothing left but a stain of blood upon the grass.

Sora continued to hold her necklace, stunned, staring at the empty grass, the open fields. Then she looked down at a larger stain, spreading across her shirt. Strangely, she hadn't felt any pain beside the initial pinch of the blade. It was as though she was staring at someone else's body.

She turned to look down at her two companions. Crash was the first she saw, and he stared back at her, his eyes wide. Burn, too, seemed frozen to the ground; his hands were wedged into the grass. He stared at her in disbelief.

Then her gaze slowly traveled to Dorian's silent form, a pool of blood around his body. His face was turned down toward the earth, his eyes open, sightless—vacant. Was he breathing?

She already knew the answer. The sight would have unnerved her, but at the moment, she seemed incapable of feeling anything.

A small stream of fluid entered her mouth, salty and thick. A trickle of blood leaked from the corner of her lip. She tried to swallow but her throat wouldn't work. She felt like her body was slowly solidifying, becoming stiff and useless.

Suddenly she was afraid. She looked back at her companions and recognized the look on their faces. A wave of nausea hit. Suddenly, she knew this was not a wound she would be recovering from.

Sora took a step toward her companions. It took a great amount of effort. Her boot bumped against Dorian's still hand.

Her hands found the blade of the sword that protruded from between her ribs, just to assure herself that she wasn't dreaming.

Her movement snapped the men into action. With her next step, Crash was up from the ground. He grabbed the hilt of the blade, giving it a fierce tug. Sora felt like the air had been sucked out of her. A scream found its way out of her throat—the pain was consuming, intense, unlike anything she had ever felt before. Like her body was splitting in two.

As soon as the blade was fully out, it flickered in the air, wavering before her eyes.

Then it disintegrated in the wind, blowing away just as the

wraith had, leaving only the black hilt.

Dizziness overcame her. Sora collapsed forward with a shudder, the pain too intense to stand. The assassin caught her.

"Are you both all right?" she managed to whisper. It was barely audible.

Crash lowered her to the ground and laid her out, his expression darker than she had ever seen. He wiped the blood from her mouth with his muddy sleeve and allowed her eyes to rove over his face, studying his cunning, sharp features, following the scar into his shirt.

"Idiot girl...." he murmured. "You should have stayed put."

"But you would have died," Sora whispered. *You all would have died.*

Crash continued to gaze at her, his mouth slightly open. No words came. Was he surprised?

It was too late to wonder. His face swam before her. Slowly her vision blurred, her ears dimmed.

Darkness.

* * *

Crash's mouth was open. He felt like his heart had just stopped. What had she said? Her last words? Not a heroic speech or the desperate promises of a fading friend. No, she had said her thoughts plainly, directly, and yet they changed everything. This girl—this spoiled, rich, infuriating girl—had given her life for his. She had saved him.

He had never felt anything like this before.

He watched her go limp on the ground, and suddenly his heart hammered against his ribs, his lungs seized. He felt like he was choking on air. Ice flowed through him. His hands gripped Sora's shoulders in an effort to regain himself. *What is happening to me?* he thought furiously. *Why am I suddenly so- so....?* Abruptly, the assassin blinked. *Could this be...fear?*

Worse than that—terror. He had never known it before. Since he was a child, he had been trained in the ways of his people, to think beyond death, to live with removed indifference, to see the world through eyes of stone. He had first killed at the age of fourteen. He had known violence his entire life. Fear was not even a word in his original tongue.

But there was no other explanation. He had never experienced such helplessness, the way his blood raced and his stomach clenched—it couldn't be anything else. Couldn't be, and yet....He closed his eyes in pain, touching the girl's golden hair. *Why now?* he wondered. *Why do I feel this now?*

It was a question to be left unanswered. Sora was nothing but a rich brat, kidnapped out of precaution, kept only because of her necklace. She was an asset as long as she had the Cat's Eye—otherwise she was expendable, nothing more than excess weight. How many times had he looked upon her in disgust? He had watched her smooth hands, butter-soft and free of callouses, grip the staff. They were hands for doing needlework and writing letters, not the hands of a warrior. He had grimaced many times at her naivete, at her senseless ideas, her assumptions about the world that only a sheltered child would have.

He didn't like a shred about her—did he? *No, of course not.* And yet...and yet....

And yet—she had saved his life.

Crash's eyes turned from the girl's soft face to the thief's dead body, lying crumpled and lifeless nearby. The Wolfy mage wasn't moving, and Crash knew that he never would move again.

He had seen countless others die, engaged in battle or sleeping in their beds, unaware. Different races, different people. It wasn't in his nature to think in terms of friends or enemies, to hold onto bodies, spirits. All beings were momentarily animated, but ultimately impermanent, destined to return to their original state. *The living are meant to die*, his mentor had once said. *They are specks of dust, momentary flashes of light. In this way, you must understand—what is alive now is already dead.*

*But...but the fields, the birds, the forest....*

*It is an illusion. Everything is Death.*

Crash shook his head—words from a long time ago, another lifetime. He had escaped that world, that realm of emptiness, but he knew that it would never leave him. Not the indifference, the huge disconnect between himself and those around him. Sometimes he truly felt like stone; felt more like the ground beneath them than the people who walked on it.

He didn't think he had changed—no, it was impossible to outgrow one's true nature—but for some reason, this girl was different. He didn't know why, but he was stricken, entranced by her silent body. *Look away,* he told himself. But he couldn't even do that.

He wasn't responsible for her, hadn't made any pretense of being so—hadn't made any promises.

*I owe her my life. We all owe her our lives....*

Crash's hand went to her face and cupped one cheek. His eyes traveled over her face, her pale cheeks, the delicate bone structure.

Then a slight movement caught his attention. He paused. Not daring to hope, he tore off his glove and rested his fingers against her mouth, and felt the constriction in his chest loosen. Yes, she was still breathing—and by the gods, he would keep her that way!

"Burn, watch her!" he shouted in urgency. "Keep her warm!"

Burn, who had been staring at Dorian's body in sorrow, shot to his feet. "She's not dead?" he asked in disbelief.

"She's not dead, but we don't have much time." The assassin's green eyes were fierce with determination. "Stay here! I must find a Healer."

The Wolfy nodded, kneeling next to Sora's still body and removing his cloak, placing it on top of her.

Crash turned and ran toward town, moving swiftly through the grass. Within seconds, he was no more than a shadow against the twilight, consumed by darkness.

*Stupid girl, you should have let me die,* he thought. Specks of light could be seen against the night sky, distant windows and flickering street lamps. How many times had he wished for death, for a killing blow? But it seemed the gods weren't done with him yet.

A shudder ran through him. He might have prayed to the Goddess at that moment, begged a favor from the deity he had never spoken to, but She wasn't his to ask. No, his people did not pray to the Wind. They worshiped something darker, something far less forgiving, whose name remained buried deep in the earth, who had stayed hidden from the world since its very creation. And it was not His way to spare a life.

He reached the gates of the town. Two figures moved to intercept him. Crash intended to bowl straight through them, but the gates were closed, and the guards stood with their swords drawn.

"Halt!" the first guard yelled.

"State your name and intention!" the second guard shouted.

Crash breezed past them, fast as a whip. He flung himself on the closed iron gates and climbed swiftly, propelling himself upward with his strong legs. He reached the top and dropped to the other side, twelve feet to the ground.

When he turned back, the two guards stared at him through the steel grates.

"Seeking a Healer," Crash said. "Is there one in town?"

The first guard pointed down the street, his face still frozen in shock. The second guard glanced sideways at him, then grabbed his hand, lowering his finger. "State your name, or we'll have to arrest you!" he called.

Crash ignored them. He turned and dashed down the street, his eyes searching back and forth, combing the closed doors and bright windows for any sign of a Healer's trade.

The town was made up of short square buildings and cobbled roads. It looked quaint and friendly, small enough for everyone to know each other. The street lamps had recently been lit and cast flickering shadows across the ground. It was growing cold, unusual for this side of the swamp—a sign from the Goddess? He hoped not.

He started down the winding street. Most of the town's inhabitants had retired to dinner, but a few still wandered outside, just in time to see the black-clad man rush past them. He would doubtlessly be the topic of conversation in the morning, but he wasn't concerned. By the time Volcrian rounded the swamp, he doubted anyone would remember him. Despite the many looks, no one called out.

A few minutes later, Crash found the kind of fellow he was looking for—a thin, honest type with large watery eyes and wispy blond hair. He was wringing his hands nervously, sitting out on his doorstep, perhaps trying to calm himself by taking in the night air. The assassin didn't linger on why he was outside; he simply acted.

"You," he said harshly, panting. He wasn't used to being out of breath, but Fennbog had taken its toll. "Where is the Healer?"

The man stared up at him, eyes wide, his face turning pale. "I-I..." he stuttered.

"Out with it!" the assassin said. "This is a matter of life or death!"

The man's eyes dropped to the daggers at his belt. His expression was obvious—full of fear. Crash groaned; he could have stabbed the man right there in irritation.

At that moment the door to the house opened. A woman appeared, outlined by the light of the room behind her, a halo of golden hair around her face. She spoke sharply, "Well? Here I am! Now who's asking for a Healer?"

Crash glared up at her. "I am. It's urgent."

The woman sighed. "How urgent? It's late and I don't have the supplies to tend cattle...."

"A girl in the field is bleeding to death. She was stabbed."

There was a pause. The man's gaze went to Crash's belt again. The assassin could read that look. He wanted to roll his eyes—*no, I'm not at fault*. At least, not entirely.

The woman came down the step and lit the lantern in her hand. Warm light illuminated her face. Crash noted that she was damp with sweat, as though she had just come from a heavy workout. She looked down at the thin man. "Oh, Jase, there you are. Your wife is fine." Then a smile grew on her face. "She only needed a few stitches. It's a beautiful boy."

The man nodded in relief. Then he scurried inside, casting one last fearful glance over his shoulder before slamming the door shut.

The woman turned back to Crash. "I'm the only Healer in these parts. It would appear that you got lucky. Now step over here so I can get a good look at you, then tell me again what the matter is."

Crash could have strangled her with impatience. *Calm,* his thoughts murmured. *Be like a stone.* He composed himself—barely.

He stepped forward from the shadows, ready to growl in frustration, then stopped in surprise.

The lady in front of him, though quite a bit older than Sora, looked almost exactly like her. From her hair, slightly less vibrant, to her short stature and firm chin. The biggest difference was how she carried herself—like a warrior. From what he could tell, her arms were tight and defined, her stance solid and straight. She wore several different knives at her belt. Definitely not what one would expect from a Healer.

The woman stared up at him with shrewd blue eyes, then let out a breath, equally surprised. "Rare," she said, "to meet an assassin this far from the City."

Crash frowned at her words, her piercing gaze. He saw suspicion furrow her brow. He shook his head, trying to clear it.

"There's no time for an explanation," he said quietly. "Will you come?"

The woman waved her hand. "Yes. Show me the girl. I'll see what I can do. Just a moment while I get my horse."

Crash watched the woman walk away, her bold stride, her fast steps. *Perhaps I am imagining it,* he thought, staring at the glow of her hair. There was no time to waste on questions. He needed to get back to Sora—now.

* * *

Crash leaned over the Healer's shoulder, sitting behind her on the horse. He saw perfectly through the darkness, easily spotting Burn and Sora in the field. The Wolfy had lain down next to her, holding Sora close to his body, trying to keep her warm as she went into shock.

He let out a breath—one he felt he had been keeping for hours. Burn wouldn't hold her like that if she were dead.

"There," he said, pointing through the darkened grass.

"I see them," the woman replied.

She reined in the horse a few yards from the fallen figures, leaped from the saddle in a fluid motion and grabbed the lantern that hung from the horse's side. She lit the lantern, holding it over her head, illuminating a wide circle of grass. Then the Healer paused, staring at Burn, her eyes becoming wide. Shock registered on her face. "A Wolfy," she murmured. Then she glanced to the side, her eyes lingering on Dorian's dead body in the grass. She blinked. "Two?" she murmured. "A friend of yours?"

Burn waved his hand. "No time for that," he said. "Please...."

The Healer shook herself, hands trembling ever so slightly on the lantern, then dropped down next to Sora's body. The girl was wrapped in Burn's cloak and the Healer carefully peeled it back.

Crash dismounted more slowly. Now he was able to see the paleness of Sora's skin, the blue tint to her lips. She looked like a small, fragile child. That terrible fear gripped him again. Perhaps it was too late.

They watched the Healer thoroughly inspect the wound. She wiped away the caked blood. Once exposed, the puncture appeared narrow and thin to the untrained eye, only about two inches wide. By the amount of blood lost, however, it was terribly deep; who knew if she had a damaged organ or lung? Blood also dripped from Sora's mouth. She had been pierced almost completely through the chest.

Crash shook his head darkly. How could she possibly still be alive? The Cat's Eye? His eyes darted to the seemingly innocent necklace. The stone would protect its host at all costs. What else did he not know about its powers?

"This is very deep," the Healer finally murmured.

Burn stared at the woman, his eyes bright gold in the lantern light. He didn't speak, but Crash knew what he was thinking. He, too, felt like he was staring at a ghost, as though Sora's image crouched over her own body.

But there were subtle differences. The woman's hands showed her age, rough and veined. Confident. On closer inspection, he could see the lines around her tired eyes, a difference in the hairline, slightly thinner lips. Sora's hair was a deeper gold.

The Healer looked up at them. "We have to move her to my cabin," she said, very serious. "Her Cat's Eye is holding her together, but it won't last much longer. She has lost a lot of blood." She motioned to the other side of the field, west of the town. "My home is in a clearing in the woods. We might be able to save her. No time to lose." She hesitated only slightly. "Are either of you hurt?"

Crash didn't respond immediately. He was surprised at the woman's knowledge of the Cat's Eye. She had identified the necklace and avoided touching it, aware of its ability to bond. For a Healer, she seemed to know a lot about the stone. Perhaps too much.

He decided not to mention it—for now. "No," he answered her question.

"Nothing serious," Burn said at the same time. "Sora is all that matters now."

The woman nodded sharply. Then she turned to the fallen girl. "Tell me, is that her name—Sora?"

"Yes," Crash said. He watched the woman's face intently.

She seemed thoughtful, momentarily withdrawn. Her eyes roamed over Sora's body, face, perhaps a bit too long. Then she turned back to them. "Come on, help me move her."

\* \* \*

Holding Sora securely in his arms, Crash charged across the field on horseback. The beast did not need urging or directions, and personally, he was far too tired to do either. Behind him, the Healer clung tightly to his waist, trying to keep him from falling off. It was working, too. He was so tired that he could have fallen asleep in the middle of a battlefield at war.

*This is a battlefield at war,* he thought, and looked down at Sora's fragile form. She had lost a lot of weight from the last time he had carried her, long before the swamp. He hadn't noticed before; hadn't cared to.

Burn followed on foot. He could run almost as fast as the

horse. The giant Wolfy carried Dorian's body slung over one shoulder.

Finally they entered a wide clearing in the woods, covered in low grass and pine needles. At its center was a log cabin. The horse slowed to a halt in front of the house. The building was much larger than he had expected, two stories high, dozens of windows, two or three chimneys—yet it appeared quaint and welcoming. Light shone from inside.

The Healer dismounted from the horse and whistled. She was answered immediately by the soft patter of footsteps. A small man came running around the building, the light shining off his bald head. He was old and hunched, with long goblin ears, a jutting nose and drooping eyes.

"Cameron? Take the horse into the stalls," she directed. "Then could you heat up what remains of the pork? Our guests will be hungry."

The man nodded hastily and made a lunge for the reins, but the Healer caught his wrist. "Cameron! Cameron, listen, take the horse into the stalls, gently, do you understand? Gently."

The man, who was obviously simple-minded, nodded solemnly and took the reins. At the same time, Burn stepped up to the side of the horse and pulled Sora from Crash's arms.

Crash was reluctant to let go. He dismounted from the horse, leaping to the ground. Then Cameron led the beast toward the stalls.

The Healer walked towards the house, opening the front door. "He was brought to me a few years ago, knocked silly from a fall off a horse," she said over her shoulder. "Cameron survived the wound, but was never quite right after that. His family asked me to look after him. We've since become quite comfortable."

She let her patients enter first. "Burn, take the girl down those stairs and through the first door on the right. You can place her on the wooden table." Her eyes slid to Dorian's body, which was still slung over the mercenary's shoulder, cold and limp. "You can place him in the next room."

Burn nodded and stepped into the house, Crash following closely.

Inside, the cabin was warm and bright; hand-woven rugs on the floor and paintings on the walls. Vases filled with wildflowers, lanterns strung on chains, a broad fireplace and ornate furniture. Obviously the Healer did quite well for herself—he wasn't surprised. Healing was a rare art and took countless years to master. Apprenticeships were hard to come by, so skilled Healers were few and far between. She probably had visitors from all over the countryside at her door, perhaps even those who lived in the foothills and mountains.

The house was cluttered; most available surfaces were covered with trinkets and candles. "Gifts from my patients," she commented, following Crash's gaze. At the end of the front room was a short step down. They entered onto the stone floor of a large kitchen, filled with copper and brass pans that hung from assorted shelves. A massive stove. Lots of floor room.

The Healer paused here, opening her cupboards and collecting a series of glass vials filled with unidentifiable liquids. Crash was a poisons expert, but these were much the opposite—naturally brewed anesthetics, disinfectants and medication.

Then she led him back to the staircase where Burn had descended. At its base, it emptied into another hallway, this one below-ground and branched off into several rooms. They passed through an oak door, already ajar. Crash could hear the Wolfy shuffling beyond it, laying Sora out on the wooden table.

The small room was well-lit by perhaps a dozen lanterns. The walls were lined with drawers and shelves. Countless jars were packed full of herbs, roots, teas, cotton swabs, antidotes, rolls of gauze. Many of the jars were unlabeled. Several clumps of plants hung from the ceiling, drying. The assassin only recognized a few.

Burn laid Sora out on the examining table and stepped back, his face pale and drawn. Crash stared at her body as well. She was completely still,; he couldn't even tell if she was breathing. He wondered if she was already dead. She seemed smaller than he remembered, miniscule on the large table.

The Healer began removing Sora's shirt, then paused. She looked up at them. "I think the patient would appreciate some privacy. When I'm done, you can come back in and take her upstairs." She looked pointedly at the assassin. "Out. Both of you."

Crash and Burn filed out of the room silently, each at a loss for words. They sat on a bench in the hallway. Every couple of seconds they glanced at the silent door. Eventually, the Wolfy got up and started pacing. Crash watched him, his body exhausted yet filled with a nervous, twitching energy.

Finally he sat back and closed his eyes, trying to rest, though he knew it would be impossible. Every time he sat back, he saw flashes of the battle, the wraith's dark, foreboding hood, the stench of magic and blood. He shook his head, trying to clear it, but there was nothing else to think about. There were no fond memories to summon, no better times.

He drew his dagger instead, intending to clean it, but he could only stare at the blade. It was long and ornately curved, decorated with fragile filigree toward the hilt. The pummel was twisted into the form of a snake, jaw open, fangs gleaming.

He had killed countless times with this knife. The only thing he had kept from his homeland. He hesitated now, watching the light glint from its surface. Unexpectedly, he remembered that night in Sora's manor, slinking along the rafters of the ballroom, waiting for a distraction great enough to finish the job. Goddess, he had killed her father! A man who had been far from innocent, but few men truly were. He didn't judge his kills—didn't weigh their acts like a tipping scale, considering their good deeds against the bad. No, he hadn't even known the man—hadn't cared about the daughter, who tripped and fell at her own Blooming.

He had only thought about the coin, about Volcrian's hatred, about how long he could run before he was caught.

And now she would die.

*What did you expect?* He had been raised as an agent of destruction. *It is what we are,* his mentor had taught. *The unseen tempest. The impartial earthquake.* Death did not judge, and neither did he.

Yet somehow, Sora was different. *I should be the one who is dead.*

His lip curled, staring at the knife in disgust. He shoved it back into his belt, a silent vow twisting in his gut. *It's over,* he thought. *I'm out.*

Eventually Burn's steps came to a halt. He sat down again, the bench creaking slightly under his weight. After a moment, he said very quietly, "We will need to give Dorian a proper burial."

Crash's eyes opened, their green light rekindled. He hadn't

thought of the thief. The cold body in the next room might as well have been a piece of wood. Was that what Burn had been pacing about—funeral rites? "Time means nothing to the dead," he grunted. "Dorian can wait."

Burn frowned calmly. "Perhaps. But I can't."

"Then bury him yourself."

The mercenary was silent for a long moment. "I suppose you *would* say that," he muttered darkly. "I'm not fooled, assassin. You may think you are removed from us—that you have come to terms with your own mortality—but I still had to drag Sora out of your arms."

Crash didn't know what to say to that.

Burn sighed softly. "After Sora is awake, then we will worry about Dorian."

Crash refused to answer, knowing for the first time that he couldn't trust his own voice. Silence was better than betraying oneself. Didn't the mercenary understand? He cared about the girl —maybe, partially, why not—but it was only because she was still alive. If she had been killed in the fight, would he have fussed over her empty body?

No, of course not. What did it even mean—to be buried? That was only a comfort to those who mourned, who grieved. No help to the ghost, no second chance for the soul.

But a tinge of guilt entered his thoughts. He had caused the thief's death, too.

He turned his face away from Burn and stared at the wall. His thoughts left a bitter taste in his mouth. *Sora is just a girl,* he thought angrily. *She will either live or die, just like anyone else.* How long was this going to take? If the Healer didn't come out soon, then he might just knock on the door and let himself in. There was nothing sacred about a healing space. He had a right to know the truth.

As he fought with himself on whether to move or not, the door opened.

The Healer was wiping her hands on a cloth, and Crash could see blood on it. His stomach did a tiny flip, though he had seen plenty of blood before. He didn't linger on the reaction.

She turned to look at them; she appeared older now, weary. "We will have to wait it out," she said. He thought he might have heard a tremor in her voice, a slight weakness. "There's nothing more I can do. But she's young; she has a good chance at recovering. There is no infection, so that's a good sign; it's mostly blood loss. Burn, can you take her upstairs to the first bedroom on the left?"

"Of course," the Wolfy said, and went into the room immediately. Crash was too relieved to follow, though he didn't admit it to himself. A moment later Burn came out with Sora in his arms, covered in a long white sleeping gown.

The assassin stood up to go with them, but the Healer—looking far too much like Sora—gave him a firm glare. She motioned for him to come with her into the room. Crash had half a mind to ignore her, but a twinge in his side told him not to. His wounds were minor, but having a Healer nearby was a rare opportunity. So he followed her and sat down on the wooden table.

The woman shut the door and turned to him. "Take off your shirt. I'm assuming your shoulder bothers you?"

Crash didn't hesitate. He lifted his shirt to reveal the stab wound on his right shoulder, where the Panthera had landed a blow. The woman took a bottle of clear liquid and dabbed a cloth into it. She wrung it out and clamped it over the wound without warning—for good reason, too, as it burned like hell.

The gash began to foam. In amazement, he saw dirt and other toxins begin to bubble out, purged from his body. His face paled in pain, but he didn't make a sound. She did this a few more times to other small scratches, her eyes traveling over his scar, then she took out a needle and a thin length of white thread.

"This is a special kind of silk—I grow it myself. It's made from silkworms and plant fibers. It will dissolve on its own in about three weeks," she said, mindlessly threading the needle. Crash nodded, looking down at her eerily familiar face, watching her deft hands. Sora had thinner fingers, he observed.

Then she knelt toward his shoulder, ready to pierce the flesh. She glanced up at him. "This might...tickle just a bit."

Crash nodded wryly, appreciating her humor. Then the needle pierced his skin, once again without warning. He hardly felt it. He watched her hands at work, weaving in and out of the wound, sewing it together inch by precious inch. She was careful and thorough, taking her time, her face drawn with concentration.

After twenty minutes, the Healer finished. Crash flexed his shoulder, feeling the gash strain against the stitches. He was mildly surprised. She was better than he had originally thought—far better than he had seen before, and he had visited quite a few Healers. Some could hardly mix cold medicine, working out of horse stalls or other unsavory places. No, this woman was quite experienced.

Crash looked back at her. Her blue eyes gazed at him steadily, a small smile on her lips. Then she spoke abruptly. "So does that tattoo on your arm mean anything," she asked, "or is it just a decoration?"

Crash raised an eyebrow. He glanced down at the green snake wrapped around his forearm, coiling up his wrist, twin fangs dripping poison. Usually he had his shirt on, so it was covered. "My namesake," he murmured.

"Viper?"

"Yes."

"Ah. I thought so." The woman grinned. "An assassin indeed."

Crash's eyes flashed, immediately suspicious. But the Healer only laughed, deep and throaty. She sounded so unlike Sora that he began to relax.

"It's obvious," she answered the unspoken question. "Your kind always have those silly tattoos."

He was absolutely shocked. He had been impressed by the woman's knowledge of the Cat's Eye, but now he was speechless. Not many came close enough to an assassin to learn such things. What else did she know? And could he trust her?

"Now tell me, Viper—or Crash, as you seem to prefer," she said, and handed him back his shirt. Then she turned and stared him in the eye, her expression far from friendly. "How do you know my daughter?"

# CHAPTER 17

Sora was floating in a black space.

Every now and then, the murmur of voices brushed the edge of her hearing, but they were mere echoes, small stars in the milky backdrop of her mind. Peace flowed through her. For the first time in weeks, she felt completely safe.

Then the darkness lightened to a shade of gray and finally to a soft white. She began to lose that fragile peace, fraying at the seams like delicate lace. Her mind stirred, rippling. Disgruntled, Sora finally accepted that she was waking up. With a small groan, she welcomed back her senses with reluctant arms.

She opened her eyes and looked above her. At first she thought she was still dreaming. A white, flat surface drifted overhead, too low and flat to be clouds. A ceiling. Her heart jolted, remembering the Catlins, her frantic race through the swamp. Had she finally been captured? Where were her companions? She listened, half expecting a vicious beast to tower above her bed.

She tried to sit up, but it was impossible. Her body felt as weak and limp as a rag doll. She couldn't even raise her hand.

She tried to remember where she was, but it was like losing her place in a book, becoming lost in the middle of a conversation.

*Something is missing.* She glanced around the room again, at the hardwood floors, scuffed and warped over countless years, small knots raised in the wood. At the crosshatch window on the opposing wall, the glimpse of tall pine trees beyond. Rafters overhead. A vaulted ceiling, like the inside of a wood cabin.

It took her a long moment, but when the memories finally came back, they were crystal-clear, full of color. She let out another groan, and this time felt the pressure of a bandage against her ribs. Her wound ached with each breath, each twitch of her muscles. She placed a gentle hand on it, wincing.

Was she really still alive? Her last waking thoughts had been of the acceptance of death. Sora raised her hands in front of her face, an action that took a peculiar amount of effort. Each limb felt leaden, full of sand. Finally her fingers were in sight and she blinked in surprise. She had been planning to pinch herself, but this was almost as good. *Goddess! My fingernails are clean!* Then something else occurred to her. *Who cleaned them?*

"Welcome back," a voice said from somewhere beyond her line of sight.

Sora didn't have to see the person to know who it was. A weak smile spread across her lips.

"You had us worried for a while. You even made an impression on Crash." Burn loomed over her bed and grinned down at her. From this position, he seemed impossibly tall, far too large for the room. He, too, was clean and wearing fresh clothes.

Where were they? How much time had passed?

"It's good to see you," she mumbled. Her lips felt numb, clumsy. She could feel her wound strain against her stomach muscles. It was a strange, unexpected sensation.

"How are you feeling?" the mercenary asked.

"All right," she murmured. "Just a little hard to...move." She tried to sit up, but a jolt of pain cut through her. She winced.

Burn frowned in concern. "Well I can tell you one thing," he said somberly. "You're stuffed full of pain killers. I'm surprised you can even feel the bed."

Sora grinned wryly. She doubted any amount of poppy extract could numb this wound.

A new voice entered the conversation. "You were badly injured. You shouldn't move."

Burn turned to the doorway, his expression not exactly welcoming. "Finished sulking, have you? Pay your respects to our little heroine. She saved our lives."

"I know," was the sour response.

Sora wasn't particularly thrilled by Crash's tone. He sounded in a bad mood. *Not that I'd recognize him in a good mood,* she thought. Still, she didn't want him to leave. It was comforting to have familiar faces nearby—no matter how ornery.

But wasn't someone missing? Where was the fourth member of their party, the one she had chatted with the most? Dorian?

For a moment she waited—maybe he would come in next? Her mind dug back through the memories, shifting and searching. She saw the wraith, dissolving like mist. The fierce wind. The pain in her gut. The images were foggy, as though she had read of them, secondhand, in a book.

When had she seen Dorian last? Back in the fields....The wraith had attacked them, yes, she remembered now....Its sword had plunged downwards. The thief had thrown himself in front of Burn. Blood had sprayed the grass.

She suddenly felt sick. Her heart plummeted. She almost choked. "Dorian!" she gasped. "Where is he? What happened?"

Burn stared down at her.

She met his eyes, trying to stay calm. "Tell me," she said. It sounded hysterical, even to her own ears.

His expression turned dark, like a light snuffing out. Those long, delicate ears twitched. The silence grew. Anxiety and fear clawed at her. Dorian...*he can't...he can't possibly be....*

"He's gone, Sora," the Wolfy whispered.

"G-gone?" she echoed, searching for any other explanation. "What do you mean, gone? Gone where? I don't...." But she did understand. She remembered what had provoked her necklace, what had caused her to act. She didn't want Burn to continue; saying the words out loud would make it more real, more inescapable.

*Should I be crying?* she wondered. She tried to summon tears. Tried to raise some sort of response—a scream, a tantrum. But she felt numb. Full of cotton.

"Burn...." she said quietly, scared by her own lack of response.

His giant hand reached down and stroked her head. "Give it time," he said.

Sora closed her eyes, trying to forget the screech of the wraith, the look on Dorian's face before he died, the way his body had fallen to the ground.

When she opened her eyes again, Burn was gone. She didn't know how much time had passed, certainly no more than a minute. She turned her head, trying to see around the room, but it was hard to move her stiff neck.

"We buried him a short ways from here," Crash said, causing her a jolt of surprise. She thought he had gone. "We were waiting for you, but you have been unconscious for more than a week."

His shadow fell across the bed. She looked up at the assassin, curious. Why was he here? He was clothed in his usual black, though the shirt and pants were patched and clean. Her eyes followed the scar from his shirt collar up to his face.

"Is that supposed to make me feel better?" she said, a wry quirk to her mouth.

"No," was his blank reply. "The body was rotting."

She glared up at the assassin, irritated by his tone, at his ambivalence. *Heartless bastard. I wish he'd just go away.*

"Is that all he was?" she asked, averting her eyes and speaking to the wall. "A rotting body? I'm sure that was a huge inconvenience." Her voice choked slightly. "He died trying to save us."

Silence. Then, "You're the one who saved us," Crash murmured.

His words didn't mean as much as they should have. *But I couldn't save Dorian. I hesitated. It's my fault.* Something cracked, and Sora's eyes filled with tears. It was all her fault. Dorian might still be alive if she had acted quicker.

"There's nothing more you could have done," Crash said, as though reading her mind. His eyes drifted over her face, watching her closely. She hated that look. It made her feel vulnerable, naked, weak and exposed.

"You say that," Sora murmured. "But I should have acted quicker."

"If you have to blame anyone, blame Volcrian," the assassin replied.

*Or I could blame you,* Sora thought bitterly, but she kept it to herself. No, this wasn't the assassin's fault. None of them could fight the wraith. Only her Cat's Eye. And she had waited too long.

"But what was that...thing?" she asked, a shudder passing

through her. She could still feel its presence, a menacing shadow hiding between the floorboards, just out of sight. Her hand went to her necklace, remembering how she had destroyed it, trying to take comfort. "Was it a...a ghost? A demon?"

"Volcrian has many powerful spells," Crash finally said. "He uses blood to create monsters, servants. Most use animal sacrifices...but there are spells that require human blood, too. They call it black-blooded. Any spell that requires one of the races is forbidden...especially those that raise the dead."

Sora frowned. "Raise the dead?"

"Yes...." Crash's gaze dropped to the sheets. "That wraith was alive, once. In some ways, it still was when it attacked us. Perhaps the Cat's Eye is not as useful against such things." Crash met her eyes. "He's growing desperate."

Sora's eyes were wide. "So...so that wraith was a dead soul...."

"Brought back from the underworld. Yes."

"That's...that's terrifying." She blinked the tears from her eyes, remembering the fierce battle, Dorian's final moments on the field. A sudden fire lit within her—hatred. It was like a knife in her gut, far worse than her father's resentment or her fear of Crash. She knew it with absolute certainty. She hated Volcrian, loathed him, wanted him dead. She hoped that he would never find them. That he would perish somewhere in the mountains, lost and starving, eaten alive by wolves.

She shook her head. It was sickening, consuming. She didn't want to feel it, but the hatred was rock-solid in her gut.

"I could have done something," she finally said, unable to hold back the bitterness. She needed to confess. "I should have acted sooner. Saved him. It was in my power." Her throat closed painfully.

Then Crash did something unexpected.

He sat down on the bed, his hand landing close to her face, gazing down at her intently. For reasons unknown, Sora felt her breath catch, her chest constrict peculiarly. She wanted to look toward the wall, the ceiling, anywhere but those moss-green depths. It was like staring into a forest pond, algae grown across its surface, the glimmer of her own reflection.

"Listen to me," Crash said quietly. His voice was soft and rich, and her heart fluttered at the sound of it. "Only the future matters, Sora. Guilt is an illusion, a way of lingering on the past. You can't change what happened." He held her eyes, carving himself into her mind. "You are alive. That is what you should worry about. Your thoughts can torture you—but not the dead. They've moved on." And he touched her head softly, as though proving a point. "Let it go."

Sora couldn't speak—frankly, was having trouble breathing. Poignant words for an assassin, but they were not reassuring. Let what go? Her guilt? Her regret? Impossible. Dorian was gone forever—how was she supposed to let *that* go?

And what would an assassin know about grief? He didn't seem to care about killing her father, about the countless other victims he had murdered. Or did he think she had forgotten? She choked suddenly, full of anger, of inexpressible sorrow.

She closed her eyes, trying to hide her pain; she didn't want him to see her anymore, exposed and vulnerable. But one tear escaped and ran down her cheek.

His finger traced its path across her skin.

Then there was a knock at the door.

Crash's head snapped up. He stood up quickly. The door opened as he moved away from the bed. Sora watched him disappear out of her line of sight, and for a moment, she didn't want him to leave....

"Good morning, Crash," a woman's voice said from somewhere out of sight.

The assassin didn't respond, but she could feel it when he left the room. There was a gentle click as the door shut.

Footsteps approached her bed. Sora knew she was about to lay eyes on the person who had nursed her back to health. She fidgeted a little nervously.

The woman came into view and stood in the exact spot where Crash had been a moment before. Sora looked up. Her eyes widened. She was momentarily breathless.

"Hello," the woman said softly.

Sora couldn't speak. *By the Wind Goddess!* She looked up at the woman's face and felt like she was staring into a mirror. Aside from the subtle marks of age, the woman looked almost exactly like her. In fact, the resemblance was so uncanny, she could have been Sora's older sister, aunt, or maybe even....

*No, it's impossible!*

"Who...who are you?" she choked out. Once again she felt close to tears, but for an entirely different reason. This was too much.

"Sora," the woman said slowly. "I think you know who I am."

She shook her head, unable to admit it even to herself.

"My name is Lorianne. I am a Healer in the village. And...this might sound strange, but...I think I am your mother."

*My mother?*

Sora wasn't sure what she felt—disbelief, to be sure. Maybe a little nausea.

"You can't be my mother," she blurted out. The words tripped over her tongue. She could barely regain her breath. "My mother is gone...I mean, she left me a long time ago...it's impossible."

"Impossible for a girl who wears a Cat's Eye?"

Sora didn't know what to say or do. Her mind raced, staring at the curve of the woman's cheek. She blinked twice. Her hand flew to her necklace, forgetting her discomfort, the pull of her sore muscles. She ran her fingers over the smooth stone.

Suddenly, she remembered a conversation from very long ago, in a mapmaker's shop. Something about discipline...about needing a direction....

The pieces were all there; she just didn't want to put them in place. This had to be a joke. "It's impossible," she repeated in a shaking voice.

Unexpectedly, the woman smiled. There was kindness in her eyes. "That's quite a word, coming from you. Your friends told me of your journey through Fennbog." She raised an eyebrow. Sora almost remembered her expression, as though from another life. "Are you truly surprised to be here?"

Sora kept running her fingers over the stone. She shook her head again, this time less vehemently. How many times had she held the necklace, how many times had she thought of her mother? Yearned to find her? Her journey through the swamp, turning this way and that, fumbling through leagues of wilderness....

All that time, she had thought she was running from Volcrian. But perhaps the necklace had been leading her somewhere else....

She stared at the woman fully, not daring to blink, hungry to study every minuscule detail of her face. She wanted to touch her somehow, make sure she wasn't dreaming. Still weak, she stretched out her hand toward the Healer, uncertain if it would go right through her.

The woman took Sora's clammy hand in her own warm, dry hand.

Then Lorianne sat down on her bed and gently embraced her. At first Sora was stiff with pain and shock, then slowly relaxed, easing into the embrace.

"Goddess be praised!" the woman said softly. "I never thought I would see you again." She hugged her closer. "I don't suppose your servants told you much?"

Sora shook her head a bit, but that was lost in the hug.

"If you'd like," Lori continued, "I can explain everything."

Lori released her and sat up, gazing down at her daughter. Sora stared, too. Once again, she was shocked by how closely they resembled each other. Blue eyes, golden-blond hair. For a moment she doubted herself—what if this was an elaborate joke? What if this woman was manic?

But, no. She knew the truth; she could feel it in her bones, in the subtle bond of the necklace. *My mother.* Somehow, out of all the acres of wilderness, the endless valleys and mountains of the world, the necklace had led her straight to this doorstep. The thought took her breath away.

"It's really you," Sora murmured. "I can't believe it."

Then tears flooded her eyes. She was no longer able to hold back. She sobbed, putting her hand over her mouth, trying to stifle the sound of sobbing. "Why?" she asked, still sniffling. "Lorianne— why?" She couldn't yet think of the woman as "mother." But she had to ask. The question had been burning inside her for years.

Lori swallowed hard. "Where do you want me to begin?" she finally asked, her voice shaking. "What do you want me to tell you?"

"Tell me why you left. Truly," Sora replied. Suddenly she was afraid—afraid of abandonment, of betrayal. What if her mother had thrown her away? What if she had been unwanted...unloved?

Her dubious thoughts were soon answered. "I was forced to leave you," her mother said, shaking her head. "It is the hardest thing I have ever done. Lord Fallcrest threatened to kill me—and you—if I stayed."

Sora was shocked. She stared at the woman, speechless. "What?" she demanded.

Her mother shook her head, her hands grasping Sora's. She closed her eyes painfully, her face growing pale. "First, Sora, you should know...that Lord Fallcrest is not your real father."

Sora didn't know how to respond. She felt out-of-body, completely numb.

"Let me explain," Lorianne said quickly. "I met your father when I was much younger. He was an adventurer of sorts. A treasure hunter. I traveled with him and his companions, chasing after lost artifacts." She took a short breath, glancing down at her hands. "We were excavating a cave some miles north of Fallcrest lands, a great crater in the earth. The cave collapsed. Your father was killed. I had just learned that I was pregnant with you."

Sora listened, her mouth slightly open, her heart beating loudly in her ears.

Lorianne continued quietly. "Word had it that Lord Fallcrest was unable to have children. He didn't have an heir, despite having remarried twice. The countryside was full of rumors; they said his seed was rotten."

"I was desperate, poor, without any prospects. You must understand, I had no way to take care of you. Dane and I—your father—owned no property. We had no livelihood." She shook her head slowly, her eyes distant, still staring at her lap. A long breath escaped her lips. "Perhaps I was mad with grief, I don't know. But I courted Lord Fallcrest. I lied and told him that I was of noble birth, the youngest in my family with nothing to inherit. Dane's friends helped me, acting as my servants. Lord Fallcrest fell in love with my beauty. We were married two months later. And when you were born, he named you his heir."

Sora's hands trembled. She couldn't hide that from her mother. Lori glanced up and met her eyes.

"Did he find out the truth?" Sora asked.

Her mother nodded slowly. "Eventually, yes. There was no record of a Lady Bloomsworth anywhere in the Kingdom. As soon as we were married, people started to talk. It was only a matter of time." She stroked Sora's hand gently. "When Lord Fallcrest discovered the truth, he told me to leave. He said he would kill me if I didn't go. Then he gave you to a midwife and forbade me to see you. He needed an heir, you see, and he thought you were his own. But if I ever showed my face again, he said he would kill us both for shaming his family." Lorianne squeezed Sora's grip, as though taking strength from it. "So I left," she said.

Sora could hear the weakness in her voice, the tears just below the surface. But she was too stunned to offer comfort. Her entire world was slowly disintegrating, piece by piece. Everything she had ever known of herself, that she had ever taken pride in, was a lie.

"I went where he would never find me," Lori finished. "I knew that you would have a good life, far better than I could give you. It took me years to settle here. I had to do things...things that you wouldn't be proud of. The world is not kind to a woman traveling alone. I was lucky enough to find a mentor and learn the healing arts. I wish I had learned them sooner. Maybe Dane would still be alive."

Sora nodded. They became silent. She considered her mother's words, letting the story sink through her skin, permeate her mind. *I'm not noble-born.* Lord Fallcrest had never been her father. In some ways, it was unexpectedly liberating. Her entire life had been tainted by a sense of failure. Her father had always treated her like a disappointment, never quite good enough. Her essays were too simple, her hands were too heavy on the reins, her singing was off-key.

Now she understood. She was peasant-born. Perhaps he had suspected that she was not his own blood. But he needed an heir. So he had kept her, since his own seed was useless.

Her mother's blue eyes focused on her hand. "I see you've found your Cat's Eye." Her lips puckered strangely. "I'd hoped you would...and also, I'd hoped you wouldn't. I didn't intend to leave it, but I had to pack so quickly....It belonged to your father." She sighed, her eyes distant. "I guess it's good that you wore it. It's the only reason you're still alive. The stone will go to great lengths to preserve the bearer."

Sora frowned at this. "My father's?" she said. She couldn't imagine the man, had no idea who he was. "How...?"

"He found the Cat's Eye on one of our expeditions. He wore it for many years. I saw it...change him...." Lori frowned. "Not in a bad way, I suppose. When he died, we used it to identify his body. It was all I had left of him...."

Her mother's expression melted into sadness, her eyes growing dim.

The new silence was uncomfortable. Sora shifted, digging around for something to say. "I always knew you loved me," she finally stuttered. "I wanted to find you so badly. And my father...I always thought he hated me, I just never knew why. I never thought...."

Her mother nodded, smiling slightly, as though waiting for something. But Sora didn't know what else to say. She was uncertain of herself and this woman before her. It was her mother, yes, but also a perfect stranger. She tried to summon up memories from her younger days, when her mother had still lived at the manor, but it was impossible. Lori had left when Sora was a baby. Her earliest memories were of the midwife.

Lorianne wiped at her eyes awkwardly, as though sensing Sora's withdrawal. "Well, I'm sure you're exhausted by all of this," she said briskly. "Dinner is cooking, I should go check on it. Of course, I think those friends of yours will eat anything." She laughed a little, but it seemed forced, anxious. "Sleep, Sora. We will speak more when you're stronger."

Sora nodded. In all honesty, it was too much. She just wanted to be alone, especially now that the excitement had waned. She could feel her body shaking from the effort of sitting up. Her breath felt strangely shallow, her eyes heavy. She nodded stiffly and lay back down.

*I found my mother. It's really her,* she thought as the woman left the room, shutting the door quietly. Not what she had expected, by far. Her fingers traveled once again to her necklace, marveling at the small stone.

Somehow, in the wake of Dorian's death, it wasn't as comforting as she had hoped.

She fell asleep, her mind heavy with new knowledge.

# Chapter 18

The forest was lush, green, and utterly alive.

It had been almost a month since her brush with death and the loss of Dorian. Her wound was almost completely healed now, except for a sore red spot that was turning into a rather impressive scar. She figured it would be her badge of experience.

But the scar of Dorian's death went a bit deeper. She hadn't seen the world quite the same since; everything had a slightly different smell and taste, even her own thoughts. For the first week or so life had been strange without him, but now it was becoming disturbingly normal. She remembered him at strange times throughout day, their conversations, the sound of his voice.

The other two men hardly spoke of Dorian, and she had not seen them mourn his death. It made her feel awkward during those times when she found herself crying. She still wondered if she could have saved him somehow.

Her thoughts were the same on this particular occasion, traveling with Burn to visit the thief's grave. The body had been burned, as Wolfy tradition dictated, and the ashes thrown to a westward wind—but for Sora's sake, they built a small monument in Dorian's honor a little way from her mother's house. She could see it now from atop her horse; a small pile of stones next to a winding stream, with Dorian's knives placed on top.

Burn rode his horse slightly behind her, silent and deep in thought, his mind probably just as far away.

Sora filled her lungs with the summer air and tried to keep her emotions steady; she didn't want to cry in front of the mercenary, and tears were becoming a waste of energy. She directed the horse around the giant roots of a tree. The forest surrounding her mother's house was large and dense, far more wild and untamed than the woodlands around her manor. She just wished she could share the sight with Dorian.

They drew up alongside the stone memorial and Sora lowered herself carefully to the ground. She was still stiff from her wound. She tied her horse to the lower branch of a tree and went to stand before the stones. She bowed her head, thinking of her fallen friend.

"Sora?" Burn's voice reached her a few moments later. "Why don't you sit over here next to me?"

She glanced at him. Usually he never spoke during these visits to Dorian's grave. The Wolfy was sitting at the base of the tree they had tied their horses to, polishing an apple on his shirt. He motioned to her. "Come on over here."

Sora paused for just a moment, then went over to sit next to him. She didn't say anything and waited for the Wolfy to speak.

"You know," he finally said, "Volcrian is the only other Wolfy I've ever heard of."

Sora nodded slowly.

"The races are perishing...and I believe the Wolfies might be the first," he murmured. "I have tried to seek them out...to listen for them on the Wind." Burn bowed his head, his golden eyes unfocused, his hair dappled with light. "Dorian might have been one of the last of our race."

Sora frowned, unsure of what to think of the mercenary's

words. She didn't know what he meant by listening to the wind, but observing his keen ears, it seemed meaningful. "Perhaps they are somewhere far overseas, in a different land?"

Burn shook his head. "The Wind speaks to us, Sora." He gave her a bleak smile. "It tells us many secrets. These ears are for more than just good looks, you know."

Sora grinned wryly. The humor faded fast, along with Burn's smile.

"It is part of our race's heritage," he murmured, "to be able to hear the Wind. There are no Wolfies left because the wind carries no knowledge of them."

"You mean the Wind of the Goddess, don't you?" Sora asked, interested. Burn had never mentioned this before. She didn't know much about Wolfy lore. "The Wind Goddess is what speaks to you?"

Burn raised his eyebrows in amusement. "There were things that existed before the gods and goddesses, Sora, and the Wind was one of them. It is that Wind that speaks to us, and there is no knowledge left of the Wolfies."

Now Sora was confused. What did Burn mean—things that existed before? "I don't understand," she said.

"The old world is being forgotten and a new world is forming." Burn smiled sadly. "The Elements came before the gods and goddesses, Sora. They created the world we live in."

"But...what happened to them?"

"Each race's lore is different. Some say they disappeared. Others say that we live inside of them. That everything is made from the Elements." Burn winked at her. "It could all just be a grand tale."

Sora sat quietly, considering his words. She hadn't met any of the other races, only the Wolfies. She just couldn't agree with him. There had to be more out there, somewhere, perhaps hidden, perhaps ignorant of their own heritage.

"That must be hard for you," she murmured. She couldn't imagine the loss of her own race, her own people. It must be terribly...lonely.

"Dorian kept my hope alive. I thought that someday, we would find a lost colony of Wolfies, some unheard-of civilization. But I suppose that's just a dream, isn't it?" Burn sighed. "Someday, I'll be dead too. And perhaps the Wolfy race with me."

Sora felt sick. She wished she could say something helpful, but there were no words. She put her hand on Burn's arm. Hopefully he would understand.

They sat in silence for a few depressing minutes, each lost in thought. Sora's mind turned to Volcrian. Had he followed them through the swamp—or was he miles away, taking the long road, traversing the mountains to reach them? She knew the hunt wasn't over yet. He had only killed one member of their party—and it wasn't Crash.

Sora wondered why Dorian and Burn had traveled with the assassin, knowing the danger they were in. Another story yet to be told.

"I thought I'd find you here," a friendly voice called from behind them.

Sora was startled from her dark reverie. She turned to see her mother striding toward them in soft pants and a white, breezy shirt. Her hair was tied up in a scarf. She smiled, her lips pressed together, as though holding back a thought. "I've been looking for you two. Dinner's on the table. You've been gone for hours!"

Sora blinked. "Hours?" It was only then she noticed that the afternoon sun was turning to deep orange, dipping low in the sky.

Her mother frowned. "And you're still recovering, too," she murmured, then turned upon the Wolfy. "Burn...."

He leapt to his feet and swept over to Sora's mother, taking her by surprise. His mood seemed instantly changed—or perhaps expertly hidden.

"Why, my gorgeous host," he said, blatantly flattering. "I knew that you, with your kind, forgiving heart, wouldn't mind Sora staying out a bit longer than planned. Especially when there is so much to talk about."

Sora's mother snorted. "So you think it's funny to leave me in the house all day with Crash? That man is horribly unsociable, you know."

This time Sora and Burn both laughed. Burn's ears twitched. "All right, all right. Sorry, it won't happen again," he said.

Her mother grinned. "Good. You're forgiven. Now if you don't mind, I'm starving."

With false enthusiasm, Burn and Sora mounted their horses and followed Lorianne back down the trail.

All was relaxed and peaceful once more, but Sora couldn't help but be troubled over Burn's story. She looked back at Dorian's grave. Life changed so quickly, so unexpectedly—how many dreams had been lost with Dorian's death? How many plans? She wondered what Burn's plans were now, if he wanted to move on or if he would just stay at Lorianne's house forever.

She wondered suddenly if her friends would ever free themselves of Volcrian's hunt, if they would get the chance to pursue a different life, one that they wanted. And what about herself? Her own dreams? *And what are those?* she wondered.

She could no longer come up with an answer.

* * *

After dinner, Sora watched Crash leave the table. He was quiet and withdrawn as usual, only offering a few comments during the meal. She wondered what was on his mind.

She excused herself, following him upstairs. Burn and Lori barely noticed her leave. They were gently arguing over the healing properties of willow bark.

She gnawed her lip, wondering what to say when she caught up to the assassin. "You seem quiet" didn't sound like the best approach.

She was surprised to find him waiting in the hallway. But of course he had heard her follow him. She paused, staring at him awkwardly, taken off-guard.

He was dressed in black, but she hadn't seen him wear his knives since he had come to Lori's house. His dark hair was slightly longer now, sweeping low around his ears, brushing across his forehead. He faced her, waiting, his eyes flickering over her. Perhaps curious.

"Crash," she said, then stopped. She felt suddenly awkward, unsure of what to say. "Uh...it was a good meal, right?" *Stupid,* she could have kicked herself.

He nodded, his shoulders loosening. He shifted his weight to one foot, slightly more relaxed.

She sighed. "I just...I wanted to tell you...." What? What had she been thinking, following him up here?

"How is your wound?" Crash asked instead.

Sora's mouth opened. "Fine," she stuttered. "Uh, almost fully recovered. Perhaps we can begin training soon."

He glanced away. She felt his withdrawal like a passing cloud pulling back over the horizon. She frowned. Perhaps she had said something wrong.

"I wanted to tell you," she started again, "that Lord Fallcrest wasn't my father."

He looked back up at her. His expression was guarded.

She took a step toward him, slightly bolder now. "I just wanted you to know," she said, pushing on. "What you did was horrible...but...well...." What was she trying to say? That killing a stranger was better than her own blood? Feelings of guilt swarmed inside of her. She had felt far more grief over Dorian's death than she had for the man who had raised her. But was it truly her fault? Lord Fallcrest had treated her as less than family. Dorian had embraced her with open arms.

"He wasn't my father," she finished lamely.

Crash waited, then shook his head, as though inwardly amused. "Is that all?" he murmured.

She nodded, gnawing at her lower lip.

"Hm," he grunted. "You should get your rest. You were out for a long time today. You're not as recovered as you might feel." Then he turned, slipping quietly down the hall, into the last bedroom on the left where he and Burn slept.

Sora watched him go. She frowned, wondering at his words, wishing she could say more. She had been doing a lot of thinking these past weeks. He was still a killer, a man capable of unimaginable destruction...but there was something else inside him.

*I'm being sentimental,* she thought, and turned to her room. *He's an assassin. He doesn't care.*

* * *

That same week, things started to change.

Crash and Burn took to locking themselves in their room, speaking softly so Sora couldn't hear what was being said. She paid no attention at first, but after a while, it began to worry her. She caught them poring over maps. Discussing roads. Making plans.

As though sensing the change, the weather turned darker. Clouds moved in. "Another bout of rain," her mother said cheerily as she brought herbs in from the garden. "The farmers will be happy. No drought this year."

The clouds lingered. As soon as one storm passed, another took its place, blowing in from the ocean. It felt like winter all over again.

It was the second week of rain when Crash caught her alone. She was looking out the window of her bedroom, bored and wishing to go outside, even if it was pouring. Her mother still fussed over her wound, convinced that she hadn't yet recovered, even though Sora felt fine. Stronger, even, than she had a year ago.

Abruptly the assassin was next to her, catching her off-guard. She squeaked in surprise, then flushed with embarrassment. *I should be used to this by now.* She looked up at him, waiting, wondering how she hadn't heard him enter the room.

He shifted. "Watching something?" he asked.

*Small talk?* "Eh...no, just the rain," she muttered, unsure of what to think.

"That's nice," he said plainly, as if he didn't think it was nice at all. Crash had been acting like this—forcibly sociable—since their moment in the hallway. However, she didn't like the silence one bit.

"You wanted something?" she asked bluntly.

Crash looked down at her and then quickly averted his eyes back to the window. He was holding something back, she could feel it. Crash—speechless? Not bloody likely. She watched him, and her irritation slowly turned to amusement. He shifted again. His mouth tightened.

"We're going to be leaving," he said quietly. He watched her carefully, and Sora realized he was waiting for a reaction.

"Well, I guessed that a while ago," she said with a shrug. All of the whispering in the bedroom had tipped her off. "When? Will it be soon?" *Why is he looking at me like that?* Was he really so surprised that she had known their plans? *I'm not a simpleton!*

"I don't think you understand," the assassin said slowly. "We're leaving you here."

Sora rocked forward. "What?" she exclaimed. This seemed to be the reaction he had been expecting. She scowled at the look on his face. "You're leaving me here? But why? How...?"

"Listen," he said, and sat down on the footstool in front of her. Apparently he had been practicing this little speech. "This is for your own good. As long as you're with us, you're in danger." He gave her a solemn look. "Volcrian will leave you alone as long as you stay out of the way. I don't think he'll find you here. Burn and I have to keep moving or else he'll catch up, and I don't..." Crash swallowed, "I don't want this to happen again."

"What to happen again?"

"*This*, Sora!" he said harshly.

She sat back, stunned by his show of emotion. She opened her mouth to speak, but he cut her off.

"You almost died!" he said sharply. "Dorian is gone, and I don't want any more innocents killed—not at my expense, not at anyone's expense!"

She looked at him seriously. This, from an assassin? "Yeah...but you need me, remember? I have the Cat's Eye. And besides, I'm just fine."

"It was too close, Sora. We thought...." He paused again, darkness passing over his face. "I don't want to have to worry about it. Burn and I both agree. You're better off here."

Sora's eyes narrowed. *I see what they're doing...I'm too much trouble.* She wasn't skilled enough, she would just get in the way and endanger everyone. Just as she had Dorian. She knew what they weren't saying. It was her fault he was dead. She hadn't acted in time. Useless.

Tears stung her eyes. She gritted her teeth.

"I understand," she said quietly, flatly. "You do what you have to do." If they didn't want her, she wasn't going to whine about it. All of this time, she had been no more than a burdensome child. That hurt far more than she was willing to admit.

Crash watched her closely again, as he seemed to watch everything.

Sora turned back to the window, pretending that she didn't care. "You certainly waited long enough to tell me," she said, annoyed.

The assassin crossed his arms, then started pacing. "I wasn't going to," he finally admitted. "Burn thought you had the right to know. We're leaving tomorrow before the rain gets any worse. We'll make a lot more headway in the summer months. We'll be long gone by the time the snows set in."

Sora tried not to show her dismay. "Will you come back?" she asked quietly.

Crash paused. She could see his reflection in the window gazing down on her.

"No," he said bluntly.

Sora purposely kept her face expressionless. She knew his reasoning, but something deep inside of her did not understand—*would not* understand. Was she really such a nuisance? To think, she had actually believed they were a team. Dorian's death had brought her immeasurably close to these men, and now they were leaving. *I'm such a fool. I should have seen it coming.*

"You'd best pack your bags then," she grunted, and waved her hand dismissively. She looked once more outside the window. This time she didn't see the rain, didn't see the trees. She focused on something deep within herself.

Because of this, she didn't see Crash hesitate. Then he was gone.

It was too soon, too quick, too painful. She couldn't believe this was finally the end.

* * *

Appropriately, it was still raining the next morning. If it had been bright and sunny, Sora would have felt even worse. She stayed in bed for a long time after waking up, staring out the window, watching the rain drip down the glass. Then she turned over and tried to go back to sleep. *Maybe if I don't get up, they won't leave.*

There was a knock at the door.

At first she ignored it, but after another series of knocks, she decided she was being childish. She rolled out of bed. "Just a moment!" she called. The knocking continued impatiently.

She stood up and tied a bathrobe around her sleeping gown, blinking her eyes tiredly, then crossed the room and undid the bolt. The door blew inward, almost smacking her in the face.

Burn rushed inside. He swept her into the air before she knew what was happening.

"If you think you can make us wait forever, I'm afraid it won't work," he said, walking into the hall and down the stairs. "Can't stay in bed if I carry you, you see." His eyes met hers, losing a bit of their cheer. "We're almost ready to leave."

Sora felt her heart sink. Burn kicked open the front door and strutted outside into the rain. He placed her lightly on the ground. She stood in the cold, her arms wrapped around herself, her hair drenched. A shiver ran through her as the gravel bit into the soles of her bare feet. At least the wind wasn't blowing too hard; otherwise she would have been completely miserable. Her bathrobe, which fell a little below her knees, was already soaked through. Her nightclothes clung like second skin.

A sound came from her right. She turned to see Crash tying something to his horse; he seemed to be having quite a time of it. His tall black boots dug into the gravel as he pulled on a rope that kept slipping out of its knot. His muscles were tense, tight. He looked irritated.

His heavy arm rested on her slim shoulders. Sora looked up at Burn. There was a slight smile on his face as he watched the assassin. Leaning over, he whispered, "Aren't you going to say goodbye?"

Sora frowned at the odd suggestion, then looked over at Crash. *Goodbye?* she thought, a bit of anger coloring her thoughts. *He wasn't going to say goodbye to me.*

Her eyes glanced to the ground.

"Sure," she said wryly, and bent down, scooping a large ball of mud out of a puddle. Burn watched her curiously, his ears twitching. She pulled back her arm, taking aim.

"Sora," he said slowly. "I don't think...."

Sora hurled the ball of mud across the small gravel drive. It struck the back of Crash's neck with a satisfying *splat!* She grinned and put her hands on her hips, standing a bit taller.

The assassin paused. He lifted a hand to the back of his neck. When he turned to look at her, she glared at him. "That's for wanting to leave without telling me!" she growled.

Crash stared at her as though she had gone mad. Sora didn't care. On impulse, she reached down and grabbed another fistful of mud, packing it into a wet, slimy ball. "And this," she said. "Is for dragging me through Fennbog!" She hurled the mud ball at him, already reaching for the next one. It struck him in the chest. Crash didn't even try to dodge.

A burst of exhilaration moved through her, and Sora kept at it, slowly stepping forward, grabbing one clod of mud after the next. "And for tying me up!" she yelled, striking his shoulder. "And for stealing my money! And for drugging me! And for kidnapping me!" This time, she pelted the ball at his face.

Finally he dodged, ducking beneath the flying wad of dirt.

She threw herself at him, full of pent-up frustration. She didn't care that he was an assassin, that he could slit her throat faster than she could say his name. She launched into the air and tackled him, trying to shove him into a deep puddle next to the horse.

Crash grappled with her, pushing her off, but she kept at it, slipping through his grip. It felt good to use her new-found combat skills. For a moment, they went toe to toe, sparring next to the horse. The assassin moved smoothly, like a snake in the grass, but Sora had anger on her side. She backed him around his steed, closer to the edge of the puddle. She got the feeling that he was letting her win.

Sora wasn't sure if he meant to fall, or if he truly slipped on the wet ground. She suspected the former. Either way, he grabbed her arm and dropped backwards, dragging her with him. Sora screamed. The two went tumbling into the puddle, splashing into the muddy water as though falling into a lake.

"Bastard!" Sora yelled, drenched. The water was cold and murky, almost a foot deep. She tried to drag herself out of the puddle, but Crash caught her ankle, pulling her back in.

"Let me go!" she shrieked.

"Not until you cool off," the assassin replied, and dunked her back into the water.

Sora came up spluttering, wiping dirt from her mouth. She glared at the assassin, taking a clumsy swipe at his head, which he easily evaded. He looked partly amused. She growled in frustration.

Then a sound reached her ears. They both looked up and across the gravel drive.

Burn was keeled over, howling with laughter, one hand to his ribs. After a moment, he sat down on the doorstep, still laughing.

"You!" Sora barked, pointing a finger. "You're just as guilty as he is!"

The Wolfy continued to laugh, choking with mirth, shaking his head.

She scooped up another handful of mud, took aim, and hurled it at the giant Wolfy. He was an easy target. It hit him square in the chin, splattering against his shoulders and neck.

Burn stopped laughing. He looked up, eyes glinting mischievously. Then he reached down and gathered his own ball of mud. "Catch!" he said, hurling it at her. He was a much larger man and it was a much larger projectile, almost like a cannonball.

Sora threw herself to one side, narrowly dodging the throw. *Splat!* When she turned, she saw that it had hit Crash in the torso, further muddying his clothes.

The assassin sat for a moment, looking down at himself, then at Burn. Then, turning, his eyes met Sora's. A sudden, silent communication passed between them.

The air erupted with battle cries and they all dove to the ground, grabbing fistfuls of mud. Before a minute had passed, the air was full of mud bombs. Burn ducked behind a large water trough, then sent a mud ball hurtling at Sora. She dropped to the ground. Crash dodged the flying mud and smoothly returned the fire, hitting Burn in the shoulder. Sora leapt up again, throwing a missile of her own. She missed Burn's head by inches.

"You almost took my ear off!" the Wolfy shouted above the pouring rain.

Sora laughed suddenly. The sound bubbled up from inside of her, joyous and unexpected. Laughing? On this day?

Then Burn launched over the water trough, charging at them headlong. Sora cried out, momentarily panicked. The Wolfy was huge, almost seven feet tall; he resembled a barreling horse. There was no time to get out of the way. The Wolfy bowled into his two companions, taking both Sora and Crash to the ground, landing them all back in the puddle.

Bodies were everywhere. Sora couldn't tell which limb belonged to whom. She tried to wiggle away but Burn grabbed her leg and dragged her back down. With a squeal of surprise, Sora felt the Wolfy run his hands up the sides of her feet. She thrashed like a caught fish and landed on top of Crash, who had been wrestling away from Burn, trapped beneath his immense weight.

"Look at that!" Burn crowed. "I can take on both of you! One in each hand!" He pinned Crash's arm behind his back, shoving the assassin back down into the water. With his other hand, he snaked his fingers beneath Sora's arms, catching her in a ticklish spot.

Now helpless with laughter, Sora begged him to stop. Rain dripped from her nose and cheeks, landing in her mouth as it fell from the sky. Hardly able to breathe, she fancied that she would drown if they kept this up.

Finally, Burn let go of her. He sat on Crash for a moment longer, then stood up, brushing off his clothes in a dignified manner. "There," he said. "That should teach you both not to fight."

Sora squirmed her way onto the driveway and sat down in the gravel, panting for breath, utterly exhausted. She could feel a deep ache between her ribs; it was the remnant of the wound, still healing internally. She sighed. Perhaps her mother had been right. Maybe she wasn't as recovered as she had thought. She glanced around, hoping the woman hadn't witnessed the mud fight, but her mother had gone to town with Cameron on errands.

Burn seemed to echo her thoughts. He paused next to her,

looking down, a fond smile on his face. "I wonder what your mother would think of all this?"

Sora blushed, though she wasn't sure why. *I just attacked an assassin,* she thought, shaking her head. When had she become so bold?

Her eyes wandered to the man in question. Crash was standing next to his steed, his back to her, brushing off as much dirt as he could. She glanced down at her ruined nightgown and tried not to feel dismayed. It was made of very fine material. Lorianne would not be pleased.

Then Burn started towards his own horse. "We should head out," he said quietly.

Immediately, all the joy and laughter was forgotten. Sora felt a gaping hole open in her chest. Her two closest friends were about to leave. She wasn't fit to go with them. The tears that stung her eyes were hidden by the rain.

"Don't go," she whispered, almost against her will.

Burn turned back to her, his gaze unexpectedly kind. "Believe me, I would stay if I had a choice," he said quietly. "I'll miss you, Sora."

She sighed. His words didn't offer any comfort. Losing Dorian was hard enough. Now she would have to let them go, too. She focused on the ground, on the tiny shards of gravel, chunks of granite and white quartz.

Abruptly a shadow fell across her. She looked up, staring at Crash's outstretched hand. His boots hadn't made any noise on the rocks.

She took his hand, surprised. He pulled her to his feet. She stood there for a moment, gazing up at him, taking in his cunning face, his smooth jaw and dark brows. His eyes, softened by the overcast sky, had turned almost gray.

"For you," he murmured. He pressed a package into her hands. The small bundle was folded in brown paper.

Sora stared, shocked. She didn't know what to say. His hands clasped hers for a moment, as though he actually wanted to linger, to say something more. Then he stepped back. "Goodbye," he murmured.

Crash turned and walked swiftly, silently on the gravel, back to his horse. It was as though he couldn't get away from her fast enough.

"Burn, let's go," he called. His voice was no longer soft or friendly, but cold and rigid, like the assassin she had come to know. She watched as he donned his cloak and pulled up his hood, obscuring his face. Just like that, he transformed into a different person, someone unknown and untouchable, as though they had never traveled the swamp together. All those months were suddenly erased. She was staring at a black-clad warrior, the kind of man one would avoid on the street. Perhaps it had all been an act —the teasing, the mud fight, the whole damned thing.

When she focused next, both men were astride their new steeds, settling into the wet saddles. Crash didn't acknowledge her again, turned his horse and started down the road at a fast trot, traveling quickly through the forest, away from her mother's house.

"Don't forget us!" Burn called, waving to her.

Sora managed a smile and a wave, but she felt sick. Her stomach sank. She watched as he followed the assassin down the road. The arch of large pine trees created a natural tunnel around them. The rain slapped against the broad leaf ferns, a soothing percussion, accented by the clip-clop of the horses' hooves.

Sora stood and followed them to the mouth of the road, wishing she could be by their side. Forget them? Never. She would probably think about them every day for the rest of her life.

The two horses moved into a canter. Numbly, she watched them grow smaller and smaller, fading into the cloudy, rain-drenched woods. Finally she allowed tears to fill her eyes, and took a faltering step forward. "Come back," she whispered, choking. *"Come back!"*

Starting to run, suddenly desperate, she yelled, "COME BACK!"

But they were too far away to hear her, not that they would have turned around. She came to a stumbling halt, her feet squishing in the mud. She had never felt so unwanted, so frustrated. So alone. Sora watched until they were mere dots against the trees, then fragments of cloud, then swallowed up by the rain.

Then she looked down at the package in her hands.

Sora walked back up the gravel drive and opened the door to her mother's house, struggling not to look over her shoulder. They were gone; it was no use. She stopped by the closet in the front room to grab a warm blanket. A hot bath sounded good, too. Next, she would set a cauldron over the fire.

She paused by the dining table. It was overtaken by herbs and flowers, each clumped into piles and then lined up into rows. Her mother's work. She cleared a small space at the end and looked at the package that Crash had given her, wondering if she dared open it. She almost didn't want to, but curiosity got the better of her. Fingers numb from the cold, she haltingly unwrapped the brown paper.

A red bundle fell out, a second wrapping. Sora frowned and picked up the soft velvet cloth. Unfolded it.

At first she didn't know what it was. A large black shape, strange carvings on the handle. It appeared to be the hilt of a weapon, perhaps a sword, though the blade was missing. She stared at it in confusion, frowning, then abruptly she remembered.

This was the same sword that had almost killed her.

Why in the world would Crash give this to her? She thoughtfully turned the object in her hands. Her fingers traced the designs carved into the thick leather wrapping. It was unexpectedly heavy and cold to the touch.

Suddenly, a small note fell out of the hole where the blade would have fit, landing on the desk. Sora blinked, surprised. She picked it up. Unfolded it. She could only assume that it was Crash's handwriting. It twisted and curled across the page.

*For the first time I felt fear.*

Clutching the note, Sora started to cry. The tears came suddenly, forcefully, unbidden. Her shoulders shook and she couldn't breathe. Her adventure was over—over, and yet she felt completely empty, drained to her core. She couldn't imagine a future alone with her mother—not after these men had changed her life. Would they ever come back? Would she ever see them again?

A small part of her mind, the part connected to the Cat's Eye, whispered—yes.

And now, a special preview of...

# VIPER'S CREED

### THE CAT'S EYE CHRONICLES
### BOOK 2

### T. L. SHREFFLER

Available Now
on Amazon.

# PROLOGUE

Crash awoke from the dream with a start.

It dissipated as soon as he opened his eyes. Stars glinted above him, pinpricks on the pitch-black horizon, the ground cold and moist. From the stillness in the air, he knew that it was early, early morning.

He stood, looking across the flat plain, a dark ocean of wavering grass. The residue of the dream lingered, its cold hand on his back, as if warning him of something....

*What?* he thought, studying the broad expanse of the lower plains. *What am I overlooking?* He felt keenly disturbed, as though a predator stood just beyond the fringe of grass, watching him, filled with murderous intent. But was the threat far away or nearby? It was like watching a heavy storm cloud approaching. *How long before it reaches us?*

A large flock of crows suddenly appeared in the sky, flapping loudly against the dead night air. They cawed and squawked to one another, rushing by overhead. Dozens, perhaps hundreds. The mass of birds was so thick, it blacked out the stars.

Crash stared. Crows flying at night?

Then he noticed a certain skittering in the underbrush. Rabbits, mice and ground squirrels dashed through the dry grass, all following the same direction as the crows. The more he watched, the more he saw. Sparrows, black birds, swallows...all darting across the plains, fleeing west.

*What is this?* he wondered. A fire? An earthquake yet to strike? Yet there was no firelight on the plains, no telltale smell of smoke. The ground remained cold and solid.

Crash pondered the animals thoughtfully. *Why are they running?* Deep in the pit of his stomach, he felt like he already knew the answer.

A bush rustled, and he turned around to find his companion, Burn, returning from his watch. Small leaves, curled and dry from the summer climate, crunched beneath his boots. It was difficult to move soundlessly. They were camped next to a thicket of spindly trees tall enough to offer shelter from the elements. Burn had spent the last several hours in the branches, taking a better look at their surroundings.

"So they woke you?" Burn asked softly, glancing at the sky where the crows were still flying by. "I wonder where they're going."

Crash nodded. So he wasn't just imagining it. "They're fleeing from something."

Burn paused next to the assassin and gazed at the horizon. He turned his face into the wind, his flared nostrils sniffing the air, his long, pointed ears twitching; Wolfies' senses were naturally heightened and sharp. Finally, he pointed toward the northeast. "There," he murmured. "Far away, at the base of the mountains." He looked troubled. "It smells like...blood."

Crash's eyes hardened. Volcrian. Had to be. The bloodmage was approaching—though Crash doubted he was close because if he was, they would know it by now.

"He wants my head," Crash replied. "We should go our separate ways. He would most likely let you go. This isn't your fight."

The Wolfy's eyes turned hard. "It *is* my fight," he murmured. "Or have you forgotten what he did...?"

Silence. No, Crash hadn't forgotten. He only wished that Burn could forget—Burn was one of those rare, upright, honorable men who deserved a good life. But if they continued traveling together, they would both end up dead.

Now Crash could feel the bloodmage's presence descending onto the plains, a malevolent force, unstoppable. He seemed larger than before, easily detectable, powerful.

"We should leave the mainland," he finally said.

"Aye," Burn grunted softly in agreement. "Might be our only option. We can travel south to Delbar, take a ship overseas...we have some backtracking to do." They were currently traveling north, and had planned to traverse the mountains to the distant ice fields. If Volcrian was close, however, they would need a faster route of escape. Overseas would do.

Crash's eyes turned to the south, tracing the constellations in the sky. To reach the port city of Delbar, they would have to pass through the region where they had left Sora more than six months ago.

*Should I warn her?* he wondered. Hopefully, Volcrian would leave her alone now that she wasn't traveling with them anymore. If they showed up at her house, they would risk drawing the bloodmage there, too. *No,* he decided. Better to stay away.

"We leave at dawn," Crash said determinedly, and turned back to the copse of trees, ready to keep watch. The crows continued to fly overhead, growing in number.

**Want more of the world?**

**Visit *The Cat's Eye Chronicles* website!**

# WWW.CATSEYECHRONICLES.COM

## LEARN ABOUT
THE RACES
THE WORLD
THE CHARACTERS
THE AUTHOR

## VIEW
FAN ART
BOOK TRAILERS
TRIVIA GAMES
WRITING PROGRESS
PERSONALITY QUIZZES

**AND BUY GIFTS FOR FRIENDS!**

# About the Author

T. L. Shreffler is a noblewoman living in the sunny acres of San Fernando Valley, California, a mere block from Warner Bros. Studios. She enjoys frolicking through meadows, sipping iced tea, exploring the unknown reaches of her homeland and unearthing rare artifacts in thrift stores. She holds a Bachelors in Eloquence (English) and writes Epic Fantasy, Paranormal Romance and poetry. She has previously been published in *Eclipse: A Literary Anthology* and *The Northridge Review.*

Feel free to connect online! She loves hearing from readers, reviewers, orcs, elves, assassins, villains, figments of her imagination and extraterrestrials looking to make contact. Her online accounts are as follows:

Email: therunawaypen@gmail.com
Author Website: www.tlshreffler.com
Facebook: www.facebook.com/tlshreffler
Twitter: @poetsforpeanuts

Made in the USA
Charleston, SC
27 April 2015